JUSTICE OURWAY

JANET CHARLES

JUSTICE OUR WAY
Copyright © 2021 Janet Charles

Library of Congress Control Number: 2021907127
Paperback: 9781736851227
eBook: 9781736851234

Printed in the United States of America

Table of Contents

Anne

My name is Anne. That is all I'll tell you about myself at this point in time. I won't even tell you where I am. You can read my story.

The Reunion

Canberra, March 1988.

'**D**on't let anything or anyone stand in the way of what you want in life. If you *truly* want something, you'll find the strength and the means to achieve it.' The words rang in Alison's ears as she left the hall. She had just attended a motivational speech by Tony Dunn.

Tony had been talking about what he'd achieved in his life. His had been one of those rags-to-riches stories. He'd founded a very successful business. He now lived in a mansion that had a heated indoor pool, and he owned a plane and a yacht. He and his family skied in Switzerland, sunbaked on the Riviera and indulged in all the other activities that are available to only very wealthy people.

Alison had attended other, similar functions and had read many self-help books, hoping that one day she'd find enough enlightenment to enable herself to release the anger, bitterness and hatred she felt towards the people who'd ruined her life. To date, not having found that enlightenment, she'd concluded that the self-help movement was all garbage.

After sitting through the most recent motivational presentation, she'd vowed to herself that she wouldn't attend another one or waste any more money and time on buying and reading self-help books. The only two reasons she'd gone along tonight were that Jean had asked her and the event was free of charge. Tonight, however, on her way to Jean's car, she found herself repeating in her mind, *'You'll find the strength and the means to achieve it.' ... But surely not for what I want to achieve.*

As she was getting into Jean's car, she thought she saw a familiar face in the distance. A strange feeling came over her. The face ... could it possibly be hers? *Could it?*

'Are you okay?' Jean asked her. 'You look like you've seen a ghost.'

'I think I *have*,' she replied.

'Who?'

'Someone from a past life.'

Jean could see that her friend was upset, so she didn't ask any more questions. Instead, she commented on how much she'd enjoyed the presentation, and she and Alison talked about Tony Dunn as she drove to Alison's townhouse.

When Alison went inside, she thought about the face she'd seen. It had been the face of Kate Scott, from a time long past. Alison hadn't seen Kate since Alison had left university – twenty-eight years ago. The two had been the best of friends, but after Alison had suddenly left university, she'd lost contact with all her friends.

Alison was restless. She made herself a cup of tea and thought about Tony Dunn's presentation. It had been billed 'Your Goals, Success and Happiness', but at no time throughout the presentation had Tony Dunn defined 'success', or, for that matter, 'happiness'. She mused that the event could have been more correctly billed as 'How I Made a Fortune.' Her interpretation was that he equated happiness with money. She thought about that assessment but concluded that no amount of money could be compensation for what she had endured. She'd never be truly happy regardless of how much money she had. What she really wanted was revenge.

She didn't feel like going to bed so decided to look for Kate's name in the White Pages. She supposed that Kate had probably married and changed her name, but she also thought that even if Kate had married, she mightn't have changed her name because Kate had once said, if she ever got married to a man who had a ridiculous surname, she wouldn't change her surname. Looking up her number in the phone book was a long shot, but it was worth a chance. After all, several times throughout Tony Dunn's presentation, he'd said that a person had to 'take chances'.

Ha! Ha! she laughed to herself. *Bigger 'chances' than seeing whether an old friend's in the phone book!*

She took the White Pages, looked up the name Scott and found that a 'Scott, C. M.' was living at 12 Cummins Street, Queanbeyan. She thought it could be Kate, whose name was short for 'Catherine', and she knew that Kate's second name was Margaret. She felt excited, but then told herself to calm down, thinking it mightn't be Kate after all. The next day would be Saturday, and she decided that at an acceptable time she'd phone the number and find out.

She started to think back to the fabulous days and fun times she'd enjoyed with Kate at university. At balls and cabarets, they'd always sat at the same table, and they'd always taken part in the annual university procession. She thought about all the fun-loving people who'd lived at Duncan College. How could she have let them all disappear? Then her anger and hatred towards the people who'd ended all the fun and friendships welled up inside her, and she thought of Tony's last sentence: 'If you *truly* want something, you'll find the strength and the means to achieve it.' Yes, she now decided: it was time to do something. She'd suffered in silence for twenty-eight years, and now someone else must suffer. As she went to bed, Tony Dunn's words rang in her ears.

She woke at about seven thirty and went outside to collect *The Canberra Envoy*, which she had delivered to her place every day. After she'd eaten her breakfast and read the paper, she looked at her watch and saw that the time was 9.12 am. She decided it wasn't too early for her to make the phone call, so feeling nervous, she dialled the number.

'Hello,' came a woman's voice on the other end of the phone.

'Is that Kate Scott?' Alison asked.

'Who are you?' the woman replied apprehensively.

'My name's Alison Roberts. I'm trying to track down an old friend, and I thought it might be you.'

'Alison Roberts?' the woman queried. 'I guess I am the old friend you're looking for. Where are you? Are you just passing through?'

'No,' Alison answered. 'I've lived in Canberra for the past twenty years. I thought I saw you at the Tony Dunn presentation last night, and I decided to see whether I could find you. How long have you been in Queanbeyan?'

'Nearly twenty-seven years.'

Oh! Alison gasped to herself. 'Did you go teaching?'

'Yes,' came the reply.

'Are you still teaching?'

'No.'

'I'd love to see you again. Why don't we meet for coffee?' Alison suggested.

She sensed some reluctance on Kate's part. However, after a brief pause, Kate replied, 'You could come to my place.'

'Great ... When?' Alison asked.

'Does two o'clock this afternoon suit you?'

Alison detected a degree of urgency in Kate's voice, as if the meeting were something she wanted to get over and done with as soon as possible. 'That's fine,' she replied. 'I'll be there at two.'

'See you then. I must go. Bye.'

Alison was surprised at Kate's almost abrupt end to the call.

At one thirty, Alison hopped in her car and headed for Queanbeyan. She felt very excited but also anxious about seeing her old friend again. She had no problem finding 12 Cummins Street but was surprised to see that the dwelling was a small, old, weatherboard house. It was in excellent condition, as was the fence, and the garden was immaculate. Nevertheless, it was a small, old, weatherboard house – not the sort of house she'd imagined Kate to be living in. *Maybe it's trendy inside,* she mused.

She tried to open the screen door, but found it was locked. Then she saw an attractive knocker on the doorjamb and tapped it. A woman opened the door, and Alison couldn't believe her eyes. Although she of course knew that Kate was now twenty-eight years older than when she'd last seen her, she'd still been expecting her erstwhile friend's eyes to have the same magic sparkle and her mouth the same priceless smile. What had happened?

'Come in,' Kate said. 'Sit here in the lounge room while I make the coffee. Is it still black, no sugar?'

'You have a good memory. Yes, thanks. Black, no sugar.'

Alison peered around the lounge room and pondered how Kate had ended up in this house. Then she remembered that Kate had sometimes gone to Queanbeyan to visit her aunt and deduced that it must be the aunt's house – but why was she living in it?

In 1960, Alison and Kate had been living in the same residential college at the Australian National University. Kate had been doing a Diploma in Education, having graduated with a Bachelor of Arts the previous year. Her parents had had a property located not far from Cowra.

Alison's tuition and residential fees had been paid by Bonram, a large pharmaceutical company, which had also paid her a generous living allowance. She'd been doing Honours in science, majoring in chemistry. It'd been a foregone conclusion that she'd obtain First Class Honours and be awarded the University Medal. After completing her Honours year, she had intended to do a PhD and take up a career as a researcher with Bonram. Her father had been a doctor and her mother a pharmacist.

Alison and Kate had seemed to have it all. They'd been physically fit, clever and attractive. They'd had everything to live for.

When Kate came back into the lounge room, she was carrying a tray bearing the items for afternoon tea. She put Alison's coffee and cake, along with a cake fork and serviette, on a small table beside the chair that Alison was sitting on.

She hasn't lost her etiquette, Alison pondered, wondering what cock-and-bull story she'd spin when Kate asked her why she'd left university without finishing her Honours year and without any goodbyes. Fortunately, Kate didn't ask, and Alison found herself wondering whether Kate already knew the reason.

Kate was also not offering any explanation about what she'd been doing in Queanbeyan for the previous twenty-seven years. Had she had a breakdown? Alison sensed that Kate didn't want to talk about it, so she didn't ask. They talked about other things: Kate's brother, Kate's nieces, her parents' deaths, the house her aunt had left her, Alison's job, her townhouse, her skiing trips, her cat, her visits to her sister Kerrie who lived on the Gold Coast and her visits to her mother and father who were still living in Nowra. The warm feelings that each woman had had for the other during their university days, seemed to re-ignite immediately – incredible, after all the years that had passed.

However, there was also awkwardness between them. Alison commented on the garden, and Kate suggested they take a walk in it. 'I love gardening,' she announced, 'I do it all on my own.'

Alison wasn't sure how to interpret the statement 'I do it all on my own.' *This often means 'I get no help from my husband or children,'* she said to herself. Alison saw that the house had nothing in it to indicate that Kate had a husband or children – no photos or anything else that might be a sign of a male occupant. She wondered whether now was an opportune moment to ask Kate about her family, but inner sense told her it wasn't. The garden was a good distraction, and both women became a bit more relaxed there.

When it came time for Alison to leave, she and Kate agreed they should get together again and that it was a shame they'd been living close to each other for so long and not known.

'I'll call during the week, and we can arrange the time and place,' Alison said as she was leaving.

Driving home, Alison thought about Kate. It was fairly obvious she was living alone. She thought she'd looked sad and that she must have had some tragedy in her life. Maybe her husband and children – how many did she have? – had died. She had no family photos in her house ... Maybe she found it too painful to look at her deceased family every day. Alison wondered whether her own tragedy showed on her face.

Alison phoned Kate on Wednesday night and suggested she come to Alison's house for dinner on Saturday. Kate expressed some reluctance and asked whether they could meet on Saturday afternoon for coffee instead. That alternative was fine with Alison. Kate then added that she couldn't drive at night.

Why not? Alison wondered.

Two o'clock on Saturday was the time they agreed on.

Alison thought about how Kate didn't want to drive at night and concluded that her friend had been driving at night and had had a terrible car accident. *Her family was killed – poor Kate,* she thought.

At two o'clock on Saturday, Kate arrived at Alison's townhouse. 'You have a lovely place,' she remarked. 'How long have you lived here?'

'This is my second place in Canberra,' Alison replied. 'I've been at this address for about six years. Take a seat in the lounge room while I make the coffee.'

Kate went into the lounge room and sat down. She thought Alison didn't look 'short of a dollar' and decided she'd ask her more about her job. She considered that was a safe question.

Alison responded, 'After I left Canberra, I went to Perth and did a Master of Science and then a PhD. After I'd finished the PhD, I stayed on at uni and did research for three years. Then I wanted to return to Canberra, so I applied for a research job with Cural, which had taken over Bonram. I got the job, and I've been in Canberra for the past twenty years.'

Alison sat poised, ready for Kate to ask, 'Why did you leave uni without saying goodbye?'

But Kate didn't ask.

Kate wondered whether Alison was happy. There was something different about her face and body from how they'd looked during her university days, and Kate surmised that the difference wasn't due to the fact that Alison was older. Kate saw no evidence of a husband or children and found that hard to understand. Alison had never been short of male company at university.

Maybe she's divorced, Kate pondered. *Maybe she lost custody of the children, but even if she did lose custody, surely there'd be some photos, but then again, not everyone puts family photos in the lounge room.* She thought it inappropriate to ask.

Then she decided that since Alison had elaborated on her employment history, she'd do the same. 'After I completed my Dip Ed,

I was posted to Dubbo High School. Near the end of the first term, I got glandular fever. When it was diagnosed, the doctor explained that ninety-seven per cent of people who get glandular fever recover without having any recurring symptoms or problems. I was among the unlucky three per cent. I won't bore you with the details. I came to stay with my aunt to recuperate because the fever had left me feeling quite weak. The doctor advised me not to return to teaching. He said I must find a job that had less stress, so I applied for a job as a teacher's aide at Dolmar Primary School, and I've been in Queanbeyan ever since. You live in a very pretty suburb.'

Alison took Kate's sudden change of topic as a cue that she didn't want to say any more about her illness. She assumed it was probably quite depressing for Kate to have ended up as a teacher's aide when she had so much potential to achieve other things. Alison also decided she was probably wrong about the car accident. 'Yes,' she said, 'it is pretty here. Would you like to go for a walk to the lake?'

Kate agreed, and they walked for about an hour. The conversation was limited and centred on the trees, the lake, the birds and a promise from Kate that she'd phone Alison during the week.

When they returned to Alison's townhouse, Kate said she'd take her leave and once again remarked that she couldn't drive at night.

After Kate left, Alison wondered what Kate would be doing that night, Saturday night. Would she be staying home on her own, watching TV? Had she become a recluse? Had she ever married, and if not, why not? At university, she'd never been without a boyfriend.

On Monday night, Kate phoned Alison and asked her whether she'd like to come to dinner at her place on Wednesday night, adding, 'That's if you're happy to drive at night.' They arranged to have dinner at seven o'clock on Wednesday.

Alison arrived on time. Kate had the table beautifully set and served an appetising, three-course meal. More talk about the past ensued, but some gaping holes remained in both women's stories. Both were surprised at how quickly the old friendship was blossoming again. They decided that the next get-together would be the jazz band at Flossie's on the following Sunday afternoon.

As Alison was leaving, Kate remarked for the fourth time how much she'd enjoyed the evening, and Alison wondered whether it'd been a big occasion for her. *What sort of life does she lead?* she pondered. *Does she have any friends?*

Kate answered the latter question when she phoned Alison to ask whether she'd mind if two friends came with them to Flossie's.

'Not at all,' Alison responded. 'I'd love to meet some of your friends.'

When Alison arrived at Flossie's, she found Kate and her two friends waiting out the front, and Kate introduced Mark Dobson and Gaye Mawson to her. They found a table and bought a bottle of wine. During the band breaks, they talked among themselves. After the band had finished playing, the foursome purchased coffees and stayed on chatting. Kate had come with Mark and Gaye, so she wasn't concerned that it was getting dark outside.

On Monday, Alison phoned Kate to see about having dinner together during the week at a restaurant in Queanbeyan. 'I'll pick you up and drop you home,' she offered.

'Sounds great,' Kate replied, 'but I feel a bit guilty you have to come to Queanbeyan. I should be going to Canberra.'

'It doesn't worry me one bit. You choose the night and the restaurant.'

'Let's make it Wednesday night, and in the meantime, I'll think of a good place to eat.'

Once again, the evening was very enjoyable, and when Alison drove Kate home, Kate invited her in for a coffee. They chatted, and Alison thought she could see a glimmer of the old Kate from their university days. As Alison was driving home, she reflected on how close she felt to Kate and mused that she shouldn't be surprised at feeling that way: they'd been the best of friends at university. Maybe she should now confide in her.

During their next get-together, which was a Saturday lunch at Alison's home, Alison asked Kate what she'd thought of Tony Dunn.

'Not much,' Kate answered. 'I think that sort of thing only works if you go to the talk believing you can change, and I don't believe I can. It's all garbage. I only went because a friend asked me to go and it was free. What about you?'

Alison concurred. 'I feel the same, although his last words are still echoing in my head: "If you *truly* want something, you'll find the strength and the means to achieve it." I wish it were true. There's something I want *so* badly.'

'What is it?' Kate queried.

Alison hesitated for a moment and then said, 'To rid the world of every person who belongs to or supports the organisation, the Right to Esse.'

'I'll endorse that,' Kate responded.

'The Right to Esse are a self-righteous lot who want to force their extreme beliefs on everyone else. They don't believe that a doctor should terminate a pregnancy to save the mother's life. If the mother dies, that's okay – she died of natural causes – but if a doctor terminates the pregnancy, he's committed murder. It doesn't matter how old the foetus is. The power that organisation wields is disgusting. At the last election, the Right to Esse surveyed every candidate to see whether they were pro-life. *Every candidate* – not just the main parties, and they published the results in all the major newspapers. The candidates who refused to give a definite yes or no were deemed by the Right to Esse as being anti-life – 'anti-life': that was the expression they used; only the Right to Esse could dream up such a ridiculous expression.'

'I saw the results of that survey,' Kate said. 'Women for Safe Abortions estimates that a third of voters belong to a church that's pro-life. What politician or would-be politician would come forward and say he or she supports abortion on demand? She'd automatically lose one-third of the votes. The Right to Esse doesn't even believe that a rape victim who becomes pregnant should be allowed to terminate the pregnancy. When I think about that, my blood boils.'

Alison nodded in agreement. 'When I think about the girls and women who weren't allowed to terminate an unwanted pregnancy, my blood boils.'

'That sends my blood boiling too.'

'Kate,' Alison began slowly, 'when I suddenly left uni, I was pregnant. All I wanted to do was terminate the pregnancy and continue with my Honours year, but I didn't know where to find an illegal clinic. I even begged my father to terminate the pregnancy. I felt as if my world had fallen apart. I'd lost everything: my Honours degree, possibly the University Medal, my happiness – you name it. I had to explain to Professor Jackson that I was sick of studying. I told him I thought I was going to have a nervous breakdown. I don't think he believed me because he said, "This has come on very suddenly." But I wasn't going to tell him the real reason I was leaving. I knew that if I told one person in that department I was pregnant, I might as well put it on the front page of Saturday's edition of the *Herald*.'

'You could have told me, Alison.'

'I didn't want to tell *anyone*,' Alison confessed. 'Mum came to get me. We packed up my things while most of the girls were at lectures and just left. We drove to Sydney. I cried all the way. When we arrived in Sydney, we went to a place called Karmoor, where I was to be turned into an incubator for some beautiful, childless couple who'd take my baby from me and bring it up in their loving family. I'd never felt so low. I actually contemplated suicide. It was a dreadful place. No one ever laughed; there was no privacy; all the girls and women were so miserable and depressed. All the misery and depression could've been cured if they'd been allowed to have a simple operation, called abortion.'

After a pause, she went on. 'Once a week, we had to listen to counsellors – that's what they called themselves – from the Right to Esse. Just thinking about the crap they spewed out makes me want to strangle the lot of them; they had no idea what we were going through.

'You wouldn't believe some of the cruel stories I heard at Karmoor. The lack of compassion shown to women who had an unwanted pregnancy is incomprehensible. There was a girl who'd been raped. Her parents contacted a pregnancy counselling service called No Regrets. It was a front for the Right to Esse. They told her parents a pack of lies about what would happen to their daughter if she terminated the pregnancy. The poor girl, as if she hadn't suffered enough. It's so hard to believe that that type of service – well, it was hardly a service – is allowed to exist. And what's more, it was government funded.'

'I've heard of No Regrets,' Kate commented. 'I can't comprehend what sort of people work in that kind of organisation. What personal satisfaction do they get from advising a rape victim to have a baby? I think your goal to rid the world of the Right to Esse members and supporters is brilliant.'

'Thanks, Kate,' Alison responded. 'Everyone in the neighbourhood knew of "the Karmoor girls" – that was what we were known as. Once it was obvious we were pregnant, we weren't allowed to go anywhere – not even for a walk. Everyone could identify a Karmoor girl. We were made to feel rotten by everyone: the social workers, the doctors, the nurses – you name it. The medical students practised on us. We were dehumanised; we were the pits. But strangely, our babies weren't. There were dozens of loving couples ready to wrench our babies from us as soon as they were born.

'I had the most dreadful birth. Some of the time, I was on my own – no friend, no mother to comfort me.'

'You mean there were times you were all alone?' Kate asked in disbelief.

'Yes, not a soul in sight. The young doctor knew I was an unmarried mother, and he was trying to avoid a caesarean. I was screaming in agony. I couldn't have cared what they did to me. I just wanted the pain to end. Finally, the doctor performed a caesar. When I came to, I wished I'd died under the anaesthetic.'

'And if you had,' Kate said, 'I bet that information wouldn't have been conveyed to the couple who were there ready to snatch your baby.'

'Of course not! I was in excruciating pain, and I had this great wound across my stomach. Mum came to see me after the birth. I should add that she, Dad and Kerrie came to see me often. I just cried and cried and cried, and so did Mum when she saw how miserable I was. The baby was a girl. I was allowed to hold her. After all I'd been through, I didn't feel like giving her away, but the social worker convinced me I'd be selfish to keep her, and I should think of the baby, not myself. Apparently, I couldn't have offered her the environment of a loving, caring family.'

Kate remained silent as she thought about the mental and physical agony Alison had endured. She couldn't find a word strong enough to describe her loathing for the Right to Esse. Kate had her own reason for detesting the self-righteous members of that organisation.

'I was boiling with rage,' Alison said angrily. 'I kept thinking, if only I could've terminated the pregnancy, I'd have completed my Honours year and started my PhD, and I wouldn't be in this miserable state.

'Four days after she was born, I was wheeled into a room. The social worker was there. She said, "I have the papers for you to sign, Miss Roberts," – as if I were signing the transfer-registration papers for a car. She couldn't get my signature on that adoption form quickly enough. I think she thought I'd change my mind and keep my baby.'

Kate was now in tears. 'Just listening to this makes me cry. Oh, Alison, you poor dear.'

Alison continued, 'I wanted to kill everyone who was remotely connected with that whole sick, uncivilised practice of forcing women to be surrogates. I didn't see Megan again – I called my daughter Megan; she was adopted three days later. I stayed in the hospital for ten days. At one of my post-natal checks, a sanctimonious doctor said I could still get married. I might be lucky and find a man who was understanding.'

Kate couldn't believe what she'd just heard. 'Did a doctor really *say* that?'

'Yes,' Alison answered. 'Mum came to take me back to Nowra. I cried all the way there. You know, Kate, when a girl has an unwanted pregnancy, she has to create a story about why she suddenly disappeared. My story was I'd had a nervous breakdown, I'd gone to Sydney for treatment, and I hadn't been allowed any visitors. Somewhere, I have a twenty-seven-year-old daughter. I know nothing about her; I only know she's been brought up by a couple who are sick in the head, because any person who could take another woman's baby, knowing the mother's still alive, is stuffed in the head.'

'I agree,' Kate said.

Alison went on. 'If my daughter's brought happiness into their lives, they've gained that happiness through my suffering, and anyone who gains pleasure through someone else's suffering is one of the lowest forms of life on the planet. My daughter's been brought up by two of the lowest forms of life on the planet!'

'That's true, Alison,' Kate agreed. 'People who take other women's babies are pretty low, but I'm sure Megan's happy. I knew a couple in Cowra who adopted a baby; they adored her.'

Alison looked unconvinced. 'I know you're trying to cheer me up, Kate, and you might be right about Megan, but I should never have had to endure what I went through. I once saw a documentary about women in some Third-World countries who sell their babies because they can't afford to keep them. I was watching it with Kerrie at my grandmother's house. Gran commented how dreadful it was. Kerrie let fly and said to Gran, "The only difference between Third-World countries and Australia is that women in Australia aren't allowed to sell their babies. They have to give them away. They receive nothing – *nothing*, not even reimbursement for fanny rags. You'd think that the effing couple who took the baby could hand over a few hundred dollars to help the poor mother get back on her feet. No woman should be made to have a baby she can't keep, but while we have bigots like you and Right to Esse pricks voting in this country, nothing'll change!" She stormed out, telling Gran she was a heartless old bag.'

'Gosh!' Kate exclaimed. 'What did your grandmother say?'

'Kerrie didn't like Gran. If she didn't agree with Gran about an issue, she always made a point of telling her so. Occasionally, she'd give her a real serve, and Gran would mumble that she didn't know where Kerrie got the bad blood from. I often think of what Kerrie said. It's so true: no compensation for lost wages, no deferment of scholarships, no compensation for broken rental bonds – nothing, not even the money for a taxi fare to get the hell out of the place, unlike sperm donors, who receive thirty-five dollars for out-of-pocket expenses. I might add, at this point, that the father of my baby never even told his parents about her. Because the caesar was so painful, I couldn't do any exercises, so I never got my figure back. I always look five months pregnant. When I went for an eight-week check-up, the doctor said it was the worst caesarean he'd ever seen.'

'How horrible and tactless of him!' Kate remarked.

'I sort of recovered. I wanted to get as far away as I could from everything associated with the trauma. I didn't want to see anyone in Nowra. Whenever I went out, I always seemed to run into someone who knew me. It's amazing how news travels. Everyone I knew always asked me how I was, told me I was looking well. They were so sorry to hear I'd been ill. I'm sure you can visualise the scene.'

'Yes, I can,' Kate replied.

'So I went to Perth and enrolled in a master's degree. After the master's, I did a PhD and then research for three years, and then I came back to Canberra. I have a nice group of friends and a good social life, and I like my job, but there's always been something missing in my life. Since the trauma, I've never been able to get close to a guy. Every time I start to get close, I can't bear the thought of explaining the huge scar on my bloated stomach, so I end the relationship. As you've probably guessed, I've never married.

'Well, Kate, that's the condensed version. There are certain things I've blocked from my memory, and I find that's the best way of coping. The power the Right to Esse organisation wields is nauseating. The members are a mob of sadists. They robbed me of a family and much happiness. The anger and hatred I have towards them has never left me. Kate, is there anything sicker, crueller or more sadistic that can be done to a woman than to force her through an unwanted pregnancy and childbirth and then take the baby away, so she never knows what's happened to her?'

Kate remained silent for a moment, burst into tears and replied, 'Yes, gang rape.'

Alison felt sick. She knew what Kate was saying. She now knew why Kate looked the way she did.

Kate took a few deep breaths and commenced her story. 'As I've already told you, after I finished my Dip Ed, I was posted to Dubbo High School. I enjoyed teaching. I had a great circle of friends, an easygoing flatmate and a fabulous boyfriend named Neil. There was never a dull moment. Life was wonderful. One night, towards the end of first term, Lorna, the PE teacher, and I went to the pictures. Lorna's flatmate drove us because neither Lorna nor I had a car. After the movie, we looked for a taxi but couldn't find one, so our only option was to walk home. We arrived at Lorna's house and I thought nothing of walking to my place on my own. I only had two blocks to walk, it was a moonlit night, and the street was well lit. I was almost home when a car with three young males in it pulled up beside me, and they offered me a lift. I said, "No thanks, I'm almost home." But before I knew what was happening, they were all around me, and one of them said, "Well, we're gunna give you one!" Then I was dragged into the car and driven to a quarry.'

Alison felt ill as she thought about Kate in the car with the three men, knowing what was going to happen to her.

'That was twenty-seven years ago. I was a virgin. Like you, I cope with the really bad parts by blocking them out. They dropped me off not far from where they'd picked me up, and I staggered home. I was in a bad state and I needed medical help.'

Alison wondered how bad Kate's injuries were, but she didn't think Kate would want to talk about them, so she remained silent.

Kate continued the recount. 'We didn't have the phone connected. My flatmate thumped on the next-door neighbour's house and told them to ring an ambulance. I was taken to the hospital, where the sister called the police. I can still remember the first two questions the policeman asked me: "What were you doing out on your own at eleven thirty at night?" and "Have you been drinking?" The questioning was indescribable.'

Alison couldn't believe her ears. 'Was your flatmate with you when you were being interrogated?'

'No,' Kate answered. 'She was told to wait outside the room. No one was with me. I thought my life was over. I felt so depressed and humiliated. I didn't want to see anyone. I knew in a day or two it would be all around the school that Miss Scott had been gang-raped. Mum and Dad came up from Cowra. When I was discharged from the hospital, we went to the flat, packed my things, left a cheque for two months' rent on the kitchen table, and drove out of town. I didn't want to go to Cowra. I couldn't face anyone asking me why I'd left Dubbo, so I came to Queanbeyan and stayed with my aunt, and I'm still here. Like you, I had to create a story about why I'd suddenly left Dubbo. My story was I'd contracted glandular fever and gone to stay with my aunt in Queanbeyan to recuperate. Also, like you, I have a nice group of friends and a reasonable social life, but I've never recovered from the trauma. This is my condensed version.'

Alison hugged Kate, trying hard not to cry.

Kate continued, 'When you left uni and didn't say goodbye, I was so hurt. I thought you might be pregnant, and I wondered why you hadn't confided in me. I always intended to find you again, but my world was torn apart, and I didn't want to see anyone, so I could understand why you didn't want to see anyone and why you left without saying goodbye.'

When Alison heard Kate's words 'I thought you might be pregnant', she felt upset, pondering how many other people had made the same assumption.

'My aunt was a widow and had no children. She was so kind to me. We got on really well. After about sixteen months, I saw a vacancy for a teacher's aide. I applied for the job and was successful, but I've never moved on. My aunt died six years ago, and as I told you when you first came here, she left me the house.'

'Oh, Kate,' Alison said, her eyes full of sympathy. 'I thought my situation was bad, but there's always someone worse off than yourself.'

'Sure is,' Kate concurred. 'My aunt and I would catch the train to Sydney on the last Friday of each month, and I'd go to a support group on Saturday afternoons.'

'Wasn't there somewhere closer?' Alison asked in surprise.

'Yes,' Kate replied, 'but if I'd gone to Canberra, I was sure that people I knew would find out I'd been raped, and I didn't want anyone to know. In

Sydney, no one knows you. You think my case was bad, but you wouldn't believe some of the stories I heard. Anyway, nothing helped. I tried everything. I was so desperate, I went with another girl to a monastery in Thailand to see if I could attain whatever I needed to find "inner peace", or some such crap, but I always drew a blank. I even tried forgiveness – what a joke!'

'Some things are unforgivable. Rape's one of them,' Alison said.

'And taking babies from their mothers is another,' Kate added. 'I tired of the questions and the advice: "How come you live with your aunt?"; "Are you going to get a place of your own?"; "Barbara's looking for a flatmate, if you're interested." Like you, I met some nice men, but when the relationship started getting more than platonic, I put an end to it. Rather than get a reputation as a frigid old bag, I stopped dating guys altogether. I kept believing that one day I'd recover, marry and have children. My mother was forty when I was born, so I thought there was still hope for me. Then one day in the staffroom, this grossly overweight woman said she was going on a special diet the following week and was expecting to lose thirty-five kilos in three months. Kelly, who called a spade a spade, almost shouted at her, "No, Maureen, you're not going on a special diet next week; you're not going to lose thirty-five kilos in three months. I've been at this school for fifteen years, and for fifteen years, you've been talking about going on a diet and losing weight, but it never happens. You'll be obese for the rest of your life. Why don't you accept it and shut up?"

'When I came home that day, I thought about what Kelly had said, and I told myself, No, Kate, you're not going to get married; you're not going to have children; you'll be on your own for the rest of your life. Why don't you accept it and shut up? Then I started to cry, and one of my fits of hatred and anger towards the bastards who'd ruined my life took hold of me.'

She'd barely finished speaking, when the phone rang.

'Do you mind if I take the call?' Alison asked.

'Of course not,' Kate replied.

Alison picked up the receiver. 'Jackie,' she said, 'how nice to hear from you.' Then the tone in her voice changed. 'Oh, Jackie, I'm so sorry to hear that.'

Kate went out on to the balcony to let Alison take the call in private.

After Alison hung up, she signalled for Kate to rejoin her in the lounge room.

Alison was now crying. 'How strange, considering what we've been talking about. That was the sister of one of the girls who'd been at Karmoor. She was ringing to say her mother had died. Joan was about seven months pregnant when I arrived. She was a lovely girl. She'd travelled down from Gunnedah on the train on her own. She said she was sick nearly all the way. A woman in the same carriage offered her some travel-sickness tablets and couldn't understand why she wouldn't take one. Four weeks later, she was rushed to hospital in the middle of the night. The next day, one of the girls asked Crabtree – the bitch in charge – how Joan was. She said Joan had had the baby and that her parents were making arrangements for her to return to Gunnedah. We all felt something wasn't quite right. I asked Crabtree whether the baby had survived. She said she wasn't privy to that type of information. A week later, I asked her again. Old Crabtree said Joan had gone back to Gunnedah. Some of us still felt there'd been something strange about Joan's departure.'

'Why did you think that?' Kate quizzed.

'Sixth sense. Some of us wanted to phone Joan's parents, but the only telephone was in Crabtree's office, which she kept locked whenever she wasn't in there. There were phone directories in the reading room, so we looked up the name Stoyles – Stoyles was Joan's surname – in the Gunnedah directory. There was only one Stoyles in Gunnedah, so we thought it had to be Joan. I wrote the number down, and most of the girls agreed someone should go the next day and phone the number from one of the public phones at the post office. We took up a coin collection, and the following day, Jenny and I went to the post office. Fortunately, we found a phone that worked. Jenny dialled the number. I saw a look of disbelief on her face. After she hung up, she said Crabtree hadn't told us that Joan had gone back to Gunnedah in a coffin. We were both badly shaken.'

'You both must've nearly freaked out!' Kate remarked.

'We *did* freak out! We went back to Karmoor and told a few of the girls. Within ten minutes, it was all around the breeding house that Joan had died. Jenny and I copped a blasting from Crabtree for creating fear. Next day, we all had to listen to a lecture from a midwife, who told us how it was very rare for a woman to die in childbirth in this day and age.'

Kate tried to visualise the terrified group of girls and young women listening to the midwife. 'It might be rare, but you had the proof it still happens.'

'That's what we all thought: *I might be the next rare case.*'

'Did the midwife say what'd caused Joan's death?' Kate asked.

'She waffled on, something to do with the placenta. For us, it was irrelevant how Joan had died – the fact was she'd *died*. No one would tell us whether the baby had survived. One time, when I was travelling to the Gold Coast, I stopped at Gunnedah and visited Joan's parents. The whole family had been devastated by Joan's death. Joan's mother told me that Joan had wanted to have an abortion and she'd known where there was an illegal clinic, but she'd persuaded Joan not to go; she'd said it was too risky. She said she'd never forgiven herself for sending Joan to Karmoor. Poor Joan, she'd never been to Sydney before. Imagine how she must've felt when she hopped off the train at Central. All alone, feeling sick, trying to work out how she could get to Karmoor. Joan's mother had been led to believe that someone from Karmoor would meet her.

'There are no words strong enough to describe the hatred I feel towards the Right to Esse. They should be exterminated. They're vermin. No, I shouldn't say that: it's offensive to rats. Not a day goes by that I don't feel anger towards the heartless staff at Karmoor and the "loving couple" who took my daughter. When she turned twenty-one, I bought all the Sydney newspapers and read every twenty-first birthday notice. I had this ridiculous idea I might be able to recognise one of the girls as being Megan. Don't ask me why, Kate – people do absurd things when grief's the controlling emotion. I also had this hope that the couple who'd taken her might've called her Megan because I'd told the social worker that Megan was what I wanted them to call her. But I don't suppose she took it on herself to pass that on.'

'I'm sure she didn't,' Kate commented.

Alison continued relating what had happened. 'After the birth, I had to have a counselling session with the social worker. I told her I'd wanted to terminate the pregnancy and continue with my studies; told her you can't compare an early termination with nine months of pregnancy, the horrendous birth I'd gone through and the end of my career. I added I didn't find it easy to turn myself into a breeding machine that had no feelings and hand over my baby like I was handing over an unwanted doll. Anyway, Kate, I mustn't go on. You've suffered more than I have.'

Kate responded, 'I can identify with your anger and hatred. One of the bastards who raped me was acquitted on a technicality. He was the worst – went first and then again, after the other two. The solicitor who got him off was beaming. She was young, she'd just opened her own practice, and it was her first big case. I was so livid I wanted killed her as well as the bastard she'd gotten off. His name was – and still is, I suppose – Wayne Keys. I'll never forget that name.

'The whole trial was a nightmare. I only got through it because of the support I had from Mum, Dad and John, my brother. It lasted five days. Returning to Dubbo was so frightening. I had visions of all the schoolkids coming out to see what kind of freak Miss Scott had turned into. Fortunately, each day, the trial ended before school finished. I was petrified during the trial that it'd be aborted, and a new date would be set. It took so much courage for me to go back to Dubbo. I knew I couldn't do it a second time. A lot of my friends, including Neil, the guy I was dating, wanted to see me, but I had no desire to see them. After the verdict, I just wanted to get out of Dubbo and never return. Dad and John wanted to ask the solicitor what type of person gloats at getting a rapist off, but Mum and I knew it was a waste of time and headed for the car.

'A year later, I wrote to the solicitor to tell her what I thought of her. I received a curt reply to the effect that any more contact from me would be considered harassment and that she'd take legal action.

'When I think about Keys and Lyn Cullen – the solicitor who got him off – I am filled with so much anger and hatred, I still want to kill them.

Sometimes I feel so miserable, I can't believe I'd be any more miserable in gaol, and I could console myself with the knowledge I'd killed them.

'Alison, you've told me what you want in life, so I'll tell you what I want: I want to throw Wayne Keys and Lyn Cullen into a dungeon and leave them there to rot. Remember the old midnight horror films? I used to — still do — visualise myself as a female version of Boris Karloff, laughing at Wayne Keys and Lyn Cullen locked in the dungeon.'

'What about the other two bastards? Don't you want to throw them in a dungeon too?'

'The three of them were granted bail,' Kate explained. 'One was killed in a car accident two days before the trial. I've never decided whether that was a good thing or a bad thing. I was glad he was killed, but I also wanted him to have suffered before he died. The other bastard was given a seven-year gaol sentence; he'd only been in gaol for a month when he was bashed. The bashing was so severe he ended up with brain damage.'

'How do you know that?' Alison asked.

'Francine, my flatmate, wrote to me. There was a lot about it in the local paper; she sent me the clippings.'

'We each have a goal,' Alison stated. 'We should strive to achieve them. I remember hearing Tony Dunn say that sometimes you have to break your goal into achievable portions. I'll start with one of the more vocal Right to Esse supporters, perhaps Senator Peters.'

'How about Gary Munkton, that horrible, bigoted Minister for Education?' Kate suggested.

'That's a good one,' Alison agreed, 'and I've just thought of another. You have two people on your list. I'll have two on mine: Gary Munkton and Colleen O'Day. She's the national president of the Right to Esse. She rears her ugly head every now and again, in the paper or on TV, to complain about something she doesn't approve of. And what's more, she lives in Canberra, very convenient Think about it, seriously. What have we got to lose?'

Kate became pensive. 'I have nothing to lose. I don't even have my life to lose; I lost it twenty-seven years ago. I should say it was stolen from me twenty-seven years ago.'

Alison looked directly at her. 'I feel the same.'

'What about the father of your baby? Don't you want him to be punished for dumping you?' Kate asked.

'He didn't really dump me. He suggested we get married, but I didn't want to marry him. He wrote to me while I was in Karmoor. As far as I was concerned, the relationship was over, so I wrote to him and said I didn't want to have anything more to do with him. ... Do you have anything planned for the rest of the afternoon?'

'No,' Kate replied.

'Would you like to go to the National Library then? There's a documentary about Madalyn Murray O'Hair. It finishes at four. We'll each take our own car. You'll have plenty of time to get home before it's dark.'

'Who's Madalyn Murray O'Hair?' Kate asked.

'Haven't you heard of her?'

'No.'

'I'm sure you'll love her when you see the documentary,' Alison assured her.

'Okay, Alison. I'll put my trust in you – let's go.'

The two women had just arrived at the Library when Alison waved to a couple and announced, 'That's Ron and Nancy. They're very active in NoFourthR.'

Kate had never heard of NoFourthR, but having shown her ignorance once already today, she decided not to ask what it was.

After the screening of the documentary, Alison spotted her friend Helen and her housemate, Anne. She introduced Kate to the two, and Helen suggested the four have afternoon tea together at the library cafe.

Over coffee, Helen remarked she'd seen a few people from NoFourthR at the documentary. Kate wondered what NoFourthR was and whether it was something she should know about. She was relieved that none of the other three women mentioned it again and that the conversation turned to the documentary.

'The most-hated woman in America. What a woman. What drives her?' Alison asked.

Helen elected to answer the question. 'Hatred – hatred of religion. It goes to show what you can achieve if you follow your convictions and never give up. So, ladies, if you have a goal in life you think is unattainable, pursue it with a passion, never give up and your goal will become a reality.'

Kate caught Alison's eye, and a knowing glance passed between them.

As the four women were leaving the cafe, Anne and Helen invited Alison and Kate to a barbecue at their house the following Saturday at six o'clock.

Alison gladly accepted the invitation, but when she noticed Kate's hesitation, she knew that Kate would be thinking about driving home at night. 'If you want to, Kate,' she said, 'you can stay the night at my place.'

'Thanks, Alison,' Kate replied. 'I'd like that.'

'That sounds like a good idea,' Helen declared. 'We'll see you next Saturday then.'

Kate felt an instant rapport with Anne and Helen. They seemed genuinely interested in Alison's long-lost friend, and she liked their sense of humour. They laughed a lot, and each time they laughed, Kate couldn't help admiring their teeth. Both had a perfect set, just like a film star's, but that was where the similarity ended. Helen had slightly wavy blonde hair and blue eyes. She was stunning. Kate imagined that as a teenager, she must have been the belle of the ball. Anne was striking in a different way. She was tanned, had thick light-brown hair, long thick eyelashes and brown eyes, which Kate noted had a mischievous twinkle in them.

New Friends

On Saturday afternoon, Kate packed an overnight bag and drove to Alison's townhouse. Alison assumed they'd go in her car, but Kate suggested they take hers. 'It'll be the first step in getting over this fear of driving at night. As you've probably concluded, this "not driving at night" has nothing to do with my eyesight; it's because of the attack.'

'Yes, I did suspect that was the reason.'

'It's not so much the driving at night; I have a phobia that the car will break down, and I'll have to walk alone to get help.'

'What about if you're with someone?' Alison asked.

'If someone picks me up and brings me home, I'm okay, but I can't offer to take anyone because it means I'd have to drive to their house on my own to collect them, and after I'd dropped them off, I'd have to drive to my house on my own.'

'Oh, Kate, I hope that fear goes one day. Anne and Helen are such fun. Anne's an architect. She has her own business, and Helen's an IT consultant with Allhue. Anne and Helen have been flatmates – or rather housemates – for twenty years. Helen was transferred to Canberra, and a mutual friend asked Anne whether Helen could stay with her for a few days. So Helen moved in, and she's been there ever since.'

'Just like that?' Kate asked in surprise.

'Not quite,' Alison replied. 'Helen wanted to buy a house, so Anne said she could stay with her until she found a place she liked. After four months of searching, Helen found a house, but she couldn't settle because the occupants – a young couple with three young children – had three months to go on the lease. About a week before settlement date, the woman became very sick. Helen settled, but she didn't have the heart to make them leave, so she said they could stay on. Anne wasn't fussed. She told Helen she could stay until the woman had recovered. It was one of those illnesses that went on and on. After two years of living together, they decided Helen would move out when one or both of them got sick of the other. Twenty years on, and they're still not sick of each other.

'They have the perfect setup. They get on really well, and they do a lot of things together, but basically, they lead independent lives. They're so capable. Wait until you see the house. They did all the landscaping, including the retaining wall at the front. The area around the swimming pool looks like something you'd see in *Home Beautiful*. They built the pergola and constructed a fabulous brick barbecue, with a chimney which draws perfectly. Anne could afford to get someone to do the work, but they enjoy doing it themselves.'

'I'm having trouble visualising those two well-dressed, immaculately groomed women building a pergola,' Kate commented.

'Let's just say they're very versatile. Anne's a bit of a larrikin. Perhaps that's not quite the correct word. No one gets away with anything with Anne. There's a big garbage hopper out the back of the building her office is in. It's always locked, and the only people who have a key to it are the cleaners. One day, Anne was coming in the back entrance to the building when she saw three green garbage bags of rubbish beside it. She opened one and saw that some of the contents were old receipts. She fished one out and wrote down the address it had on it. On her way home that afternoon, she stopped outside the house and dumped the three bags of rubbish all over the front lawn and drove off.'

'That was taking a risk!' Kate gasped.

'She doesn't mind taking risks. Another time, she bought an evening dress. When she tried it on at home, she found a little tear in one of the sleeves, so she took it back to the shop. The saleswoman said it was strange that Anne noticed the tear at home but not in the shop. She said the dress was undamaged when Anne had bought it and implied that Anne had torn it, so she refused to give Anne a refund. Anne being Anne, though, wasn't going to take it lying down. She stood at the entrance to the shop and showed the damaged dress to everyone who came in and advised them not to buy anything from the shop because the owner didn't give refunds for damaged garments.'

'Did it work? Did the woman give her a refund?' Kate asked, surprised.

'Anne really wanted the dress, so she went back into the shop and told the woman she'd go away if she gave her a discount. The woman agreed, and Anne left.'

'Would you be game to do that?'

'No way!' Alison asserted. 'The anonymous phone call is her specialty. The son of one of her staff was working as a bowser boy at a local petrol station. He wasn't getting the award wage, so Anne rang the service station and said she was from the Department of Industrial Relations; said she was doing a random ring-around of businesses to remind them that paying any employee less than the award was illegal. She thanked them for their time and hung up.'

'Did it do any good?'

'Yes. Three days later, the man told Anne his son had received a pay rise.'

'Has she ever been caught out?' Kate enquired.

'No. We all say Anne could get away with murder. She can be quite naughty. One day, she returned to her car to find the tail-lights on one side smashed to pieces. There was a note on the windscreen from someone who'd seen a woman sideswipe the car and drive off, but before the woman had driven away, the witness had written down the number plate. Somehow, Anne found out where the woman lived. One night, she went to her house and saw the car parked outside. It had a large scrape along the side, so Anne slashed two of the tyres. She said that even if she'd gone to the police with the woman's number plate, the police wouldn't have done anything. Anne is one of those people who believe if you can't get justice through the proper legal processes, you take the law into your own hands.'

'I agree with her; I couldn't get justice through the proper legal processes. I just wish I could do something about it.'

'You know, Kate, I'm sure if you told Anne what happened to you, she'd help you get some sort of justice. That's the kind of thing that gets her seething, and once Anne's seething, action follows.'

'Sounds like the world could do with a lot more Annes,' Kate commented.

'You're right. Too many of us, including myself, just sit back and take shit.'

'I wonder what drives her.'

'I honestly think it's her passion for justice. In a way, she's a strange mixture. Sometimes she can appear so cold and uncaring, but she'd take enormous risks to help a friend.'

'She'd have to take some big risks to help me get justice,' Kate stated.

'Don't underestimate her. Her friend Malcolm does the same sort of thing. He found out that a financial adviser was advising all his clients to invest in a company that was giving him a commission. The financial adviser's office was on the seventh floor of a large office block. Malcolm put a notice in each lift advising prospective clients about the adviser's commission. I could go on about Anne's and Malcolm's antics, but I think I've said enough for you to get the picture. I'm always telling Malcolm that if he gets caught, he'll be deregistered and lose his job. He's a solicitor.'

'I don't like solicitors,' Kate declared.

'Malcolm's different though,' Alison assured her. 'He's the most principled person I know, despite the fact he sticks notices in lifts. He and his business partner, Wendy, have a very modest practice. Neither of them is interested in material possessions. Malcolm often jokes that he and Wendy are the only solicitors you'll find on the beach because the cats will've covered all the others with sand.'

'What about Helen? Does she get up to the same antics?' Kate asked.

'No, but she usually endorses Anne's actions. Helen's one of the kindest people you could meet. She sponsors two girls in Afghanistan, and she's been to one of the Pacific islands – I forget which one – twice, at her own expense and in her own time, to teach computing. She also shares Anne's passion for justice. She's very active in Lawfail. Maybe you've heard of it.'

'I have,' Kate replied. 'My aunt went to one of their meetings. She really went to check it out for me – to see if Lawfail could help me in any way. She said I'd have to tell Lawfail everything before they decided whether they'd take my case on. I wasn't prepared to do that, so I didn't think about Lawfail anymore.'

'Some of the members are victims who feel they've been let down by the legal system. They all say attending Lawfail meetings is beneficial. Belinda, who's a victim of road rage, says that just knowing that other people support you is worth a lot.'

'Do you belong?' Kate asked.

'Yes, but I must confess I'm not what you'd call an active member.'

'Maybe I should join; get myself really involved; get passionate about something. I've often noticed that people who have a passion for something are happy. Maybe I should get passionate about my goal.'

'So should I. Anne and Malcolm also belong to Lawfail. It's not only the injustices in the legal system that Lawfail want to publicise; they want to make judges, magistrates, lawyers and shrinks more responsible for their decisions. How did I get on to this?'

'You were telling me about Anne and Helen,' Kate reminded her.

'That's right, I was. They're two fabulous women. I've known Helen for twenty years. I regard her as my best friend.'

When they arrived, Anne introduced Kate to John, Don and Carmel, and ten minutes later, Peter arrived. Helen asked the guests to move outside. Peter poured everyone a glass of wine, and Helen passed around a plate of hors d'oeuvres. Peter offered to do the cooking. Everyone helped themselves to steak, sausages, onions and salads. They sat around the table eating and drinking.

Peter declared, 'We have excellent company, perfect weather, hearty meat, healthy salads and fine wine – what more could we ask for?'

'Stimulating conversation!' Don replied. 'I hope you're all going to the NoFourthR meeting on Wednesday night.'

'We never miss them,' Carmel said. 'What about you, Kate?'

Oh help! Can't pretend any longer! Kate thought. 'I must confess, I don't know what NoFourthR is.'

Don explained, 'It's an organisation that wants the government to ban the teaching of religion to anyone under the age of sixteen. There are far too many people in Australia – in the world, to be more precise – whose lives are screwed up because of what they were taught, and in some cases, because of what was done to them, all in the name of religion. I should know: I'm one of them. NoFourthR also has a support group for people who are experiencing problems because of what was instilled in them when they were growing up.'

'I'll support that,' Kate responded. 'It's beyond my comprehension how anyone can believe in a loving god who's all-powerful. How can an all-powerful, loving god look down on a child who's being sexually abused and say, "I have the power to stop this, but I won't because I've given the abuser free will."? Don't get *me* started on religion.'

Don was relieved to hear Kate's reply because as soon as he'd opened his mouth, he realised he knew nothing about her. For all he'd known, she might have been a Sunday school teacher. He now viewed her as being a willing listener. Don never missed an opportunity to recruit a new member for NoFourthR. Once he'd started talking about his pet subject, it was hard to shut him up. He continued, 'A person who's been screwed up is like a piece of wire that's been screwed up: no matter how hard you try to straighten it, a few kinks will always remain.'

He was on a roll now. 'I was sent to boarding school at the age of eleven. It's unbelievable, the things we were taught – "indoctrinated" or "brainwashed" is probably more like it. We were taught that masturbating's a sin. We were told it increased the risk of cancer – no specific organ was ever mentioned – and it drained the marrow out of your spine. I was a very good cricketer, a fast bowler. One day, I wasn't able to bowl because my back was hurting. I was scared stiff the nurse would find that the cause of my back pain was diminished marrow in the spine and that I'd be expelled for masturbating and sent home in disgrace. I didn't know how I'd be able to face my parents.

'We were also taught about a place called hell. If you commit a mortal sin and die before you have the opportunity to confess your transgression, you go to hell. Once in hell, you're there forever. You're in constant pain, and no matter how bad the pain gets, you won't black out. I didn't know what'd be worse, hell or being expelled from school for masturbating. What sort of government allows this evil teaching? It's child abuse.'

'Speaking of hell,' Anne said, 'when I was in First Class, I remember going home from school one day and seeing Patrick O'Connor. He was bawling his eyes out and saying he was going to go to hell. I asked him how he knew, and he said he'd eaten a sausage roll. He said he was walking past a house where there was a birthday party. One of the kids at the party had offered him a sausage roll over the fence. He'd taken it and eaten it. After Patrick had eaten it, he remembered it was Friday, and he'd gone troppo. Then Mary Maguire had come along and told him he had to go to confession. I said I'd heard Mrs Clifford telling my mother about a woman who'd swallowed too many pills and had had her stomach pumped. I suggested to Patrick he go to the hospital and get the sausage roll pumped out. Mary Maguire said that wouldn't save him. She told him that as soon as he arrived home, he had to ask his mother to take him to confession, but she warned him to be careful crossing the road because if he was hit by a car and killed before he'd confessed, he'd go straight to hell.

'Poor Patrick. He was almost paralysed with fear; I can still see the image of that petrified boy. What sort of person would teach innocent children that rubbish? What a way to live: always terrified you might do something that would send you hurtling into the fiery furnace forever. Today, if Patrick O'Connor ate a sausage roll on a Friday, it wouldn't be a sin. How can something be a sin one Friday but the following Friday, it's not a sin?'

'So what happens to the souls in hell who committed a sin that's no longer a sin?' Peter asked.

Carmel replied, 'I guess a committee's formed to decide their fate. Can't you just see it? Some saying it was a sin when they committed it, so they have to stay in hell; others saying it's no longer a sin, so they can come out. I suppose after a lengthy discussion, they take a vote. Who makes up this voodoo crap?'

'Some religions don't believe in blood transfusions,' Peter said. 'I used to work with a chap who belonged to that type of religion. His wife had a miscarriage. They had three young children. Her husband was told that if she didn't have a blood transfusion, she'd die. She refused, and of course she died. What was achieved through leaving three young children without a mother?'

'Nothing,' Don replied. 'Nobody feels threatened by that religion because they don't have the numbers at the ballot box. What if one day they did? What if they got into power and made blood transfusions illegal? What would Gary Munkton think then? How would he feel if his daughter died because she couldn't have a blood transfusion? But he doesn't care if someone else's daughter dies because she can't have an abortion.'

'Abortion!' Alison said. 'He believes abortion's murder and that God said, "Thou shalt not kill." But God's not in a position to say, "Thou shalt not kill." He did his share of killing. One estimate is two million, two hundred and seventy thousand, three hundred and sixty-five, and that doesn't include Noah's flood, Sodom and Gomorrah, the firstborn Egyptians and the closing of the Red Sea.'

Don started up again. 'What if the atheists got into power and we forced our stance on the entire nation – made religion illegal, destroyed all the churches and threw the worshippers in the clink? We don't force our views on anyone, so why do Gary Munkton and his cronies think they have the right to force their irrational nonsense on us? In some religions, they don't believe in drinking. Imagine if they got their way. How would that pisspot Munkton survive without his daily fix? He wanted the government to give a grant to the Right to Esse.'

'The Right to Esse!' Helen exclaimed. 'When I used to organise abortion rallies, the Right to Esse would always turn up. We'd get the permit and do all the publicity, and they'd cash in on our efforts – turn up and stage their own demonstration. At one rally, there were about eighty of them. I was wishing I had a bomb. I could have dropped it on them and got eighty in one hit!'

'Eighty fewer Right to Esse supporters in the world – that'd have to be a good thing!' Don remarked. 'Hopefully NoFourthR will achieve its goal, and the government will legislate to make it a crime to fill the heads of children and young teenagers with such sick ideas.'

There was a pause, and Peter said light-heartedly, 'Well, Kate, do you have a better understanding of NoFourthR now?'

'I sure do,' she replied.

Everyone gave a little laugh.

Don spoke almost apologetically. 'You'll have to excuse me, Kate: I'm passionate about NoFourthR. I get so worked up when I see the needless suffering that religion's caused to so many people. Religion! Religion! Religion! If we could only rid the world of religion – religion and greed – how much better off would we all be!'

'I don't have to excuse you for anything,' Kate said. 'I feel quite passionate about it myself.'

'The ridiculous things some people believe!' Peter threw in, and he asked John, 'Does Mike still believe that God was right over the bald head incident? Are he and Laurie still arguing about it?'

'Yes,' John replied. 'Mike reckons God was right, but Laurie doesn't agree. We'll seek an independent opinion. Kate, what would you say about this? A bloke named Elisha was going somewhere – forgotten the name of the town, and on the way, some boys made fun of his bald head, so he cursed them in the name of the Lord. Then two bears came out of the wood and tore forty-two of the boys to pieces. Mike reckons that's fair punishment for any brat who mocks a guy's bald head, but Laurie thinks it was too harsh. What do you think?'

'I'm not a man with a bald head,' Kate answered, 'so I'm probably not in a position to say. I take it Mike's bald and Laurie's not.'

John commended her: 'Excellent detective work, Kate. Some people say a good detective makes an astute criminal, but I don't think that's true of you.'

Soon it will be, Kate thought, and she asked, 'Why did God give Elisha the burden of a bald head if he couldn't bear it? I was told, "God never gives us a burden we cannot bear."'

'Good question, Kate,' John said. 'Poor Mike can't bear his, particularly when he has to bare it; he'll wear a hat whenever he can.'

'How come we didn't see you at the library on Sunday?' Helen asked Don.

'I wanted to go, but I'd committed to a bushwalk. How was the documentary?'

'Extremely interesting,' Carmel replied. 'She certainly is one hell of a woman. I don't think I can find the words to describe her courage and commitment. She's so courageous.'

'Next week's documentary should also be interesting,' John said. 'It's called *Peter Stiller*. He was sentenced to death for killing the guy who murdered his wife, the barrister who defended the murderer and the judge who disallowed the crucial evidence that would've been proof that the accused was guilty. His final words were "Justice has been done. The feeling is euphoric. I have attained nirvana."'

'How come the evidence was disallowed?' Kate asked.

John answered, 'Well, some cops went to Grayson's, the murderer's, house. The search warrant was being processed. A constable was going to bring it to them. However, there was a delay in issuing it, so the cops broke in and obtained the evidence they needed. When the constable arrived at Grayson's house with the warrant, the cops already had what they needed, so they all left. At the trial, Grayson's barrister said the evidence couldn't be used because it'd been obtained illegally: that is, the cops had broken in at something like 1.50 pm, and the warrant had been issued at 2.03 pm, and the judge disallowed the information. Can you believe it? I mean, *can you believe it*? So Stiller shot the lot.'

'What a great bloke!' Anne remarked. 'That's exactly what he should've done. If someone commits a crime against you and gets off, you should get your own justice!'

'Like that woman who shot the Family Court judge,' Peter added. 'What's wrong with shooting a jerk in a wig who tells you when you can and can't see your kids?'

'Like Tore in *The Virgin Spring*, my favourite Ingmar Bergman film. He did the right thing, killing those men. That's exactly what every father should do to any man who rapes his daughter. What do you think, Kate?' Carmel asked her.

Kate considered her response. 'A father might be able to get away with killing the men who raped his daughter in medieval Sweden, but in Australia today, the consequences of an act like that would add to the victim's suffering. Her father would be sent to gaol.'

'You're right,' Carmel said. 'I guess if you take the law into your own hands, you have to be prepared to wear the consequences.'

I am prepared to wear the consequences, Kate said to herself. 'The consequences mightn't be as bad as you think; the sentences some of those judges hand down are a joke – not a joke, an insult – an insult to the victims.'

Carmel nodded in agreement. 'Well, Kate, if you do decide to go to a meeting of NoFourthR, the next one's on Wednesday night, eight o'clock, at 22 Rhime Place, Kenton. It's a private house. We hold our meetings in Ron and Nancy's garage. It always helps if you bring your own chair. Everyone throws in ten dollars to cover the cost of supper and to try to boost our not-so-healthy coffers. It's interesting – or perhaps I should say disturbing – you haven't heard of NoFourthR. It comes up at every meeting. How can we get more publicity? Would you believe that neither the *Queanbeyan Hermes* nor *The Canberra Envoy* will allow us to advertise our meetings?'

'Is NoFourthR only in Canberra?' Kate asked.

'No, it's a national organisation. Each capital city has a branch, and many of the larger country towns have a branch too. The *Adelaide Trust* is the only paper in the whole of Australia that's willing to advertise the meetings.'

'Well, Don,' Helen said, 'we've certainly had some stimulating conversation.'

'We have indeed,' Don echoed. 'And what's more, we all managed to eat our food and drink our wine while engaging in this stimulating dialogue.'

Anne and Helen cleared away the plates and served coffee and cake.

'How's Allhue treating you, Helen?' John asked. 'Or perhaps I should say, "How are you treating Allhue?"'

'Funny you should ask that,' Helen replied, 'given what we've been talking about. I received what one would call "a strong reprimand" from Roger, one of the top blokes, last week. I forgot to tell you, Anne.'

'Struth!' Anne exclaimed. 'What did you do?'

'I had a disagreement with Shelley.'

'It must've been more than that,' Anne persisted.

'Shelley was showing everyone pictures of her daughter's twenty-first birthday party. Everyone in the office knows the daughter is adopted. She asked me whether I wanted to see the photos. I said, "No. It would only bring tears to my eyes, thinking of the birth mother. I bet she wasn't celebrating."'

'Crikey, Helen. That was a bit rough,' Anne said, aghast.

'Could have been worse! At least I didn't say what I was thinking.'

'Which was?' Carmel asked.

'God made you barren for a reason!'

'Phew! It *is* just as well you didn't say that,' Carmel agreed.

'There is no way I would have said that,' Helen assured them. 'But Shelley's one of those people who thinks everything happens for a reason. It doesn't matter what tragedy befalls a person; she always tries to offer some explanation.'

'What happened after you told Shelley that you didn't want to see the photos?' Don asked.

'Shelley started bawling, and I went back to my office. But we all know about office grapevines. About fifteen minutes after my little homily – would you call it a homily?'

'No,' Don replied, 'I wouldn't.'

'Well, whatever,' Helen continued, 'the phone rings, and it's Roger, says he wants to see me. So I go up to Roger's office, and his secretary tells me to go straight in, so in I go. I tell him to dispense with the intro: I think I know what he wants to talk about. He raves on about how he can't believe I said such horrible things and that I'm to apologise to Shelley and tell her I didn't mean what I said. And I say to him, "I'm not apologising because I meant what I said. I didn't want to look at the photos. I would be thinking of the birth mother and I bet she wasn't celebrating."'

'What did Roger do?' Don asked.

'Sat there like a stunned mullet then waved me away.'

'Did you find out who the mole was?'

'I think it was Maree. I passed her in the corridor later in the day. I smiled sweetly at her, and she had the decency to look embarrassed.' She turned to John. 'Anyway, before you asked me how Allhue was treating me, John, I was on my way to get some more serviettes.' She went into the house.

'She wouldn't get away with that where I work,' Carmel commented.

'Helen could moon at Roger, blow a raspberry in his face and walk out, and he'd be begging her to come back before she reached the car park,' Anne said.

'She's a smart cookie,' Carmel declared. 'Gerry always says I-SOFT would snap her up tomorrow.'

'Sweet, kind, soft-hearted Helen,' Anne said. 'That must've come as a shock to the office workers who haven't seen that side of her. Beneath that face that could launch a thousand ships ...'

Helen returned holding the serviettes, and the group continued to chat and tell jokes. Anne put on some music. Helen and Peter started dancing.

John asked Kate to dance. She felt nervous. She hadn't danced since Lorna's twenty-first birthday party in Dubbo. *Dancing must be like riding a bike,* she mused. *You never forget how to do it.* John was a good dancer, easy to follow, and she was enjoying the activity. Soon, though, a dark feeling came over her. She'd always enjoyed balls, parties, singing and dancing. She started thinking about her wasted years and became filled with hatred. She resolved that nothing was going to stand in the way of her goal: Wayne Keys and Lyn Cullen were going in a dungeon.

Shortly after midnight, everyone decided it was time to go home. All agreed it had been a great night. The guests offered to help with the cleaning up, but Anne and Helen said it could wait until the next day.

When all the guests had left, Anne said to Helen, 'One day, what you say will get you into real trouble.'

Helen replied, 'One day, what you *do* will get you into real trouble.'

'But no one knows what I do; I don't have witnesses,' Anne reminded her.

'You're always one up on me, Anne.'

'Nonsense!' Anne exclaimed. 'I'm going to bed. Goodnight, see you in the morning.'

'Goodnight, Anne.'

Alison and Kate were the last to leave, so Kate was surprised to see a big four-wheel-drive vehicle in the driveway. 'Who owns the four-wheel drive?' she asked.

'Anne.'

'Why doesn't she put it in the garage?'

'She has a car in there. She usually parks the four-wheel drive in the carport, but as you can see, right now there's no room. The barbecue, pot plants and outdoor furniture belong to a friend who's in the process of moving to a new house. Anne has two vehicles: a BMW that does everything except find you a parking spot and that big four-wheel drive. She likes to go off the beaten track, and she's a keen skier, so the four-wheel drive gets plenty of use. Anne's not short of a dollar.'

'I guessed that,' Kate said. 'Her clothes didn't look like they came from the op shop.'

'You won't find any cheap clothes in Anne's wardrobe,' Alison assured her. 'You won't find any cheap things in the entire house.'

'Did she start up her business?' Kate asked.

'No, her uncle did. After she graduated, she went to work for him. He was a bachelor. He died six years ago and left her a thriving business, and under her ownership, it continues to thrive. Helen told me she's just won a huge contract to design a new office block. Anne never talks business at social gatherings – much too plebeian for Anne.'

'How old is she?'

'One year older than us, forty-nine. Helen's three years younger than Anne. Helen's pretty well-heeled herself.'

'Helen has such a gorgeous face,' Kate commented. 'I find it hard to believe she said those things to Shelley.'

Alison laughed. 'Helen's little outbursts are like a private joke among the group. Malcolm estimates she averages 1.8 a year.'

'Well, I guess everyone's safe from her next serve for a while.'

'No, there's no pattern to them. The next one could be tomorrow or in five months' time.'

They arrived at Alison's house, and Alison showed Kate her room. Kate hopped into a comfortable bed that Alison had made up with fresh-smelling sheets. She lay there thinking, *What fabulous people. Why didn't I try to find Alison? I should've known she'd have great friends. I can still hear Anne saying, 'If someone commits a crime against you and gets off, you should get your own justice.' All the insults I had to listen to: 'Kate, you'll have to accept the law.'; 'Kate, you'll have to forgive them.'; 'Kate, you'll be a stronger person because of this.'; 'Kate, it's time you put this behind you and got on with your life.'* Then she told herself, *Don't get yourself worked up. Your revenge is coming. Go to sleep.* She went to sleep and didn't stir until morning.

When she rose, she found Alison already up.

'How'd you sleep?' Alison asked.

'Really well, though I had my doubts for a while. You're the only person I've told about my ordeal since I moved to Queanbeyan – but of course, some people found out about it and I started to think about some of the things people had said to me. I remember a counsellor saying to me, "Don't let this ruin your life." As far as I was concerned, my life was already ruined. And the biggest insult of all came from Reverend Flynn, a minister in Cowra. I can still remember his exact words: "Kate, God never gives us a burden we cannot carry. God has forgiven those men; you must do the same."

'Then he quoted something from the Bible, about vengeance. "'Vengeance is mine: I will repay,' said the Lord." Well, I haven't seen any evidence of it. What would *he* know? I was livid. I told him there was no God. I told him I had the proof because I'd pleaded with and begged God to save me, but God had said no. Is that what you call a loving God? I asked him what else he believed in: the Easter Bunny, fairies at the bottom of the garden. He started up again about how I was God's daughter and that God was also feeling my pain. What a load of rubbish! I told him I was now a committed atheist and he wasn't to come to the house again, trying to find some reason for what'd happened to me.

'As a parting shot, I asked him whether he thought God had watched me being tortured or whether he'd he been busy creating an earthquake to kill a few hundred people. Religion's all man-made – and I'm being politically correct when I say "man". Anyway, enough of this. I don't want to go on. Your friends are so different from mine. My friends are kind, caring, they all have a great sense of humour, but there's no way any of them would condone what Peter Stiller did.'

'I do,' Alison affirmed.

'So do I.'

'Let's eat,' Alison beckoned her. 'I've prepared breakfast.'

Alison and Kate had breakfast on Alison's balcony in the sun – fresh fruit, yoghurt, croissants and filtered coffee. They read the Sunday papers, and then Kate went home because she'd arranged to play tennis in the afternoon. She felt heartened as she was driving home. She was on a high – not a huge high, but a high nevertheless. She'd met some people who thought as she did, and although Alison had been with her, she'd driven at night. She recalled what Peter Stiller had said: 'I have attained nirvana.' She said aloud to herself, 'I will attain my nirvana.' With that, she recalled memories of her grandmother's funeral. Her grandmother had spent the last five years of her life in a nursing home. She'd been frail, bored and very unhappy. Old age frightened Kate, but death didn't; in fact, she sometimes longed for it.

On Monday night, Kate rang Alison to tell her she was going to the NoFourthR meeting. 'I'm bringing Brett, and what's more, I'm driving. I'm picking him up at seven thirty. I'm going to overcome this fear of driving at night. But now I have to change my story. I always said I couldn't drive at night because of my eyes. Now I'll have to convince everyone I can see. That might be a bit hard to explain. I sometimes feel that for the past twenty-seven years I've been living a lie.'

'Who's Brett?' Alison asked.

'Brett Hall. He's a new teacher at the school. When I say "new", I mean new this year. I thought he might be interested because he refused to attend the beginning-of-term church service, and he doesn't think religion should be taught in state schools. He couldn't believe it when I told him about NoFourthR. He hadn't heard of it. Don sure has one new member in Brett.'

'I'm so glad you have someone to go with because I can't make it,' Alison said. 'I have a work commitment. I'll send an apology with Helen.'

On Wednesday night, Kate drove to Brett's house, where she found him waiting for her at the front gate. Brett navigated, and they found Ron and Nancy's place without any trouble. They took their chairs and made their way to the garage. It was a huge garage with enough space for four large cars.

Kate was pleased to see Don and Carmel there. Don greeted them and introduced them to Ron and Nancy and some of the other members.

It wasn't long before Helen arrived. John and Peter, who'd been at the barbecue, were also there.

At eight o'clock, Don asked everyone to take a seat and called on Steve to chair the meeting. Steve welcomed Kate, Brett and Fiona, who was also attending for the first time. Kate estimated there were about sixty people at the meeting.

The meeting had the usual format: apologies, minutes of the previous meeting, treasurer's report, president's report and other business to be discussed. At this meeting, the two items for discussion were Carol's support group and the monthly newsletter.

Carol spoke briefly about the support group. The aim of the group was to help adults release the religious fear they'd been indoctrinated with when they were young, a fear that most attendees said hung over them like a curse. Feedback was that whoever attended the support-group meeting found it extremely helpful.

When Carol finished speaking, Steve asked Mary to talk about the newsletter. Mary thanked the people who'd contributed to the newsletter and also thanked Elaine, who'd printed the newsletters free of charge. As was the usual practice, Mary had done up the newsletters in bundles of one thousand, and on top of each bundle, she'd included a map of the delivery area. She informed the people who'd volunteered to do the deliveries that they could collect a bundle of the newsletters when Steve had closed the meeting. She also said she had spare copies if anyone wanted to deliver more and reminded anyone who had contributions for next month's newsletter to get them to her by the end of the following week.

Steve thanked Mary, and because there was no other business to discuss, he declared the meeting closed and invited everyone to stay on for a cuppa. As soon as Steve had finished speaking, almost everyone headed to the table on which Mary had placed the newsletters and took a bundle. Brett offered to drop some copies in Queanbeyan. Kate was too embarrassed not to take part in the action. Brett told Ron he'd take whatever was left over and that he and Kate would work out an area in Queanbeyan between them. Everyone was delighted that Queanbeyan was to receive some newsletters. Kate was a bit concerned about doing the deliveries. Letterbox dropping was not quite her forte. She couldn't deliver them at night, so she'd just have to wear a hat and sunglasses and hope no one recognised her.

Supper was very basic – a teabag or instant coffee in a polystyrene cup and a biscuit. Everyone was very friendly, and Kate was enjoying herself. Once again, she thought how different Alison's friends were from her own. Most of her friends would be horrified to learn she'd gone to a NoFourthR meeting.

Brett told Kate and Fiona he was going to get a membership form from Nancy and asked them whether they each wanted one. Both said they did. Three new members in one night was quite something. Brett struck up a conversation with Don, telling him how pleased he was that Kate had asked him to attend. He also expressed his dismay that he'd never heard of NoFourthR. Don explained the difficulty they had in publicising NoFourthR because there was so much opposition to it. Don introduced Brett and Kate to Kevin and Clare. Brett was sure he'd seen Kevin and Clare before, but he couldn't recall where.

Kate and Brett chatted as Kate was driving home. Both agreed how friendly everyone was. When they arrived at Brett's home, he said he'd work out two areas for the letterbox drop and that he'd come around the next day after work. After he'd hopped out of the car and Kate realised she was alone at night outside the safety of her home, she thought she was going to have a panic attack, but she managed to control herself. She locked the passenger's door and drove home. She parked the car in the carport, picked up her bundle of newsletters and went inside. She felt good. She'd achieved something that night.

It wasn't late, so she decided to look at the newsletter. She took one from the top of the pile. It was a single A4 sheet, printed on both sides. She read the newsletter and was impressed. It was simple, to the point and well presented. At the top of the newsletter was a little spiel about NoFourthR and a contact number. That part was followed by articles from two women who'd written about the negative effects religion had had on their lives, and under the heading 'Learn More about God' were some of the atrocities that God had committed, followed by a Bible reference for anyone who wanted to check them out. Kate was surprised to learn that God had killed a man named Onan because he had practised coitus interruptus when God told him not to.

Because Alison hadn't attended the NoFourthR meeting, she decided to visit Kate the following Sunday. When she arrived, she was surprised to see that Kate had a male visitor. It was Brett. He'd come to borrow Kate's vacuum cleaner.

'I turned mine on and saw smoke,' he said. 'That was enough for me. I wanted to clean the house, so I thought I'd ask Kate. Oh, by the way, Alison, Kate tells me it was you who introduced her to NoFourthR. I intend to become a very active member. They seem like a great group. Don introduced me to Kevin and Clare. I knew I'd seen them before, and now I remember: they were helping out at one of the stalls at the RSPCA fete.'

'That could be where you saw them,' Alison said. 'Clare's a real animal lover. Kevin was the president of NoFourthR last year. His story is very sad. He's quite open about it. He was studying at the university in Armidale. He was in his third and final year of a science degree. He was a member of a band that played every Saturday night at the uni. Often, townies, as they were called, came to the dances. One night, one of the townies latched on to him. She then started to attend regularly, and they'd go somewhere after the dances. One night – they'd only known each other for eight weeks – she told him she was pregnant, and they'd have to get married. He was shell-shocked because she always told him it was safe. He asked her to have an abortion, told her he knew where there was an illegal clinic. She belonged to a religion that reckons abortion is murder. He didn't want to marry her, but before he knew it, her father had everything arranged and was threatening him with all sorts of legal action. Not that there was any legal action he could've taken, but Kevin didn't know that. Kevin said it was like he was caught on a conveyer belt: everything was being decided for him, and he was being carried along.

'He took a crash course in her religion and passed with flying colours once he'd signed a document agreeing that he and, more importantly, the forthcoming bastard and any other children they might have, would join the flock. Then he told his parents he was getting married. They were devastated. The girl's father wasn't exactly on Skid Row, so Kevin was able to complete his degree, but as soon as he'd sat his last exam, he went to work in his father-in-law's business, selling trucks.'

'*Selling trucks!*' Brett exclaimed.

'Yes, Brett, selling trucks,' Alison affirmed. 'His wife wouldn't use any type of contraceptive, and she wouldn't let him wear a condom. At the age of thirty-six, Kevin had a wife he didn't love, five children and a controlling father-in-law. After the birth of the fifth child, Kevin had had enough. He slept on the lounge couch and started an affair with his father-in-law's secretary. When his wife heard about it, all hell broke loose. The secretary was immediately sacked, and Kevin said he was leaving town. He said that as he drove out of town, his father-in-law was yelling at him and threatening to have him arrested because the car he'd taken belonged to the business. Kevin said his father-in-law controlled everything and that that was the first time he'd stood up to him. He came to Canberra and met Clare.

'Like so many people, he resents the path he was forced to take because of something that was never meant to be. Why should someone's life be ruined because of something as trivial as a bang on the wrong night?'

Brett agreed with every word Alison had said and proceeded to tell them about his friend. 'One of my best friends, Tom, had to get married at the age of nineteen. Neither he nor the girl wanted to get married. They both wanted to terminate the pregnancy and get on with their lives. But that wasn't possible, so they got married.

'When I was young, my grandmother told me I shouldn't hate anyone. Well, I hate every member of the Right to Esse. That organisation must be the most powerful lobby group in Australia. No politician would dare speak out against them.'

'I hate them too,' Alison said.

'Tom's story's very sad,' Brett continued. 'The baby was a boy. They named him Tim. About three years later, they had a girl. After eight years of fighting and arguing, they finally split up. Tim's thirteen now. Regrettably, Tom and Tim don't have a very close relationship.

'Tom once said to me he'd wipe out every member of the Right to Esse if he had the means. I think I'd start at the top; start with the national president, Colleen O'Day. Lock her up and not let her out till she recanted. Next on the list would be Toni Crawford. She's the vice president. Colleen lives in Canberra. You might've seen her in the paper or on the local news, whingeing about something she wants banned just because she doesn't agree with it.'

'I have,' Alison said, 'though I haven't heard of Toni Crawford.'

Brett went on, 'She lives in Wagga Wagga, where Tom lives – 34 Ceseum Road. Remember when the government wanted to introduce "no fault" divorce?'

'Yes.'

'She headed up a group to protest against it. What more can one say?'

'Not much, Brett. We get the picture.'

'I must go now: I've a few chores I want to do before it gets dark. Thanks for the loan of the vacuum cleaner, Kate. I'll return it tomorrow after work. Bye, Alison. I'll see you at the next NoFourthR meeting.'

'Bye, Brett,' both women said in response.

Kate saw Brett to the door.

When he'd left, Alison asked, 'What's the story on Brett? He's very knowledgeable about the upper echelons of the Right to Esse.'

'I don't know a lot about him,' Kate replied. 'I know he went to Sydney Teacher's College and his first appointment was Gundagai. Dolmar's only the second school he's taught at.'

'How old is he?'

'He must be about thirty-five because he told me he'd been in Gundagai for sixteen years. He never volunteers any information, and I don't ask – probably why we get on so well. He has a very active life. In summer, he coaches Kanga cricket. Every Saturday morning he goes to watch his team play, and in the afternoon he plays club cricket. He's a keen bushwalker too. He's a member of the local bushwalking club, and he reads a lot. For every book I read, he'd read two. He's also a good cook. He brought a delicious carrot cake for morning tea last week. He's a great guy, very popular at school, and – would you believe? – he offered to do my share of the NoFourthR newsletter deliveries.'

'Did you accept?' Alison asked.

'I did. He convinced me he was perfectly happy to do it, and I offered to feed his dog next weekend. He's going away.'

'What Brett's friend said about wanting to wipe out the entire Right to Esse movement reminded me of our goals: mine to throw Gary Munkton and Colleen O'Day into a dungeon and leave them there to rot, yours to throw Wayne Keys and Lyn Cullen into a dungeon and leave them there to rot. We have to start working on our goals. Never forget what Tony Dunn said: "If you *truly* want something, you will find the strength and the means to achieve it."'

Kate's attitude to life was changing. Her parents were dead, so she didn't have to worry about upsetting them. She thought back to some other things Tony Dunn had said on how to achieve your goals in life: 'Visualise your success. Never lose sight of your goal. Do not think of what might go wrong. Think of what will go right.'

'Alison, I'm going to achieve my goal,' she announced. 'For twenty-seven years, I've harboured anger and hatred towards Wayne Keys and Lyn Cullen. I think if they suffer, it'll help me heal. It'd be as if they took on some of my suffering. People talk about justice. Justice is merely the politically correct term for revenge. I want revenge.

'How long have you been a member of NoFourthR?'

'About ten years. I don't seem to be able to release the last bit of my faith – no, it's not faith – it's fear. When I was in primary school, there were girls who told me that God kept a list of all the wrong things you did, and when you died, you were punished for each one, and if there was more than fifty on the list, you didn't go to heaven. Some things seep into your head like a stain, and you can't remove them.'

She went on. 'My maternal grandmother was very religious. She went to church every Sunday, said her prayers, and read the Bible every day. Mum and Dad weren't very religious. Mum went to church every so often and usually Christmas and Easter. My sister and I went to Sunday school every Sunday. I think it was only to keep Gran happy. Sometimes Gran would come around to our house for Sunday dinner. She'd always ask Mum whether she'd been to church. The answer was nearly always no, and Gran would say, "You'll have some explaining to do at the Pearly Gates, my girl!"

'At Sunday school, I learnt about heaven and eternal life. There was never any "fire and brimstone", but somehow, I just can't shake off my last thread of fear that maybe there's something out there – particularly when I hear about people's near-death experiences. That's the main reason I go to NoFourthR.'

'I can assure you, Alison,' Kate said, 'there is nothing.'

'Thanks, Kate. I just wish I could be as certain as you are. When we're young, we're taught about a man in a red suit who lives at the North Pole and once a year delivers a present to every child in the world. We're taught about a rabbit who delivers chocolate eggs and a fairy who comes around at night, takes away your tooth and leaves some money. As you get older, you realise that these things aren't possible, and you wonder how you ever believed such nonsense. But religion's different: we keep believing.'

'Some people keep believing,' Kate commented. 'I didn't. I have proof there's no God.'

Alison continued, 'I remember one Christmas holidays when we were young, the children next door were playing with my sister and me in our backyard. Their mother was calling them to come home, and they were taking no notice of her. She said, "I'll tell Santa Claus you've been naughty!" That had no effect; they just went on playing. Then Gran came out the back door and said, "If you kids don't go home this minute, I'm going to tell Jesus you've been disobeying your mother!" Well, you should've seen them charge for home! Took off like blue-arsed flies! And Gran said, "That put the fear of God into them." And that's my problem: I can't shake off that last remnant of fear.'

'I tell you, Alison, you've nothing to fear. Controlling by fear is evil,' Kate assured her.

'But I do fear,' Alison confessed. 'I just wish that last skerrick of "What if Gran's right?" would vanish.'

'If you're having trouble releasing your fear, imagine how hard it must be for people who were indoctrinated with the threat of hell when they were young.'

'I know. There should be a law against it. Well, I guess it's time for me to go home.'

'I'll see you out,' Kate said.

Kate and Alison were becoming very close and were now seeing each other at least once a week. Both felt they'd confided more in each other than they could ever have imagined.

The Plans

Kate was keen to reciprocate Anne's and Helen's hospitality. A fortnight after the barbecue, she invited them and Alison to her place for dinner and a game of Five Hundred. She rang Alison first. Alison was free and said she'd be delighted to come.

'Good, I'll ring Anne and Helen, and see if they can come.'

'I must tell you something strange,' Alison said. 'Toni Crawford was mugged on the weekend.'

'*What?*'

'I'm not deaf, Kate.'

'Sorry,' Kate said. 'It's just such a coincidence, considering we were talking about her. How do you know?'

'There was a tiny bit in *The Canberra Envoy*,' Alison replied.

'What did it say?' Kate enquired.

'Just said she was mugged by two men in balaclavas a short distance from her home, treated at the hospital and allowed to leave.'

'Was she robbed?'

'It didn't say she was.'

'Did they find the men?'

'No,' Alison responded.

'If she was allowed to leave the hospital, she couldn't have been that badly hurt.'

'I guess not,' Alison agreed. 'It's a shame she wasn't pounded to a pulp. Well, I'd better hang up, so you can ring Anne and Helen. See you Saturday night.'

Kate had to compose herself before she rang Anne and Helen. Had the muggers been Brett and Tom? Obviously, Alison hadn't made a connection. Then Kate remembered she hadn't told Alison where Brett was going. Although Kate had known that Brett was going to Wagga Wagga, she'd merely told Alison he was going away for the weekend.

Kate put on a delicious meal, and all four women enjoyed the Five Hundred. Towards the end of the evening, Alison asked Anne and Helen, 'When was the last time you visited your block of land in the country?'

'About two months ago,' Helen replied.

Kate was very interested. 'Where is it?'

'It's about forty kilometres from our house, on Grawback Road.'

'How long have you had it?' Kate asked.

'About four months,' Helen replied. 'We should all go there one day for a picnic.'

'One day? How about next Saturday?' Kate suggested.

'Does that suit everyone?' Anne asked.

'Yes,' came the reply.

'Okay,' Helen said. 'We'll take one car. What say we meet at our place at twelve o'clock? BYO everything. There's nothing – I repeat *nothing* – out there.'

One consistent thing about the group of women was their punctuality. Alison and Kate arrived at five to twelve and found Anne and Helen ready to leave. They hopped in Anne's four-wheel drive, and she drove to the property. The gate to the property was locked, and on it was a sign that read 'PRIVATE PROPERTY'. Helen jumped out and unlocked the gate. Anne drove through, and Helen relocked the gate. They drove about half a kilometre up an unsealed road and stopped.

'Here we are. Everybody out!' Anne announced.

'Wow, what a fabulous place!' Kate exclaimed. 'So private; all those trees.'

'Yes,' Anne replied.

Helen joked, 'You could commit a few axe murders out here without anyone knowing.'

Then Kate saw a large metal shed and close by it an enormous hole that had a huge steel framework in it. 'I thought you said there was nothing out here.'

'I meant nothing in the way of home comforts,' Helen clarified. 'I'll explain the shed and hole over lunch.'

Anne brought out a fold-up picnic table and four chairs, and each woman put her food and drinks on the table. The talk was trivial until Helen commented that the previous night, she'd watched a documentary about the Holocaust. 'It's hard to comprehend how one man could turn so many people into such evil creatures. How did he get them to carry out such atrocities?'

'He did it through hate,' Alison responded. 'He was able to convince them that the Jews were responsible for their suffering. Hatred can turn a person into an evil being.'

'I agree,' Anne said. 'My grandmother's best friend was the victim of a robbery. A guy snatched her handbag while she was waiting for a taxi. She lost her balance, fell over, broke her wrist and split her lip. Psychologically, she was a mess after the incident, almost too frightened to leave her house. Of course, the guy got off with some piddly weekend detention. I took Grandma to the hospital to visit her. She looked dreadful. I honestly believe if that'd been Grandma, I'd have gone after the guy with my softball bat. I even worked out a plan.'

'Do you really think you'd have carried out your plan? Sometimes the consequences aren't worth it,' Kate said.

'Knowing Anne, she'd have risked the consequences,' Helen said, in a very convincing tone.

Without giving Anne time to respond to her question, Kate continued. 'I knew a girl who was raped. The rapist was acquitted on a technicality. Her father and brother wanted to smash him to pieces, but they realised they'd only create a worse situation: they'd be sent to gaol, and the girl and her mother would be on their own. They knew that if they were in gaol, they couldn't help their daughter and sister try to recover from the trauma.'

Anne was adamant. 'If I had a daughter and she was raped, and the guy got off, I'd *have* to do something – but I don't have a daughter.'

'What about a friend? Would you do the same for a friend?' Kate asked.

'I'm sure I would,' Anne replied.

'You still haven't told me about the shed and the hole,' Kate said impatiently.

Helen responded, 'The couple we bought this block from were very committed greenies. They were going to build an eco-friendly cottage. Anne drew up the plans. They built that shed, purchased everything for the first stage of the cottage, had it delivered and constructed that steel framework, and then they fell behind with their repayments. They were desperate to sell, but no one was interested. They asked Anne whether she'd buy it. She discussed it with me, and we decided to buy it together. We thought it might be fun to have a block in the country.'

'That's not the reason you bought it,' Alison said teasingly. 'That couple was desperate to sell. You got a good deal, and knowing you two, you'll sell it in four or five years and make a killing.'

Anne and Helen laughed.

'Not many of our friends know we have it,' Helen admitted, 'because when we were thinking about buying it, we mentioned it to some of them. All except Alison told us they thought it was a waste of money, so we didn't bother telling anyone we'd bought it. Now we have a block of land with an enormous hole in it and a shed full of tools, sheets of plywood steel-mesh concrete reinforcers and a long ladder. And underneath that poly tarp is a load of sand.'

'How big's the hole?' Kate asked.

Anne answered, 'About 5.3 by 4.3 metres, depth 4 metres.'

'I know what I could use it for,' Kate announced.

'Tell us, Kate,' Anne said.

Kate thought there was 'something' about Anne and Helen; she felt very close to them. She knew they'd be sympathetic, so she told them about the night she'd been raped at the quarry and the trial she'd had to endure.

'So I'd like to turn the hole into a dungeon, and lock Wayne Keys, Lyn Cullen and Colleen O'Day in it. Colleen O'Day is the national president of the Right to Esse. The Right to Esse doesn't believe in abortion under *any* circumstances. So, if I'd become pregnant as a consequence of the rape, the Right to Esse believes I shouldn't have been allowed to terminate it. What a mob of evil scum!'

When she'd finished talking, Alison and Helen were crying, and Anne was shaking with rage.

Helen stopped crying. She looked at Anne and saw an expression, which she'd never seen before, on Anne's face. 'What are you thinking?' Helen asked her.

Anne remained silent for a minute before replying, 'I'm thinking I should help Kate get justice.'

'Are you serious?' Kate asked.

'Yes, I'm serious. I promise you, Kate: Wayne Keys, Lyn Cullen and Colleen O'Day will end up in that hole. You and I will construct a dungeon and put them in it. It'll be our goal. I'm looking forward to it.'

'Oh, Anne, I don't know what to say,' Kate responded. 'Can we really do it?'

'Yes, Kate. We can *really* do it.'

'Can I help you achieve your goal?' Helen asked.

'I'd like to help too,' Alison added, not having given much thought to what she was saying.

Alison had never told Anne or Helen about her baby, so she was thinking how tactfully Kate had included Colleen O'Day in the list.

'Of course you can both help,' Anne replied. 'Several people can have the same goal, but you must be committed to it. Helen, remember when we went to hear Tony Dunn speak? Remember what he said about goals? "Set your goals. Don't let anyone stand in the way of your goals. Don't dwell on things that might go wrong, or you won't move forward. Think about what will go right." He also said it was important to write your goals down and read them morning, noon and night, but given the nature of our goal, I don't think that's wise.'

'Wow, you have a good memory!' Helen replied. 'I can remember hearing him raving on about goals, but I can't remember that much.'

Kate was surprised that Anne and Helen had gone to hear Tony Dunn. 'Did you go to hear Tony Dunn?' she asked.

Helen answered, 'One of the heavies at work believes in all that nonsense. I was under great pressure to attend, so I dragged Anne along.'

'I've set my goal,' Anne said. 'Wayne Keys, Lyn Cullen and Colleen O'Day will end up in that hole. We'll start our mission today. *Whoopee!* Perhaps this is the reason I was put on this planet – yours too, Helen: you're always questioning the meaning of life.'

Helen was upset. 'Anne, given the reasons for putting these monsters in the dungeon, I think you're being a bit insensitive. Yes, I do wonder about the meaning of life, but I don't believe that some people have to suffer to give other people their purpose in life.'

'You're right, Helen. I'm sorry. It's just that I haven't felt like this before. I almost feel like it's my duty to lock these evil creatures away.'

Alison was feeling strange, thinking that this was just one of those idle threats that Anne and Helen made in a fit of rage. *Wasn't it?* They couldn't be serious. Maybe they were. She really did believe that Colleen O'Day should be punished for being the president of an organisation that had enough power to bring so much needless misery to thousands of women.

Anne announced, 'We can start to plan our strategy right now. Everything we need to construct the cellar, dungeon, or whatever you want to call it, including the tools, is out here.'

'Can we build it ourselves?' Kate asked.

'Yes, Kate,' Anne replied. 'The hardest part – constructing that steel framework – is done. And more importantly, it's been inspected and approved. I'll draw up new plans for the cottage. "Cottage" isn't the correct word: it won't look like a cottage, more like a cabin. It won't be a very attractive construction. I don't think I'll put my company's name to it.

'There'll be no problem getting the changes approved. I'll make the changes as soon as I get to work on Monday. It won't take long. I should be able to take them to the Lands Office in the afternoon. I'll have to rethink the air vents. They were quite visible on the plans, but now we'll have to conceal them.'

'What about lighting? Or do we leave the prisoners in the dark?' Helen asked.

'The greenies were going to use solar lights.'

'Solar lights!' Kate exclaimed. 'How do they work?'

'They're powered by batteries that are charged by solar panels during the day.'

'*Solar panels!* Aren't they still in the experimental stage?'

'Apparently not. In 1979, Jimmy Carter had solar panels installed on the roof of the White House. Don Grimshaw, the bloke we bought the property from, told me about solar panels. There's a store in Brisbane that imports solar lights, and Solar Hot, in Fyshwick, is an agent.

'Don explained that the lights come in a kit. You get a panel, another piece of equipment – I think he said it was a controller – a battery, the light, cables and the instructions for how to put it all together.'

'Will our panels go on the roof?' Kate asked. 'What'll our roof look like?'

'I'll change it to flat metal,' Anne answered. 'That'll be the easiest to construct. I hope a flat roof will be okay for the panels. Helen, can you and Alison make some enquiries into solar lighting at Solar Hot?'

'Sure,' came the reply.

Anne continued, 'I hope groundwater won't be a problem. I raised that with Don when I was drawing up the plans. He reckoned it wouldn't be a problem. He said the hole was on top of a rise; the soil was clayey; there was a lot of rock – would probably have to do some blasting, which they did. I think the project's going to get out of hand if we try to line the cellar with bricks and seal the bricks.'

'I agree, Anne,' Helen responded. 'Let's take our chances. If groundwater becomes a problem, we'll just have to find a solution.'

'What were the greenies going to use the cellar for?' Kate asked.

'To grow mushrooms; store pumpkins for a year; wrap apples in straw and keep them fresh for months – all those sorts of things.'

Anne continued to tell them what was involved in constructing the first stage. It all sounded quite feasible. She said they should get together in a week's time. They agreed they'd go to Kate's on Saturday night.

'Come at six thirty,' Kate said, 'and we can have dinner together.'

Alison arranged to go with Anne and Helen. As soon as Kate had served the drinks, Anne started talking about what they now referred to as 'The Plans'. 'So, we all agree Wayne Keys and Lyn Cullen should be punished for what they did to Kate, and Colleen O'Day should also be punished for pushing the line that rape victims who become pregnant shouldn't be allowed to abort?'

'Yes,' came the group reply.

'Good, so we're all in this together. Once we start construction, we must be on our guard all the time not to let anything slip that we're building a dungeon. Whatever we do in relation to the dungeon, we mustn't leave any trails. That's vital. It's imperative that nothing can be traced back to us. And remember, we're a team: no one must do anything without consulting the other three.'

Helen was feeling uneasy. She'd gone along with many of Anne's hare-brained ideas and turned a blind eye to lots more, but none of them was on this scale. She didn't really believe that Anne would see the project through. Nevertheless, she told herself that she'd go along with it. Besides feeling uneasy, she was feeling excited.

Alison felt nervous. Building the dungeon would be fun; however, that was about as far into the future as she could see, or more correctly, that was as far as she wanted to see. She was frightened to think that The Plans might become a reality.

Kate was euphoric. She had an indescribable feeling when she thought of having Wayne Keys and Lyn Cullen in the dungeon.

Anne continued, 'It's nearly six months since that hole was dug. We can't be sure how many people know about it. The point is that some people do know it exists, so if anyone ever asks you what happened to it, don't lie. Say straight away that we built a cabin over it. Don't say we filled it in because you'll get in a hole yourself. The questioning might start, and then you'll be gone. For example, did you hire a loader? Where did you get the soil? The previous owners used the soil to build a dam, didn't they? How did you get the loader to the block?

'One other very important thing: financing the project. Are we happy to split the cost of everything by four?'

'Yes,' the others replied.

'I'm assuming that also means the mortgage payments,' Alison said.

'Are you happy with that?' Anne asked Kate.

'Absolutely,' Kate answered. 'I was also assuming that was part of the deal.'

'In that case,' Anne said, 'we'll get the property put in all four names. It'll be hard work building the dungeon and the cabin, but it can be done. Think of all those people who pay a fortune in gym fees. We'll get more exercise, and for free.

'During the week, Helen and I worked out how we'll construct the dungeon. "A picture paints a thousand words." First diagram: the gaol layout, approximate measurements:

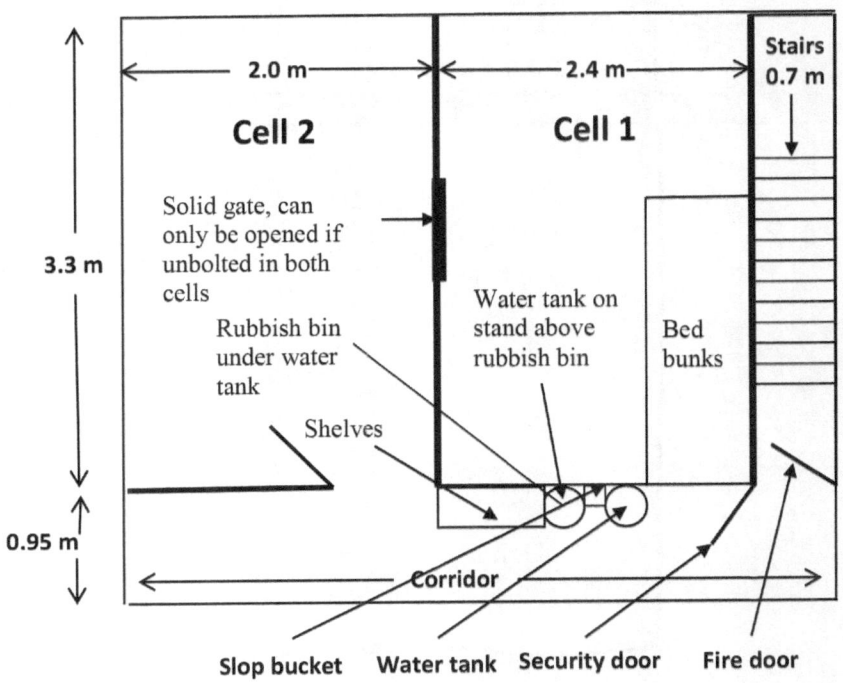

It was Helen's brilliant idea to have a solid security gate – more like a hatch – between the cells. This'll have bolts on each side, and it can only be opened if the occupants of each cell release the bolts. She decided on that just in case, sometime in the future, one or both cells require maintenance. We'd have to put all the prisoners in the one cell.

'Second diagram: the ventilation. The concrete bricks we'll be using to build the cabin are hollow and slightly porous. It's through this hollow section that air will get into the dungeon. Inside the cabin, we'll leave a small gap between the top of the wall and the roof supports, and before we have the concrete poured for the cabin floor, I'll mark out precisely – and I mean *precisely* – where the hollow part of the bricks will sit. I'll strategically put some pieces of wood over the areas I don't want concreted:

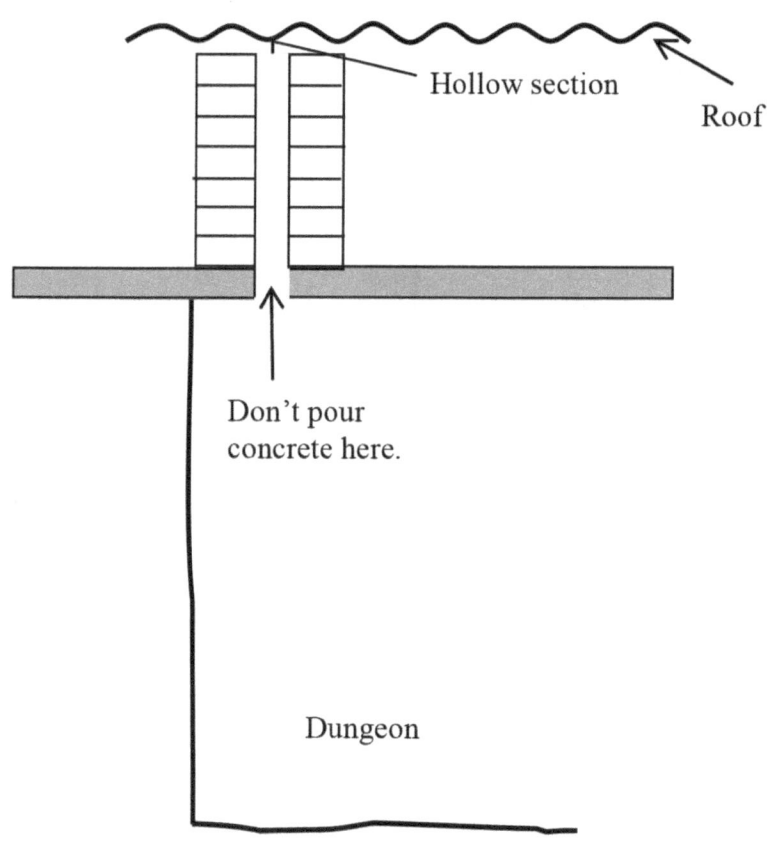

Hollow section

Roof

Don't pour
concrete here.

Dungeon

'I believe this setup will provide enough oxygen for the prisoners. The dungeon's a large volume compared with a motel room. Consider having three people in a motel room with the windows closed. The only air getting in is under the door. They survive the night. Helen also intends to make use of the cavity to run the cables from the solar panels.'

'Do you think noise will come up through the hollow section?' Kate asked.

'Helen and I thought of that. We don't think it will, but we will *thoroughly* test it before we put any prisoners there. If people in the cabin can hear people in the dungeon, we will have to come up with another way of getting air into the dungeon.'

'Sorry I interrupted you, Anne,' Kate said almost apologetically.

'Not at all, Kate. Great to see you are thinking of these things.'

'Unfortunately, there some things we can't test along the way,' Helen added. 'Keep going Anne.'

'Third diagram: getting the carbon dioxide out. We buy some plastic pipes that will fit through the cavity in the bricks. Put the pipes through the roof, through the cavity into the dungeon, and sit a little whirlybird on top of each pipe. *Huge problem*: any visitor to the cabin – and we can't rule out that that will never happen – might think it strange we have our whirlybirds over the cavity. I think I have destroyed some of my brain cells trying to come up with a believable answer, should anyone ask. The best I can do is: "The bricks the cabin is made of are porous. I thought if we installed some whirlybirds over the cavity, it might help keep the cavity dry should damp become a problem." So if anyone asks the question, that's the answer you give. Nothing more, nothing less!

'We will have four whirlybirds: two whirlybirds will sit on top of pipes which go into the dungeon in the corridor, and the other two will sit symmetrically on the other side, but those pipes won't go into the dungeon. If they did, they'd be in the cells – too risky. The prisoners might try to use them to scream for help.

'Sorry about that long-winded waffle, but this is very important.'

'It wasn't waffle,' Kate said. 'It *is* important.'

'Thanks Kate. So, to get back to the *real* reason: do you think this'll work, Alison?'

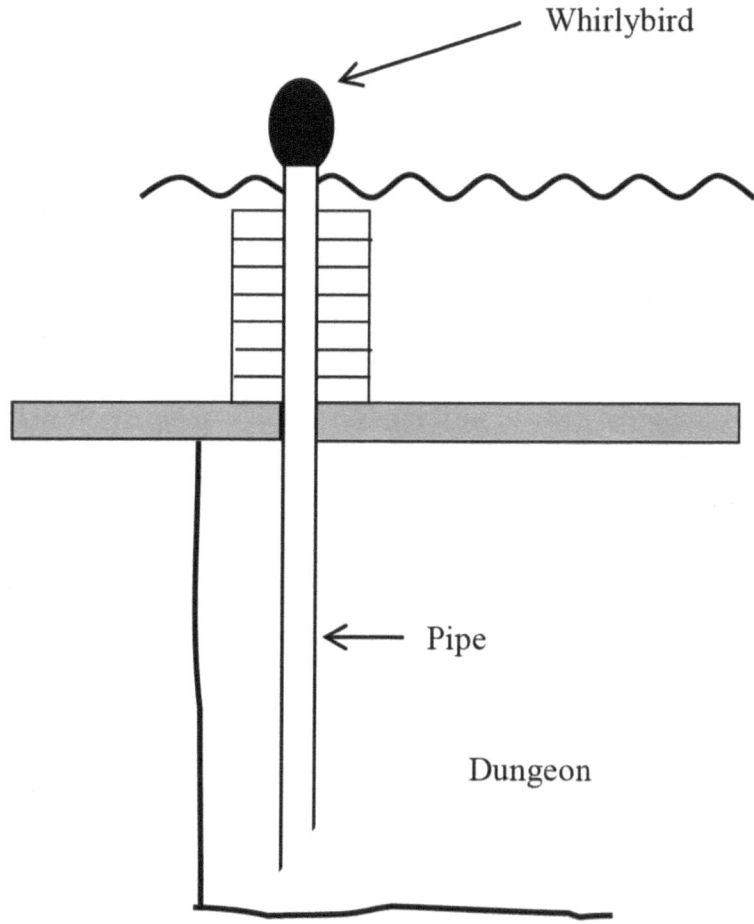

Whirlybird

Pipe

Dungeon

'Yes, I do,' Alison replied. 'That setup should extract the CO_2. You're brilliant, the way you come up with a solution to everything.'

'Fourth diagram: the front of the cells. I've gone over *and over* about what's the best way, and this is my plan. Most of the big hardware stores and the plumbing and fencing suppliers sell metal pipes that are used to construct fences and other things such as dog runs and aviaries. The pipes come in various lengths and diameters. I propose to construct the front of the cells out of them. The pipes can be joined in any way. There are corner joins, two-way joins, three-way joins and four-way joins. The front of the cells will be like a giant grid. This is what it'll look like:

'The blank parts are of course where the gates will go. We'll attach, in a very flimsy way, wood-veneer panels to the lower half to make it look less like a gaol. Once the prisoners are inside, we'll remove the panels.

'I've done some calculations, and I've worked out how many pipes we'll need. When the time comes, I'll tell each of you how many to buy.

'Last: how do we hide the entrance to the dungeon? We'll construct a trapdoor, and on it, we'll sit a cupboard, one that's bench height. We'll screw the cupboard to the wall in four places, from the inside. The screws won't be seen from the outside, and the cupboard will be on invisible castors. Each time we go into the gaol, we'll have to undo the screws, roll the cupboard off the trapdoor and open the trapdoor. When the trapdoor's opened, it'll lean against the cupboard, so we'll have ready access to the stairs.'

Alison and Kate stared at the dungeon plans, hardly able to believe that Anne and Helen had achieved so much in so short a time.

'Alison and Kate, do you have any questions?' Anne asked.

'No,' Kate replied, 'but I think your plans are brilliant.'

'So do I,' Alison added.

'I want to say something, but it's not about the dungeon plans,' Kate said. 'Once, when I was on the phone, I must've got a crossed line, and I could hear every word of another woman's conversation. I mentioned this to a friend, and he said he'd had a similar experience. What say we make a rule we never talk about The Plans on the phone?'

'Excellent idea,' Anne replied. 'Now, Alison, do you want to tell us what you've found out about solar lights?'

'Sure. The batteries charge during the day and the lights come on at night, so the prisoners' day will be our night and their night will be our day—'

'Sorry to interrupt, Alison,' Anne said, 'but I've just thought of a problem. If it's daytime and the solar lights aren't on, we might have trouble persuading someone to walk into a very dark hole.'

'We can get around that,' Alison said. 'If we cover the panels with something opaque, the panels will think it's night-time and the lights will go on, but there is an optional on/off switch.'

'That's a relief,' Anne commented. 'Keep going, Alison.'

'I propose we have an on/off switch for the light in the cabin and leave the ones in the dungeon automatic. We'll have to give the prisoners torches for their night, and depending how much they use them, we could go broke buying batteries. We will also need torches because if we go into the dungeon during the day, the solar lights won't be on. I suggest we all buy a battery-operated camping lantern which takes rechargeable batteries, and a battery charger. We can hammer some hooks into the corridor wall to hang the lanterns on when we are there.'

Anne agreed. 'Good idea. I intend to get each cell a CD player, and those things will also chew up the batteries. But remember, make sure your lantern or some other gadget takes size D batteries. We don't want a friend to see you recharging size D batteries if you don't have something to put them in.'

Helen was next to speak. 'I've made a list of everything we'll need to buy for the cells: one camp stretcher, one set of camping bunks, three mattresses, three water tanks, three foam cubes to sit on, two plastic tables, two slop buckets, two camping thunderboxes, two camping showers, sand to put under the showers, two rubber shower mats to put on the sand, outdoor carpet for the floor, linen and kitchenware.'

'We don't have to buy any sand,' Anne stated. 'There's no shortage of sand. Under that poly tarp is enough sand to cover 160 square metres.'

'That's good,' Helen said, 'because I intend to cover the floor of the dungeon with sand before we lay the carpet.'

'Do you think there'll be a drainage problem with the shower?' Alison asked.

'I don't think so,' Helen responded. 'They won't be showering every day, once a week at the most, and it'll be a very short shower. We'll dig a large pit under the shower and fill it with sand. If it becomes boggy, the prisoners will have to refrain from having a shower till the bog dries out. For the dunny, we'll dig a big hole in the corner of each cell. We'll knock out the bottoms of the thunderboxes and sit the thunderboxes over the dunny holes.'

'Last time I was in a national park, I went to an eco-toilet,' Alison mentioned. 'There was a sign on the back of the door to inform the user how the toilet worked. Perhaps I should go back and write down the instructions.'

'Forget it, Alison,' Anne said. 'I've read all that stuff, and in my opinion those toilets are just glorified long-drops. There's no useful information on the back of those doors.'

'How deep do we make the dunny holes?' Helen asked. 'Does anyone know how long it takes a turd to seep away completely?'

'No, but if the loo overflows, we'll be in deep shit!' Kate joked.

'Ha! Ha! Good one, Kate!' Alison responded.

Helen continued, 'We're dealing with a lot of unknowns. I'm taking a wild guess that we make the holes, which will be square, about thirty centimetres wide and seventy centimetres deep.'

'Won't one hole have to be twice as deep as the other one?' Alison queried.

'I'm assuming that size will be adequate for two inmates. We'll make the holes the same size. You never know: Keys might crap at the same rate as the two women.'

'Don't you think there'll be a problem with smell?' Alison suggested.

'Possibly,' Helen replied. 'We'll have to play that one by ear.'

'Don't you mean "rear"?' Anne jested.

'Play it by nose,' Kate added.

'Okay, let's get serious again,' Helen said. 'We'll use the temporary fencing panels that are now around the hole to – for want of a better expression – line the cells, to stop the prisoners from tunnelling their way out. Mind you, I think it'd be just about impossible, but we won't take any chances. We don't want people reading about one of those incredible escape stories: "Four women arrested after a man tunnelled his way out of a four-metre-deep dungeon using a plastic spoon." It'll have to be the last thing we do because once we've put the panels *in* the gaol, there'll be no fence *around* the hole. We'll have to have the concrete for the gaol roof, which is also the cabin floor, poured the very next day. How's everyone bearing up? I still have more to say.'

'Keep going, Helen,' Kate said.

'Okay. The gates for the entrance to the cells are made of wrought iron, and you don't need the key to lock them. Once the gates are closed, they lock automatically. The vertical bars on the gates have an eleven-centimetre gap between them. I've worked out that there's nothing in the way of groceries or toiletries that won't fit through the gaps. We buy some shelves, the open metal ones used in sheds. We stand them in front of the gates. The prisoners can put their hands through the gaps and take what they need from the shelves, and they can push their washing through and leave it on the bottom shelf. Does anyone have any comments?'

'No,' was the unanimous reply.

Anne, Helen and Alison had thought of everything, and Kate was feeling guilty she hadn't contributed anything.

'I want to talk about purchasing things for the gaol,' Anne said. 'Always pay cash and be discreet. For example, the pipes for the front of the cells: don't buy them all in one go. Go to different stores. A woman putting five pipes in a car mightn't be as memorable to a shop assistant as a woman struggling to fit fourteen pipes in. Never draw attention to yourself when you're buying something for the gaol. I'll buy the gates.'

'Anne, can I buy the gates?' Kate asked.

'No, Kate. It'll be simpler if I buy them. You'd have to have them delivered, and that'd mean giving an address.'

'Maybe I could borrow your four-wheel drive,' Kate suggested.

'No, again. If your neighbours are nosy, they might notice that Ms Scott, who owns a silver, two-door Lancer, was seen driving a four-wheel-drive vehicle that had a large roof rack and two security gates on the roof rack.'

'Aren't we being a bit paranoid?' Helen asked.

'No,' Anne replied. 'We have to be on guard all the time. We have to have a ready answer for any question someone might ask. I'll call it our "Q&As". I'll buy the gates.'

'Okay, Anne,' Helen said. 'Here's another Q&A: we have ten temporary fence panels around the hole. I estimate we'll need eight of them for lining the cells so how do we get rid of two temporary fence panels?'

'We'll think of a way,' Anne replied. 'And you've given me an idea. We'll hinge one riser at the top so we can push it back and drop any rubbish that might be risky for us to dispose of. I can't think of anything right now, but you never know. On a totally different note, wills: we'll all have to amend our wills in order to take care of this property. Does next Saturday suit everyone for our first working bee?'

'Yes,' the others replied.

'Bring a pair of light-duty gardening gloves. We don't want any broken finger nails,' Helen added.

Shortly after midnight, Alison, Helen and Anne decided it was time to go home. On the way home, they talked about Kate. They felt very sorry for her, knowing she'd been robbed of her life.

'Sometimes, when I look at Kate, I can see the sadness in her eyes,' Alison said. 'At uni, her eyes positively sparkled, and her mouth was in a constant smile, those gorgeous eyes and her beautiful white teeth.'

'I hope having Wayne Keys and Lyn Cullen in our private gaol, where they belong, will be therapeutic for her,' Helen said. 'I believe in "an eye for an eye".'

'So do I,' Anne added. 'Maybe the sparkle and smile will return.'

At nine thirty the following Saturday, the four women were at the block.

Anne got right down to business. 'The first thing we should do is bolt the supports for the cabin floor. Bolting them in place should be easy. The only danger is that a beam might fall on someone's foot or someone might fall in the hole. We must be very safety-conscious. Laying the beams also means we can cover the hole with that huge poly tarp.'

As soon as they'd placed the four horizontal beams in position, they ate lunch. After lunch, they dug some trenches: one for the grid, one for the dividing wall between the cells, and another for the wall between the staircase and Cell 1. Then Helen said, 'Let's call it a day.'

All agreed they should. They covered the hole with the poly tarp, put boulders on the edge of the tarp to prevent the wind from dislodging it and closed up the safety fence.

'Anne, you said no one must know we're building a gaol,' Alison said. 'Do you think it's possible someone will come on to the property and check things out when we're not here?'

'That thought's crossed my mind too,' Anne admitted. 'The gate to the property's always locked, the hole is now covered with a tarp, and the hole has a fence round it. We could go on and on about security. Someone could open the safety fence; someone could climb over the safety fence; someone could set fire to the tarp. Ever since we've owned the property, we've seen no evidence that anyone's trespassed on it. I'm not saying it hasn't happened, but I think we can be pretty certain no one will come prying. If we come out here one day and there's evidence someone's been snooping around, what do we do, abandon the project? I don't think so.'

That night, Anne and Helen went over the gaol plans.

'I'm in uncharted waters, Helen,' Anne said. 'It's awkward not knowing the precise dimensions of the hole. I hope I've worked out those pipe lengths correctly, and I hope Lyn Cullen's not a Two Ton Tessie who can't fit down the stairs or that Keys hasn't got a twisted hand that won't fit through the gate.'

'Assuming he doesn't have two twisted hands, he shouldn't have any problem getting his supplies off the shelves. I've checked that out. I opened a kitchen cupboard eleven centimetres and had no trouble getting out a large can of beetroot, and I think it's highly unlikely Lyn Cullen's more than seventy centimetres across the beam.'

Anne felt responsible for the gaol's success, being the one who'd promised Kate vengeance. She mustn't let her down.

Helen was enjoying building the gaol, although she wasn't sure about the structure's future use. One thing clear to her was the other three women's determination. She'd have to do her part. They'd made a deal.

On Sunday, Kate played tennis, had coffee with her tennis friends and went home to catch up on the household chores and get ready for another week. She loved the days they'd spent at the block, building the gaol. She was thrilled and yet frightened at the thought of having Wayne Keys and Lyn Cullen in the dungeon. She was very moved by the other three women's commitment to attaining justice for her. She mustn't show any fear. They were all so positive. She'd have to do her bit.

Alison had one of her typical Sundays. She went for a bicycle ride with some friends, had afternoon tea with them and went home to finish a book ahead of her book-club meeting scheduled for Tuesday night. That night, she thought about The Plans. It was fun building the gaol, but were Wayne Keys, Lyn Cullen and Colleen O'Day really going to end up in it? She must never show her doubts because showing them would equate to betrayal. The other three women were committed to the project. She must do her share.

Helen had a relaxing Sunday. She and Peter went to the National Gallery to see an exhibition and then went to a six o'clock movie.

Anne went to golf.

The women were very careful not to let the construction of the gaol take over their lives. They didn't go to the property every weekend.

After four months of hard work, the gaol was ready for the prospective prisoners.

The four women sat in the gaol to make sure they hadn't forgotten anything. Helen said with pride, 'Try with all your might, Wayne Keys, Lyn Cullen and Colleen O'Day: you'll never pull that barrier down. The top's bolted to the metal cross-beams and the bottom's set in twenty centimetres of concrete.'

Kate produced a large vacuum flask and a packet of biscuits. 'What say we have a cup of coffee and a biscuit in this five-star accommodation? We only have three cushions, so I'll sit on the plush carpet.'

All four couldn't help but marvel at what they'd constructed.

It was now time to construct the cabin floor, or the gaol ceiling, whichever way you looked at it.

On Monday, the truck arrived with the concrete. Anne, Helen and Alison worked frantically, spreading and smoothing it. Kate was feeling guilty she hadn't helped, but the others assured her not to worry.

The following Saturday, they all went out to see how the concrete had set.

'Perfect,' Anne declared. 'Now we have to build the cabin. I'd like to get it finished before Christmas. If we all agree, we should take advantage of daylight saving and come out after work some days.'

All agreed it was a good idea. The cabin would be visible, so there was no need for any secret purchases. This part wasn't going to be as exhausting as the building of the gaol.

On the way home, Anne thought about the fun they'd had constructing the gaol. She also thought about why they'd built it, and she felt nervous. If they made any slip-ups, it would be Alison, Helen, Kate and she ending up in a state gaol rather than Wayne Keys, Lyn Cullen and Colleen O'Day ending up in the gaol the four women had built. That night, Anne told Helen she was working on a plan to get Wayne Keys into the gaol. 'I won't go over the plan now; I'll take you through it when I'm satisfied with it.'

Helen was relieved. She wasn't sure she wanted to hear it.

'I want him to meet us at the Hapley shops because they're the closest shopping centre to the property. But we have to make a few visits to the shops before we arrange to meet him. I don't want our first visit to them to be on the same day Keys disappears. We'll have coffee a few times at Zig's. We'll also have coffee a few times after he disappears. We'll go next Sunday. I think three visits will be enough.'

Helen asked no questions and was willing to go for coffee at Zig's the following Sunday.

Finally, the cabin and gaol were finished. The four women were checking to see that they hadn't overlooked anything.

'The only thing which we haven't addressed is cooking,' Anne said. 'I've been thinking about cooking and heating water. I've seen a little hiking stove with a flint. It uses disposable cylinders. I think we should try it, and if the inmates abuse the privilege by trying to burn something, they lose the stove – not that we'll go into the cell and retrieve it, we just won't buy them any more cylinders, and they'll have to eat cold food.'

'Struth, Anne!' Helen exclaimed. 'With cooking, breathing, farting and methane gas from the dunny, those little whirlybirds will be working overtime!'

'Methane's lighter than air,' Alison informed them, 'so theoretically, when we lift up the trapdoor and open the downstairs doors, the methane will escape.'

'Thanks for that information, Alison,' Helen said. 'That'll be a nice thing to greet us every time we visit the prisoners. By the way, Alison, what's up? You look worried.'

'Er ... nothing,' Alison mumbled.

'If something's troubling you, tell us,' Anne insisted.

'Er ... sometimes ... sometimes I get nervous about what we're doing,' Alison said softly.

'Criminals get caught through their own slip-ups. We won't make any. It's our duty to punish Keys, Cullen and O'Day.' Anne didn't add that she and Helen also felt nervous and that she was sure Kate felt the same. 'Keys will be our first prisoner. I've worked out a plan. Now I want your advice.'

'Are you feeling okay, Anne? Since when did you want anyone's advice?' Helen asked light-heartedly.

Anne took no offence. She and Helen often ribbed each other. 'Do we invite a few friends out here? Secrecy can lead to suspicion.'

All agreed it was a good idea.

'Next Sunday will be our last chance before Christmas,' Helen remarked.

'Settled,' Anne said. 'I'll invite Malcolm and Peter for afternoon tea next Sunday.'

Kate suggested she and Alison not go to the afternoon tea. 'I think it best if Alison and I distance ourselves from the block. Obviously, Malcolm and Peter will ask questions. The fewer people around who can answer them the better. I can't explain exactly what I'm trying to say, but—'

'Yes, Kate, I can see what you mean,' Anne said.

The following Sunday afternoon, Anne, Helen, Malcolm and Peter went to the block for afternoon tea, and Malcolm and Peter certainly asked some questions.

Visualising

Kate rang Helen to ask how Malcolm and Peter enjoyed the afternoon tea.

'They enjoyed it very much,' Helen said. 'No one would suspect a thing. From time to time, we'll invite the odd person or two to the block. We all agree secrecy can lead to suspicion. Kate, you sound a bit down. Are you all right? Did you go to tennis this afternoon?'

'Yes,' Kate answered. 'I had a very pleasant afternoon, but I'm a bit depressed: Friday was my birthday ...'

'Kate!' Helen exclaimed. 'Why didn't you tell us? We'd have taken you out to dinner or a show or both.'

'Well, I guess that's *why* I didn't say anything. I always get down on my birthday, but Friday was particularly bad. We always have a cake when someone has a birthday. At recess, we were in the staff room and Denise produced a cake with three candles on it. She lit them, I blew them out, and everyone sang "Happy Birthday". I put on a brave face. Then Martha, the deputy principal, sang that stupid song "Why Was She Born So Beautiful?" When she sang the line "Why was she born at all?", I nearly lost it. Luckily, the bell rang – talk about "saved by the bell" – because the truth of the matter is, ever since that dreadful night at the quarry, I've often asked myself the same question: *Why was I born at all?* Do you know what Sophocles said?'

'He said a lot of things,' Helen stated. 'Which one comes to mind?'

'"To never have been born may be the greatest boon of all."'

Helen was doing all she could to hold back her tears. 'Do you want me to come over?'

'No thanks, Helen. I really appreciate your offer, but I'll be okay. I'm going to have a few games of solitaire and then go to bed.'

'Kate, ring me if you want anything,' Helen implored her. 'It doesn't matter if it's two o'clock in the morning, I'll come over.'

'Thanks, Helen. No one could ask for a better friend. On a different note, I can't get over our achievement: finishing the gaol before Christmas was really something.'

'Yes, it was.'

Christmas 1988 came and went, and late January 1989 was now upon them. It was always the time of year that Kate was at her lowest. She was depressed at the thought of another year on her own, doing the same things and being one year closer to old age. She felt like crying. All the group members except Brett were back from their holidays, and he'd be home the next day. Kate had one more day of feeding his dog and taking her for a walk. In four days, she'd be back at work. She was almost ready to go to Brett's house when the phone rang. It was Alison. Kate could tell by the way Alison spoke that she too was feeling down.

'I'm going to Brett's place to feed Gandee and take her for a walk. Why don't you come over and come with us? I'll wait for you.'

Alison agreed, and twenty-five minutes later, they started walking to Brett's house. 'Where's the dog food?' she enquired.

'At Brett's. He left me a key to the back door. It only takes about fifteen minutes to walk to his house.'

When they were inside the gate, Gandee ran to greet Kate.

'What a beautiful dog!' Alison remarked.

'She *is* a beautiful dog,' Kate agreed. 'Just like her master. Brett's such a lovely person. Remember the story he told us about the father who didn't have a close relationship with his son?'

'Yes, I remember.'

'The boy's his godson. Brett was taking him to Disneyland and then to San Diego to visit the zoo.'

'Brett's wasted,' Alison commented. 'He should be married to a lovely woman and have two beautiful children.'

'I agree. Come on, let's go inside and get the dog food.'

When Kate unlocked the back door, Alison saw a sparkling-clean, tidy kitchen.

Kate put the dog food in a bowl and put the bowl on the grass, and she and Alison chatted while Gandee ate her food.

'I was admiring that little silver cactus on Brett's windowsill,' Alison said. 'I bet he got it in Tijuana.'

'What makes you say that?' Kate asked.

'I saw ones like that when I was in Tijuana.'

'He sometimes talks about where he's been, but he's never mentioned Tijuana. Maybe it was a gift.'

Gandee finished her food and stood perfectly still while Kate clipped the lead to her collar.

'What a good dog!' Alison commented.

'She sure is. As I said, just like her master. And she never pulls on the lead. She's so easy to walk.'

Kate and Alison walked Gandee for almost an hour. As soon as they'd returned to Brett's house, Kate removed the dog's lead. Gandee immediately raced to her water bowl and had a long drink. Kate topped up the water bowl and made sure everything at Brett's place was secure. Then the two women walked back to Kate's house.

'Do you want to stay for dinner?' Kate asked her friend. 'I'm not expecting a knight in shining armour to come knocking on my door.'

'Join the club! Thanks, Kate. I'd love to.'

'Dinner won't be the greatest,' Kate confessed. 'The larder's a bit empty.'

'I'd rather eat a stale scone with you than a six-course meal on my own,' Alison said in response.

'That's a nice thing to say, Alison.'

Kate made a tasty omelette and served it with hot toast, and the two chatted away between mouthfuls.

Suddenly, Alison said, 'Kate, I keep forgetting to tell you this: you must come to the Lawfail meeting on Wednesday night. Have you ever heard of Alex McAlpine?'

'No,' was the response.

'He'll be at Wednesday night's meeting. I'm sure you'll find his story interesting. In a way, his story's similar to yours. His niece was brutally murdered. The guy who killed her got off. Smart-arse judges disallowing evidence; you've heard it all before. So Alex McAlpine went and shot the guy.'

'The first part of the story's similar,' Kate said diffidently. 'I hope someday the second part's the same.'

'If you decide to go, the meeting's at Polly's. Some of our mob are getting together at six thirty for dinner before the meeting. Well, I guess it's time for me to go home.'

After Alison left, Kate felt very lonely. She suspected that Alison would have the same feeling when she arrived at her empty townhouse.

Next morning, just before eleven o'clock, someone knocked on Kate's door. She was surprised to see Brett there. 'Brett, I didn't expect to see you so soon. I thought you'd still be jet-lagged.'

'No, we had a fabulous trip back. Lots of empty seats. I slept all the way. So did Tim.'

'Come in.'

'I brought you a bracelet from Tijuana.'

'I didn't know you were going to Tijuana,' Kate commented in a surprised voice because Brett had given her his itinerary before he'd left, and there was no mention of Tijuana.

'I hadn't planned to, but as we were so close, I decided to go.'

'Have you been before?' Kate asked.

He hesitated for a moment before replying, 'No.'

'Brett, have you heard of an organisation called Lawfail?'

'I have,' he answered, 'but I don't know much about it.'

'I was wondering whether you'd like to go to the Lawfail meeting on Wednesday night.'

'Yes, Kate, I'd like to go. Is it all right to go in your car? I lent mine to Paul. I told him he could keep it till Friday.'

'That's fine.'

Kate was glad they'd be going in her car: she wanted to take every opportunity she could to drive at night. It'd be dark when they were driving home. She and Brett agreed they'd meet the other partakers at six thirty for dinner.

After he left, she got to thinking about his visit to Tijuana. Had he planned to go there? Had he been there before? *Forget it, Kate!* she commanded herself. *Brett wouldn't lie!*

Lawfail meetings were held on the first Wednesday night of each month at eight o'clock in the function room at the back of the Polly Hotel. The owner of Polly's, Jack Dawe, didn't charge the Lawfail members room hire; he was a member of the organisation and was pleased to provide the room free of charge. Although it wasn't much of a function room, the Lawfail members were very grateful to Jack for letting them use it.

When Brett and Kate arrived at the hotel, Anne, Helen, Alison, Malcolm and Wendy were already there. Everyone was always glad to see a new face at a Lawfail meeting. The menu was somewhat limited, but they all enjoyed what Malcolm described as 'a hearty counter tea'.

At a quarter to eight, Kate and Brett went to the function room, the others having said they'd be along as soon as they'd finished their drinks. A woman at the door was handing out copies of the agenda and some notes about a new Lawfail case. Kate and Brett took a copy of each document. They were reading the agenda when a man approached them and introduced himself. His name was Trevor Orchard. 'Is this your first meeting?' he asked them.

'Yes,' was Kate's and Brett's response.

'I hope we see you again,' Trevor said. He then pointed out the president. 'That's Jim Clunes. He's a wonderful president. He manages to control the divisions within the group. Unfortunately, we have some very definite factions. We have some people who want the death penalty reinstated; we have some people who want the victim to be able to confront the accused; we've got the very militant who almost believe that when justice fails, someone should shoot the criminal and the judge; and we've got people who take a more orthodox approach, as in publicising the injustices and lobbying the politicians. One faction is called the Religious Wrong. When they first came to prominence, they were referred to as the Religious Right. One night, someone asked, "What's *right* about them?" And from then on, they were known as the Religious Wrong. Did you come tonight to hear Alex McAlpine?'

'Yes,' Brett replied, 'but that doesn't mean I won't come to the next meeting.'

'This is where our factions come in,' Trevor explained. 'It'll mainly be the militants here tonight. Some of us think Alex is a hero. Many members disapprove of what he did. I predict some'll make their point by walking out when he starts speaking. Not all cases get the full backing of Lawfail. We have a new case being presented tonight. I've read the notes. The Religious Wrong won't support it. Most of the Religious Wrong support the Right to Esse. They won't want Lawfail to take on the new case. Hopefully none of them are here tonight.'

'Will you support the new case?' Kate asked him.

'I sure will.'

'I take it you're not a fan of the Right to Esse,' Kate said.

'No, I am not,' Trevor answered. 'I think they're a mob of evil germs. Are you a fan?'

'No, I'd like to shoot the lot of them.'

'I wouldn't waste the bullets, Kate,' Trevor advised her. 'I'd like to find a great, big, open-cut mine and herd them into it – send them over the edge, like lemmings. My wife … my wife … my wife had a … my wife says the only thing beneath a sea snake's duodenum, lying on the sea bed, is the Right to Esse.' He was about to cry. 'Sorry, Kate,' he said. 'I get so … It's almost eight, perhaps we should find a seat.'

Kate noticed Helen, who indicated there were some spare seats near her and the others.

The meeting started at eight o'clock on the dot. Jim Clunes welcomed everyone and asked whether everyone had a copy of the agenda and the notes about the new case. After he'd given the apologies, discussed the minutes of the previous meeting and read out the president's and treasurer's reports, it was on to other business: three progress reports, the new case and the special guest speaker, Alex McAlpine.

Each case was given a name. The first progress report was about the Dr Bloomer case. A woman by the name of Penny Jacobs spoke for approximately fifteen minutes about what action the members were taking to make Dr Bloomer accountable for his decision to allow a psychiatric patient to take day leave, so he could attend his grandmother's birthday party. Dr Bloomer had ignored the advice of two junior doctors and the sister in charge, and his decision had led to the death of an innocent woman. The anger that the family of the murdered woman had towards Dr Bloomer was amplified because of his arrogant attitude. He didn't believe he should have taken the advice of two junior doctors, let alone that of a nurse. The case had received national coverage, and the Lawfail members were hoping to give it more publicity. Penny gave the details of two demonstrations that had been arranged.

Kate noted that Brett wrote down the time and place for both demonstrations.

Another woman then spoke about the Rodney Fuller case. Rodney Fuller had been on his fourth drink-driving charge, but Magistrate Penn had let him off with a fine and a warning. Two weeks later, while under the influence of alcohol, Fuller had hit a woman who was walking on a pedestrian crossing.

David Best then gave a progress report about the Harry Willis case. Harry had been ignoring an AVO his former girlfriend had taken out on him. He'd threatened her several times and thrown a brick through her lounge-room window, but 'no one' was doing anything to ensure he was complying with the AVO.

After the progress reports had been delivered, it was on to the new case, and for that, Jim introduced Keith Davies. Jim informed the audience that the committee had agreed to take on Keith's case and that Mike Baker was to coordinate it.

Keith thanked Jim and said all he wanted to say was in his report, so he'd read it out: 'I come from Coomesville. We don't have a Lawfail group in Coomesville, so I've come to Canberra to seek Lawfail's help.

The victim in this case is my sister. I'm tackling a very sensitive subject. We talk about separation of church and state, but we don't talk about separation of church and law.

'My sister's a widow. She has a daughter, Glenda, who's mildly retarded. When Glenda turned fifteen, she became promiscuous. Glenda would go out at night after Betty had gone to bed; she'd wait at the front gate, and some guy would come by and pick her up.

'Betty was beside herself with worry. She wanted to have a tubal ligation performed on Glenda, but no doctor in Coomesville would perform the operation. She came to Canberra and saw a gynaecologist. He told her he'd perform the operation, but she'd need a court order. She spent a lot of money on legal fees, to no avail. Why? Because the magistrate assigned to the case was Michael Dutton. Michael Dutton's a very vocal member of the Right to Esse. Due to his personal beliefs, he opposes any form of sterilisation, for both males and females. He raved on about Glenda's right to have a child and that it's not up to someone to deny her the right. The solicitor presenting Betty's case explained that Glenda's condition was genetic and that there was a ninety per cent chance that any child of Glenda's would have the same condition. Dutton considered the fact irrelevant.

'In a trial by jury, the accused has some say in who the jurors will be. Betty had no say in who the magistrate would be. The solicitor cited the case of Marilyn X, in which Magistrate Maria Dunstan granted permission for a tubal ligation. Again, Michael Dutton said the fact was irrelevant. Betty and I both feel that if she'd been able to choose Maria Dunstan to preside, the outcome would've been quite different. Betty appealed. Judge Brendan O'Farrell, of the same ilk as Michael Dutton, also refused to grant permission.

'The inevitable happened: Glenda became pregnant. Betty tried to have the pregnancy terminated, but of course, termination wasn't allowed. Betty took Glenda to Sydney to a place called Karmoor. She assumed that Glenda would be well looked after there. After the baby was born, Betty went to Sydney to bring Glenda home. Betty wanted to have the baby adopted out because she knew that Glenda was incapable of caring for her, and Betty felt that she herself was too old to look after the child. However, Glenda was only mildly retarded, not completely stupid, as half the town thought she was, and refused to sign the adoption papers. The baby girl, who Glenda named Tiffany, has the same condition as Glenda's, so now my sister has the responsibility for a mentally handicapped daughter *and* granddaughter.

'I've come to Lawfail tonight hoping to obtain some support for Betty's case and, as you also say in Lawfail, to make judges responsible for their decisions. It's fine for Judge O'Farrell to talk about Glenda's right to have a child, but he's not the one left holding the baby – literally.'

Jim thanked Keith and again told the attendees that Mike Baker had volunteered to coordinate the case.

The last item on the agenda was the presentation by Alex McAlpine. Jim introduced Alex and informed the members, most of whom already knew, that Alex was the author of the book entitled *The Injustice in Justice*. Eight months earlier, Alex had been released from prison. He'd served almost ten years for killing Craig Waugh, the man who'd murdered his niece. Waugh had been found guilty by a jury, but of course he'd appealed. The most important bit of evidence had been disallowed by two of the appeal judges.

As Trevor Orchard had predicted, two people left as soon as Alex was introduced.

Kate was on the edge of her seat, wanting to hear every word Alex said.

Alex didn't speak for very long, saying he'd said everything he wanted to say in his book. He concluded, 'Now, I'd like to ask you a question: has anyone been through what my family's been through?'

There was no response.

'Then please don't judge me.'

Almost everyone clapped, and Kate nearly laughed, thinking, *Here's a group of people applauding a murderer!* She was on a high and kept hearing Alex say, 'A story in which I tell how an honest, law-abiding citizen from a loving, caring family became a murderer.' She modified it to apply to herself: 'A story in which I tell why an honest, law-abiding woman from a loving, caring family incarcerated a man and a woman in a dungeon.'

Jim Clunes asked whether anyone had any questions, and several people asked some. A woman named Sue asked the last one: 'Some members might find my question offensive, but I want to ask Alex, did you find a god in gaol?'

'No,' Alex replied, 'and I can assure you I had plenty of opportunity, but I didn't find a god of any description in gaol.'

Jim thanked Alex, declared the meeting closed and invited everyone to stay for tea, coffee or something stronger. He also reminded everyone that Alex had copies of his book for sale. The profit from book sales was to go to Lawfail. Many members, including Kate, Brett and Helen, bought a copy.

It didn't take Kate long to see evidence of the factions within Lawfail. She was standing near Sue when she heard a man say, 'Your question was totally inappropriate!'

Sue replied, 'I bet if he'd answered yes, you wouldn't have considered the question inappropriate; you would've been on Cloud Nine. I'm surprised you stayed to hear him speak.'

'Just because you don't agree with what he did, doesn't mean you can't listen to his story,' the man remarked in response.

'Provided there's no danger you might be brainwashed into agreeing with what he did,' Sue added.

The man left without making any other comment.

Then Kate overheard two women talking about the new case: 'I won't be supporting it: it's a woman's right to have as many children as she chooses.'

'I agree, and I don't support sterilisation, under any circumstances.'

Penny Jacobs approached Kate and Brett and introduced herself. 'Hi. I'm Penny Jacobs. Is this your first time at a Lawfail meeting?'

'Yes,' Brett answered. 'I'm Brett, and this is Kate.'

'I like to make new members welcome,' Penny said. 'As you would've heard, I'm coordinating the Dr Bloomer case. I'm passionate about it. That man has to hang. This isn't the first time Dr Bloomer's made an incorrect assessment that's had disastrous consequences. My husband's an engineer. If he certifies a bridge as being safe to walk over and it collapses, and someone's killed, he's in deep shit – pardon the French. I see you both have a copy of Alex's book. Does that mean you agree with what he did?'

'I sure do,' Brett replied.

'So do I,' Kate added.

'What about the new case?' Penny asked. 'Will you be supporting it?'

'Yes,' Brett and Kate replied in unison.

'Good,' Penny declared. 'Not everyone will be supporting Keith Davies.'

'Which factions won't?' Kate asked.

Penny laughed. 'I saw you talking to Trevor; I guess he told you about our factions. Keith's case won't get the support of what I and many others among us call the Religious Wrong. They're so inflexible, always convinced they're right. Some of them get very nasty with people who disagree with their beliefs. I hope they took note of Alex's last words: "Then please don't judge me." It's been lovely talking to you. Now, if you'll excuse me, I have to catch up with some other people. Don't forget: I expect to see you at the next meeting!'

'You will,' Brett said.

Helen joined them, carrying two cups of coffee, and Brett was happy to let Kate have the second one. He said he was going to find Mike Baker.

Kate and Helen were drinking their coffee when Tracy Marlin joined them. 'How are you going, Tracy?' Helen asked her.

'I was feeling okay till I ran into Olga Mikhailovich. She just can't get the point Keith Davies is trying to make about separation of church and law.'

'Olga doesn't get anything,' Helen declared. 'She's as thick as two bricks; she wouldn't know if her own bum was on fire. I'm surprised she came tonight. Oh no, speak of the devil, she's headed this way. I'm feeling like a proper shit, so if she has one of her self-righteous digs at me, I might retaliate.'

'Don't overdo it, Helen,' Tracy advised her.

'Hello, Helen,' Olga said to her.

'Hello, Olga. This is Kate.'

'Hello, Kate. So what do you three think of this nonsense that Keith Davies is rabbiting on about, separation of church and law? I've never heard of anything so ridiculous.'

Helen responded, 'No, Olga. He's making a valid point. One's judgements will always be skewed because of one's religious convictions. Imagine yourself on the jury of an abortion trial.'

'Oh!' Olga exclaimed. 'That's totally different. Abortion's murder, it's a sin. So's sterilisation.'

'That's the point he's trying to make,' Helen shot back. 'Not everyone thinks sterilisation is a sin.'

'It *is* a sin,' Olga said emphatically.

'That's your opinion, Olga,' Helen stated. 'Think of Keith Davies's sister: at the rate Glenda's going, Betty could end up with ten retarded grandchildren to look after.'

'Well, they're all God's children, and God loves them,' Olga said.

'But God doesn't have to look after them,' Helen reminded her. 'Betty's stuck with them. She can't drown them in the Red Sea or turn them into pillars of salt.'

'Nothing can be used as justification for sterilisation,' Olga said in a very forceful voice.

'I can think of one reason right now! It's a shame your mother wasn't sterilised – preferably before the Russian Revolution!'

Olga was gobsmacked and stared at Helen in disbelief. 'You're a despicable woman, Helen Davis!'

'That's your opinion, Olga. Some people think I'm very nice, so don't you go trying to ram your opinion down their necks.'

Olga left.

'You're right, Tracy,' Helen said. 'Olga just doesn't get it.'

'Along with all her other cronies,' Tracy added. 'I must go. See you at next month's meeting.'

Gradually the people left, and just before eleven o'clock, Jack called out good-naturedly, 'Last drinks!'

The last of the crowd said their goodbyes and made their way to their cars.

'I like Trevor Orchard's wife's description of the Right to Esse,' Brett said to Kate as they were driving home. 'They're the pits, Kate. I saw Colleen O'Day on television about eight months ago – the self-righteous so-and-so.'

'What was she on about?'

'There was a couple in their seventies. They had a fifty-year-old son who needed constant care; he couldn't do anything for himself. They'd looked after him for fifty years, and their only respite was when they propped him up in front of the TV during cartoon hour, and he'd look at the colour and movements on the screen. Then they learnt he was going blind, so they poisoned him with phenobarbital. They were charged with murder, found guilty and given a two-year suspended sentence. Colleen was outside the court speaking on behalf of the Right to Esse. The Right to Esse was going to seek legal advice to see whether they could appeal against the leniency of the sentence. After the interview, I wanted to go to her house and strangle her!'

'So, Brett, if Colleen O'Day's found strangled, you'll be the number-one suspect,' Kate jested.

Brett laughed. 'If she mysteriously *vanishes* one day, I'll be the number-one suspect. But I'd make sure no one found the body. I wouldn't leave any trails.'

That's exactly what Anne says, Kate said to herself.

'Brett, you shouldn't say that. What if she *does* disappear?'

'The world should be so lucky. I *loathe* that organisation. I think of Tom, and I think of my grandfather. He developed Alzheimer's and ended up in a nursing home. For eleven years, my parents and I visited a man who didn't even recognise us. Mum used to say she'd rather visit his grave. After what you said tonight, I feel I can safely tell you I'm a member of Smooth Egress. I'm careful whom I tell. It doesn't get you Brownie points with many people.'

'Maybe it's time for you to shout it out, Brett. Shout it out, and don't worry who gets upset.'

'Maybe it is,' Brett agreed.

'Helen doesn't worry about upsetting people if they deserve it. Tonight, she told one of the Religious Wrong it was a shame her mother hadn't had her tubes tied before the Russian Revolution!'

'Helen said *that*?!' Brett asked, wanting confirmation he'd heard correctly.

'She did,' Kate answered.

'I can't believe it. Don't get me wrong, good on her. It's just that she seems so sweet – that gorgeous face; she reminds me a bit of Olivia Newton-John. I can't hear her *saying* that.'

'She's sweet to people who deserve it.'

'What was the significance of the Russian Revolution?' Brett asked.

'I think she wanted to insult Olga even more by implying she looked older than seventy,' Kate replied.

Kate dropped Brett off at his house, and as soon as he'd closed the passenger door, she leant over and locked it. Her fear of driving on her own at night was lessening. She drove home, parked the car in the carport, went inside and tried to get ready for bed, but her mind and body were 'out of sync'. Her mind was racing. Parts of Alex's presentation kept repeating in her head: 'How an honest, law-abiding citizen from a loving, caring family became a murderer ... I could see Mum crying ... I kept telling my parents someone had to do it ... Why doesn't someone do something? Well, I *did* do something.'

Alex's talk was the last nudge that Kate needed: she could now see Wayne Keys in the dungeon. Again, she admonished herself for losing contact with Alison 'all those years ago'. She thought about all the fantastic people she'd met through her, and she also recalled other parts of Alex's presentation: '... able to put some sort of closure on what was the most dreadful time of my life ... festered with hatred till I died.'

She felt that what Anne, Helen, Alison and she were going to do should have been done twenty-seven years earlier. Maybe then, she could've had some sort of closure to what had been the most dreadful time of her life. If she'd kept in contact with Alison, Keys and Cullen might've been in a dungeon years ago.

Over the next few days, Kate read Alex's book, and it was like a manual for her. She identified with every issue Alex had raised. There was only one step left now: *do it*.

The Sunday after the Lawfail meeting, Kate went to Brett's house to help develop a plan for the Keith Davies case. Mike Baker and two women, Leonie and Margaret, were there. When they'd worked out what they intended to do, Kate mentioned she'd read Alex McAlpine's book. The group then discussed what Alex had done.

'I really believe what he did was right,' Mike said. 'The law's not always right. People should rebel against a legal system in which a child killer is allowed to go free. Of course, the Religious Wrong disagrees with what Alex did: they believe that one should obey the law. But imagine if euthanasia became legal, they'd be the first ones to rebel. I can't stand them.'

'Neither can I,' Margaret said, 'and neither can Trevor Orchard. One night, Rose Chilton was going on about how Lawfail seemed to be more about revenge than justice. "We mustn't have an eye-for-an-eye attitude!" she said. So Trevor gave her a blast; told her that according to Leviticus, if someone breaks one of your bones, you can break one of his. Same if someone knocks out your tooth or pokes out your eye. That silenced her.'

Leonie, who hadn't yet contributed to the discussion, spoke pensively. 'The thing I have trouble comprehending is the line between wanting to kill someone and actually doing it. I imagine it's a very wide line. What makes a person cross it? I've read his book. He was aware of all the consequences, yet he had the courage to kill Waugh. Do you understand what I'm saying?'

Kate knew exactly what Leonie was saying because she was going to cross that line.

Mike replied, 'I understand what you're saying. If I knew that someone had murdered my daughter and hadn't been found guilty, I'd want to kill him, but I don't know whether I'd have the courage, or whatever it takes, to do it. I think Alex McAlpine's a hero.'

Kate enjoyed the afternoon and arrived home feeling great. She rang Alison to tell her about Sunday.

Alison was surprised how happy her friend sounded.

Kate then rang Anne and Helen. Helen answered and suggested she come over for dinner. When Kate arrived at their home, Anne was there and offered to do the cooking.

'I've finished reading Alex's book,' Kate said. 'I'll read parts out to you while you're cooking.'

When Kate had finished reading excerpts from the book, she announced, 'That guy's my hero. I love his last sentence. "In some countries, under the law, a woman who has committed adultery must be stoned to death, and we in Australia say that is dreadful. How can it be allowed? Why doesn't someone do something? I say that in Australia, we have a legal system under which murderers are allowed to go free, and I say that is dreadful. How can it be allowed? Why doesn't someone do something? Well, I *did* do something."

'There are some things in my life I'll never forget hearing. To name a few: I can still hear my mother saying, "You received a credit and a distinction. Congratulations, darling. You have a BA." I can still hear John saying, "Vanessa had a healthy baby girl." And I can still hear John saying, "Kate, Dad died." And I now have another one. I'll never forget it: Alex McAlpine saying how an honest, law-abiding citizen from a loving, caring family became a murderer.'

Dinner was now ready. Anne served up cannelloni with a green salad and homemade garlic bread.

'This is better than you'd get in a five-star Italian restaurant,' Kate said to Anne while she was eating the meal. 'You're a top cook – you're good at everything.'

'I don't know about *everything*,' Anne replied.

'You're good at everything you *do*,' Helen said.

'But there are lots of things I don't do,' Anne insisted. 'I don't draw or paint, or sew or knit, or play mahjong. I could probably draw up a long list.'

'Well, let's just say whatever you do, you do it well. I'm sure you could become a champion mahjong player if you wanted to,' Helen said.

'Thank you, Helen,' Anne said in response. 'I could say the same about you.'

'That's very kind of you to say that, Anne. I'm flattered.'

Kate thanked them for their hospitality and went out to her car to drive home.

Cell 2

Cell 2 was now ready for the first guest, Wayne Keys. The bed was made up with fresh linen and a new pillow, and neatly stacked in a cardboard box was a torch and enough food, water and toiletries for twenty-four hours. Had the cell been in an opal-mining town, everyone would have said what a cute place it was.

The women were having afternoon tea at Alison's townhouse when Anne announced she'd finalised her plan for luring Wayne Keys to the gaol. It was no secret he was still living in Dubbo – the women had checked that fact out before they'd started building the dungeon. He was in the telephone directory, and they knew his address.

'I've worked out how we'll get Keys in the gaol,' Anne said. 'Kate, I think it's best if you're not involved. Helen and I will do it.'

Helen looked surprised, having assumed they'd all take part in his capture.

'We won't discuss the stratagem with you or Alison,' Anne stated, 'and neither of you must ask us anything about how we intend to do it. I know we're all in this together, but I'm working on the principle that the fewer people who know, the better.'

Alison didn't know how to interpret the last part of Anne's statement; all she knew was that when she heard that sort of talk, she felt nervous.

Anne continued, 'You know, with a creep like Wayne Keys, it'd be nice to have a gun, just in case we have trouble.'

Alison wasn't quite sure whether she was hearing correctly.

'I have one,' Kate announced.

'What! Where'd you get *that?*' Alison asked her.

Anne and Helen also were surprised to hear it.

Kate explained. 'When I went to the support group in Sydney, there was a woman who said we should all carry a gun, so something like that could never happen again. She had a friend in the US who used to send them over. That was more than twenty-five years ago. All she had to do was declare what was in the parcel. She'd put something like a toy model of Yosemite Sam's gun, a birthday gift. In those days, there were no problems with Customs. I didn't want one, but she kept on, and in the end, it was easier to give her £30 just to shut her up. I still have it.'

'Do you know how to use it?' Anne asked her.

'No, but the instructions are still in the box it came in,' Kate replied.

That night, Anne told Helen her plan to trap Wayne Keys. 'We have to get him to Canberra. We can't go to Dubbo because we'll probably have to go there to get Lyn Cullen. That really would look suspicious if we just happened to be in Dubbo the day Wayne Keys disappeared, and the day Lyn Cullen disappeared. I just hope Keys falls for what I have in mind. I'm going to send him a letter. Have a read: it's on the screen. Oh, by the way, I checked the post-office boxes. There's no post-box number 2256 – just in case the creep decides to reply.'

GOODE and TAYLOR
SOLICITORS

GPO Box 2256
Canberra ACT 2601
Telephone XXXXXXXXXX

Mr W. G. Keys
26 Pace Road
Dubbo NSW 2830

Dear Mr Keys,

DO NOT SHOW THIS LETTER TO ANYONE OR DISCUSS THE CONTENTS OF IT WITH ANYONE.

I am acting as executor of a will in the name of JOHN BAXTER GRAY, in which Wayne Gary Keys is named as one of the beneficiaries. I have done an extensive search, and you are the only Wayne Gary Keys I have been able to trace.

The name John Baxter Gray might not mean anything to you, but you might have come in contact with him and not known you had. He was a recluse who had no

---

known relatives. I have been in legal practice for twenty-seven years. During that time, I have dealt with more than thirty cases in which the beneficiary had no recollection of ever having met the deceased. Sometimes, people who have no family or friends will choose to leave their possessions to someone who has shown them an act of kindness. It could be something as simple as lending a spanner. Often, these eccentrics have an incredible memory, and according to our records, Mr Gray lived in Dubbo for a short time. To claim the inheritance, all you have to do is show evidence that you are the Wayne Gary Keys who is named in the aforementioned will. I feel quite sure you are. A simple meeting to which you bring some form of identification is all that is required. Your driver's licence would be adequate.

Three weeks ago, my partner and I were given only two weeks' notice that our office lease was not to be renewed – the office block is to be demolished to make way for townhouses. We have not yet found a suitable office; hence, I am unable to supply you with a telephone number.

In the meantime, we have moved all our active files, which includes your file, to safe storage at my hobby farm located not far from Canberra. In a few days' time, I will telephone you, and we can arrange a date and time to meet in Canberra. For your greater convenience, I suggest we make the meeting on a weekend. The most convenient place for us to meet is the seat outside A. J. Benson, Chartered Accountant, in Canberra, at the Hapley shops. I am enclosing a map to show you the location, which I have marked with a cross. I doubt you will have any trouble finding it. I will then take you to the farm where you can sign the documents.

It is imperative you not discuss this letter with anyone, not even the members of your immediate family. Why? I refer to a similar case, which a colleague of mine was handling. A jealous relative tried to prove he was the intended recipient. The processing of the will was delayed, and the amount of money was reduced because the legal fees incurred were taken out of the estate.

If I telephone at a time when you cannot talk, please simply say, 'You have the wrong number,' and I will hang up and try again later.

Please sign and date on the line below, and make sure you bring the letter with you when you come to Canberra.

Yours faithfully,

Sally Goode

_____   _____
Signature   Date

'What do you think?' Anne asked Helen. 'Do you want to make any changes?'

'No, I don't.'

Anne continued, 'Today, I bought a ream of paper, a box of envelopes, a book of stamps and a box of disposable plastic gloves, and I took a sheet of sticky labels from work. I'm not worried about using my own printer. Lots of people have the same type of printer as mine, and hopefully Keys will take me seriously and not show the letter to anyone. I can't print it yet because I need to date it before I post it, and I'm not sure exactly when I'll be able to.

'After we post the letter, I ring Keys and arrange to meet him outside A. J. Benson's office on a certain date at a certain time. By the way, I rang Telecom today and told them I'd received an STD nuisance phone call and asked whether they could trace it. The woman I spoke to told me there was no way it was possible to trace it. I asked about phone bills. She assured me that unless Telecom puts a trace on the phone, those calls are untraceable. So I meet him, take him to your car and introduce you as my business partner, and we drive him to the gaol. On the way, I rave on about storing our active files at my hobby farm till we can find a new office and how I've constructed a fireproof subterranean room to store our archived files in.

'I'll have to get the gun from Kate, but it won't be loaded. If things don't go according to plan, I don't want my reflex action to be "shooting Keys". I don't want to be up on a murder charge.'

'What if Keys senses it's a trap?' Helen asked. 'What if he asks to see your driver's licence?'

'I'll tell him I don't have it on me. I know what you're thinking: what if he then asks to see yours. Helen, there are a few what-ifs in what we're doing. You'll be driving so you can tell him you'll show him when we stop.'

'It's not like you to have any what-ifs,' Helen remarked, in a surprised voice.

'Even if he senses a trap, he'll probably want to see what the trap is. I'm sure his curiosity will get the better of him. And by the time he knows for certain it *is* a trap, he'll be locked in Cell 2. In the meantime, we have to find out whether he lives alone. If he doesn't live alone, the trickiest part in phoning him will be getting him at a time he's on his own. There's a limit to the number of times he can say, "You have the wrong number."'

'That's assuming he answers,' Helen pointed out. 'There's a limit to the number of times *you* can say you have the wrong number.'

'True,' Anne agreed. 'What I plan to do is pretend I'm doing a survey. How does this sound? I ring Keys's number. If a kid answers, I'll ask to speak to his mother or father. Once I know I am talking to an adult, I'll give my spiel: "Good evening, my name is Tamara Gill. I'm from Potter and Meldrum Research, and I was hoping you could give me three minutes of your time." I don't give him or her time to say no. "You might already know that over the past four months in New South Wales, three elderly people have been found dead in their homes. In each case, the death wasn't discovered until neighbours complained that a foul smell was coming from the deceased's dwelling. I'm conducting a survey on loneliness. It's completely anonymous. Your number was dialled at random, and I'd be grateful if you'd answer seven simple questions. If you participate in the survey, your number goes into a draw. The prize is a week's holiday for two on the Gold Coast."

'Without pausing, I launch straight into the survey:

'Question 1: How many males and females live in your house?

'Question 2: How many of the occupants are employed?

'My next question will depend on his or her answer to Question 2. If it's a house full of dole bludgers, I go to Question 5.

'Question 3: What time do the employed occupants leave home for work?

'Question 4: What time do the employed occupants arrive home from work?

'Question 5: Do you have a set time each week at which you or any of the other occupants are alone?

'Question 6: Do you feel you spend too much time on your own?

'Question 7: How often do friends visit?

'I'll phone him next week. I hope he doesn't live in one of those houses where people are coming and going all the time.'

Helen had no amendments to make to Anne's plan, believing that Anne was much more competent in that area than she herself was.

The following Saturday, Anne and Helen drove to the Hapley shops and had a coffee at Zig's café.

The following Wednesday, Helen had dinner with some of her work colleagues, and when she arrived home, she was momentarily stunned when Anne told her she'd made the survey phone call.

'It went like clockwork,' Anne assured her. 'A woman answered, and she volunteered more information than I'd requested. There are three people living in the house: one male and two females. I'm assuming the male's Keys. They all work. The women leave for work at seven forty-five, and the man leaves at about eight fifty. We've made enough visits to Zig's; we can send the letter now.'

She put on a pair of disposable gloves and printed the letter and an address label.

'Now I have to peel off the label and stick it and a stamp on the envelope – not all that easy, with these gloves. I'm going to burn the rest of the labels and envelopes so that if anyone comes searching this house, they won't find a label or an envelope like the one Wayne Keys received his letter in.'

Helen always felt uneasy when Anne said those sorts of things. Could anyone really trace the letter back to them?

'Mind you,' Anne went on, 'I'm still hoping he won't show the letter to anyone, but one can't be careful enough. Posting it won't be a problem: I often post the mail when I go to lunch. I just have to be careful not to touch the letter.'

Next day, Anne posted the letter. 'I posted the letter,' she informed Helen when Helen returned home from work. 'I'll ring on Tuesday morning, at eight thirty.'

I'll make sure I've left for work before eight thirty on Tuesday, Helen said to herself.

'If a woman answers, I'll ask to speak to Xeenie – surely there won't be anyone by that name living in the house. Assuming she says there's no one there by that name, I'll say, "I must have the wrong number," and hang up. But according to my little survey on loneliness, if I ring at eight thirty, the women will have left for work and Keys should be home alone.'

At eight thirty on Tuesday morning, Anne made the unbelievable phone call.

'Hello,' came a male's voice on the other end of the phone.

'Mr Wayne Keys?' Anne asked.

'Yeah.'

'Sally Goode here. Did you receive a letter from me?'

'Yeah.'

'Are you able to talk now?'

'Yeah.'

'Great. When would be a convenient time to meet? I'd prefer a weekend because I'm snowed under with this office move. The sooner we get this business settled, the better.'

'I can drive down this Saturday. I can be there by eleven thirty.'

'Good. Make sure you bring the letter. I hope you haven't mentioned it to anyone.'

'No. How much do ya think I'll get?'

'About $65,000.'

'Wow!'

'I trust you still have the map I enclosed.'

'Yeah.'

'Park in the large car park near Coles, not the small one outside Benson's, because unless things have changed since I last visited the Hapley shops, parking in the small car park is limited to one hour. Just wait on the seat outside, and I'll come and take you to sign the declaration. That's all. Goodbye, Mr Keys.'

'See ya.'

Anne hung up.

On that Tuesday, Anne arrived home from work before Helen did. 'It's all set,' she said to Helen as Helen was entering the front door.

'What's all set?' Helen asked her.

'Our encounter with Keys: eleven thirty next Saturday, outside Benson's. I want the two of us to go to the gaol on Friday night; give it the final check. The bed must look like a couch. We'll put a sheet – make it look like a dust cover – over the ablution section. I'm going to put a box of hanging files just inside the entrance to Cell 1. I suggest we hang some cheap framed prints on the corridor wall and perhaps put an artificial pot plant on top of the shelves – do anything to help remove the appearance of a gaol.

'The gate to Cell 2 will be opened about fifty degrees. Keys has to be able to walk straight through, and I have to be able to reach it easily to close it. I'll be the one to close it. That's another thing we must rehearse: our roles – who does what.

'I want the cabin to have a "legal look" about it. I'm going to create a fake certificate: "Member of the Law Society" or something like that. I'll frame it and put it on the cupboard. We'll also leave a few books on the cupboard. I'm exhausted now. Let's have a glass of wine.'

At ten thirty on Saturday, Anne and Helen parked Helen's car outside the office of A. J. Benson, Chartered Accountant and went to Zig's for a coffee. Anne had the unloaded gun and a can of hairspray in a large leather shoulder bag. Helen was wearing a denim jacket; in two of the pockets she had a small can of hairspray. Anne kept looking at her watch. At eleven twenty-two, they left Zig's and walked to where they could see Benson's office. And there, sitting on the seat outside, was a man. They stopped to look at him, and saw he was wearing a black T-shirt and jeans and that he was unshaven and bald. He yawned, and they saw he had some teeth missing. He wasn't a pretty sight. Anne also noted that he wouldn't have any trouble going down the seventy-centimetre-wide staircase. Anne and Helen looked at each other as if to say, 'Poor Kate'.

'Helen, go straight to the car and start the engine,' Anne directed her.

Helen did just that, and Anne approached the man. 'Wayne Keys?' she asked him.

'Yeah.'

'Good morning. Sally Goode.' She offered to shake his hand. 'Here's my business card. I'm afraid the only up-to-date information's the postal address. The car's right here.'

She opened the back door for Keys, quickly hopped in the front beside Helen and introduced her to Keys. 'This is my business partner, Linda Taylor.'

'How do you do, Mr Keys?' Helen said to him, and as soon as she heard Keys close the door, she drove as fast as the speed limit would allow, towards the highway.

Anne started talking to Keys. 'The termination of our office lease came as a huge shock to us and the other tenants. About four months ago, the landlord wrote to all the tenants, advising us our leases wouldn't be renewed. The tenants got together and lodged an appeal. We lost it, but we all thought we could stay for another eight months regardless. That was when the last lease expired. Then suddenly, Linda and I were given two weeks to vacate. We still haven't found an office we like. As I mentioned to you in the letter, your file's at my hobby farm, so that's where we're going.

'There are many costs involved in running a legal practice, but one big cost that people often overlook is for storage of archived files. We have to keep files for years. Security companies charge a fortune, and you can't always be sure the files will be safe from fire. *And* you can't always access them when you want to – security firms don't operate twenty-four-seven. So, when I had the shack built on my hobby farm, I had a fireproof room constructed underneath it. Until we find a new office, Linda and I are storing our active files there. When the underground room is finished, we'll be moving all our archived files into it.

'It'll only take about twenty-five minutes to get to the farm. You can read the will and sign the declaration to state you're Wayne Gary Keys. Then we'll take you back to your car, and you can head back to Dubbo. It'll probably take about four weeks to finalise everything. I'll post you a registered letter with the cheque enclosed. Do you have the letter, Mr Keys?'

'Yeah.'

'Have you signed it?'

'Yeah.'

'Could I have it, please?' Anne asked him. 'The law's a strange business. If there's any mix-up with this will – mind you, I don't for one minute think there will be – I'll have to show that the person I've authorised payment to has signed the letter. While we're at it, I might as well see your driver's licence.'

Without turning her head, she put her right arm over the seat and took the letter and licence. She looked at the licence and then gave it back to him. 'Thank you, Mr Keys, that's fine.'

Anne was relieved to have the letter in her possession: she didn't want to have anyone find it in Keys's house after he'd disappeared. The letter would certainly be the police's most crucial lead.

They had to go through only two sets of traffic lights before they were on the highway. Ten kilometres on, they turned into the back road that led to the property.

So far, so good, Helen thought.

'My subterranean room's like a huge cellar,' Anne said. 'Four metres deep, with a twenty-five-centimetre-thick concrete slab over it. A friend of mine who's a wine buff tells me files don't deserve such luxury. He's always hinting what a great place it'd be to store wine. I told him wine bottles don't have to be stored in a fireproof area: they can always be replaced. You should've seen the look on his face! Told me ninety per cent of his cellar's irreplaceable. Oh well, each to his own!

'The approach to the stairs isn't finished yet. I intend to have a neat, little wooden railing with a matching gate constructed. The steps to the repository are a bit steep, and they're not well lit. The fellow who installed the solar lighting told me he couldn't put a light in the stairwell. When I asked him why, he couldn't give me a satisfactory answer. I think he just didn't want to put it in – probably a bit fiddly – so he told me it wasn't possible. I couldn't argue with him because I know nothing about solar lighting. I've divided the repository into two rooms: one where I'll store files that are more than seven years old, the other where I'll store the more recently archived files.

'I'm still waiting for the builder to complete the lining. He keeps promising he'll come on such-and-such a day, yet when the day arrives, there's always some reason why he can't come. It's so frustrating! One of my friends likes the "natural earth look"; she says I should leave it as it is. However, I think it's a bit off-putting.'

Anne, you're brilliant! Helen said to herself.

'Goodness me! I've been doing all the talking!' Anne declared. 'Did you have a good trip? What time did you leave?'

'About six thirty. What if there's another Wayne Gary Keys?'

'Once I've authorised probate, it's too late,' Anne explained. 'No other Wayne Gary Keys has come forward. I've fulfilled all my legal duties in relation to this will; my partner will vouch for that. Won't you, Linda?'

'I sure will,' Helen said. 'Sally's very conscientious about her work.'

'How come you're not in the phone book?' Keys asked.

Helen's mouth went dry, and her bowels almost gave way. She didn't know whether to try to answer the question or not. She was still thinking when Anne, whose large intestine was also giving warning signs, spoke. 'Linda and I have only been in partnership for three months. I had another solicitor working for me, but she retired. My business was growing, and I was keen to take on a partner. Linda was working for a solicitor who made it clear he wasn't going to offer her a partnership, so she joined me. Did you try to find us in the phone book?'

'Yeah.'

'That thought crossed my mind, but I thought if I tried to explain it to you in your letter, you might think I sounded a bit whacky. I'm recently divorced, and I've gone back to my maiden name – "maiden name" – I hate that expression. Because I was deregistering my old business and registering a new business, I decided to use my maiden name in the title of the new business. Goode is the name that's also on my degree.'

'What sort of work do you do?' Keys asked her.

'Wills, conveyancing, family law … anything else, Linda?'

'Compensation claims,' Helen added.

'Do you do any criminal stuff?'

'No, we don't do criminal law,' Anne replied.

'Why not?'

Helen answered, 'When you first go into practice, you work with a solicitor, and she decides what sort of work you'll do. You don't have much say. I was given the type of work I'm doing now. I liked it and didn't have any desire to change. What about you, Sally?'

'I think you've answered for me, Linda.'

'I like solicitors who get criminals off. Would you like them?' Keys asked.

Anne replied, 'I'd be completely neutral.'

'So would I,' Helen added. 'Emotions and the law don't mix.'

Anne was relieved when she saw the gate to their property come into view; she didn't think she could keep up the trivial chat or Keys's interrogation for much longer.

As soon as Helen stopped the car, Anne jumped out and unlocked the gate. Helen drove through, Anne relocked the gate and hopped back in the car.

'Nearly there!' Helen announced.

They arrived at the cabin and Helen unlocked the doors. She pushed the timber door open and held the security door open for Keys and Anne to enter. When they were inside, she subtly relocked the timber door.

Over Anne's right shoulder was the shoulder bag that had the gun in it. She and Helen had left the trapdoor open, leaning up against the cupboard, and over the back of the cupboard they'd hung a bright cloth, so Keys couldn't see the hinges. Also, they hadn't locked the downstairs doors.

'Until things are complete,' Anne said, 'I have to keep this cupboard in front of the hole. Just go down the stairs, Mr Keys. I'll be right behind you. The file's on the little plastic table in the second room. Take care in the corridor: there are some metal shelves. I haven't decided where to put them. There's also the equipment for the solar lighting and a step stool for getting files off the top shelves. Whatever you do, don't trip over any of it.'

Keys went down the stairs, followed by Anne and then Helen. He went through the metal gate into Cell 2 and picked up the file. As soon as he'd picked it up, Anne closed the gate.

Keys turned around to see what had caused the noise. 'What the fuck! What *is* this?'

'We'll explain later, scumbag!' Anne replied.

Keys rushed towards the gate and shook it with all his strength, and the veneer panel fell off it.

Anne produced the gun and pointed it at him. 'Move to the back of the cell and face the wall.'

She and Helen were relieved to see that Keys was obeying. She kept the gun fixed on him while Helen removed the veneer panels from the front of both the cells. Then she padlocked five chains around the gate: two around the hinged side, two around the other side and one at the top. They closed the gate to Cell 1 and left to the sound of obscene threats emanating from Wayne Gary Keys.

'Rapist!' Helen yelled at him.

They locked the two downstairs doors, closed the trapdoor and screwed the cupboard in place.

Anne and Helen were exhausted. The tension had taken its toll. They wanted to get off the property as fast as they could.

'I just have to burn this letter,' Anne said. She put the letter and envelope into the barbecue and burnt them, and she and Helen made sure there was absolutely no trace of the paper in the ashes.

They locked the cabin and headed for the Grongo pub. Grongo was a very small village located about fifteen kilometres from their property. They'd planned to have lunch there. This would be their alibi should anyone ask them what they were doing driving along Grawback Road. When they arrived at the pub, they sat in the car for a few minutes.

'I'm not sure if I'm hungry; I have a strange feeling in my stomach,' Helen said.

'I know what you mean,' Anne replied. 'Nevertheless, I've decided I *am* hungry. I was going to say, Let's buy a bottle of champagne to have with our lunch; however, we mustn't look as if we're celebrating anything.'

'Spot on.'

After the lunch, they went home and flopped on a couple of the lounge chairs. They'd expended a lot of nervous energy and were now feeling tired.

'You were so cool, Anne,' Helen remarked. 'How did you manage it?'

'Me, cool? I thought my heart was going to explode. I thought *you* were cool.'

'No way!' Helen said. 'I was nearly crapping myself! I was wishing I'd worn brown track pants with tight elastic around the ankles. When you spoke to me, I wasn't sure I could reply. For a brief moment, I thought my jaw was locked, like in the horror movies when the victim's so scared, she can't call for help. Fortunately, it wasn't.'

When they'd rested, Helen rang Kate and then Alison, but neither was home. 'Oh well,' she said. 'We'll keep trying. They have to come home eventually.'

At four o'clock, she phoned Kate again. Kate answered that time, and Helen said, 'I've found your keys.'

Kate was confused for two seconds, but then knew exactly what Helen meant. Her legs almost gave way. 'When?'

'About eleven thirty today.'

'Can I come over?'

'Sure.'

'See you in twenty-five minutes.'

Kate couldn't find words to describe how she was feeling. She wanted to know how they'd done it, but she remembered the agreement: she mustn't ask any questions.

Helen tried Alison's number again, and this time she was home. Helen told her the news, and Alison froze, feeling very nervous. She'd never really believed that The Plans would become a reality. She now wanted to visit Anne and Helen and see if she could find out anything about Keys's capture. She remembered the agreement and knew Anne and Helen would not reveal any details; nevertheless, she still wanted to see them.

Alison arrived at their house about the same time Kate did.

'What did you say to him?' Kate asked Anne and Helen.

'Nothing,' they replied. 'Our nerves were giving out, so we locked up and left.'

'*You* can explain to him why he's there, Kate,' Anne said.

'For twenty-seven years, I've said over and over to myself what I'd like to say and do to him. I can't believe the day is here. Now it is, I don't know what to say.'

'Just say to him what you've been rehearsing for twenty-seven years,' Helen offered. 'Doing to him what you want might be a bit more difficult.'

Kate had a shopping bag with her. She put it on the table and pulled out three masks: Alice from *Alice in Wonderland*, Snow White and Cinderella. Each was a moulded rubber mask and had hair attached to it. 'I stopped off at the Joke Shop on my way here and purchased them,' she explained. 'We have to convince Keys we'll let him out some day, otherwise he might do something stupid, like go on a hunger strike. I'll tell him I have cancer and I have only two years at the most. When I die, the others will let him out. But the guy's a criminal: he knows you mustn't have witnesses to a crime. I know he's seen your faces – never let him see them again. Always wear a mask and call each other by that name. I won't wear a mask: my identity's no secret. Keys will know who I am. I'll show you how to put on the mask.' She picked up the Snow White mask. 'See this split up the back? You open it and pull the mask over your head. When it's on, the split closes and the hair covers the split. Once the mask's on, the only part of the head that can be seen is the eyes. Can I go and see him now?'

'Yes, but don't go alone,' Anne said. 'No one must ever go to the gaol alone. Alison, do you want to come with me and Kate?'

Alison wasn't sure she wanted to go, but she felt she couldn't say no. 'Er, yes, of course,' she replied unconvincingly.

'Anne, I think it's too soon for Keys to see you, even with a mask on,' Kate said.

Anne was paranoid about there being any slip-ups. She also wanted to see whether Keys had destroyed anything. 'I agree with what you're saying. However, I just want to check for myself.' She'd made her point, and everyone knew it was no good arguing with her. 'I'll change my clothes. I won't wear what I wore this morning. I'll wear a mask and I won't speak. He'll think I'm a different person.'

'You were so phoney this morning, I don't think Keys will recognise your voice if you do say something to him,' Helen remarked.

'Well, I won't say anything today, but I can't guarantee I won't give him a blast next time.'

'That ring you often wear on your right hand,' Kate said to Anne. 'Did you wear it this morning? He might've noticed it.'

Anne was delighted with Kate's awareness. 'Spot on, Kate, but I didn't wear it this morning.'

'Okay,' Kate said. 'You get changed, and we'll go. Can I carry the gun?'

'Of course,' Anne replied.

Kate calmly took the gun and put it in the camera bag she'd bought to carry it in. She surprised herself at how calm she was.

Alison felt ill. She wondered whether it was all a bad dream, but she knew she had to face the facts: it *was* real, and she was involved.

'I might as well go too,' Helen said. 'We have to take the rugs off the solar panels. Another thing, Kate: do you want to give Keys a tirade in private, or do you want someone with you?'

'I have no secrets from you or Anne or Alison: I think I'd like someone with me.'

Kate drove to the cabin, unlocked the doors and went inside. As soon as the other women were inside, she relocked the timber door, unlocked the cupboard and took out two large screwdrivers. She gave one of them to Alison, and together they unscrewed the cupboard, rolled it forward and lifted up the trapdoor. Alison, Anne and Helen each put on her mask. Alison was feeling very nervous and she was amazed at how calm Kate seemed to be. Kate took the gun from the camera bag. All four women went into the stairwell. Kate unlocked the fireproof door at the bottom of the stairs, opened it, unlocked the security door, opened it, moved to the front of Cell 2 and saw Wayne Gary Keys. All she could do was stare at him.

'Who are you?' he yelled. 'What the fuck d'ya think you're doin'? Let me out!'

'In two years' time, maggot,' Kate replied, 'but only if you behave; otherwise, it'll be for the term of your natural life.' She pointed the gun at him. 'Do you recognise me, gutless creep? I've waited a long time for this day, and I promise you—'

'Never seen ya before in me life!' he shot back.

'Well, take a good look, because before we release you, I'm going to blind you. That's just one of the many things I'm going to do.'

The expression on Keys's face changed, and Kate was certain he was afraid. She was delighted.

'Well, who are ya?' Keys asked her.

'Do you remember a night at the Dubbo quarry, back in 1961? Or is that sort of thing the norm for you?'

'I don't know what you're talkin' about!'

'Stop lying, Keys. And tell me: whatever happened to Ernest Derek Sullivan?'

'I don't know any Ernest Derek Sullivan.'

'Stop lying! Tell me what happened to Ernest Derek Sullivan.'

'Ernie ended up in the nuthouse.'

'How come?'

'He got bashed up in gaol. After he got out, he went to live with his mother. When she died, he went to a nuthouse in Sydney. That's all I know.'

'Is he still alive?'

'I s'pose he is.'

'I promise you: you'll be sorry for what you did that night. I'm going to torture you and turn you into a eunuch, and I mean it. It'll give me great pleasure. In fact, it's one of my goals in life, and it's very important to achieve one's goals.'

'I—'

'Shut up!' Kate shouted at him and indicated to the others, who were standing in front of Cell 1, that she was ready to leave.

Anne, who was wearing the Snow White mask, whispered to Kate, 'I want to take a quick look around. Give me the gun, please.'

'What are you goin' to do to me?' Keys asked Anne.

She decided to ignore him. Instead, she surveyed the dungeon and satisfied herself he was trapped.

Kate locked the doors, and the four women went up the stairs. Kate and Anne lowered the trapdoor and then rolled the cupboard back and screwed it in place.

'We might as well leave the masks here,' Helen said, 'but what about the gun?'

After a short discussion, they decided they wouldn't leave the gun in the cabin.

Helen climbed on the roof, removed the rugs from the solar panels and reminded Anne and Kate that from now on, every time they went into the dungeon during the day the solar lights would not be on.

As they were walking to the car, Anne remarked to Kate, 'You didn't say much to him.'

'No,' Kate replied. 'I don't want to give him the satisfaction of knowing he ruined my life.'

They drove back to Anne and Helen's house, and Helen made them all some coffee. Usually all four of them were never lost for words, but at this point, the conversation was a bit limited. They were emotionally exhausted.

Helen was first to perk up. 'You know, Anne, we should give the property a name. I quite like "Glocca Morra"; it has a good ring to it – "How are things in Glocca Morra?"'

'I agree we should give it a name,' Anne said, 'but not Glocca Morra. We want an original name.'

'How about "Socamora"?' Helen asked.

All agreed that Socamora was a good name.

As they were drinking their coffee, Anne said she wanted to discuss some of the practical things involved in keeping Keys in the gaol.

'One: toiletries and food shouldn't be a problem. When you're doing your own shopping, buy a few extra cans of fruit and vegetables, some tinned fish and meat, crisp bread, cheddar cheese, long-life milk, tissues, Wet Ones and any other things you think Keys'll use to make his spell in our gaol more comfortable. Send them through the checkout last so we can keep a tally of how much each of us spends.

'Two: gas cylinders. We'll have to buy them from a camping store.

'Three: rubbish. I don't see any problem in that department. On each visit to Socamora, one of us will take the rubbish back to her place and drop it in the garbage bin.

'Four: washing. We'll take it in turns to do his washing, but for heaven's sake, don't hang anything on the line that might look remotely out of place with your normal washing. Don't leave any of his washing drying inside your house because an unexpected visitor might see it there. Which brings me to my next point: Keys has only the clothes and shoes he's wearing, so we'll have to buy him some unisex-type clothes. Have I forgotten anything?'

'No, that's sounds complete,' Helen replied. 'Just remember to take your camping lantern every time you go.'

'Thanks, Helen,' Anne said. 'Kate, do you want to go with me to Socamora tomorrow? We can ask him what size clothes and shoes he takes. Phew, I'm exhausted; I'm glad I'm not going out tonight.'

'Yes, Anne,' Kate replied, 'I'll go with you tomorrow.'

'I'll go as well,' Helen said. 'We have to load up the shelves and put the water tank, the garbage bin and the slop bucket in place.'

Alison and Kate finished their coffee and went home.

The next day, they all turned on their televisions and waited for the news. There was no mention of a missing man; nothing in the papers.

On Sunday, Anne, Helen and Kate went to Socamora.

They entered the dungeon. They hung two camping lanterns in the corridor and were pleased to see they gave off plenty of light.

Anne told Keys to move to the back of the cell. She kept the gun aimed at his head while Helen and Kate were putting the water tank, garbage bin, slop bucket and shelves in place and stocking the shelves. When the two had finished the tasks, they moved back from the cell, and Anne explained the procedures to Keys.

'Well, Mr Keys, you're so lucky we're nice people: we're going to buy you some new clothes and shoes. You can't wear *those* clothes for two years, can you? That wouldn't be very pleasant. So I need to know what size you are. Footwear, I think slippers will be fine. So I also need to know your shoe size. Underpants are another thing, though: the best we can do for you are large Cottontails. The decision's yours. If you don't agree to the Cottontails, I guess you'll have to put up with a few "loose ends". You don't have to rush into deciding right now, and if you change your mind over the next six months, we'll oblige.

'Pyjamas are also out: you see, Mr Keys, we have to do your washing. We can't take the risk that someone'll see a pair of jocks or striped pyjamas in our laundry. How would we explain the foreign objects in our washing to our friends and neighbours?

'We'll probably visit you once a week, but we'll make sure you have enough food and water for two weeks, just in case some unforeseen circumstances arise, and we can't make it here.

'Each time we visit, we'll top up your supplies, including your water, and return your washed clothes and linen, and we'll take away your rubbish and washing, and empty the slop bucket.

'Your water tank holds eighty litres, your camping shower nine. We estimate that even if we visit you fortnightly, you'll be able to have one shower a week and still have enough water for drinking, brushing your teeth and washing up. Your weekly shower will be brief – but then again, I guess you're not going to get very dirty in this lovely suite. Only use the water in the tank for drinking, cleaning teeth and washing up; if you want to clean your hands, use a Wet One. We'll ensure you have plenty of Wet Ones. Empty your washing-up water and teeth-cleaning water in the slop bucket, not down the toilet.'

Keys was snarling under his breath, but it was obvious he was scared.

Anne continued, 'Read the instructions on how to use the camping stove. Don't leave it burning too long because there's limited oxygen in the gaol, and you should conserve it for breathing. Let us know if you have trouble breathing, and we'll measure the oxygen level.

'Have you decided whether you'll shave each day or grow a beard? I suggest you grow a short beard; you'll use up more water and gas if you shave. You can use your nail scissors to keep your beard trimmed. Haircuts shouldn't be a problem: that's quite a shine dome you have.

'Also, Mr Keys, we're concerned about boredom. Would you be interested in learning to do cross-stitch or perhaps in making a latch-hook rug? Let us know what books or magazines you like to read and what sort of music you like to listen to. We'll purchase the magazines and CDs if we can find them.

'Apart from the odd bout of boredom, I think you'll be very comfortable here for the next two years. Look on the bright side: you don't have to go to work; you don't have to do any shopping or washing; you'll be a kept man. Now—'

'You fuckin' bitch!'

'Don't interrupt me when I'm speaking!' Anne said firmly. 'That's bad manners, and I don't like bad manners. As I mentioned earlier, we're nice people; nice people don't like foul language. Any foul language whatsoever will result in removal of your privileges. I hope I have made myself clear. Do you have any questions?'

'You won't get away with this!'

'That's not a question!'

'What makes you think we won't?' Helen asked him. 'Come on, pus bag, answer the question: why won't we get away with this? No one seems to know you're missing so don't sit here wondering when someone'll find you because no one's looking for you. Now, just to reconfirm: clothing large, shoes 10, and we'll estimate size 20 for the Cottontails. Last but not least, get this into your head: you're at our mercy. You're powerless. Do you understand? How does it feel? How does it feel to be outnumbered four to one? How does it feel to be at the mercy of four evil bitches?

There's no saying what we might do to you, you detestable creep! Do either of you want to say anything else to this loathsome being?'

'No.'

'In that case, we'll depart.'

During the week, the women purchased some tracksuits, T-shirts, slippers and Cottontails.

On Saturday, Anne and Kate went to Socamora. Keys swore and shouted at them and told them they wouldn't get away with what they were doing because he'd worked out how he was going to escape.

'How?' Kate asked him.

'As if I'd fuckin' tell *you!*'

'That's enough, Keys! If you don't mind your manners and control your foul tongue, we'll leave you so little food and water you won't have the strength to crawl from one side of the cell to the other, let alone escape. Now, let's get this straight: you're not in a position to be giving cheek. Any bad behaviour and your sentence could be extended to three years.'

They topped up the food and water, dropped off the clothing and left.

The following Saturday, Keys's second week in the gaol, Helen and Kate went to Socamora and completed the weekly tasks.

When Kate arrived home, she thought about Keys. She thought he had looked more angry than frightened. She wanted to see fear on his face. She took the unloaded gun, pointed it towards the television and pulled the trigger. It gave a little click. She did it again.

It was now Keys's third week in the gaol. While Anne and Kate were driving to Socamora, Kate told Anne she intended to pretend to shoot Keys to scare him. Anne had no objections to the idea.

Once inside the gaol, they went through the usual routine, but as they were about to leave, Kate pointed the gun at Keys. She kept it aimed at his head and pulled the trigger.

Keys jumped. 'What the fuck!'

Kate laughed mockingly. 'I love playing Russian roulette – with someone else's head!' She glared at him, challenging him to say something, but he didn't react.

Anne and Kate locked up and left.

It was almost four weeks before Wayne Keys's disappearance was reported in *The Canberra Envoy*. It was only after a shopkeeper had reported that an abandoned car, which was traced back to him, was sitting in the Hapley shops car park that the police looked into his disappearance. The shopkeeper couldn't remember exactly when he'd first noticed the car. The police were now appealing to anyone who'd seen anything unusual in the vicinity of the Hapley shops over the past three or four weeks. The newspaper article featured a photo of Keys and a little blurb about him. He had a criminal record; he'd served two gaol terms: two years for causing grievous bodily harm and three for armed robbery, and he was also supposedly involved in car rebirthing. In the end, the police didn't know whether he'd been murdered or whether he'd staged his own disappearance. His disappearance ceased to be news very quickly.

Anne and Helen went over their story again and again. If the police approached them, this would be their story: 'Yes, we were at the Hapley shops around that time: we sometimes have coffee at Zig's there. No, we didn't see anything unusual. No, we didn't see the man shown in the photo.'

They weren't worried, knowing that a criminal such as Wayne Keys probably had quite a few enemies. They were extremely confident that no one would link Keys's disappearance to them. The only 'Achilles' heel' in the entire operation was if someone had seen Keys get into Helen's car at the Hapley shops or if someone along the way to Socamora had seen him in the car and recognised him. As far as they knew, neither of those two scenarios had happened.

Alison wasn't as confident. She was almost paranoid, even though she'd had nothing to do with Keys's disappearance. Every time she heard a car drive past her house and slow down, she imagined it was the police. One time, she saw the breathalyser on the roadside and felt ill, thinking it was a roadblock to stop her. The day after Keys had been reported missing, a Salvation Army officer who was collecting money knocked on her door. She almost threw up when she saw the officer's hat. He noticed her anxiety and asked her whether she was all right. She gave him a donation, and when he'd left, she sat down in her favourite chair to regain her composure. She started thinking, *This isn't good. I can't spend the rest of my life living like this or I'll go mad. Anne and Helen aren't the slightest bit worried, so why should I worry? I'm not sure about Kate, but I dare not ask her. I have to say to myself three times a day, 'No one will find that hole!'* She calmed herself down and told herself not to be ridiculous: *Why would anyone associate me with Wayne Keys's disappearance? Besides, I was nowhere near the Hapley shops. Get a hold of yourself, girl!*

Keys had now been in gaol four weeks. Although he had enough food and water to last for two weeks, Anne thought it important to visit him weekly while the gaol was in its testing phase. That idea suited Kate because seeing Keys in the dungeon 'did something for her'. Restocking the shelves, topping up the water, emptying the slop bucket, removing the rubbish, collecting the washing and performing the other routine tasks took two women about fifteen minutes. They left the dungeon as soon as they'd completed the chores. Conversation between them and Keys was very limited. After inspecting the dungeon thoroughly over the four weeks, Anne was convinced Keys couldn't get out. It was important for Alison to go there to learn the ropes, and Kate suggested she go there with Alison in two weeks' time. Anne and Helen agreed to the plan.

'One thing that troubles me is these short visits,' Anne commented. 'I feel that someday soon, someone'll ask us what we do when we come here. I suggest I buy some boules and a badminton set. Have a game. I also suggest all four of us come here and have a picnic soon.'

Two weeks later, Kate arrived at Alison's house to take her to the gaol. Alison was nervous.

'I know the routine off pat,' Kate assured her. 'Once in the gaol, hang up the lanterns, take the washing off the bottom shelf and put it in the clothes bag; put the clean clothes and linen on the bottom shelf; replenish the supplies; empty and replace the slop bucket; empty the garbage bin and replace the liner; top up the water tank. Filling up the water tank's the biggest chore.'

'Aren't you worried Keys'll make a grab for you when you're stocking the shelves?' Alison asked her.

'That's why you never go there alone,' Kate explained. 'We always make sure Keys sees the gun. He knows to stay at the back of the cell. I told him if he didn't co-operate, he wouldn't get any food, but you never let your guard down.'

As soon as they opened the door, Keys yelled, 'What took ya so long?'

Kate was delighted to hear the question, thinking he'd obviously been worried he might have been abandoned. 'Get used to the fact we mightn't come here every week! Don't use up all your water in the first week!'

Alison felt more relaxed when they'd locked up, and Kate suggested they try out the badminton set. They played for almost thirty minutes, and both thoroughly enjoyed the game. Then they had a game of boules. Alison realised it was impossible for Keys to get out and as good as impossible for anyone to find the dungeon. She thought back to a conversation she'd overheard at work soon after Wayne Keys had been reported missing. One of her work colleagues had been reading about the disappearance in *The Canberra Envoy*. 'He's staged his own disappearance,' the colleague had stated. 'I think someone's sorted him out. He seems to have a lot of enemies,' another commented. No one suspected Alison Roberts of having anything to do with Wayne Keys's disappearance.

Kate was always willing to go to Socamora because she loved seeing Keys as powerless as he was. Keys had now been in the gaol for seven weeks. This day, Kate and Helen were there, and Helen was wearing the Alice mask. Keys was refusing to go to the back of the cell.

'Well, that's it, Alice,' Kate announced. 'Let's go.' She turned to go.

Realising he wouldn't be getting any fresh supplies, Keys started moving towards the back of the cell. As Helen was putting some canned food on the shelves, Keys suddenly charged to the front of the cell, thrust his right hand through the bars, knocked over the shelves and made a grab for her. Fortunately, she was well out of reach of him. She and Kate were a bit shaken up and decided to leave immediately.

'What about my supplies?' he bellowed as they were leaving. 'Are you sure you know how to use that gun? It's so old, it prob'ly doesn't work!'

'Oh, it works, all right!' Helen yelled back at him. 'I'll show you next time! Goodbye, you sorry excuse for a human.'

Helen and Kate calmed down once they were in the car and talked about their close shave and what they would've done if Keys had actually grabbed one of them. They drove back to Anne and Helen's house, and Helen invited Kate in for a drink.

Anne was home and asked, 'How are things at Socamora?'

'We had a bit of a scare,' Kate replied. 'Keys made a grab for Helen. As she was putting some cans on the shelves, he charged towards her. He sent the shelves flying and tried to grab her. We just left; we didn't even put the shelves back. So he'll be without food until our next visit. That should be a lesson for him.'

'We always said he might try that,' Anne said. 'How close was he to grabbing you?'

'Not very close,' Helen answered. 'Still, I wonder what we'd have done if he *had* grabbed me. The gun's never loaded; I think he suspects that, because he said, as we were leaving, we didn't know how to use it.'

'Well, we'll have to put him straight on that point, won't we?' Anne said in response. 'Kate, you said the instructions for how to use the gun are still in the box.'

'Yes, they are.'

'I don't like what Keys said. It's essential we show him the gun works: we're in charge. When you leave, I'd like to follow you to Queanbeyan and read up on the instructions. I'm going to show Keys the gun *does* work.'

'I hope it works,' Kate said. 'It's never been put to the test. Do you think we should go back to Socamora and put the shelves in place?'

Helen answered, 'If he goes a week without food, he mightn't have the strength to charge at the gate and make a grab for one of us.'

'I think we should put the shelves back. I don't want him to die before he's finished serving his sentence,' Kate said.

'He won't die,' Helen assured her. 'He has plenty of water. Anne, what say you and I go out on Monday after work?'

'Okay,' Anne said.

'Sorry to put you to the inconvenience. But after what happened, it seemed like a good idea to get the hell out of the place.'

'That's okay, Kate. You and Helen did the right thing.'

Anne and Kate finished their drinks and drove to Queanbeyan. Kate found the gun instructions and gave them to Anne, who sat down to study them. It didn't take her long to work out how to use the weapon: the instructions were clear and had accompanying illustrations.

'It's a revolver,' she announced. 'It holds five cartridges. The spent cartridges remain in the chamber. According to the instructions, you should use ear and eye protection if you're practising. My biggest concern is that a bullet would ricochet. Where am I going to fire the gun in the gaol? We'll have to have a practice go; let's make it next weekend. The sooner we put Keys straight about this issue, the better. The whole process of showing him that the gun works is going to be a bit taxing. I suggest all four of us go to Socamora next Saturday or Sunday. I'll tell Helen. Can you see whether Alison can come, and if she can, what day she prefers?'

'Sure,' Kate answered.

'Good. I'll take the gun and instructions, so I can have another read, but I won't take any bullets. I'll ring you during the week to finalise the day and time. Now, I must go home.'

When Anne arrived back from Queanbeyan, she informed Helen. 'I have the instructions for how to use the gun – I should say revolver. We have to show Keys the gun works.'

'Why? I don't think we should fool around with the gun. It's served its purpose.'

'No,' Anne said. 'Keys has to know that the gun works and that we know how to use it.'

Helen didn't reply, knowing that Anne was in what Helen called one of her 'Anne has spoken' moods. There was no point engaging in any more discussion: Anne was going to show Wayne Keys that the gun worked.

On Tuesday night, Anne received a call from Kate, who asked, 'Did you and Helen go to Socamora and put the shelves back?'

'We did. He was obviously a bit worried. He moved to the back of the cell obediently. He probably won't try that again, but all the same, I think it's important we show him that the gun works.'

'I phoned Alison about trying out the gun,' Kate said. 'She was very nervous about it. I think we should count her out.'

'Okay. Which day do you prefer?' Anne asked.

'Saturday morning.'

'Good. Is nine thirty too early for you?'

'No,' Kate answered. 'I'll be at your place at nine thirty on Saturday, with the bullets.'

'Just bring three,' Anne instructed. 'And bring some earplugs.'

Kate arrived at Anne and Helen's house on Saturday morning, and Anne opened the door to her.

'Come in. Helen's just getting her earplugs. I have, in this sports bag, the gun, a pair of earmuffs and my clear cycling goggles. I'm going to have a practice shot. As soon as I fire, I'll drop the gun, the earmuffs and the goggles in the sports bag, so if anyone hears the shot and comes running over, we'll just say we heard the shot, but it wasn't on our property. I don't think anyone will appear.'

'We might as well go in my car,' Kate offered.

When they arrived at Socamora, Anne hopped out of the car to unlock and relock the gate. In her absence, Helen and Kate had a brief conversation, which Helen initiated. 'You know, Kate, I'm dead – no pun intended – against this trying out the gun. What do you think?'

'I've detected on more than one occasion that once Anne's decided to do something, it's a *fait accompli*,' Kate stated. 'I have great faith in Anne. I bet she scares the living daylights out of Keys! I agree with her, Helen: it's essential Keys knows the gun works and we know how to use it.'

'I guess you're right.'

'Do you think people such as Anne ever come a cropper?' Kate asked.

'Some do. Let's hope if Anne does, it's not today.'

'Be like me, Helen,' Kate implored her. 'Trust her implicitly.'

'That's all we *can* do.'

Anne got back into the car and said, 'Park in the usual place, Kate.'

Kate parked the car, and the three hopped out.

Anne took charge. 'I'm going to make that tree over there my target. I've absolutely no idea what'll happen. Will the bullet lodge in the tree? Will parts of the bark go flying off? Will it ricochet and hit me? If it does, it was nice knowing you!'

'Don't talk like that, Anne,' Helen said. 'How far back from the tree are you going to stand?'

'About four metres. Kate, give me one bullet, please. Now, you two stand near the cabin.'

Kate and Helen obeyed.

Anne went over to the tree, wedged a leaf in between the cracks in the bark and called to Helen and Kate, 'That's my target!' She moved back from the tree until she was about four metres from it and put the sports bag on the ground.

Helen and Kate saw her crouch down and load the gun. She put the gun on the ground, pointed it towards the tree, and stepped back about a metre. She put on her goggles and earmuffs. She moved towards the gun, picked it up, pointed it towards the tree and pulled the trigger.

There was a loud noise. Although the leaf was intact, it was obvious she'd hit the tree and that she was still standing. Part one of the mission had been successful.

Anne quickly put the gun, earmuffs and goggles into the sports bag and walked over to Kate and Helen. 'Well, we know for sure it works.

Now we have to show Keys, but before we do, let's take a look at the tree. Can anyone see a bullet in it?'

They all had a good look and could see no sign of the bullet, just a small hole. Anne picked up a piece of bark and wedged it into the hole. She inspected her work and was satisfied that anyone snooping on the property wouldn't know that the tree had been used for target practice.

They went into the cabin and locked the doors behind them. Kate and Helen unscrewed the cupboard and wheeled it away. They then raised the trapdoor.

'Can one of you go down and unlock both doors and hang up a lantern?' Anne asked.

Kate descended the stairs, unlocked the doors, hung up a lantern and went back up.

Because of the wall between the cells, you had to be almost in front of Cell 2 (the cell Keys was in) before you could see into it.

'I'm going to stand in front of Cell 1,' Anne announced. 'Keys won't be able to see me from there. That's good: he won't see how shaky I am.'

Kate and Helen looked at each other as if to say, 'Anne, shaky?'

'Now both of you stand back while I load the gun.'

Helen couldn't remain silent any longer. 'Anne, please load the gun at the *bottom* of the stairs. They're steep and not well lit, and there's no hand rail. You'll be going down them wearing earmuffs and goggles, holding a loaded revolver. What if you go A over T?'

'I'll be fine, Helen,' she assured her. 'I'm going to put the bullet in chamber three. That means first click, nothing happens; second click, the bullet's fired.'

She loaded the gun, placed it on the floor, pointing away from herself and put on the goggles and earmuffs.

Helen and Kate put in their earplugs, and Helen put on the Snow White mask.

'You stay in the stairwell while I fire,' Anne instructed them, and she descended the stairs. When she'd reached the bottom, Kate and Helen entered the stairwell.

The next phase was a bit of a blur to everyone. Anne fired the gun. She saw some dust at the end of the corridor, and despite the earplugs, Kate and Helen could hear Keys screaming, 'What the fuck d'ya think y're doin'?'

Anne entered the stairwell, gave Kate the revolver, and indicated to her to show Keys she'd been the one who'd fired it.

Kate stood in front of Cell 2 and said, 'Just showing you that the revolver might be old, but it works – and what's more, I'm a pretty good shot! Remember what I told you before: If you ever give me any trouble, I'll turn you into a eunuch!'

Keys didn't reply.

That was all anyone said until the three women had gone upstairs again.

'What now, folks?' Anne asked.

'A game of boules,' Helen suggested.

'What do I do with the third bullet?' Kate asked.

'Take it home and put it with the rest of the bullets,' Anne replied. 'I was going to allow myself two practice shots.'

'I owe you an apology, Anne,' Helen said. 'I was against trying out the gun, but you're right: Keys has to know it works. I suppose seeing as we're here, we might as well top up the water – everything else can wait till next week.'

The shooting incident had quite an effect on Keys in that he genuinely now believed that Kate might make good her threat. The women had also convinced him they'd release him in two years' time if he behaved himself. 'We don't want to be looking after you for the rest of our lives,' Helen told him.

Anne felt that Keys had now accepted he was powerless. He had a temper and had trouble controlling his foul mouth. Anne thought there was no purpose in provoking him and suggested that she, Alison and Helen try to establish a bit of gaoler-prisoner rapport with him. But Alison and Helen wouldn't have a bar of it. They loathed Keys for what he'd done to Kate and they had no intention of having any sort of rapport with him. Anne was always civil to him and made polite, though very limited, conversation with him. She'd never mentioned the rape incident to him.

Eight weeks after the gun trial, Anne and Alison were at Socamora when Anne broached the subject with him.

'Yeah, that was a good night! I broke her in. Not often a bloke gets that opportunity. It's a great feeling. For some reason, she wasn't—'

'Shut up! Shut up, you bastard!' Anne screamed. She went upstairs and took off her mask.

Alison followed. Anne sat on a chair, put her head on the table and proceeded to cry. Alison was so shocked to see her crying she forgot what Keys had said.

Anne stopped crying and said, 'I want to torture him! Can you get some nitric or sulphuric acid from your work?'

'I guess so.'

'I'm going to buy a big water pistol, fill it with acid and squirt him with it!' She sat in silence for almost three minutes and then asked Alison to get the lanterns and lock the downstairs doors.

They drove to Anne and Helen's house, and Anne invited Alison in. Helen was home and she could tell something was wrong by the look on Anne's face. When Anne told her what Keys had said, Helen was filled with rage. 'I'm going to Socamora this minute to … to …'

After a brief silence, Anne said, 'Forget about the acid, Alison; I won't go ahead with my plan. Also, forget about trying to have any gaoler-prisoner rapport with him. I can hardly bring myself to speak to him. I was wrong to even suggest it.'

'Well, it's not often you're wrong, Anne,' Helen assured her. 'And when you are, you have the grace to acknowledge it … But what were you going to do with the acid?'

Anne told her how she wanted to torture Keys when he'd bragged about what he'd done to Kate.

'He needs another shake-up, Anne. As you once said, he has to know we're in charge. I thought he'd been behaving himself since we showed him the gun works. He can't say things like that and get away with it.'

'I was the one who brought up the rape,' Anne admitted.

'Irrelevant,' Helen said. 'We should go back with a water pistol full of acid and show him what he can expect if he ever says anything like that again. Anne, you're too upset to go back. Alison and I'll do it. I'm fuelled by rage. We have to do it *now*. Once my rage subsides, I'll be overcome with grief and incapable of anything. Do you have a key to the laboratory, Alison?'

'Yes.'

'Good. You go and get some acid, and I'll buy a water pistol. I'm not going to squirt it on him, Anne; I just want to show him what I'll do to him if he ever says anything like that again. He's shown what an evil creature he is by saying that. He's not one bit remorseful.'

'Don't worry about the pistol, Helen,' Alison said. 'I'll get some zinc sheeting. I'll put it on the ground outside his cell and tip the acid on it. He can watch the zinc being eaten away while we remind him what it can do to his skin.'

'Be careful,' Anne said to Helen and Alison as they were leaving.

Helen and Alison returned two hours later.

'That was very successful,' Helen announced. 'Alison tipped the acid on to the zinc. You should've seen the panic in his eyes when I said to him, "Can you imagine what this does to flesh? In future, if you ever say anything to make any one of us upset, I'll squirt this on your tongue!" He got the message. I wish Kate could've seen it.'

'Well done!' Anne said.

'We'll tell Kate what we did, but we won't tell her what he said. We'll just say his language was so filthy we had to show him we weren't going to listen to it. Are you okay, Anne?'

'I'm really upset about what he said; I feel quite depressed.'

'Join the club,' Helen said, and she started to cry. 'As I said before I left for Socamora, my next emotion after rage will be grief. I was right.' Through her tears, she tried to comfort Anne.

Alison suggested she make some coffee, and while they were drinking it, they ceased talking about Keys. Helen stopped crying, and Anne recovered from her little bout of depression.

Just Deserts

Seeing Wayne Keys locked up was 'doing wonders' for Kate. She was more confident, did more entertaining at home, attended NoFourthR meetings and dabbled in Lawfail. She even looked different. Alison thought some of that old 'uni magic' was returning to her face. Friends commented how well she was looking, and there was the odd tongue-in-cheek question about whether she'd had a facelift.

Keys had been in the gaol for five months now. Fortnightly visits were rare. Between the four women, two usually visited him weekly. Even though they loathed him, they felt he was being well cared for. They did his washing regularly and kept his toiletries, food and water in plentiful supply. They made sure not all his food was canned or dried, often buying him fresh rolls, cold meat and fruit. Sometimes they brought him leftovers from their meals, and they occasionally gave him a few cans of beer. Anne purchased a gauze toaster, which sat on top of the camping stove, so he could make toast if he wanted to. They supplied him with vitamin tablets and ensured the CD player and torch always had charged batteries. They purchased CDs and magazines of his choosing.

However, they could not persuade him to take up an activity to ease the boredom. Helen suggested he make a matchstick model of the Sydney Harbour Bridge. Alison suggested he give weaving a go. Anne and Kate suggested he write his autobiography, for which Kate even proposed the title *Falling from Behind*. He didn't get the meaning of the word 'behind' in the title, so Kate explained it to him. He rejected all the suggestions. He succumbed to the Cottontails and grew a beard, which he kept short. He wasn't backward in asking for anything he wanted. If it was something that was feasible, the women usually got it for him.

Kate didn't say much to him. Anne always said hello and goodbye, and sometimes asked him whether he was enjoying his new CD or magazine. Alison and Helen delighted in taunting him.

The only hitch during those five months was the toilet, which had started to smell. Helen said it was an added punishment and told Keys, 'When you're perfect, your shit doesn't smell, so when that happens, we'll let you out.'

Anne said the problem had to be fixed. 'If fresh air can get into that cell, Helen, bad odours can get out. You agree we should bring people out here occasionally. Well, we can't bring them out if the place smells like an unflushed toilet.'

Helen had to agree. 'Yes Anne, you're right.'

They purchased disinfectant and sawdust and so managed to control the problem. Helen gave Keys a stern warning to use the sawdust sparingly, telling him that if the toilet filled up, he'd have to use a plastic spoon to dig another one.

Kate was keen to get Colleen O'Day in the gaol. She hoped having her locked up would help Alison in the same way having Wayne Keys locked up had helped her, but she wasn't certain it would, knowing that Alison directed her hatred towards many people. There was no doubt in Kate's mind that revenge was the greatest cure for an injustice, an eye for an eye.

The four women were having dinner at Kate's house when Kate announced it was time to put Colleen O'Day in the dungeon and that she'd worked out a way for her and Alison to do it. Alison almost had an attack of diarrhoea.

'Do I tell all of you the plan, or do I just tell Alison?' Kate asked.

'The only advantage in telling Helen and me is we can look for weaknesses,' Anne responded.

'Okay, I'll tell all. I intend to get Colleen to park in the Cactus Bar car park. The Cactus is a regular haunt for us, so there'll be nothing unusual about the fact we were there the night Colleen disappeared.'

'Sorry to interrupt,' Helen said, 'but Colleen might think it's a strange place to meet.'

'We'll have to think of a reason, so we can convince her it's a good place to meet,' Anne put in.

Kate continued, 'Yes, I'll put my thinking cap on. It's not a big car park, so if we know her car's number plate, she won't be hard to find. Alison and I collect her, drive to Socamora and throw her in the clink. After we throw her in the clink, we go and have dinner at the Grongo pub. How do I get her to park at the Cactus? I'll go home for lunch one day and ring her. I've rung Telecom about tracing of nuisance calls. They still can't do it unless a trace is put on. As I was saying, I'll ring her during the day. The weak bit in the plan is getting her at a time when she's alone. I know she doesn't work: she's such a creep she still thinks women should stay home and look after their children. I'll tell her I know where there's an illegal abortion clinic and I want to show it to her. I can't tell the police because some policemen are paid hush money. I'm taking a big risk, but it's up to the Right to Esse to close the evil place. I'll arrange a time – eight o'clock in the evening – and tell her to park in the Cactus car park. I'll ask what car she'll be in and the number plate.'

'Good,' Anne said, 'but as you mentioned, Kate, the weak spot's getting her at home on her own. I know your working hours are pretty inflexible. There's more chance she's on her own in the morning than at lunchtime. We know her husband works at James & Partners and all her kids go to school. Let me know when you and Alison are ready, and I'll make the call.'

'We are ready,' Kate declared. 'But what about voices? What if Colleen says I don't sound like the woman on the phone?'

'Tell her you're not surprised. You were very jumpy when you phoned.'

'Well, *you* had better sound jumpy when you phone!'

'Don't worry, I will,' Anne said reassuringly. 'Helen, can you find any problems with Kate's plan?'

'I think Kate and Alison should go to the Grongo pub for dinner on a weeknight before they kidnap her, also a few times after the kidnapping. I know we've been to the pub quite often, but I don't recall any of us going for dinner during the week.'

'Good suggestion,' Kate replied. 'We'll do that.'

Alison was feeling nauseous. Her goal was about to materialise, but she was 'going to water'. All the thinking and planning had been done; she would simply have to follow instructions.

On Tuesday night, Kate and Alison went to the Grongo pub for dinner, and a fortnight later, they went to the Cactus Bar for a drink and then to the Grongo pub for dinner.

Kate told Anne that she could now ring Colleen O'Day. Kate and Alison had no commitments at that time and had agreed they wouldn't make any until Colleen was where she belonged.

Anne was an expert at the type of phone call required. She now dialled the number and waited.

'Colleen O'Day,' came a voice on the other end.

'Mrs O'Day,' Anne began, 'I'm ringing you because you're the national president of the Right to Esse. I'm taking a great risk making this phone call. Are you alone?'

'Yes,' Colleen replied, sounding wary.

'Good. My name's Pat Dobson, and I happen to know where there's an illegal abortion clinic, not far from Canberra. I can't go to the police because some of the police are paid what you might refer to as hush money. I don't know who I can trust, but if I can't rely on the national president of the Right to Esse to do something, who can I?'

'How do you know about this clinic?' Colleen asked hesitantly.

'I'm a trained nurse. I was tricked into "helping out" there. It's a long story. I'll tell you when – I hope it's when – I see you. I was told a few facts about the clinic and I was also given a stern warning not to tell anyone about it. After what I'd been told, I knew my only way to expose the clinic was to take someone from the Right to Esse there. My goal was to get a set of keys to the clinic. After ten weeks, my dream came true: I had to lock up. I had a set of keys cut the next day. I then went to the clinic and informed the boss that I no longer wanted to work there. He accepted that but gave me another threatening reminder not to tell *anyone* about the clinic.

'I'd like to take you there. You mustn't mention this phone call to anyone – *anyone*: the people who operate the clinic are ruthless. They have spies in the Right to Esse. They could dismantle the clinic in forty minutes if they got wind someone had found out about it. Once I've given you the details and shown you the clinic, you can enlist trusted members of the Right to Esse to help you close it. Could I meet you soon?'

Colleen sounded excited. 'Yes, I could meet you Wednesday night.'

'*Good!* Wednesday night I'm having dinner with a group of work colleagues at the Cactus Bar. I'll slip away at eight o'clock. Can you be in the car park at eight?'

'I can,' Colleen replied. 'But would you like to make it a night you're not going out for dinner?'

'No,' Anne answered. 'The truth is: I don't really want to go, so if I meet you, I'll have the perfect excuse to leave early. Just sit in your car. Try to be discreet while you're waiting for me. Now, what colour and make of car will you be driving, and what's the registration number?'

Colleen obligingly supplied the details.

'The Cactus car park's not very big; I'll find you. Mrs O'Day, I must re-emphasise the need for you to not mention this call to anyone.'

'I think I understand.'

'Sorry, Mrs O'Day, I don't mean to be rude, but it's not good enough just to think.'

'I understand.'

'Thank you, Mrs O'Day.'

Kate and Alison drove to the Cactus Bar on Wednesday night. They parked in the car park, went inside and had a soft drink. At eight o'clock, they returned to the car park and saw Colleen's white Mazda. Alison drove up behind it. Kate hopped out and approached the driver. 'Mrs O'Day?' she asked.

'Yes.'

'Pat Dobson. I've brought a trusted friend for support. Her car's here.'

She opened the back door and Colleen hopped in. Kate hurriedly jumped in beside Alison and continued talking to Colleen. 'This is June.

If June and I seem a bundle of nerves, it's because we are. June's the only other person I've told because I know I can trust her. I didn't want to involve her, but I needed support for what I'm doing. You wouldn't believe the lengths they go to hide the clinic. It's underground. When we arrive, I'll have to unscrew a cupboard and lift up a trapdoor, so I can get access to the stairs. Oh, I'm so nervous!'

'So am I,' Alison said.

'You're doing fine, June.'

They arrived at the cabin. Kate had the gun, which wasn't loaded, in the pocket of her duffle coat, and Alison had a can of hairspray in her pocket. Neither conspirator was expecting any trouble from Colleen. It seemed they'd completely fooled her.

As Kate and Alison were unscrewing the cupboard and opening the trapdoor, Kate said, 'As I told you in the car on the way, they've gone to incredible lengths to make sure they don't get sprung.'

Kate started to go down the stairs. 'I'll go first, Colleen, because I have to unlock two doors at the bottom. You come next, and June can bring up the rear. Take care on the stairs.'

As quietly as she could, Kate unlocked both the doors at the bottom of the staircase, wanting to get Colleen into Cell 1 before Keys said anything. She quickly unlocked the gate to Cell 1. Colleen was now in the corridor.

'Through here, Colleen,' Kate instructed her.

Colleen entered Cell 1 and Kate closed the gate. It all happened so quickly that Colleen didn't have time to protest. Alison raced upstairs, put on the Cinderella mask and returned.

'What *is* this?' Colleen yelled. 'Who's behind that wall?'

Kate took the gun out of her pocket and aimed it at Colleen. 'Cinderella will explain someday. In the meantime, move to the back of the cell.'

Colleen obeyed, and Alison put the five chains around the gate.

By that time, Keys was at the front of his cell, trying to see what was happening. 'What's happening next door?' he asked in a reasonably civilised voice.

'Colleen can tell you when we leave,' Alison replied. 'I must warn you, Colleen, that the guy in the cell next to yours is a rapist. There's a cardboard box in the corner. In it is enough food, water and toiletries to keep you going for twenty-four hours.'

'Please explain what this is all about!' Colleen begged.

'As I've told you,' Kate responded, 'Cinderella will explain all – probably next time she visits you.'

'When will that be?' Colleen pleaded.

'Soon.'

That was all Kate and Alison said before they left Socamora and headed for the Grongo pub. Like Anne and Helen when they'd brought Wayne Keys to the gaol, Kate and Alison were exhausted and too terrified to stay and explain anything to Colleen; they just wanted leave.

When they arrived at the pub, Alison wanted to know whether Kate could see her heart pounding through her jumper. Kate assured her she couldn't.

'Kate, do you think a heart can just blow up or explode? I think mine's going to self-destruct, along with my bowels.'

'We'll stay in the car for a few minutes,' Kate said, 'till our heartbeats slow down – mine's also beating dangerously fast. I don't feel like eating.'

'Neither do I, but we'll have to force something down: it might look a bit odd, coming all the way to Grongo for one drink. How about a toasted sandwich?'

They went inside the pub and ordered two toasted sandwiches. When they'd finished eating, they left.

'We'll have to come back to the pub a few more times on a weeknight,' Alison said.

'I know – and we'd better feel like a proper dinner next time – the barman must think we're weird coming all the way to Grongo for a toasted sandwich.'

They drove back to Alison's house where Kate had left her car. Alison invited Kate in for a hot chocolate, and Kate accepted. She made the hot chocolates and took them into the lounge room, where she found Kate sitting in silence.

'We didn't even tell Colleen why we put her in the clink,' Alison said. 'I remember when Anne and Helen put Keys in the clink, they said they'd just put him in the cell and left. I thought it strange they didn't give him a blast and tell him why he was in our private gaol, but now I know how they felt: exhausted. That was how I felt tonight. I just wanted to get the hell out of the place.'

'So did I,' Kate added. 'Also, the more time we spent at Socamora, the more unexplained time we might have to account for.'

'Don't say that: it makes me feel ill!' Alison pleaded.

'Relax, Alison. Our story's watertight. We just say we went to the Cactus Bar for a drink and then to the Grongo pub for dinner. We've done it before, and we'll do it again.'

By noon the next day, it was on the news that Colleen O'Day was missing. Colleen's husband was extremely worried. He said his wife was involved in many community activities and often went out without specifying exactly where she was going. Her car had been found in the Cactus Bar car park. The police had questioned staff at the Cactus Bar and had undertaken a thorough search of the car. However, no one had been able to supply any useful information.

The following day, Colleen's disappearance was on the front page of *The Canberra Envoy*. It wasn't the first time her name had appeared in the paper: about five years earlier, a picture of her had been published on the second page of the *Envoy*. In the photo, she was leading a group who wanted to have the Wallo Bar closed down. The Wallo Bar had been a popular place among the members of the gay community. Also, on local radio and TV programs, Colleen had said, 'Homosexuality isn't acceptable, and homosexuals should be prepared to accept treatment for their illness!' Whatever 'treatment' meant!

About two years after that incident, she'd made herself very unpopular by trying to cover up a sex scandal in which a teacher at her sons' school was involved. And more recently, within the past eight months, she'd tried to stop a developer from building townhouses on some land that had originally been designated for a church. The land had been rezoned.

Colleen had said that the proper legal procedure hadn't been followed and that the developer should therefore not be allowed to build the townhouses. She'd put up quite a fight and sought legal advice, and for a while it looked as if she and her supporters would win. Her husband had reported that she'd received threatening phone calls at the time. No one had suggested that her disappearance had anything to do with her being the national president of the Right to Esse.

At about four o'clock in the afternoon on the day after Colleen's disappearance, Kate heard a knock on her front door. She felt nervous: no one knocked on her door at that hour on a weekday. She opened it and was surprised and relieved to see Brett standing there, but he looked worried.

'Brett, come in. Is anything wrong?' she asked.

'It's about Colleen O'Day,' he answered. 'She's gone missing.'

Kate went numb. Why would Brett come to tell her that? Had he seen her at the Cactus Bar? *Impossible,* she thought. *Brett wouldn't have been in Canberra on a weeknight.*

Brett got straight to the point. 'Remember the night we were driving home from Lawfail and I said, "If Colleen O'Day mysteriously vanishes, I'll be the number-one suspect."?'

'I'd forgotten,' Kate lied, 'but now I do recall it, yes.'

'Kate, you don't think I had anything to do with it, do you?'

'Gosh, no, Brett! I can assure you I don't!'

'I couldn't believe it. I'll never say anything like that again.'

'Well, you can relax, Brett. I don't think you had anything to do with it. Would you like a drink?'

'No thanks, Kate. I'd better go home and take Gandee for a walk. I was stupid to say that about Colleen O'Day.'

'We all say stupid things without thinking they might come back to haunt us. I can assure you, Brett, I don't think you had anything to do with her disappearance.' She saw him out, thinking, *But I'm not so sure about the mugging of Toni Crawford.*

Helen agreed to go with Alison the following night to stock the shelves and put the water tank, garbage bin and slop bucket in place and to explain the gaol rules to Colleen and why she was in the gaol.

When they arrived home, Anne was there and asked the standard question: 'How are things at Socamora?'

'Not the best,' Helen replied.

'What! What's up?' Anne gasped.

'Keys raped Colleen.'

'Oh no! How did that happen?'

Alison answered, 'He made some coffee and asked her to have a game of cards with him. Like a fool, she went into his cell. She got back to her cell when he went to sleep, and she bolted the adjoining gate from her side. I warned her he's a rapist.'

'Is she all right?'

'Okay physically, but mentally, I don't think she's too good. We gave Keys a serve, told him if he ever tried it again, we'd give him just enough food and water to keep him alive. He'd be so weak, he wouldn't be able to get himself erect, let alone anything else. His demise would be long, slow and painful. Colleen pleaded with us to let her go, said she wouldn't tell anyone where she'd been. But Alison told her she had to serve her sentence for heading up the Right to Esse.'

'Kate and I are going to Socamora on Saturday,' Alison said. 'We'll reassure her again that Keys can't get into her cell.'

Kate arrived at Alison's townhouse on Saturday morning and found Alison waiting at the gate. 'Gosh, you're keen!' she said to her as she hopped in the car. 'Helen told me about Colleen. Is she all right?'

'Physically, she's okay,' Alison replied. 'That's all that matters. Because of her ordeal, I didn't fully explain to her why she's in our gaol. I thought I'd hold off for a few days. But I sure am going to tell her what I think of her today. I hate that woman, Kate; I loathe her!'

When they arrived at Socamora, they found Colleen almost hysterical. 'Please! Please let me out! I won't tell anyone about you! He keeps shouting and saying he's coming to get me. I'm terrified.'

'There's no way Keys can get into your cell if you keep your side of the gate bolted,' Alison assured her.

'He keeps banging on the gate!' Colleen pleaded. 'He says he'll find a way to get it opened.'

'I *will* too!' Keys shouted from the other side. 'She's not such a bad lay!'

Kate stood in front of Cell 2 and yelled back at him, 'You disgusting bastard! If you bang on the gate again, we'll chain you to your bed. Cinderella's a vet. She has access to a stun gun, used when large animals get out of control. We'll knock you out with one of them and chain you up.'

'Bullshit!' he yelled back.

'Don't push me, Keys!' Kate shouted. 'I hate you. In fact, while you're out cold, I might get Cinderella to remove your organ. She's done it to a bull that had cancer, so she can do it to you.'

He said nothing in response to that one.

Kate was about to leave when Alison said, 'I have to have a little chat with Colleen. As I told you on Thursday night, Colleen, you're being punished for being the national president of the Right to Esse – that evil, sadistic organisation. I'd like to put the lot of you in a dungeon. Unfortunately, that's not possible, so in a way, Colleen, you're carrying the sins of all the Right to Essers – a heavy burden. But remember, Colleen, God will not give you a burden you cannot carry. I've left an A4 writing pad and two biros on your shelves. The pad has one hundred pages, and each page has thirty-three lines on it. You're going to write, six thousand, five hundred and ninety-nine times, "Surrogacy is inwomane." I was going to get you to write, "Surrogacy is inhumane", but it can only happen to a woman, so I've invented a new word: "inwomane". I've written the first one for you. You can fit two to a line. And as you write, you'd better start to believe what you're writing because that's the only way you'll get out of this dungeon. In some countries, what I'm doing to you is called re-education.'

Kate hadn't known that Alison was going to deliver that tirade to Colleen.

Alison indicated she'd said all she wanted to say, so she and Kate locked up and left.

Anne was concerned for Colleen. She and Helen went to Socamora on Wednesday after work to see how she was and to re-emphasise that there was no way Keys could get into her cell.

'Has he been banging on the gate?' Anne asked her.

'No,' Colleen answered, 'he's stopped.'

'Is he saying anything to upset you?'

'Sometimes he does.'

Anne then talked to Keys. 'You should've valued Colleen's arrival: you've someone to talk to, and you have a common goal – namely, how to get out of the dungeon. Together, you could discuss how you might be able to escape. You've turned your greatest ally into an enemy, you stupid idiot! There's an old saying: "Two heads are better than one." Maybe if one of the heads is yours, that saying's not true.'

'You—'

'Keep quiet! I don't want to hear your voice!'

'And I don't want to hear yours!' he yelled, knocking a can of fruit off one of the shelves.

Anne picked up the can, put it on one of Colleen's shelves and said to him, 'You're not getting this back. If your manners don't improve, your rations will be reduced.'

Keys stared at her, a defiant look on his face. Anne was annoyed that although he was in such a powerless position, he had the gall to yell at them and make out he was the one who would win in the end.

'Are you ready to leave, Alice?' she asked Helen.

'I am.'

'Good fuckin' riddance!' Keys roared.

Anne and Helen didn't react to the remark.

As they were turning to leave the dungeon, Colleen told them she'd completed the writing of the lines and that she believed what she'd written. They didn't know what she was talking about. Colleen held up the writing pad. Both noted the word 'inwomane'.

'Who told you to do this?' Anne asked her.

'The woman wearing the Cinderella mask.'

'Well, keep it for Cinderella. Don't cry, Colleen. When you genuinely believe what you've written, we'll let you out.'

'I don't believe you! My family must be worried sick!'

'We'll find a way to let them know you're okay.'

Kate and Alison went to Socamora the following Sunday.

Colleen showed Alison what she'd written, and said, 'And I believe it.'

'I'm sure you do, Colleen,' Alison said in response. 'It's the meaning of the word "surrogacy" we need to clarify. I've left another writing pad and biro on your shelves. This time, you have to write, "The Right to Esse is a mob of sadistic scum." You only have to write it three thousand, two hundred and ninety-nine times, once on each line.

'Have you looked in the mirror today, Colleen? I can hardly recognise you as the confident, self-righteous prick who stood outside Parliament House surrounded by your disciples, spruiking the evils of abortion, IVF, voluntary euthanasia and God knows what. Why do you think you have the right to ram your stinking, warped religious beliefs down the throat of the entire nation?'

'I won't do it anymore if you let me out.'

'I don't believe you!' Alison said.

'Neither do I!' Kate added.

Kate and Alison locked up and left.

The following Wednesday, after work, Anne and Helen went to Socamora with a cassette recorder, a blank tape, an envelope and some stamps. They instructed Colleen to record this message, which she did: 'Dear all, Sorry I left without explaining. I must be having a midlife crisis. I'm ashamed I was ever associated with the Right to Esse. What sort of people believe that a rape victim shouldn't be allowed to terminate her pregnancy? I'm staying with a friend.'

'Now,' Anne said to her, 'stick some stamps on the envelope, address it to your family, put the tape inside, put the envelope on the shelf and move to the back of the cell.'

Colleen did exactly as she'd been instructed.

Anne, who was wearing disposable plastic gloves, took the envelope and asked Colleen, 'How's Keys behaving? Do you talk to each other?'

'Sometimes, he asks me questions about myself. Sometimes, he boasts about terrible things he's done, but I don't want to talk to him.'

Anne looked into Cell 2, saw Keys there and said to him, 'You were so quiet, I thought you must've been asleep!'

'I was tryin' to work out what ya were doin'!'

'Colleen can tell you when we leave.'

'She doesn't want to talk to me,' Keys replied.

'Who would?' Helen snarled at him. 'You evil snake! Goodbye, pus bag!'

'Goodbye, Alice in Fuckland!' he retorted.

As they were walking to the car, Helen said, 'I don't think we should send the cassette: the cops will get another lead from it.'

'I have no intention of sending it. I'm going to burn the envelope and cassette right now. The disposable gloves were just a ploy to convince Colleen we intended to send it to her family.'

Anne put the envelope and cassette in the barbecue and set fire to them. Then she threw some kindling on the fire and waited until there was no evidence of what had been burnt.

Kate and Helen went to Socamora the following Sunday. As soon as they entered the dungeon, Colleen asked them, 'Did you send the cassette?'

Helen answered, 'We did. There was a picture of your husband and all your children in the paper. The eldest daughter – I've forgotten her name.'

'Frances.'

'Frances, that's right, she was holding the cassette. According to the newspaper, your family's delighted you're ashamed you ever had anything to do with the Right to Esse.'

'That's a lie!'

Helen became angry and yelled at Colleen, 'What makes you think you're always right, you self-righteous ghoul? Frances said she was so glad you'd seen the light!'

'Frances wouldn't say that!'

'There you go again, know-all! Frances *did* say that! As if Frances or any of your other kids would've been game to tell you they didn't agree with your stance on abortion or any other Right to Esse crap. You would've had their guts for garters. Now, get this into your bone dome, Colleen: You are not always right!'

'How come ya didn't send *my* family a tape tellin' 'em *I'm* still alive?' Keys bellowed.

'Because no one's worried about you!' Helen yelled back. 'Everyone's glad you're gone. I wouldn't want to disappoint anyone by telling them you're alive.'

'Shut the fuck up, bitch!'

Helen didn't reply. She'd had screaming sessions with Keys before and she wasn't in the mood for one now.

She and Kate completed the routine tasks, locked up and went upstairs. Helen took off her mask; she was sweating. 'Let's go to the pub for lunch and a cold beer.'

'I'm happy to do that,' Kate said, 'but I think we should have a game of boules or badminton. Our last few visits have been fairly short.'

'You're right, Kate: let's play boules.'

Alison loathed Colleen and, over the ensuing weeks, continued to make her write lines and, to use her own expression, 'monitor the progress of her re-education'.

Anne felt a tad sorry for Colleen. She persuaded Helen to go to Socamora with her again the following Wednesday after work.

'Okay,' Helen said, 'but this is the last time during the week. I don't know why you care about her: she epitomises everything you abhor. Have you forgotten she's the national president of the Right to Esse? You know their position on abortion. If Kate had become pregnant after she was raped, Colleen and her ilk believe she shouldn't have been allowed to terminate it. Remember what Keys said to you when you asked him about the rape? Remember the despicable things he said, not to mention what he might've said if you hadn't told him to shut up? Poor Kate, imagine if she'd had to carry that scumbag's baby for nine months. I feel sick just thinking about it.

'According to Colleen's god, Keys should've given Kate's father fifty shekels of silver and married her. But if he'd screwed a donkey, he should've been put to death, along with the poor, unfortunate, innocent donkey – work that one out.'

Helen always felt angry when she thought about what had happened to Kate. She felt other people's pain. Anne knew that Helen's next emotion would be grief, followed by depression. Anne didn't want Helen depressed, so she decided not to suggest any more midweek visits to Socamora.

The following Wednesday, after work, Anne and Helen went to Socamora, and Anne gave Colleen an explanation: 'This is the last midweek visit. I emphasise again that Keys cannot get into your cell, and I want to reassure you, you won't be harmed. When Cinderella's satisfied with your re-education, we'll let you go. Of course, we'll have to do a bit of plea-bargaining, but we'll face that when the time comes. I'm confident you'll be co-operative.'

'What's being said about my disappearance?' Colleen asked.

'Nothing, now, Colleen,' Helen replied. 'You're old hat. People get bored with the same news.'

'My family must be beside themselves with worry!'

'I don't think so: the cassette was very reassuring for them. Now, concentrate on your re-education. The sooner you're re-educated, the sooner we release you.'

'Are the police looking for me?'

'I doubt it,' Anne answered, 'because you said on the tape you're staying with a friend – although no one's found which friend it is. Do you have any friends your family doesn't know about?'

'Now I wish you hadn't sent it.'

'Don't let yourself get upset by that, because if the police were looking for you, they wouldn't find you. We've made sure of that. Also, according to the news, the police have no leads, and no one's come forward with any information. Now, for the last time, concentrate on your re-education. Alice in Wonderland told you your family's delighted with your newfound wisdom.'

'What's her newfound wisdom?' Keys called out.

'She now believes in backdating abortion to get rid of scum like you!' Helen snapped.

'What about scum like you, bitch?'

Helen didn't reply.

'Please! Please let me out!' Colleen pleaded. 'I'll swear on a Bible I won't tell anyone about you! I'll just say I was blindfolded and kidnapped! I'll say I don't know what the kidnappers look like! I'll say they let me go when they realised they'd kidnapped the wrong woman!'

'Nice try, Colleen,' Helen said angrily.

Five weeks after Colleen's ordeal, she told Anne and Kate she was pretty sure she was pregnant. When they arrived at Anne and Helen's house, Anne invited Kate in. Helen was home and asked the standard question: 'How are things at Socamora?'

'Bad,' Anne replied. 'Colleen thinks she's pregnant.'

'Oh hell!' Helen shrieked.

'She probably isn't,' Kate said, 'but she sure is worried. Still, there's no point getting our knickers in a knot till she's certain.'

'Maybe we should put her out of her misery. What say we buy a pregnancy-testing kit?' Helen suggested.

'Hopefully the results will also put me out of my misery. God, I hope she isn't pregnant,' Anne said.

'I'll buy the kit tomorrow,' Helen offered. 'I don't imagine the chemist assistant will do one of your Q&As, Anne: "Excuse me, Ms Davis, but why are you purchasing a pregnancy-testing kit when it must be nearly five months since your last roll in the hay?"'

'Well? What would you say?' Anne asked her.

'I'm just checking for an immaculate conception. On second thoughts, I could say it's for you – what is it, three months since that one-night stand with Clive?'

'*Helen!*'

Suddenly, Helen realised how insensitive she was to talk that way in front of Kate. She apologised profusely. 'Sorry! Sorry! I'm sorry, Anne! Sorry, Kate! I'm sorry I said that!'

'I think buying the kit is a good idea, Helen,' Kate said. 'If you buy it, I'll go out with you after work during the week.'

'Thanks, Kate. How does Tuesday suit you?'

'That's fine.'

Helen and Kate delivered the kit to Colleen on Tuesday night, and after the next visit, they returned with the news: 'Colleen *is* pregnant.'

'Oh no,' Anne sighed. 'You know what that means? It means we have to bring Lyn Cullen in as soon as we can. I haven't even thought about a plan to catch her. We'd all better start thinking, fast.'

'Why do we have to bring her in as soon as possible?' Helen asked.

'She has to be the midwife.'

There was a stony silence. The women did not feel well. Not even Kate wished this on Colleen, but she did think there was a touch of poetic justice.

'What did Colleen say?' Anne asked.

Helen replied, 'She raved on that she wouldn't tell anyone anything if we let her out, kept asking what sort of women could treat another woman so inhumanely. She also asked for a Bible.'

'What did Keys say?'

'Surprisingly, he was civilised: he didn't raise his voice the whole time we were there. Colleen hadn't told him she suspected she was pregnant. When he heard all the weeping and wailing, I told him. He said, "I'm going to be a daddy!" There's nothing we can do, Anne, except take one day at a time.'

Anne made no comment.

'I suppose I should go home now. I'll stop off on the way and tell Alison.'

'I'll see you out, Kate,' Helen said and walked with Kate towards her car. As they were walking, Helen said, 'Tonight I saw something I didn't think I'd ever see.'

'What was it?' Kate asked her.

'A worried Anne. All the years I've known her, I've never known her to worry about anything. She's obviously very concerned about Colleen. How do you think Alison will react?'

'I'm not sure.'

Kate called on Alison on her way back to Queanbeyan. 'I've just come from Socamora. Colleen's pregnant.'

'That's fantastic!' Alison said. 'Now the bitch can experience first-hand what she preaches. I'm going to Socamora tomorrow after work to congratulate Colleen on the wonderful news.'

'I've just come back from Socamora. We don't have to go there till next weekend.'

'I know, but I thought you might come with me. I don't want to wait a whole week before I tell her how "blessed" she is.'

'She wants a Bible,' Kate added.

'I'll buy her one in my lunch hour on Monday. Do we have to clear it with Anne?'

'Surely not.'

'She might insist we do one of her Q&As,' Alison kidded. 'Excuse me, Ms Roberts, but where's the Bible you bought at Loony's bookstore on Monday? How come you bought a Bible when you profess to be an atheist?'

'Alison, we shouldn't talk about Anne like that,' Kate said sternly. 'Look what she's done for us.'

'Yes, Kate, I agree,' Alison said, feeling a tad guilty that she had 'mocked' Anne. 'If I clear it with Anne, will you come with me to Socamora after work tomorrow?'

'Sure.'

'I might also take her a copy of *The Power of Positive Thinking*.'

As soon as Kate had left, Alison rang Anne to see whether it would be okay for Kate and her to go to Socamora the next day and take a Bible for Colleen.

Anne had no objections, although she thought it strange that Alison was so keen to get Colleen a Bible. *I guess it's just Alison being kind to Colleen,* Anne said to herself. *She is a kind person.*

Kate was barely in the door when the phone rang. It was Alison: 'I phoned Anne. It's okay for us to go with a Bible tomorrow. In fact, she's glad we're going, she thinks the more often Colleen sees us the safer she'll feel. I'll leave work early. Can you be at my place by four thirty?'

'Sure.'

'Great, see you tomorrow.'

Alison purchased the Bible during her lunch hour, left work early and was waiting at her front gate when Kate arrived. They drove to Socamora. Alison put on the Cinderella mask and went to talk to Colleen. Kate waited in the stairwell.

Alison commenced the address: 'Colleen, I've just heard your wonderful news. What a blessed gift! And I've brought you a Bible; I'll leave it on the shelves before I go. There is something in the Old Testament about God punishing women by increasing their troubles in pregnancy and their pain in giving birth. And why is he punishing *us*? Because Eve gave Adam an apple and he ate it! And she wasn't supposed to give it to him. Work that one out! You might like to find the verses and study them. You have plenty of time. Hopefully, you can then explain them to me, and I will fully understand why some women are punished by botched caesars!'

Alison went on and on, and Kate thought how she'd never heard her talk that way before. She could never have believed that Alison had such venom in her. Kate could hear Colleen sobbing.

After the rant, Alison locked the doors and said to Kate, 'I can't believe this has happened. Do you think Colleen will change her views about allowing rape victims to terminate their pregnancies?'

'I don't think so, Alison. The poor woman's so brainwashed by her religion she can't think for herself.'

'Don't you feel that some sort of justice has been served?' Alison asked. 'What if *you'd* become pregnant? Scum such as Colleen believe you should be made to have the baby – and then what? Do you keep it?' She started to cry. 'Oh, Kate, my life would be so different now if I could've terminated that pregnancy. I don't feel sorry for Colleen. She heads up an evil, sadistic organisation that ruins people's lives.'

When Kate started thinking about her own life, she also began to cry. The two women were now sobbing and sobbing. It was as though the plug on a geyser had been removed.

Alison was first to stop crying. She remained silent until Kate regained her composure. 'Do you feel like dinner at the Grongo pub?'

'Sure,' Kate replied, 'though I think we should wait till our eyes don't look like someone's squirted pepper in them.'

For Colleen's sake, Anne was desperate to get Lyn Cullen in the gaol. She thought that if Colleen had a cellmate, she'd cope with her frightening situation better. Within four days of the confirmation of Colleen's pregnancy, Anne told Helen her plan to get Lyn Cullen into the gaol: 'Initially, I thought we'd go to Dubbo and kidnap her, but I've scrapped that idea. We'll get her to come to Canberra. We have to be so careful. The cops will link the disappearance of Lyn Cullen with that of Wayne Keys – both from Dubbo, both lured to Canberra. They'll go back through their records. You never know, they might even question Kate. I'll tell her when we're bringing Cullen in, so she can have an alibi.

'Lyn Cullen has her own practice. I ring it and ask to speak to her. If I am put through to her, great! But if Lyn Cullen's practice is like all the solicitors' practices I deal with, the receptionist will say she's busy, and if I leave my name and number, she'll call back. I say my name's Anthea Crisp. Anthea Crisp's a real person; she's a bigwig in the Department of Finance. I tell the receptionist the matter is very private. If she rings back, my secretary will answer the phone and ask who's speaking, and I don't want my secretary to know. Hopefully, I get some idea of what time I can ring her and speak directly to her.

'Now, this is the line I spin: I used to work in the Department of Development. About three years ago, the department called for tenders for developing the shopping centre for a new suburb. I was on the panel that was to assess the tenders. One of the tenderers came to the department to get some more information. A colleague and I met him. He suggested we go and discuss it over coffee at a rather up-market restaurant. He drove us in his car. When we arrived, it was almost midday, so he suggested we have lunch. He bought a very expensive bottle of wine and paid for both our lunches. During the lunch, he mentioned he had a penthouse on the Gold Coast. He said he hardly ever stayed there and that he wished it was used more often. Then he said, "If you and your families ever want to stay there, let me know." He added we could use the car he had in the garage.

'I took him up on the offer. My husband, two children and I stayed there for a week, during the Christmas holidays. After we'd returned to Canberra, he rang me and asked me how we'd enjoyed the holiday. He said how pleased he was that the penthouse was being used. Then about four weeks before Easter, he rang me and asked me whether I wanted to take the family to Vanuatu for Easter. He said he had a bungalow at a resort. He'd been planning to go but the plans had fallen through. He had four airline tickets booked, said he'd change them into our names. I accepted. Now, someone's found out about this, and I could be accused of accepting a bribe.

'You might be wondering why I've contacted you. I'm always seeking legal advice in my work, and I'm friendly with the upper ranks of the Canberra legal fraternity. I want someone who's not a friend or an acquaintance – *or* a friend of a friend or a friend of an acquaintance. I was wondering who I should contact when I remembered that a work colleague had told me, some time ago, about the Judas List. It's a list of lawyers who've knowingly got guilty criminals off on technicalities. The list was composed by an organisation called Lawfail. I asked her whether I could see it. Your name was on it. Because you're the lawyer on the list who practises closest to Canberra, I decided to contact you. I'm hoping you'll take me on as a client.'

'Okay, Anne,' Helen responded. 'I'm sure you can pull it off.'

The following day, which happened to be a Tuesday, Anne rang Lyn Cullen's practice. The receptionist said that she herself went home at five o'clock, but that Mrs Cullen seldom left before six o'clock. Sometimes

Mrs Cullen answered the phone, sometimes she let the call go to the answering machine.

At five thirty, Anne rang the office again, and that time Lyn answered. Anne gave her the spiel and added, 'I have so much to lose. Could you come to Canberra? I'll arrange the accommodation.' She was extremely surprised when Lyn agreed to come to Canberra on the Friday. 'I'll book your accommodation and get back to you with the details.'

'When you do,' Lyn said, 'I'll give you my ETA.'

'I'll phone you tomorrow. Goodbye, Lyn.'

'Goodbye, Anthea.'

Anne then hastily booked the accommodation, giving Lyn as the contact person. She asked the receptionist for an end room located on the ground level and then phoned Lyn to give her the details.

'Thank you, Anthea,' Lyn said. 'I never make appointments for Friday afternoons, so I'll leave here after lunch and stop along the way for tea, and I should be in Canberra before seven o'clock. I'm looking forward to meeting you.'

'Thank you, Lyn. I'll knock on your door at seven o'clock, and we can go to my house to discuss my predicament. I'm also looking forward to meeting you. Bye.'

All four women were concerned about how they'd get Lyn Cullen into the cell. It'd been okay while the cells were empty, but this time, the door of Cell 1 would have to be opened while Colleen was in there. Also, they didn't think Lyn Cullen would be as easily fooled as Colleen O'Day had been as to why they had to unscrew a cupboard, lift up a trapdoor, go down some stairs and unlock two doors at the bottom of the staircase. They agreed that Alison and Helen would go to Socamora, unscrew the cupboard and open the trapdoor before Anne arrived with Lyn Cullen. They would also unlock the downstairs security door, move the shelves away from the gate to Cell 1, and remove the chains around the gate, so all Anne would have to do would be unlock the fireproof door and the gate to Cell 1.

'Colleen's bound to ask us why we're moving the shelves and chains. What do we tell her?' Helen asked.

Alison answered, 'Tell her we're bringing a doctor to see her, a doctor who believes that all Right to Esse supporters should be locked in a dungeon.'

'Don't say anything!' Anne said. 'I don't want to give Colleen any prior warning we're going to open the gate. I don't think she'd let Keys into her cell, but you never know. If they know we're going to open the gate, they might try something.'

'I'm sure she'll work out for herself we're bringing in a cellmate,' Alison said.

'You're probably right, but even so, don't confirm it with her.'

Alison would park her car behind the shed, where it wasn't visible. She and Helen would wait out of sight near the cabin. When Anne entered the cabin with Lyn, she'd leave the timber door wide-open. Alison and Helen would then move close to the open door, taking care they couldn't be seen if Lyn Cullen were to look straight back at the open door. Anne would descend the stairs and say, 'Come down, Lyn.' This would be Alison and Helen's cue to wait a few seconds then enter the cabin, lock the timber door and follow Lyn Cullen down the stairs. Helen would have the gun. Anne and Alison would have cans of hairspray at the ready, hairspray being standard issue for that type of operation.

Anne continued, 'The one thing we must try to estimate is timing. You don't want to enter the cabin until Lyn's head is below the floor, otherwise she could look up and see you. Also, you want to be sure you can hear me. We have to rehearse what we can tomorrow night. I estimate I'll arrive at Socamora with Lyn at seven thirty. Let's be there at seven thirty tomorrow night.'

Anne, Alison, Helen and Kate were at Socamora on Thursday night. Kate was playing the role of Lyn Cullen. Helen and Alison had no trouble hearing Anne. The only problem was how long it would take from the time Alison and Helen heard Anne say, 'Come down, Lyn.' to the time Lyn's head was below floor level.

Helen suggested, 'Forget about timing. Once we hear you speak, we can assume – although I know, Anne, you'll say we can't assume anything – Lyn will start walking down the stairs. One of us will have to take a peep to see when her head disappears. We have to be realistic. She's descending steep stairs, in not the brightest of lights; she's hardly going to be looking at the door; she'll be looking to see she doesn't fall down the stairs and bust her arse.'

'Okay,' Anne agreed.

'She'll think she's hallucinating if she looks back and sees Alice in Wonderland and Cinderella!' Alison remarked.

On Friday night, Anne drove to the Portal Motel, checked that no one was in sight and knocked on the end door. A woman opened it. 'Mrs Cullen?' Anne asked.

'Yes,' came the reply.

'Anthea Crisp,' Anne announced. 'My car's this way.' She opened the passenger door for her, quickly ran around the back of the car, hopped in the driver's seat and drove off immediately. 'I don't think I told you, Lyn, I live on a hobby farm. It's only twenty minutes from here. As well as the paper files, I have some electronic files and emails on my computer I want to show you. I'm worried sick about this whole affair.'

She continued making small talk with her passenger as they were heading for Socamora. 'We love living on the farm. We've been there for nearly five years. When we told our friends we were going to build in the country, some of them said we'd waste a lot of time commuting to and from work. I laughed. It takes me less time to get to work than it does a colleague who lives in Banks.'

When they arrived at the gate, Anne said, 'Having to open and close this gate is the only thing I don't like about our country residence!' She performed the unlocking and re-locking tasks, hopped back in the car and declared, 'All done! Our home's just over that rise. We were going to build on top of the ridge but decided it was too windy up there. I have to stop off at what we call our bodega and get a bottle of port for my husband. Friday nights, he loves to watch the football and have a glass or two.'

She parked the car very close to the cabin and said, 'I won't be a minute!' She left the parking lights on, hopped out and closed the door. She then opened the driver's door and said, as an aside, 'Come and have a look at my husband's wine collection!'

She unlocked the cabin doors and held the screen door open for Lyn. 'The cellar's downstairs.' She descended the stairs, unlocked the fireproof door and said, 'Come down, Lyn.'

Lyn Cullen went down the stairs, and as soon as Helen saw her head disappear, she and Alison entered the cabin and locked the timber door. Helen stood at the top of the stairs. When she saw that Lyn had turned into the corridor, she quickly descended the stairs. Alison followed. They tiptoed, and Lyn wasn't aware of their presence.

Anne saw that Colleen was lying on her bunk, and Colleen started to get up when she saw her.

Helen produced the gun. 'Stay where you are, Colleen. Don't move!'

Anne unlocked the cell gate and commanded, 'Get in, Mrs Cullen!'

Petrified, Lyn Cullen entered the cell. Anne closed the gate, raced upstairs, put on the Snow White mask and returned to the dungeon. Helen pointed the gun at Lyn and ordered her to move to the back of the cell and face the wall. Alison and Anne put the chains around the gate and put the shelves back in place.

'What *is* this? Let me out!' Lyn screamed.

'What's going on next door?' Keys shouted.

'Lyn can tell you!' Anne replied. 'I believe you two know each other. You can have a chat over old times!'

'Please tell me what this is all about!' Lyn begged.

'I don't have time to tell you now,' Helen said. 'I'm going out to dinner.'

She put the second water tank in place, and the three women filled it up. Then they locked up and headed for the Grongo pub, in disbelief at how smoothly the assignment had gone.

When Lyn Cullen had failed to return to Dubbo on the Saturday night, her husband contacted the police. Her disappearance was in the paper and on the TV the following Monday.

'Time for a phone call,' Anne told Helen after they'd finished watching the news.

'What are you going to do?'

'I worked out my spiel today at work. I'm going to ring the police hotline. Any calls to that number are anonymous.' She dialled the number. As soon as the phone was answered, she gave her rehearsed speech: 'I have some information about the missing Dubbo solicitor. There's a mob in Canberra involved in money laundering. They got a tip-off that the cops were closing in on them. They decided to get some legal advice. One in the group was from Dubbo. He wanted to hire Lyn Cullen, reckoned she could get them off if the tip-off was true. After she'd been given *all* the info, she decided the case was too big for her. The mob was mighty annoyed, and they weren't happy that she was privy to their top-secret dealings. I guess you know what that means.' She hung up.

Anne was concerned about Colleen's pregnancy and the pending birth. She was relieved to learn that Colleen's previous two births had been home births. She provided her with iron and vitamin tablets, and she and Helen discreetly purchased all the things a newborn baby would need – anything Colleen asked for, Anne bought.

Whenever Helen started to worry about Colleen, she thought of Damien – beautiful Damien – having married that 'moron of a woman' because she was pregnant. Helen remembered Damien crying the night he told her he was getting married. She thought of her classmate Sandra during her final year at school. One day, Sandra had stopped going to school. No one had believed she'd suddenly developed a dreadful skin condition and gone to stay with a family who lived in a warmer climate. And of course she thought of Kate. Whenever she thought of Damien, Sandra and Kate, she became angry. She got so angry, she couldn't care what happened to Colleen.

Kate seemed indifferent to Colleen's plight. Contrary to what Anne and Helen had expected, Alison wasn't the least bit worried about Colleen; in fact, she almost seemed pleased.

The only baby needs the women couldn't fit through the bars of the security gate were a bathtub and a bassinet. They decided they wouldn't bother about the bathtub; besides, there wasn't enough water to bath a baby every day. In order to get the bassinet to Colleen, they had to open the gate to the cell that had two prisoners inside it. Although the prisoners were outnumbered, the operation wasn't without risk. Who knew what Lyn and Colleen had been planning? All four women went to Socamora on the day they'd decided to deliver the bassinet.

'Just as well we have a gun,' Anne said.

'Yes, but it's not much use if it's not loaded,' Helen pointed out.

'Well, it's good scare tactics.'

Helen had the gun, and each of the other three women had a can of hairspray. The four of them stood outside Cell 1, and Helen pointed the gun at Colleen. 'Colleen, if you want this bassinet, you and Lyn move to the back of the cell.'

'What if we don't?' Lyn asked.

'Questions like that make me angry, Lyn. Let me give you some advice: it's *not* a good idea to make a woman holding a gun angry – just *do it!*'

'Yeah, do as you're told!' Keys called out mockingly.

Lyn and Colleen obeyed.

Anne and Kate moved the shelves, removed the chains and opened the gate. Alison pushed the bassinet through and quickly closed the gate. They put everything back in place and went upstairs. Normally, they would've stayed for a game of badminton or boules, but no one was in the mood today.

Helen was feeling quite drained and said, 'I hope we don't have to do that again.'

Well, we will! Alison said to herself.

They drove back to Anne and Helen's house. Alison and Kate had activities planned for the day, so they went their separate ways.

That night, Anne and Helen discussed Colleen's plight. 'There's nothing we can do,' Anne said. 'If we let her out, the four of us would be dead ducks – worse than dead ducks: gaolbirds. The pregnancy wasn't part of The Plans.'

'The best-laid plans of rats and women ...'

'... go awry,' Anne said. 'Everything associated with the birth stays in the dungeon. We'll push it through the hinged riser.'

'What made you think of constructing the hinged riser, Anne? That was a brilliant idea.'

'I'm not sure. I guess I thought one day there might be something we need to get rid of, but we can't risk putting it in our garbage bin. I don't know what I had in mind. It certainly wasn't anything to do with a birth.'

'Putting disposable nappies in our bin might be a bit risky,' Helen said.

'I know, but we'll have to take that risk. I hope Colleen will be all right.'

'This'll be her sixth child. And remember, she had the last two at home, with a midwife. "Do not dwell on things that might go wrong or you won't move forward. Think about what will go right." Boy, I never thought I'd be quoting Tony Dunn; I thought he was such a phoney!'

'I bet those motivational speakers never think anyone will use their advice for the wrong reason,' Anne said. 'We've provided her with everything she's asked for. Let's not dwell on it anymore.'

The women never discussed the forthcoming birth. It was just too horrible to think about it. You might say life went on as usual. The women ensured the inmates had plenty of food and water, batteries for the CD players, books, newspapers, magazines, clean clothes and clean linen. They also brought them little treats. Colleen asked for a cross-stitch kit and a Scrabble set. At Anne's request, Alison reluctantly agreed to put Colleen's re-education on hold.

It would be difficult to describe the relationship between the gaolers and the prisoners. The gaolers loathed the prisoners for what they'd done, and the prisoners loathed the gaolers for keeping them in the dungeon.

Helen and Alison often taunted Keys, Lyn and Colleen. Some days, Alison loved reminding Colleen about her 'precious gift'; other days, she delighted in telling her what an evil bigot she was and that she was now being punished.

Kate no longer spoke to Keys. She'd made all the threats she'd wanted to, and she knew that if she kept them up, he'd know she was bluffing. However, she loved to mock Lyn and Colleen, often asking, 'How's Lynette in the oubliette?' or 'How's Colleen of eighty O'Days?', referring to the number of days Colleen had been in the dungeon.

Anne didn't engage in any diatribe, feeling that the other three were giving enough.

Occasionally, the prisoners retaliated, and a little slanging match took place.

Colleen and Lyn continued to plead to be let out, swearing they wouldn't tell anyone about the dungeon. Sometimes they begged and cried; sometimes they asked the women how they could treat two of their own sex so inhumanely. Alison was unmoved by Colleen's pleading. It would be incorrect to say the other three women were completely indifferent to Colleen's pleas, but they knew it wasn't possible to let her out.

Whether or not the prisoners were afraid of the gaolers no one knew because no one asked.

Colleen had the baby, a girl, and she named her Gertrude Lynette. She didn't give her a family name, and the four women thought it wouldn't be very tactful to ask why.

Wayne Keys didn't have any children and was quite chuffed at being a father.

Gertrude was now six days old and seemed to be quite healthy. All four women agreed she shouldn't be in gaol because she hadn't done anything wrong. They'd have to work on a plan to get Gertrude out of the gaol. They all liked her, she was very cute.

'I wish I could take her home,' Alison said. 'She might be some consolation for my stolen daughter. One thing's for sure: I'll take her from

Colleen O'Day so she never hears about her again. Maybe there's a tad of justice in the world after all. Leave it with me; I'll work something out.'

Anne and Helen looked at Alison. They didn't understand what she was saying.

Alison decided it was time Anne and Helen knew about her daughter, so she told them. 'That's the sort of warped practice the Right to Esse endorses. It's one of the cruellest, sickest things that can be done to a woman: to make her have a baby and take it from her so she never – *never* – hears from her again. The pregnancy, the birth, the recovery, the whole trauma; trying to get your life back on track when all could've been solved if you'd been allowed to have a simple operation. And that bitch – that bitch also known as Colleen O'Day – thinks it's an acceptable thing to do to a woman! Well, it's not! When Kate told me Colleen was pregnant, I was so glad. I said to myself, "If that baby survives, I'm going to take it away from her and tell her she'll never know what happened to it. Maybe there's a God after all. The Lord has repaid; Colleen has been punished."'

The next time Alison saw Kate, she told her of her plan to take Gertrude from Colleen. 'Every time I go home from Socamora, I drive along Burns Road. Number 58 Burns Road is one of those houses that always has cars parked outside it, and all those cars have spoilers. Last night, I went through the phone book. It took me nearly three hours, but I found the phone number of 58 Burns Road and, for good measure, 56. When we feel up to it, we'll all go and have dinner at the Grongo pub. Then we'll go to Socamora. We'll tell Colleen we have a friend who'll give Gertrude a medical check-over; tell her to put Gertrude in the bassinet, put the bassinet near the gate and go to the back of the cell. In other words, we get the bassinet plus the baby out of the cell, the same way we got the bassinet in.

'We leave the bassinet there. It's covered in fingerprints. You and I wear plastic gloves for this one. We change Gertrude's clothes and nappy, and we put her in the baby cocoon I bought some months ago. It's still in the plastic wrapper. Then you, Gertrude and I head off. We drive along Burns Road; put the cocoon on the boot of one of the cars – I'll use the spoiler to wedge it in; drive to my place; ring the number and tell them there's a baby on the boot of one of the cars outside their house. I ring again in five minutes to see if they've found the baby. I'll run it past Anne and Helen to see whether they can find any weak spots.'

'When did you buy the cocoon?' Kate asked her.

'Not long after Colleen's pregnancy was confirmed. I bought it in Sydney, and when I was buying it, I was wearing a hat and glasses, which I threw in the garbage bin afterwards. I said to myself, "I'm going to take that baby away from her." and I figured that the easiest way to transport a baby was in a baby cocoon.'

Alison was keen to get Gertrude away from Colleen as soon as possible. The following night, she phoned Anne and Helen and asked whether she could go over to their house and tell them her plan. She said she welcomed any suggestions. She drove to their house and told them the plan.

When Anne had heard it, she made two suggestions. 'One: when we've finished dinner, we stay on and chat for at least an hour. You don't want to drive down Burns Road before eleven o'clock; the later it is the less traffic there is. Hopefully there'll be no traffic at that hour on Burns Road; if there is, you'll have to drive around the block. Also, the news of an abandoned baby will miss the morning papers. I always think that the longer a piece of news is kept from the public, the better. Two: I'll make the phone calls. You phone me when you get home. It's better I make the calls: you could be a bit flustered. I'll put on a bit of an accent, otherwise, I think the plan's good. Oh, one more thing, I'll make the calls from work, using Terry's phone. I don't think our phone's tapped, but we can't be too careful.'

'What makes you even *think* that?' Alison asked, horrified.

'Keys and Cullen are a link to Kate, and Kate is a link to us.'

'Using that logic, Kate and all her friends' phones could be tapped.'

'That's true, Alison,' Anne admitted. 'As I've already said, I don't think our phone is tapped, but as an added precaution, I intend to make the calls from work. I sometimes go to the office at odd hours, especially if I want to make an overseas call. How long will it take you to drive home from Burns Road?'

'About ten minutes.'

'And it'll take me about fifteen to get to work, so Gertrude will have to stay on the car for at least twenty-five minutes. We'll make sure Colleen's given her a big feed, and we'll see she's rugged up. The fresh air will do her good. The longer the time lapse from when you get home to when I make the phone call, the better. Do you want to add anything, Helen?'

'What if Gertrude's screaming her head off?' Helen asked. 'We'll have no control over that.'

'I know. We did buy some dummies. We'll get one, and Kate or Alison will have to shove it in her mouth if she starts screaming. Make sure you're wearing gloves if you do have to put a dummy in her mouth.'

'It's too late now,' Alison said, 'but we should've thought of some way of keeping Gertrude. I could've pretended I was pregnant and had a home birth.'

'I don't think we could've pulled that one off, Alison,' Anne said.

Alison started to cry, and Helen consoled her. Alison's tears were good therapy for Anne because they eased the guilt feelings she had for Colleen's children who had lost their mother. Whenever Anne had those little pangs of guilt, Helen reminded her that Colleen's children were better off having no mother than having a mother who filled her children's head with her warped religious beliefs.

When Alison stopped crying, she left.

'You don't think Alison's going to do something dumb and try to keep Gertrude, do you?' Helen asked Anne.

'I've had the same thought, but I don't think she will. She's not stupid.'

'Yes,' Helen agreed, 'but emotions can drive people to do stupid things – just ask *us*.'

'Kate will be with her. I'm sure Kate will bring her to her senses if she tries to do something stupid.'

'I hope you're right,' Helen said guardedly.

Three nights later, all four went to the Grongo pub to have a counter tea. They finished their meal and then ordered coffee. They took their coffees into the lounge area and sat down in front of the television. The TV was a good distraction for them because none of them felt like talking. At nine forty-five, they headed to Socamora.

They removed the cupboard, lifted up the trapdoor and went into the dungeon, hoping it would be the last operation for which all four of them were required. Anne, Helen and Kate moved the shelves while Alison spoke to Colleen: 'Put Gertrude in the bassinet and put the bassinet near the gate. A friend of mine's a doctor. She'll check Gertrude over. She won't ask any questions.'

'You mean to tell me you're going to take Gertrude to a doctor for a health check and that the doctor won't ask any questions?' Colleen queried. 'What sort of doctor would do that?'

Alison replied, 'By now, Colleen, you should know we're very good at fooling people with our cock-and-bull stories. What sort of woman would fall for going to an illegal abortion clinic? You fell for it! Keys fell for our story about the unclaimed will, and Lyn fell for the one about the bribery case. Don't worry: we'll concoct some feasible story the doctor will believe.'

'When will you bring her back?' Colleen asked.

'Tonight,' Alison answered. 'Put her in the bassinet. Put the bassinet near the cell gate. Then you and Lyn go to the back of the cell.'

'No!' Colleen wailed. 'I won't let you take her! What if you don't bring her back?'

'Colleen, your mind will be put at rest because you know she's in good health. Of course we'll bring her back. Don't be ridiculous! How could we possibly explain to everyone how we have a baby?'

'How do I know you're not going to kill her?'

All four women flew into a tirade simultaneously. 'How dare you say that? How dare you imply we'd kill a baby?'

Alison continued, '*She*'s innocent, but *you*'re evil. You're evil because you think it's acceptable to make a woman have a baby and take it away from her. You and your bloody organisation, you ruin people's lives. Keys is evil because he's a rapist. Cullen's evil because she lets a rapist go free and gloats about it. But Gertrude's innocent. Put her near the gate, and step back! I'm absolutely fuming, and I might just use that gun! Now, for the last time, put her near the gate and get back!'

Colleen put the bassinet near the gate and went to the back of the cell, where Lyn Cullen was.

Helen opened the gate and Alison picked up the bassinet. Alison and Kate put on their plastic gloves. Alison picked up Gertrude and hugged her. She held Gertrude in front of her and looked at her. She brought her close to her chest and hugged her again. Alison started to cry. She tried to wipe the tears away through the Cinderella mask.

'Be careful, Cinderella,' Anne said. 'We don't want fibres from your jumper on Gertrude's jumpsuit. Colleen, drop another jumpsuit in the bassinet and return to the back of the cell.'

'You harm that baby and I'll rip this wall down and kill ya!' Keys screamed. 'I wanna see 'er!'

Kate turned to him in a fit of rage. 'Harm? Harm? Since when have you been so concerned that someone might be harmed? Think of all the people you've harmed in your life! I won't hurt Gertrude, but now you've raised the matter, I might come back and harm *you*! I might just use our gun to ... to ... to enlarge the diameter of your anus – a modern-day Canterbury Tale. I've been taking lessons at the local pistol club. I'm actually quite a good shot. Come on, Cinderella. We must go.'

'Let's show the doting father his daughter,' Alison insisted and stood with Gertrude in front of Cell 2. Keys couldn't take his eyes off her.

'Take a good look at your daughter,' Alison snarled at him. 'What if one day she's gang-raped? What would you like to do to the bastard who leads it?'

Colleen was now crying uncontrollably. Keys was swearing and threatening to smash the gaol to pieces, and Lyn Cullen was screaming that they wouldn't get away with what they were doing.

'I'm sure a good lawyer like you could get us off, Lyn!' Kate shouted. 'In fact, we might be able to make a deal! Now, come on, Cinderella. We really *must* go!'

'No, Kate,' Alison said. 'I want to spend another sixty seconds watching Colleen experience the indescribable grief of having her child taken away.'

'You're not bringing her back, are you?' Colleen screamed.

'Calm down, Colleen!' Helen yelled. 'Don't get upset! You didn't get upset when Alison's baby was taken from her, so why would you get upset now Alison's taking your baby away from you?'

Alison and Kate went upstairs. Alison put a new jumpsuit on Gertrude, changed her nappy, and asked Kate to remove the cocoon from its plastic wrapper. She put Gertrude in the cocoon and then said to Kate, 'I have to do one more thing. It won't take long.' She opened the cupboard and picked up a mallet and a large tent peg from inside. She went downstairs, hammered the tent peg into the corridor wall, and hung the bassinet on it.

'There, Colleen,' she teased. 'You can stare at the empty bassinet and wonder about your baby every day of your life: Where's my daughter? Is she happy? Is she being abused? Is she still alive? Will I ever find her? And in two years' time, you'll look at every two-year-old girl you see and wonder whether she's Gertrude. And in three years' time, you'll look at every three-year-old girl you see and wonder whether she's Gertrude. And in four years' time, you'll look at every four-year-old girl you see and wonder whether she's Gertrude. It'll never stop – *never*! You stinking germ!'

Alison went back up the stairs, took off her mask and wiped away the tears. She put the cocoon on the table and looked at Gertrude. Kate heard her murmur, 'Megan'.

They put the cocoon on the back seat of the car and strapped it in. Alison took off her gloves and drove to 58 Burns Road. There were two cars outside the residence, and the street was deserted. Kate jumped out, put the cocoon securely on the boot of one of the cars and jumped back in, and Alison drove to her townhouse. She parked the car in the garage, and she and Kate raced inside.

'Kate, can you ring Anne? I'm about to crap myself! I also think I'm going to spew!'

Kate dialled the number and Anne answered, 'Hello.'

'It's Kate. Did you pick up my glasses?'

'No.'

'Oh, it's all right. Alison's indicating she picked them up.'

They'd agreed on a cryptic way of conveying they'd placed Gertrude on the car boot.

'The food was quite rich. Are you two okay?' Anne asked.

The food hadn't been rich, but Kate knew what Anne meant. 'Just! Thanks, Anne. Bye.'

'Bye, Kate.'

As soon as Kate had put the receiver down, she said to Alison, 'Now it's my turn for the dunny. These operations take quite a toll on the large intestine, don't they?' When she returned to the kitchen, she found Alison pouring two brandies and dry.

'Let's sit down and have a drink,' Alison said.

'Are you going to keep yours down? Which end did you put in the china?' Kate asked her.

'The rear. I feel okay in the stomach now, and the brandy will help settle me. I was terrified someone would drive up the back of me, and we'd have to call the police. Do you think we could've convinced the police the baby was mine? I'm sure they'd know she was only a few days old. Do you think the truck driver at the lights could've seen the cocoon?'

'The answer to your first question is yes, and the answer to the second one is no. Now, let's not talk anymore about it.'

Alison poured two more brandies. Kate knew she shouldn't have the second drink if she was going to drive, but she wanted it.

Alison looked at the TV guide. '*The Fun Factory*'s on in ten minutes. Sometimes, it's quite amusing. Why don't we watch it? It only goes for half an hour.'

'Okay, let's watch it.'

The show was amusing, but Alison and Kate were having trouble laughing. They were still feeling nervous about the night's escapade and anxious for Anne to call and tell them Gertrude was safe.

At eleven forty-five, Anne phoned 58 Burns Road. A male answered. He sounded a bit groggy. Anne put on an accent: 'I am werry sorry to disturb you at dis hour of dee night, but someone has just left something on dee boot of your car, and it looks like a baby. Could you please check for me?'

'What?'

'I'm serious. Could you please look on dee boot of your car?' She hung up and phoned back five minutes later. 'Dis me again – waz it a baby?'

'Yes, who are you?'

'A concerned neighbour.' She hung up again and then rang Alison.

'Hello,' Alison answered.

'Gertrude?'

'No.'

'I'm so sorry. I have the wrong number.'

'Gertrude's safe,' Alison told Kate. They both heaved a sigh of relief.

At about midnight, Kate said, 'I suppose I'd better head home.'

'You'd better stay a bit longer: you could be over the limit. They were large brandies. The last thing anyone wants is for you to be picked up by the breathalyser. You never know, the cops might ask you where you've been. Which road did you take to get here?'

What Alison had said 'put the wind up' Kate, and she knew Alison was right: the last thing she wanted that night was to come face to face with the police.

Alison suggested she stay the night, and Kate thought about the suggestion. She was tempted, but the thought of having to get up early and then go home and shower before she went to work was too off-putting. She decided she'd go home.

'Thanks, Alison, but I think I'll go home now. I don't think there'll be anything in the papers tomorrow: it's too late. You're fine with our story: "We drove up Burns Road; we always do after the Grongo. Time? Can't be sure … about eleven. No, we didn't see anything unusual." End of story.'

'Yes, Kate,' Alison assured her, 'that's fine.'

'Anyway, Alison, who'd suspect us of kidnapping a baby?'

'No one. But when I say that to myself, I think of Mr Dawson, and I get a bit edgy. Mr Dawson was the deputy principal when I was in Third Class. Everyone said what a lovely man he was; the parents were always singing his praises. Then one day he disappeared. All we heard was he'd engaged in inappropriate behaviour with some of the boys who'd stayed back for extra tuition in reading. When I was a few years older, I realised what "engaged in inappropriate behaviour" meant, and I could hardly believe it – lovely Mr Dawson. Who would've suspected him?'

'He left witnesses,' Kate pointed out. 'Do you think anyone would suspect you of kidnapping a baby? *Do* you?'

'I guess not,' Alison answered.

'*Pardon?*'

'No, Kate.'

'That's right. Anyway, we didn't *kidnap* her; we *saved* her. I don't mean to be cruel to you, but next time you see Colleen, you can tell her Gertrude will go to a good home.'

'I'll tell her more than that. I can't wait.'

Kate drove home, parked the car in the carport and went inside. She turned on the television to see whether there was a news flash. Sometimes, she couldn't believe what she was doing, but twenty-nine years earlier, she hadn't been able to believe what was being done to her. Nor could she forget Alison's suffering. Those people deserved to be in a dungeon.

What Next?

Anne was right: the morning papers contained no news that a baby had been left on the boot of a car. However, the evening news and the following day's papers were a different story; the incident was on the front page of the *Queanbeyan Hermes* and *The Canberra Envoy*.

The police were now appealing to the mother to come forward. They'd issued a photo of the baby in the hope someone would recognise her or her clothing. They'd also issued a photo of the cocoon. A policewoman had said they were confident they'd be able track down where the cocoon had been bought because not many of that type had been sold, having been recalled for safety reasons soon after they'd gone on sale.

The four women agreed that even if the police did manage to find the shop, they'd have a hard time finding the person who'd bought the cocoon. One instruction that Anne had drummed successfully into all of them was 'Leave no trails.' When Alison had purchased the cocoon several months before, in Sydney, she had worn a hat and a pair of glasses. She'd disposed of both soon after the purchase.

Alison wondered whether any of Colleen's family members could see any resemblance between Colleen and Gertrude.

A week after Kate placed Gertrude on the boot of the car, Helen was on her lunch break, walking back to work, when she saw a man coming towards her. She started to feel uneasy. She couldn't place his face, but she had a feeling it spelt danger. She looked the other way, but the stranger walked right up to her and said, 'Helen, have you forgotten me? It's Don!'

Helen remembered who Don was: he and his wife, Susan, were the greenies from whom Anne and she had bought Socamora. 'Oh, yes,' she responded.

'What a coincidence running into you!' Don remarked. 'I was going to phone Anne about buying the block back. Susan and I are on our feet now. We used to say if we ever got on our feet again, we'd make you an offer you couldn't refuse. What did you do with it?'

'Er ...' Helen stumbled. 'We built a cabin over the hole and sealed it off. We didn't want to leave the hole there. You know what it's like: someone'll fall down it and sue you and besides, it looked ugly, like a construction site.'

'You mean you didn't make use of the hole?'

'That's right.'

'What a waste! Are you interested in selling the block?'

Helen laughed. 'No! We'll never sell Socamora. We named the property Socamora. We love going out there on weekends. We play badminton and boules. When did you get back?'

'What do you mean?'

'From Wollongong. I thought you went to live with Susan's mother.'

'We did. She moved to Queanbeyan. She *used* to live in Wollongong. Could I go out one day and have a look?'

Helen was taken off guard but managed to reply, 'I guess we can arrange it – not now though. I must get back to work. I'll call you.'

'You don't have my number,' he pointed out. 'I'll call Anne. Is she working at the same place?'

'Er ... yes. Must fly! I'm late! Bye!'

That night, she told Anne about the encounter, and both agreed they'd take him out if he phoned. And phone he did – Anne at work the next day. She wanted to get the visit over and done with as soon as possible, so she agreed to take him out on the Saturday morning, at ten o'clock. He then explained that his wife and two children also wanted to come, so they'd meet Anne at Socamora. Anne didn't like that development and knew Helen wouldn't either, but she felt they had no choice. She arranged to meet Don and his family at the entrance to Socamora at ten o'clock on the Saturday.

When Anne and Helen arrived at nine forty-five on Saturday, they could hardly believe their eyes: there, parked outside the locked gate, was a car that had no one in it. Anne and Helen drove to the cabin, and once there, they felt angry upon seeing all four members of the family trying to look inside the cabin.

'We just couldn't wait to see it, so we decided to start walking!' Don called out to them. 'You remember Susan? And this is Jackson and Walker.'

'There isn't really much to see,' Helen said. 'As I told you when I saw you in the street, we built the cabin over the hole.'

'We'll make you an offer you can't refuse.'

'No, Don. Helen and I will never sell this place. We like it too much.'

'Here's my card if you ever change your mind.' He handed Anne a business card. 'I like your tank. What's with the whirlybirds?'

Helen looked at Anne who did not respond to his question. He didn't persist for an answer and asked, 'Can we look inside?'

Reluctantly, Helen unlocked the doors and opened them, whereupon the two children rushed inside like kids racing for the last chair in a game of musical chairs. Mum and Dad were close behind them.

Susan looked up at the roof and asked. 'Where're the whirlybirds?'

Anne launched straight into the 'reason'. 'So that's why you can't see them: there're over the brick cavity.'

'I haven't heard of whirlybirds being used for that purpose!' Don queried.

'Neither have I!' Susan added.

'There's always a first!' Helen retorted. 'That's all there is to see inside. Let's lock up and go.'

'Not everything,' Don probed. 'Is that a solar light?'

'Yes,' Helen replied.

'Do you come out here at night?'

'Sometimes.'

'Where's the panel?'

'On the roof.'

Don rushed outside and stood on the barbecue, trying to see the panel on the roof. 'I think I can see more than one panel. How many've you got?'

Adhering to Anne's rule of 'Do not lie.' Helen answered, 'Five. We're only using one panel, but one day we might want to install some more lights outside the cabin.'

'Those lights are for internal use only,' Don informed them.

'I know,' Helen agreed. 'Let's just say we're allowing for future expansion.'

'Did you buy five light kits?'

'Yes.'

'Where's the rest of the equipment?'

'At home. Anything else you'd like to know?' Anne asked the question in a tone to imply he should shut up.

'Wow, I can't believe our beautiful, environmentally friendly hole is below us!' Susan said, and she started jumping up and down on the floor of the cabin. She laughed. 'Just thought the floor might cave in and I could see it!'

Then the two boys started jumping up and down.

'That's enough!' Anne said firmly.

'One night I'll come 'round here with a jackhammer and take a look!' Don roared.

'Ha! Ha! Have you forgotten? There's no electricity here!' Helen reminded him.

'Have you seen some of the equipment you can operate from petrol-driven generators?' he asked.

'Time to go,' Helen snapped. 'I'm going out for lunch and I have to take a salad; I haven't even prepared it.'

'What time's your lunch?'

'Er … twelve o'clock. Now let's go!'

'You go,' he instructed. 'We can walk back and climb over the gate.'

'No. You should know it's not good for the gate. And besides, we don't want anyone taking you for trespassers. Now, let's go. Squeeze in the back, and I'll give you a ride to the gate.'

When they arrived at the gate, Don said, 'If you're really serious about keeping cars out, you should invest in something more secure than one padlock: those padlocks aren't hard to pick. I've picked one or two.'

'I wouldn't be boasting about that!' Anne said.

'Oh, they were my locks.'

Helen parked the car on the roadside while Anne relocked the gate. Anne and Helen didn't want to leave till the Grimshaws had left, but the family was showing no signs of wanting to go. *Just rack off!* Helen said to herself.

'We might take a bit of a drive and see if any of the surrounding properties are for sale,' Don announced. 'Are you absolutely *sure* you don't want to sell?'

'Positive, Don,' Anne answered, not trying to hide the annoyance in her tone, 'so don't keep asking.'

Anne and Helen drove home feeling angry. Don and his family had wasted their Saturday morning. The two women were also feeling nervous: the last person they wanted living close by was Don Grimshaw.

'I'd better keep moving. I'm teeing off at twelve forty-five,' Anne said.

'I want to buy a few things at the mall. I'll have lunch there, at least I can say I went out for lunch. Bye, Anne. Enjoy your golf.'

'Bye, Helen.'

Helen completed her shopping, had lunch, put her parcels on the back seat of her car and headed for home. As she turned into her street, she saw Don's car parked outside the house. She was furious and uneasy: what did he want? She wondered how he knew where she lived. Then she remembered that her address would've been on the title transfer when she and Anne were buying Socamora. Normally, she would have put the car in the garage, but today she stopped in the driveway. She hopped out of the car and saw Don, Susan, Jackson and Walker charging towards her.

'Hello!' Don said at the top of his voice. 'I told Susan if you were having an early lunch, you might be back by three.'

Helen saw him looking at the parcels on the back seat and wondered what he was thinking.

'How was lunch?' he asked suspiciously.

'Lunch was cancelled. I went shopping,' Helen replied.

'Oh, why was that?'

'The hostess was not feeling well. What do you want?'

'After you left, we drove around the countryside. We saw three properties for sale. I wrote down the contacts. One was quite close to yours: Dameyarden. Do you know anything about it?'

'No. We only go to Socamora on the weekends, and we don't see anyone.'

'You said you sometimes go at night.'

'Not very often, and if we don't see people on the weekend, we're hardly going to see anyone at night.' She'd had enough of this pain in the butt. 'Don, you'll have to excuse me: I have the usual weekend chores to attend to.'

'Okay,' he said. 'I'll keep in touch.'

'Please don't!' she said under her breath and went inside.

When Anne arrived home, Helen told her that Don had come to the house.

'I saw him looking at my parcels on the back seat. I don't think he believed my story about going out to lunch, so I told him lunch was cancelled and I went shopping. Then the nosy so-and-so wanted to know why! I told him the hostess was sick. He's now probably wondering why I was so keen to leave Socamora. I forgot one of your rules: never lie.'

'Yes, you did! But he can't read anything into that. I think we both made it obvious we'd wasted enough time there.'

How was golf? Did you win again?'

'Yes. Besides the queries about Dameyarden, did Don say anything else?'

'He said he was going to keep in touch, but don't ask me why. He's a worry; he's so nosy. I was so sure they'd gone to Wollongong for good. And what do you make of his reference to picking padlocks?'

'I hate to think!' Anne replied. 'I have this awful feeling he might've been snooping around while we were building the gaol.'

'I was glad you remembered your story about the whirlybirds! I was also worried he was going to check out the cables from the solar panels. He'd have to climb on the roof. Do you think he'd have the gall to do that?'

'I wouldn't put it past him,' Anne replied. 'Don't worry: We'll make sure he and his family never set foot on Socamora again.'

'He'll end up in the dungeon himself if he doesn't watch it!' Helen declared. 'I was thinking how smoothly everything was going: the prisoners in the gaol, Gertrude safe. And now this nosy parker has to reappear. I'm going to make some coffees and read the paper.'

'Can I have the crossword?' Anne asked.

'Of course.'

They drank their coffees in silence, Anne doing the crossword and Helen reading the paper. 'Oh no!' Helen cried, after about ten minutes of reading.

'What?'

'Listen to this: "MAN QUESTIONED: Police have questioned a 42-year-old Canberra man over the disappearance of Colleen O'Day. Mrs O'Day disappeared ten months ago. Her car was found abandoned in the Cactus Bar car park. Police believe she has met with foul play. The man, whose identity police have not yet made public, is assisting them with their enquiries." That's all it says.'

'Crikey!' Anne exclaimed. 'Is this good news or bad news?'

'I don't know,' Helen replied.

According to all the newspapers, Gertrude had been placed in foster care and was to be adopted if the mother didn't come forward. No journalist had given any indication of how long the mother had to 'come forward'.

It was Kate and Alison's turn to do the chores at Socamora, and Colleen was pleading with them to tell her what they'd done with Gertrude.

'No!' Alison replied. 'You'll never know, and I promise you there won't be a day in your life you don't think of Gertrude. Let's have a long talk, Colleen.' She proceeded to tell Colleen about the unplanned, unwanted pregnancy that had occurred while she was studying at university and how her life had been ruined because of it. 'Can't you see, Colleen? Can't you see what unnecessary suffering and misery you Right to Esse people bring to women? I'm almost begging you, Colleen: try to see what your organisation does to women and, in some cases, men who agree to going into a loveless marriage. You see nothing wrong with the fact that two people who are totally unsuited to marriage sign that vow because the woman's pregnant, when a termination would be the solution to everything. You'd condemn two people to a life of misery. You don't know the difference between living and existing.

'You, as the national president of the Right to Esse, are one of the lowest forms of life on this planet. You can't compare an early termination with a full-term pregnancy and birth. Even *you* know that now. When you learnt you were pregnant to a rapist, you nearly freaked out and hoped you'd have a miscarriage, but when you saw Gertrude, your heart changed. The same thing happened to me. When I saw my daughter lying there in the baby trolley, and I knew she was going to be taken from me and I'd never hear another thing about her, I wanted to commit suicide. I didn't think I could recover from the trauma, and I was right.

'Now, you'll experience the same pain until you renounce the evil organisation you belong to. And it's not only abortion, Colleen: what about voluntary euthanasia? Why does your organisation condemn old people to years of suffering? You're a self-righteous prick trying to force your religious beliefs on the whole of society. You and your cronies can all end up incontinent zombies in nursing homes if that's what you want, but *I* don't. If I can't wipe my own bum, I don't expect anyone else to do it. Why should anyone have to wipe your backside? I think that's expecting too much of anyone.'

She called out to Wayne Keys. 'And what about you, pus bag? Have you given any thought to what you are? Have you repented? And while

I'm at it, the same applies to you, Cullen: what are you? What sort of person tries to get a rapist off?'

'I was only doing my job,' Lyn replied.

'You didn't *have* to do it,' Alison snapped.

'And she did a great job!' Keys called out. 'Not too many guys can take a virgin against her will and get away with it! Ernie went to gaol, and Sam probably would've too if he hadn't wiped himself out in his car. You weren't so good on the armed-robbery charge though.'

Alison yelled at Keys, 'You'll regret you said that, Keys! You'll eat cold food for the next month!'

Alison and Kate went upstairs. Kate was enraged and distressed, and Alison tried to comfort her. 'I want to physically hurt him!' Kate confessed. 'Sometimes I think I'll throw darts at him, but I know he'll throw them back! Sometimes I think I'll get a javelin and stab him, but I know he'd grab the other end and pull it, and I'd have to let go!'

'We'll think of a way,' Alison said in response. 'Let's have a cup of tea. I have a few more things I want to say to Colleen before we leave.'

They drank their tea, and Alison then went into the dungeon. 'Colleen, do you want to get out of this gaol?' she asked.

'Of course I do!'

'Well, there *is* a way. I'm going to leave you a nice box of stationery, a book of stamps, and a letter I've written – not my *best* literary effort: feel free to correct any grammar or spelling mistakes. Read it over and over, and when you agree with every word in it, write it on the writing pad, put it in the envelope, stick a stamp on the envelope and address it to your family. And swear on the Bible – Lyn can be your witness – you'll do everything humanly possible to ensure no other girl or woman ever has to experience the horror of what I had to endure. You might be wondering why I've given you a box of stationery and a book of stamps. I haven't opened the stationery box or the stamps, so I know my fingerprints won't be on anything your family receives.'

Alison put the stationery, stamps and letter on the shelves, and stood back.

Colleen took the letter and began reading it.

Alison went upstairs to where Kate was waiting, and she and Kate proceeded to lock up. They decided to call in at Anne and Helen's house and tell them what Keys had said.

When they arrived there, they found that Anne was the only one home. Anne agreed that Keys wouldn't be given any more cylinders until he'd eaten cold food for a month.

The next time Alison went to Socamora, Colleen showed her the letter she'd rewritten in her own handwriting:

Dear Bernie, Frances, Pat, Mary, Michael and Therese,

I didn't leave you; I was led away. I was led away because I was one of the lowest forms of life on earth and because some higher power wanted to make me see I was and help me change.

On the night I disappeared, I heard a very loud noise. I went out the front door to see what had caused the noise. I saw a semi-trailer coming up the road. As it rounded the bend, the headlights shone right into my eyes and I was temporarily blinded. It was probably only about twenty seconds before I could see again, but in that short time, I had a vision. The vision was of a woman. She told me to go to the Cactus Bar. The vision was gone, and I could see again.

An indescribable feeling came over me. A higher power was controlling me. I drove to the Cactus Bar. I went inside, and I saw a woman sitting alone at a table. She was the woman I had seen in my vision. Her eyes were the most melancholy I have ever seen. Her face portrayed a life of sadness. I went and sat beside her. She told me it was her daughter's birthday. Then she told me how she had had to give up her studies because she was unmarried and pregnant. She had to leave town. Twenty-seven years ago, she had given birth to a baby girl. She had seen her for a few hours, after which the baby was taken away.

Then she told me what she thought of the Right to Esse. She said her suffering could have ended with a simple termination of the pregnancy. It was beyond her comprehension how anyone could treat a woman so cruelly. We continued to talk, and I knew that my vision was telling me something: she was right, and I was wrong.

I left the Cactus Bar and rang an acquaintance – you haven't met her – from my uni days. At uni, we had opposing views on life. She said she was thrilled I'd changed my position. She collected me from the Cactus Bar car park and took me to her home, where she said I must stay until she was convinced, I have completely relinquished my wicked beliefs.

Love,
Mum

Colleen told Alison she'd read the letter many times, seen the error of her ways and agreed with every word in the letter.

Alison replied, 'I'm not convinced. I think you're telling porky pies: your conversion was too quick. No, I'm not convinced. You weren't thinking of pretending you agreed with the letter, so I'd let you out of gaol, were you, and then going to the police and telling them you were kept in a dungeon with Wayne Keys and Lyn Cullen?'

Colleen started to cry.

'Tears will get you nowhere, Colleen – just as they got *me* nowhere.'

'Is Gertrude alive?'

'I don't know, Colleen – just as I don't know whether my own daughter's alive. Keep reading the letter. Some people have incredible conversions, just as you might in this dungeon. How long have you been here? It must be nearly twelve months. How often do you pray to God to let you out of this hell? Three times a day? That's a lot of prayers. Why won't he answer your prayer? I wouldn't have thought you were asking too much. Do you think he can't hear your prayer? Is the concrete slab too thick? Think about it. Think about it, Colleen: why won't God answer your prayer?' Alison was now shouting at Colleen. "Oh, what needless pain we bear, all because we do not carry everything to God in prayer." Who wrote that rot?' She turned and left the dungeon.

Hope

It was now the end of July 1990, and Keys had been in the gaol seventeen months, Colleen eleven and Lyn nine. Helen and Kate were on their way to Socamora.

'Helen,' Kate said, 'remember when I first went to see Keys, I told him I had cancer and the most I was expected to live was two years? We gave the same spiel to Colleen and Lyn. The last time I went to Socamora, Keys told me that the cancer story was a "fucking bloody lie". He was pacing up and down his cell, ranting and raving like a mad man. I think it's time I disappeared. Tell them I'm in hospital. I'm quite willing to do my share of washing and shopping and still come here, but I think it's time we resurrected the "cancer story": they're starting to despair. We must give them hope; everyone needs hope.'

'Is that tongue-in-cheek, Kate?' Helen asked her. 'I agree with you. I don't know that everybody needs hope, but I agree it's a good idea to tell the prisoners they'll be released soon.'

'Next time I come to Socamora, I'll borrow some clothes I know Alison's worn here, and I'll wear the Cinderella mask,' Kate suggested.

'It's probably best if they don't see you at all. You can come to Socamora, but only Alison, Anne and I will go into the gaol. We'll get the plan moving next weekend. Anne's going away. I'll see whether Alison can come with me.'

Kate called in to see Alison on her way back to Queanbeyan. She told her about the plan to tell the prisoners she was in the hospital and that they'd soon be released.

The following weekend, Alison arrived to collect Helen, who was wearing a pair of slacks and a jumper that Alison had never seen before. 'Have you bought some new clothes?' Alison asked her.

'No, they're old. I know I've never worn this outfit, including the shoes, to Socamora, and I've bought a new mask, Sleeping Beauty. I'm going to pretend to be another person. I'm going to speak in a different voice and tell them I'm the one who'll let them out.'

'Don't you think they'll know you're Alice?' Alison queried. 'They might think it's strange that the new woman and Alice are exactly the same height and shape.'

'I thought of that,' Helen responded, 'so I'm going to walk with a slight limp and wear a black leather glove on my left hand, as if I'm trying to hide something. Besides, I haven't always been Alice: I've had a few turns as Snow White. *You* be Snow White today.'

They arrived at Socamora and went through the standard unlocking and locking procedures.

Helen entered the gaol first. 'Hi, guys! How're we all doin'? Wow, look at your five-star accommodation! I'm new 'round here. I've come to case the joint 'cause I'm the one who's gunna let yous out, just as soon as Kate passes away.'

'When will that be?' Colleen asked.

'We can't be sure,' Helen answered. 'But you're not wishin' it, are you? Because I tell you, that ain't very nice to be wishin' someone to die.'

'How are you going to let us out?' Lyn asked.

'Well, I was intendin' to keep it a secret, but since you asked so nice, I might just as well tell ya. Now, you don't think I'm just gunna unlock these gates and stand by while yous exit, do ya? I might look stupid with this mask on, but I *ain't*. I've got a van, an ex-paddy wagon. I'm gunna back it right up to the door upstairs, and then I'm gunna come down here and toss yous the keys. There are two for each unit. I believe that Snow White and her friends call them cells; I think they're so cute I'll call them units. One key unlocks the chains, and the other unlocks the gate. By the time yous have opened the gates, I'll be sittin' in the paddy wagon with the engine runnin'. Yous hop in the back and lock the door, which once locked can only be unlocked from the outside, and I drive away.'

'What if we don't hop in the wagon?' Keys put in.

'Crikey, Mr Keys,' Helen said, 'you're soundin' mighty ungrateful – borderin' on the *rude* side, and I don't like rude people. Since I'm polite, I'll answer your question: if ya *don't* hop in the back of the van, you'll be overcome with carbon-monoxide fumes and pass away – a bit like gettin' shot on the last day of the war, wouldn't ya say? And by the way, this is a *team* effort. I don't drive away in the paddy wagon 'less yous are all in. I drive to a very remote place, and who'll be waitin' for me there? My good friend Alice in Wonderland! I hop into Alice's car, and we drive away.

'You'll be in the paddy wagon for three days. It'll be a bit cramped. Nevertheless, a person can put up with almost anything if the end's in sight. Ain't that a fact? And because we're *real* nice people, we're gunna give yous three days' supply of food and water. We've even installed a porta-potty with a cane screen 'round it in the wagon. One porta-potty for three people for three days. That's askin' quite a lot of one little porta-potty; go real easy on the paper! I suggest you practise the ancient art of origami: fold one, fold two, fold three – ya with me? Yous don't want to be puttin' an "Out of Order" sign on it at the end of day one, do ya, now?

'Three days is what it'll take us to raze this structure to the ground. When there's no trace of these cute little units, three or four men armed with shotguns and wearin' balaclavas will come and let yous out. There's no need to be afraid. They'll order yous to move about fifty metres from the paddy wagon, and they'll hop in and drive it away. When the paddy wagon's safely in its garage, one of the men'll phone the cops and give them your exact location. Yous mustn't leave that location. We estimate it'll take about two hours from the time the men drive away to the time the cops find yous, so just be patient.

'Now, this is gunna be "big headline" stuff: the photographers will want to get a few snaps. Make sure you're lookin' pretty. Now, you can't call me inconsiderate, can yous, *eh*?'

'You'll never get away with this!' Lyn yelled.

'Well, if you're thinkin' like that,' Helen snapped, 'I might as well abandon the plans to release yous 'cause I don't intend to spend any time in the clink for givin' you three scumbags a bit of a rough-up!'

'What did ya say that for, ya stupid bitch?' Keys bellowed.

'Yes, why did ya say that, Lyn?' Helen asked her, pretending to sound worried. 'You've got me worried. What makes ya think we won't get away with this?'

'I won't say a word!' Colleen said. 'Just let me out. I'll say I must've had amnesia!'

'Now you're talkin', Colleen!' Helen said, feigning enthusiasm.

'So will I!' Lyn echoed.

'Two out of three! What about you, turd head?' Helen called out to Keys. 'Can *you* dream up a story to explain ya extended holiday?'

'I'll think of somethin',' Keys retorted.

'That's the spirit!' Helen replied. 'Give it a go, eh? Have I forgotten anything, Snow White?'

'Yes,' Alison replied. 'You've forgotten to inform these despicable women they'll be safe from any sexual abuse from Mr Keys. Colleen and Lyn, just before Sleeping Beauty tosses you the keys, I want to carry out a bit of target practice on Mr Keys.'

She moved so she was standing in front of Cell 2 and pointed the gun at Keys. 'On the day of departure, I'm going to get you to drop your dacks, and according to what mood you're in, you'll stand side on or face me. You'll have to remain perfectly still, Mr Keys; so will I. In fact, I'm seriously thinking of bringing a stool in for me to sit on, so I can steady my hand and be on the same level as my target. My aim's improving, but I do need more practice. After my little shoot-out, you'll be at the mercy of those lovely ladies in Cell 1. You'll need their help, so mind your manners and language! Maybe I'll allow you one four-letter word immediately after your operation. As we keep reminding you, we're *nice* people, so I'll provide you with a three-day supply of Migone. It's the most powerful painkiller you can buy over the counter. Read the dosage instructions carefully. You don't want to use it all on the first day, and remember: "If pain persists, see your doctor." If I was a gambling lady, I'd bet a lot of money your pain *will* persist.'

'You're not serious!' Keys exclaimed in a tone that indicated he was worried.

'Is that a statement or a question?' Alison asked him. 'If it's a question, I'm serious. We were going to do this long ago, but we were worried you might die of septicaemia before you'd served your sentence. I hate you, Keys! I hate you for what you did to my friend! People can be driven to do unbelievably cruel things because of hatred!'

'If ya feel a bit shaky with the revolver, Snow White, ya can try the acid gun,' Helen suggested.

'That also requires a steady hand.'

'Ain't that a fact!' Helen agreed. 'I saw an inexperienced operator with the acid gun once. He had several goes. The guy's organ ended up lookin' like a piece of Gruyere cheese! He *sounded* like an organ too – a pipe organ. Well, we all had a good laugh! It's important ya keep your sense of humour. You'd agree with that, wouldn't ya, Mr Keys? I'm sure after ya operation you'll still be included among the Lord's people. There's a verse in Deuteronomy that's rather frightenin' for any guy who's not intact. Colleen, can ya find the verse and read it to Mr Keys? That edition has sub-headings, so it shouldn't take ya long to find it. And while we are waitin' for Colleen, yous can think about ya sins.'

'I found it,' Colleen said, and she read it out: '"No man who has been castrated or whose penis has been cut off may be included among the Lord's people."'

'Thank you, Colleen. I think you'll be okay, Mr Keys. Ya don't intend to do that much damage, do ya Snow White?' Helen asked, professing to be serious.

'I'm not intending to, but if my aim's bad on the day, you never know what the end result could be.'

'Get Colleen to take a look at your organ,' Helen teased. 'She'll know. She knows all about the Lord. Well, Snow White, ya don't have to decide right now which gun you'll use.'

'Yes,' Alison agreed. 'I'll make my decision closer to the date. Now, I want to give all of you some advice about counselling. You've all undergone a very traumatic experience. If you're thinking of seeing a counsellor when you get out, don't bother. Save your time and money: it doesn't work. Think about it: someone you've never seen before in your life, someone who can't have any comprehension of your trauma, is going to give you advice! I tell you, you'll only end up wanting to bop the counsellor on the head.

'Mr Keys, it's more than likely Mrs O'Day will bring a charge of rape against you. I want to give you the name of a lawyer you should get to defend you. Her name's Lyn Cullen.

'Now, in preparation for your release, I should update you about things on the outside. Things can change so much in nine months – that's how long Lyn's been in our dungeon.

'First you, Keys: you were never officially declared missing. No one wanted you found; everyone was glad you'd vanished. Now, Colleen and Lyn, the news for you is also not good. Well, Colleen, that holier-than-thou husband of yours recovered very quickly from his loss. He's now shacked up with a woman whose morals aren't to your high standard.'

'You're lying!' Colleen screamed.

'Now, that ain't nice, Colleen,' Helen interjected, 'to call my good friend Snow White a liar. That ain't nice at all!'

'Sorry, Colleen,' Alison continued, 'but it doesn't take men very long to get over the loss of their wives. I remember Mr Sanders – lovely Mr Sanders. He lived in Nowra. His wife of thirty-five years died. He wept and wailed, said he couldn't go on without Fay, and then what happens? Four months later, he's introducing everyone to his Filipino bride.'

'Can I just interrupt ya for a moment, Snow White?' Helen asked her. 'There's something I've always wanted to know. I'm sure Colleen'll know the answer. Colleen, eventually Mr Sanders and his Filipino bride will die and, I guess, go to heaven. Therefore, in heaven, Mr Sanders will have two wives. Do they, whoever they are, allow bigamy in heaven?'

Colleen remained silent.

Helen shouted at her, 'Come on, smart arse. Answer the question! There are only two possible answers, yes or no. How come ya don't know? You seem to know everything else that happens to ya when ya die.'

'There are no husbands and wives in heaven,' Colleen said in an irritated tone of voice.

'Well, that's a plus point for heaven. Still, I think it's a pathetic answer … Sorry for the interruption, Snow White. I really want to know about bigamy in heaven, and I was so sure Colleen would have the answer.'

'That's okay, Sleeping Beauty,' Alison said. 'As for you, Lyn, well, I don't like telling bad news, but Frank — yes, Frank — was number-one suspect in your disappearance. When someone disappears, and the cops suspect foul play, they look for a person who has a motive. And what was Frank's motive? He was carrying on with your receptionist.'

'I don't believe you!' Lyn blubbered.

'However, I do have some good news for you: your staff's kept your practice going. So when you return to Dubbo, you can go straight back to work. Of course, you'll probably want to get a new receptionist.

'Now, Kate's not too well. I estimate you have another six weeks to serve. You should think about your sentences. Personally, I believe they're too light. Why'd you get Keys off, Lyn? Come on, answer me! You knew he was guilty. What are you? What sort of person are you? And as for you, Colleen, what does your organisation hope to achieve? Do you think that because you're the national president of the Right to Esse you'll have a shorter stay in purgatory? You poor, brainwashed fool!

'In the meantime, I think we'll make some changes to the accommodation: I think it's time Colleen had a room to herself. Next time I come, we'll put Colleen in Cell 2, and Wayne and Lyn can share Cell 1. That'll be a change. As they say, a change is as good as a holiday.'

'That's a great idea, Snow White!' Helen remarked, with feigned enthusiasm.

'I won't complain about that: I think Lyn'll be a great cellmate,' Keys commented in a mocking tone.

Lyn started to panic. 'How can you women treat another woman so sadistically?'

Alison was quick to respond. 'I think "feeling pleased about getting a gang rapist off on a technicality" is sadistic. If he rapes *you*, you'll be able to get him off – what a laugh!'

'Keys can't get into our cell unless we undo our side of the gate,' Colleen pointed out.

'We can get around that little problem,' Alison replied. 'Just think, Lyn: if you hadn't got Keys off, you wouldn't be here.'

Lyn sobbed. 'I was only doing my job.'

'I wish Kate could see ya bawlin'!' Helen put in.

'So do I!' Alison added. 'We'd better top up your food and water and do all the other things we have to do to keep you scumbags happy. Will you lend a hand, Sleeping Beauty?'

'Of course, Cinderella. Just tell me what I have to do and I'll do it.'

Keys laughed. 'Can't wait for your next visit!'

Helen and Alison went about the routine tasks in silence and then locked up and left. On the way home, they laughed about how they'd scared Lyn.

'I wonder what they discussed after we left,' Helen said. 'We're too nice to them – Lyn probably knows we're bluffing.'

'She can't be sure, so she can sweat it out till our next visit. As we've said so many times before, it'd be nice to be a fly on the wall.'

Alison dropped Helen at her front gate and then drove home, intending to finish reading the newspaper before she went out for dinner. A horrible feeling came over her as she was reading a small news item, in which the journalist said the police were expecting to charge a man 'over the disappearance of Colleen O'Day'. She wondered whether any of the other women had seen the story. *Oh well,* she decided. *He hasn't been charged yet, so no point getting your knickers in a knot over something that mightn't happen.*

It was now six weeks since Helen and Alison had given the prisoners their release plan.

'We can't string them along any longer,' Kate said. 'Alison and I'll go to Socamora and tell them the bad news.'

Kate entered the gaol first. 'I have some good news and some bad news,' she told the prisoners – 'good for me, bad for you: I'm in remission. I could be like this for years, so we have to resort to Release Plan 2. For Plan 2, I need a good lawyer, and how fortunate I am to have one right here. How would this story stand up in court, Lyn?

'About two years ago, I was drinking at the Cactus Bar. I started talking to three women I'd never seen before. They were very friendly. One of them said I looked sad, and I guess because I was under the weather, I told them my story. They were horrified. They told me they had a dungeon and they'd fix everything. I gave them my name, address and phone number, and then they left. It was dark inside the Cactus Bar, and by that stage I was quite blotto, so their faces were a blur, and they still are. I'd never be able to recognise them again.

'One day, out of the blue, I received a phone call; it was one of the women who'd been at the Cactus Bar. She told me they had Wayne Keys in the dungeon. I felt sick; I didn't believe her. She told me to go to the park opposite the Hapley shops, sit on the bench closest to Flower Road, look straight ahead at the old pine tree and never shift my gaze. She said she'd be there in half an hour.

'I went to the park opposite the shops. I sat on the bench closest to Flower Road and stared straight ahead at the old pine tree. I'd been sitting there for about five minutes when someone came up behind me and said, "Keep looking straight ahead, and put these on. Don't be scared." A hand reached over my shoulder and handed me a pair of wraparound sunglasses. I put them on, and I couldn't see a thing: the lenses had been painted over with an opaque paint. Then a woman – I could tell by her voice it was a woman – sat down beside me. She said, "Remember the night at the Cactus Bar? We've got Wayne Keys in our dungeon. Can you remember what any of us look like?" I apologised and said I couldn't. She said I didn't have to apologise: she'd been hoping I'd forgotten. That was a good thing. She led me to a car and told me to hop in.

'I sat in the back. Two women in the car said hello and called me by my name. Obviously, they were the other two women who'd been at the Cactus Bar. The woman in the back gave me a pat on the knee and told me not to be scared. She could've saved herself the effort because I was terrified, and her little reassuring pat did nothing to reduce my terror.

'We drove for what seemed like two hours, but when the women allowed me to remove the glasses, I looked at my watch and realised that the drive had been more like half an hour. The women were wearing masks of fairy-tale characters: Alice in Wonderland, Snow White and Cinderella. The masks were made of moulded rubber and had hair around them, and what's more, the women called each other by the name of the character whose mask they were wearing.

'They took me to the dungeon. I saw Wayne Keys. Some months after that incident, they'd put Colleen O'Day in the dungeon, and about three months after that, they'd put Lyn Cullen in.

'I was very scared of the women: one of them was always carrying a gun. I was always picked up from the same park bench, and I wasn't allowed to take the glasses off till they'd told me I could.

'One day, they told me I could let the prisoners out when I was satisfied they'd served their time. I jumped at the chance. The women said I had to keep the prisoners captive for thirty-six hours after we'd left the dungeon so the women could destroy it.

'*Phew!* That was quite a spiel! How do you think it'd stand up in court, Lyn?'

'I think it'd stand up perfectly,' Lyn replied. 'I don't think anyone would argue with it.'

'You can't be serious! There are umpteen holes in that waffle! You're meant to think about it; you were too quick to be convincing!' Kate said in a loud voice.

'Like you, Colleen,' Alison added. 'You were too quick with your conversion. By the way, how's it coming along? Are you reading the letter every morning, noon and night? Are you starting to believe what's in it? Are you wondering where your god is? Crikey, Colleen, think of what you've been through! Sorry, Kate, I interrupted.'

'That's okay, Cinderella. You've given Lyn some more time to think about Release Plan 2. What do you think, Lyn?'

'Yes, Kate. There are holes,' Lyn admitted. 'Though I'm sure we can work together to close them. How would you stand up to the police interrogation? They can—'

'Don't talk to *me* about police interrogations, you rotten maggot!' Kate cut in. 'You think the *police* are bad – what about the *defence lawyers*? What about the way *you* interrogated me? What about the way *you* humiliated me? You despicable bitch! You stinking arsehole! You've just reminded me you should spend a few more years in gaol!'

'You dumb, stupid whore! Now you've fucked up another chance to get out of here,' screamed Keys.

Kate decided to leave the dungeon and go upstairs, and Alison locked the doors and followed her.

Kate was now sitting on one of the camping chairs, white and trembling, her lips quivering. She was trying to speak, but nothing was coming out.

Alison was scared, thinking Kate was having a fit, and she didn't know what to do. 'Kate, are you all right? Kate! Kate! Can you hear me?'

Kate nodded.

'Kate, what *is* it?'

'I'm … I'm … I'm reliving it.'

Alison now felt completely useless and decided to sit beside Kate and try to comfort her.

Finally, the trembling stopped, and Kate was able to speak. 'It's just as well the gun's not loaded, otherwise I'd go downstairs and shoot Keys and Cullen – and I might as well finish off O'Day.'

'What say I make us a cup of tea and we sit outside and drink it?' Alison suggested.

Kate was grateful for the suggestion. 'Thanks, Alison; I'd like that.'

'It's a lovely day. You go and sit in the sun, and I'll bring the tea out when I've made it.'

By the time Alison had brought the tea outside, Kate had recovered. They drank their cups of tea in silence while admiring the view.

Alison broke the silence: 'We didn't restock the shelves.'

'I know,' Kate responded, 'but I can't do it now. The sight of Keys and Cullen ...'

'Are you all right to drive?' Alison asked her.

'Yes.'

As they were driving home, Kate talked about wanting to shoot Keys and Cullen. 'I've read the instructions for how to use the gun. It's simple: you load the chamber, or chambers, depending on how many bullets you want to fire; you point the gun at your target and you pull the trigger. Even if I don't shoot Keys and Cullen, I think it's time we reminded them the gun works. In fact, Colleen and Cullen have never seen the gun fired: next time we go to Socamora, I'll bring some bullets. I'm sick of Keys's language. He needs to be taught a lesson, though maybe after today's outburst I'm not in a position to talk about bad language. I'm going to point the gun at him and tell him I'll shoot his mouth off if he doesn't control his foul tongue. Re supplies: can you come next weekend?'

'Of course,' Alison replied.

'Good. I'll bring some bullets.'

Alison didn't know what to say. She didn't like the idea of Kate with a loaded gun, although she did agree she was sick of hearing Keys's foul language.

Kate dropped Alison at her townhouse and then drove home to Queanbeyan.

Alison felt very uneasy about Kate and the gun. She wasn't sure Kate would bring some bullets the next time she went to Socamora or whether she'd said she would in the heat of the moment. She decided to discuss the matter with Anne and Helen.

When she arrived at their house, she found Helen the only one home. She told Helen about Kate's incident at Socamora and about her intention to take some bullets there and threaten to shoot Keys's mouth off.

Helen wasn't overly perturbed to hear about the plan. 'I can still remember Kate's very first visit to Socamora. I can remember her story so vividly. I can understand why she wants to shoot Keys and Cullen. If you want me to, I'll go with you next time you and Kate go there.'

'Thanks, Helen, I'd appreciate that.'

'I'll bring some earplugs just in case she does decide to shoot Keys's mouth off.'

Alison concurred. 'I will too.'

'I thought you might've come to tell me the police have charged that guy over Colleen's disappearance,' Helen commented. 'Did you see it in the paper on Friday?'

'Yes, I did.'

'Did Kate say anything about it?' Helen asked.

'Yes. We talked about it on the way to Socamora. She's very upset. We agreed the four of us should get together and see what we can do.'

'It'll be interesting to see what happens. How are they going to link this guy to Colleen? What's his motive?'

'What if he's found guilty of her murder?' Alison asked in a worried voice.

'We'll face that when – if – it happens. I like the bit where it said he couldn't recall where he was on the night Colleen disappeared. That's not much to go on. Who can?'

'Me, I was in the Cactus Bar car park!' Alison joked.

'Good one, Alison, though I wouldn't be saying it too loudly.'

'Don't worry,' Alison replied. 'I won't.'

'I'm not concerned this guy will be found guilty. What's his name? Lex Woodlock? I bet he's rotten to the core and the cops haven't been able to pin anything on him. Still, it's puzzling why they've chosen Colleen. I guess we'll learn more about this guy as the case is reported more in the papers.'

'I guess so, but isn't there something we can do to prevent the trial? The poor guy, he has to face a trial and the legal costs will be horrendous. What does Anne think?'

'She thinks the same as I do: the guy is rotten, and this is the cops' way of getting back at him.'

'I hope you're right,' Alison said, not convinced.

'Be realistic Alison. This guy must be known to the cops. There must be some reason why they have "chosen" him. When are you and Kate going to Socamora next?'

'Next weekend. After all the drama, we didn't get around to stocking the shelves. Are you available?'

'I am,' Helen replied.

Alison went home.

Alison, Kate and Helen went to Socamora the following Saturday, and along the way, Kate almost boasted how she was looking forward to scaring the shit out of Keys and Cullen. 'I have five bullets – that's as many as the gun will hold.'

When they arrived, Kate gave the orders: 'You two put your earplugs in before you put your masks on. Now stand well back while I load the gun.'

Helen and Alison did exactly as Kate had instructed them, and both noticed that Kate put all five bullets in the gun.

'Now I'm going to scare the hell out of the prisoners!' Kate announced. She put her earplugs in and went into the dungeon, holding the loaded gun.

Helen and Alison followed, and waited on the stairs. Their earplugs weren't very effective: they could hear Kate giving the prisoners a real tongue-lashing. They then heard the gun being fired and the prisoners screaming. They thought they heard Kate laughing. The tirade started up again, and they heard two more shots and more screaming. They looked at each other in disbelief.

Kate then appeared. She took out her earplugs and shouted to Alison, 'Come and look at Colleen!'

Helen followed, not knowing what to expect. She saw that Colleen and Lyn were still standing. She then moved along to Cell 2 and saw that Keys was still 'intact'.

Kate was revelling in the moment. 'Alison, look at the fear on Colleen's face!'

Alison started up: 'Not so brave now, are we, Colleen? Are you feeling scared? That's how all the poor women in Karmoor felt: scared as we faced the impending birth of a baby we'd have taken from us; scared as we wondered whether we'd be able to find a job when we were released;

scared about whether we'd get postnatal depression and end up in the nuthouse; scared we mightn't recover from our trauma.

'The Right to Esse doesn't believe in surrogacy. In that case, what was I, and all the other poor women in Karmoor? *Well?* Answer me, you germ! If we weren't being forced to be surrogate mothers, what were we? I'm waiting for an answer, Colleen! There are two more bullets in that gun, and if you don't give me a satisfactory answer, I'm going to blast a hole in your foot. Kate, give me the gun, please!'

Kate handed her the gun.

'I get so frustrated with you, Colleen!' Alison yelled. 'You're not learning! Now, answer my question: was I forced into being a surrogate mother?'

'Yes,' Colleen replied softly.

'Speak up! I have earplugs in my ears,' Alison bellowed.

'*Yes,*' Colleen shouted.

'You don't believe that!' Alison roared. 'You're only saying that, so I won't blast a hole in your foot. Earplugs in, Kate!'

Kate barely had time to put her earplugs in before Alison fired the gun, twice. There was more screaming from the prisoners.

Helen saw dust at the end of the corridor and felt relieved Alison hadn't shot Colleen in the foot.

Alison announced to the prisoners, 'That's enough for one day! You're lucky we're nice people: despite the fact you're three of the lowest forms of life that have ever crawled along the surface of this planet, we're going to replenish your supplies.'

The women completed the standard tasks, locked up and went upstairs.

Kate was first to speak. 'Alison, isn't the feeling of having a loaded gun in your hand something else?'

'Sure is!' Alison said jubilantly.

Helen was curious as to why Alison had fired the last two bullets and asked her.

'Two reasons. One: I wanted to try the gun out, and two: I didn't want to take any bullets home.'

'Who's going to remove the shells and dispose of them?' Helen asked.

'I will,' Alison answered. 'I think, from now on, every time we come to Socamora, we should load the gun.'

'I agree,' Kate said.

Helen was surprised at what was transpiring during the conversation, but she decided not to say anything.

'Where to next, ladies?' Alison asked the other two.

'Lunch at the Grongo pub. My shout,' Kate replied.

'Good idea, Kate, but you don't have to shout.'

'Well,' Kate said, 'let me buy a bottle of wine to celebrate our newfound power.'

They had lunch at the Grongo pub and then went home.

When Helen arrived home, she found Anne getting ready to go for a walk with Magda. Anne asked her the standard question, 'How are things at Socamora?'

Helen told her about the gun incident, and how Kate and Alison had relished their newfound power.

Anne also expressed surprise to hear about the incident. 'Who was taking the gun home?'

'Alison.'

'I haven't been for a while,' Anne said. 'Maybe I should go next time.'

'Maybe we should all go,' Helen proposed. 'Anyway, to get back to your original question "How are things at Socamora?": I think the prisoners are starting to despair about when they'll be released.'

'We'll talk about that when I get back. I must go, or I'll be late.'

Helen sat down to read the paper, thinking how she and the other three women couldn't believe that the police had charged Lex Woodlock with Colleen's murder. *The Canberra Envoy* featured a large report about the development on page 2. The most damning evidence against Lex was that his son who was attending the same school as Colleen's sons, and four other boys, had been molested by one of the teachers there. Colleen had wanted to hush the revelation up. The boys' parents had been livid on hearing about Colleen's approach, and Lex Woodlock had threatened to 'smash her head to pieces'.

Also, Lex Woodlock held a lot of shares in a company that wanted to build townhouses on a section of land that had been zoned for a church, and Colleen had taken legal action to try to stop the company from building them. She'd made herself very unpopular with Lex and the other investors. Her husband had now reported she'd received several threatening phone calls in which the caller advised her to drop the case. Lex Woodlock's lawyer said the evidence was circumstantial and had posed the question that because the teacher had been found guilty and been given a gaol sentence, and because the townhouses had been built, why would his client now want to kill Colleen O'Day?

The *Envoy* article featured three photos: one of Lex, one of Colleen's husband and the couple's children, and one of Colleen, within a smaller article, about her. The journalist wrote about what a wonderful wife and mother Colleen was, listed her community involvement, and added she'd been the national president of the Right to Esse.

All four women went to Socamora the following weekend. Alison and Kate had recovered from their 'trigger-happy' incident, and this time the gun wasn't loaded. They completed the weekly tasks, had a picnic and played badminton and boules. On the way home, Alison brought up the Lex Woodlock case. 'What are we going to do if he's found guilty?'

'Let's take this case one step at a time,' Anne replied. 'He hasn't been found guilty and he's out on bail, so we don't have to worry about anything right now.'

'I'll feel awful if he's sent to gaol,' Alison admitted.

'We all will,' Helen and Kate added.

'Relax, Alison,' Anne advised her. 'As we've said before, he's not guilty of bumping off Colleen, but I bet he's done something dastardly and gotten away with it, so the cops are trying to pin this one on him. Don't let it bother you if they succeed.'

Helen tried to give reassurance. 'When I was in Third Class, there was a horrible girl in the class, Narelle Dormer. She was a nasty bully. One day, I was behind her in assembly. She kept pulling the hair of the girl in front of her, so I decided I'd "make her pay". Tuesday was sewing day; we had the sewing class between recess and lunch. I was the sewing monitor, and it was my job to put the sewing baskets on each girl's desk during recess. The Tuesday after the hair-pulling incident, I put my pencil case under Narelle Dormer's desk. When we came back from lunch, I told Miss Daniels my pencil case was missing. She told everyone to look under her desk. I knew she'd say that: it was always her first directive when anything went missing. My plan worked: Narelle Dormer found it under her desk. After some interrogation, Miss Daniels concluded that Narelle had stolen it. She sent her to the headmistress's office, and the headmistress made her stay in every lunchtime for a week. And you know what, Alison?'

'What?' Alison asked.

'I didn't feel one ounce of guilt! I was glad. Okay, she got away with the hair-pulling incident, but she got punished for stealing the pencil case, something she didn't do. The point is, she got punished and she deserved it. People should be punished if they hurt other people. This is what Anne and I think about Lex Woodlock. He's done something wrong and got away with it, so the cops are going to get him on something he hasn't done. He's done something *bad*. The cops just didn't go through the telephone directory and pick him out.'

'I guess you're right. But concerning Narelle Dormer, weren't you worried someone'd find out you were the one who'd put the pencil case under her desk?' Alison asked.

'No, not one bit. No one would've suspected me of doing something like that.'

'I'm more worried about Don and Susan, the greenies,' Anne stated. 'I somehow don't think we've seen the last of them.'

When they arrived at Anne and Helen's house, Anne invited Alison and Kate in to discuss the prisoners' morale.

Kate was first to speak: 'We have to create another release plan, another carrot on a stick, to keep them going. The thing I'd like to know is: can they remember what you three look like? When we brought them to Socamora, Keys saw Anne and Helen … Colleen saw Alison … Lyn saw Anne … and Colleen saw Anne when she put Lyn in Cell 2.'

'I often wonder about that,' Anne admitted.

'I'm going to find out,' Kate said. 'I have an idea; I'll fine-tune it during the week. Who's coming to Socamora next weekend?'

Alison and Helen agreed to go with her.

Kate collected Alison and Helen the following Saturday. Helen noticed there was a briefcase and a bag of clothes on the back seat and enquired, 'What's with the briefcase and clothes, Kate?'

'I'll explain everything on the way to Socamora,' Kate replied.

When they were inside the cabin, Kate changed into a tracksuit, which she'd never worn to Socamora before. She put on a balaclava that had the mouth hole sewn up and light-green cellophane stitched over the eyeholes, and a pair of fingerless gloves. She then opened the briefcase and took out some cardboard signs she'd written. She went into the dungeon and stood in front of the dividing wall so Keys, Colleen and Lyn could see her. She held the index finger of her right hand to her lips, indicating they should remain silent.

Alison and Helen stayed in the stairwell.

Kate held up the first sign:

> I CAN'T TALK,
> BECAUSE THIS
> PLACE COULD
> BE BUGGED.

She then held up the second sign:

> HOPEFULLY, I'LL
> HAVE YOU OUT
> OF HERE SOON.

Next, she held up two more signs:

> CAN YOU DESCRIBE
> THE PEOPLE (excluding
> Kate) WHO BROUGHT
> YOU HERE?

> IT'S OKAY TO
> TALK. PRETEND
> YOU'RE TALKING
> TO EACH OTHER.

Kate, Helen and Alison listened as Colleen described Alison, and as Lyn described Anne. Lyn's description of Anne was quite accurate.

Kate then held up another sign:

> WOULD YOU
> RECOGNISE THEM
> IF YOU SAW THEM?

Keys was adamant he wouldn't recognise 'the two bitches' if he saw them again. Colleen wasn't sure if she be able to identify June, but Lyn said she was certain she'd recognise Anthea Crisp 'although I don't believe that's her real name.'

'You silly goose!' Kate said and pulled off the balaclava. 'Now you've ruined Release Plan 3. We're running out of ideas!'

Keys yelled abuse at Lyn, and Colleen started crying.

Kate decided to leave the dungeon, and the three women went upstairs, from where they heard a lot of yelling and crying coming from the gaol. When the noise had ceased, Alison and Helen completed the routine chores. After performing her mean trick, Kate decided that she wouldn't go back in the gaol that day.

When Helen arrived home, she reported to Anne what had happened at Socamora. 'Lyn gave a very flattering description of you, said you were "striking"! How about that? She said, "She was tall; had an athletic body and light-brown hair; was immaculately dressed and groomed; and had long, thick eyelashes."'

Anne laughed. 'Did Kate tell her, "Flattery will get you nowhere."?'

'No, she didn't. Lyn couldn't remember the colour of your eyes.'

'Speaking of eyes, wasn't Kate cluey to put cellophane over the eyeholes of the balaclava,' Anne remarked.

'She sure was,' Helen agreed. 'She completely fooled them; they couldn't see her eyes *or* her lips. Both would've been a dead giveaway: her eyes are unique, almost haunting.'

'So is her smile,' Anne said. 'I'll dream up Release Plan 4 during the week and present it to them next weekend.'

All four went to Socamora the next weekend, straight down to the dungeon, where Anne addressed the prisoners: 'We now have to resort to Release Plan 4, and might I say this is probably the last plan, so don't mess this one up!

'First, I must give you a bit of background information about the organisation. We don't operate alone: we're part of an extended network. I've belonged to the organisation since I was a student in my fourth year at university and let me tell you, not all members treat their prisoners as well as we've treated you.

'From what Kate tells me, Lyn, you'd recognise the woman who brought you here, and of course you all know Kate, but we'll deal with Kate separately. The problem is that Lyn would recognise Anthea Crisp. However, that problem can be solved if you co-operate, Lyn. All you have to do is convince yourself you've forgotten what the woman who brought you here looks like – that you wouldn't recognise her again – and we'll let you go.'

'What do you mean "the woman who brought you here"?' Lyn asked her. '*You* brought me here: you're Anthea Crisp – although I don't believe that's your real name. Now I think about it, maybe you're not Anthea Crisp. I don't think I would recognise the woman who brought me here; I'm sure I wouldn't.'

'Not so hasty, Lyn!' Anne said sharply. 'I'm going to describe a situation to you. Suppose the woman who brought you here decides to visit Dubbo Zoo. She takes an elephant ride – if there is such a thing – and who should be sitting next to her on the ride? None other than Lyn Cullen. You recognise her; you recognise her as the woman who'd locked you in this gaol. What are you going to do?'

'I don't know!'

'Well, you *have* to know because I *need* to know!' Anne snapped. 'Your answer's very important in relation to the release plan. If you all agree you've forgotten what the people who brought you here look like and you'd never recognise them, we can think about Release Plan 4.'

'I agree!' Colleen said.

'I don't want your answer yet, Colleen,' Anne retorted. 'You have two weeks to come to your decision. What about you, Keys?'

'I was sitting in the back seat of the car,' he replied. 'I didn't get a good look.'

'What about when you hopped out of the car?' Anne enquired.

'I couldn't recognise those fucking bitches!'

'As if you'd say you could!'

'I'm tellin' the truth!' Keys barked.

'That must feel strange!' Anne quipped. 'Who brought *you* here, Colleen?'

'Kate and a woman called June; I believe she's the one who wears the Cinderella mask.'

'Picture this scene, Colleen,' Anne instructed her. 'You're in a shopping mall; you see June having a cup of coffee; you recognise her as the despicable being who brought you to this gaol and caused you so much misery. What are you going to do? I should add that June – not her real name, of course – is a highly intelligent, respected woman. If you went to the police and told them June had locked you in a dungeon, there'd be more chance you'd be taken away by the men in white coats than the police bringing such a ridiculous charge against June. Think about it. You might even like to try forgiveness; that'd be nice, wouldn't it? And remember: what was it you told me once, Kate, about the Lord and vengeance?'

'Oh yes, never take revenge, let God's anger do it. "I will take revenge, I will pay back, says the Lord."'

'Well, that should be a load off your mind, Colleen! How do you think we'll be "paid back"? Do we get punished in this life or the next?' Helen asked.

'Stop mocking me!' Colleen sobbed.

Helen replied sternly, 'I'm not mocking you, Colleen; I'm asking you a valid question.'

'I don't know,' Colleen whimpered.

'How come you don't know?' Helen asked, angrily. 'I thought you were an expert about the afterlife. Maybe we'll be tortured in our next life.'

Alison chimed in: 'One person's pleasure can be another's torture. Every Sunday, for one hour, my grandmother listened to Faith Long sing songs of praise. Listening to Faith Long for an hour every Sunday for the rest of my life is my idea of torture. That really *would* be payback! Have you heard her sing that one with the lines "The vilest offender who truly believes / that moment from Jesus a pardon receives"? That means, theoretically, that Keys could be pardoned: he fits the category of "the vilest offender". And that's not right: his crimes are unpardonable.'

'They sure are,' Helen stated. 'Anyway, it's not up to someone else to pardon him; only the victim can do that. Has it occurred to you, Colleen, that you're being "paid back" for something wicked you've done? Maybe God's working through us to pay you back for being the president of that evil, barbaric organisation you call the Right to Esse.'

'God gave you free will, and you've chosen to abuse it,' Colleen told them.

'We didn't *choose* to set up this gaol!' Helen sneered. 'We were *forced* to! And if God *is* all-knowing, he must've known the danger in giving everyone free will. Why didn't God save Kate? Nothing makes sense! Can you make sense of any of this, Colleen?'

'I only know that God is watching over me.'

'You can't be serious!' Helen shouted. 'How can you still believe that? Think of what you've been through! What about you, Lyn?'

'I think you're evil people,' Lyn answered.

Helen flew into a rage. 'How dare you call *us* "evil"? How dare you! *You're* the evil one! You're the one who gloated at having let a rapist go free! The only way to rationalise this situation is to accept that God is *livid* with *all* of you! But don't ask me why Kate had to suffer!'

'I'm afraid what faith I had in God has gone,' Lyn declared.

'Now you're talking, Lyn!' Helen yelled back. 'This little stay in gaol's been very positive for you. All you have to do now is repent to Kate, but I don't expect Kate to forgive you. I don't understand you, Lyn: what made you want to defend Keys? I just don't understand it!'

'Don't try, Helen,' Anne advised her. 'Put a sock in it, and let's get back to the release plan. Now for some chilling advice: don't *ever* tell anyone or inform the police about your stay in our dungeon. If you do, you'll wish we'd never let you out! Do you understand?'

'Yes!' the prisoners answered in unison.

'As I've already said,' Anne continued, 'we don't operate alone: someone'll "fix you up" – that's the expression the "bad boys" use – if you ever tell anyone about your "little holiday" with us! Once you've made your decision, I'll notify X. X will have to work out a strategy. It'll take six to eight weeks. X won't release you all on the same day or at the same place. I'll probably suggest you first, Colleen. Once the plan's been activated, that'll be the last we see of you. Some other members of the organisation will take over. You'll be moved around and held at various locations.

'Kate's going underground to work for the organisation full time. X will ensure she's in the same town the day you're released, Keys, so if we get any trouble from you, we hang her disappearance on you. Any questions?'

'What about Gertrude?' Colleen asked.

Alison responded, '"The best thing you can do is forget you ever had that baby!" They're the sick, cruel words that were said to me when I had my baby taken away. When I comprehend that you were the national president of the Right to Esse – that evil, destructive organisation – I think you haven't been punished enough. By the way, how's your re-education coming along? Have you learnt anything over the twelve months you've spent in this dungeon, or do you still believe all that voodoo? How *can* you, Colleen? You don't know the difference between faith and fear!'

'Any other questions?' Anne asked. 'No? Well, I guess we'd better do the chores, then. Our next visit will be in two weeks.'

When the two weeks were up, all four women went to Socamora. Anne entered the gaol, and the other three remained on the stairs. 'Well, what's your decision about Release Plan 4?' she asked the prisoners.

All agreed they'd go along with the plan.

'Okay,' Anne said. 'Two other things. One: after you're released, you're not to have any contact with each other. Someone'll be watching you. Two: you all have to create your own individual story about where you've been. I'll leave you plenty of paper and biros for that part. You must write your stories, and I then have to present them to the committee to see if they're acceptable. One story that was going around after you vanished, Lyn, was that Keys had bumped you off because he was so angry you hadn't gotten him off on an armed-robbery charge. What *are* you, Lyn? Why did you try to get him off? You must've known he was guilty! Yet you tried to defend him. How would you feel if a charge of deprivation of freedom – or whatever it's called – was brought against *me*? There I am, standing in the dock. You're looking face to face with one of the women who kept you in this hellhole, and some smart-alec lawyer gets me off on a technicality. I grin from ear to ear. What would you like to do to the lawyer?

'As for you, Keys, there's a religion in which the followers believe there's good in everyone. I suggest you find out which one it is and join it, and then they'll then have to admit they're wrong.

'Dear me, I feel quite exhausted. These little pep talks are very draining. Just as well my good friends Kate, Alice and Cinderella are here to help with the chores. Oh, here they are now! Have I forgotten to tell the prisoners anything?'

'Yes,' Alison answered. 'You've forgotten to tell Colleen she has to sign a form to say she gives up all rights to Gertrude. So, Colleen, if you ever find Gertrude, you have no claim to her; she's not yours. I'll draw up the form. It's a shame I can't trust Lyn to check it.'

Colleen blubbered. 'What if I don't sign it?'

Alison responded, 'I hold the loaded gun to your head, and you have the option of your signature or the contents of your head going on the form. Isn't that what happened to me? Didn't someone hold a gun to my head? Did I have a ...' Alison broke down. She leant forward and almost fell over.

Helen took her upstairs and sat her down.

Anne and Kate remained in the dungeon and they could hear Alison crying hysterically. Anne, who wasn't usually lost for words, could only stare at Colleen, as could Kate, both too upset to speak. It was Anne who broke the silence: 'Right now, Colleen, I feel like walking into that cell and choking you!'

She went upstairs, and Kate followed.

Alison was comforted by her friends' genuine love and concern for her, and eventually she stopped crying. Helen stayed with her while Anne and Kate completed the chores in silence. They locked the dungeon, and then all four sat outside the cabin and admired the countryside. They next had a game of badminton and decided to have lunch at the Grongo pub.

'I can't go to Socamora next Saturday,' Kate announced. 'I'm going to the airport to collect Brett and his mother. He's been taking some long-service leave. He's such a sweetie: he's taken his mum to Disneyland, Hollywood and San Diego. He said she'd always wanted to go but his father hadn't been interested.'

'That's okay, Kate,' Anne assured her.

Kate drove to the airport to meet Brett and his mother, Hazel, the following Saturday. She was standing with Hazel while Brett was collecting the luggage from the carousel. 'How did you enjoy the trip?' Kate asked her.

'I loved it!' Hazel replied. 'We had a wonderful time: Disneyland, Hollywood, San Diego and we had a day trip to Tijuana.'

'I didn't know you were going to Tijuana,' Kate remarked.

'Neither did I. Brett kept it as a surprise.'

Kate drove Brett and Hazel home.

On Sunday, Brett drove his mother to Dome Beach. On his return to Queanbeyan, he visited Kate to thank her for having looked after

Gandee. 'Mum thoroughly enjoyed the holiday; I'm so glad – she certainly deserved it.'

'How did she enjoy Tijuana?' Kate enquired.

'Pardon?' he replied. 'We didn't go to Tijuana – didn't have time.'

Kate was gobsmacked and didn't know whether to tell Brett his mother had said they'd gone on a day trip to Tijuana. Although Hazel had seemed to have all her faculties, Kate decided she wouldn't say anything about the trip to Tijuana, just in case Hazel had gotten her facts wrong. The two chatted for a while, and Brett then went home.

Kate now felt upset: why was Brett telling lies? She decided to visit Helen, knowing that Helen would cheer her up.

She and Helen were chatting when someone rang the doorbell. Helen answered it and returned with a woman Kate hadn't seen before. Helen introduced Kate to Magda, who was one of Anne's friends. She was tall and vivacious, and had a louder-than-average voice, which she used to announce, 'I've just been visiting Auntie May in the nursing home. She has dementia; didn't have a clue who I was. The poor old dear looked dreadful. She was wearing an orange dressing gown and a ridiculous green beanie; she reminded me of a carrot. It's a disgrace what happens to some old people. She used to be way ahead of her time, had a PhD in physics and rose to the rank of associate professor – almost unheard of for women in that era. She used to be a champion bridge player, and she could swing a mean golf club. She'd die if she could see herself. She'd also object to the money that's being spent to keep her existing. She used to be all for education – said you couldn't spend enough money on it.

'That stinking organisation, the Right to Esse; they're the scum of the earth! The power they wield over the government *stinks*! Poor old Auntie May should've been euthanased five years ago, and I know that's what she would've wanted. That guy who's supposed to have bumped off the president of the Right to Esse should be given a medal, not eighteen years in the clink. I don't believe he did it. The evidence against him was pretty flimsy – just because he had a share in that development company.'

'Oh well, I guess he'll appeal and get off,' Helen said.

'No, he wasn't granted an appeal.'

'How do you know?' Helen asked, trying to hide her anxiety.

'It was in *The Canberra Envoy* on Wednesday. His trial must've been one of the quickest murder trials in history. No one I know thinks he bumped off the old bigot. Mick, a guy at work, thinks it's all to do with the fact he got off on an arson charge about five years ago.'

'Arson! What arson?' Kate probed, trying to sound nonchalant.

'Can you remember the fire at the Brax shopping mall?' Magda asked.

'Yes,' Helen and Kate responded, almost in unison.

'Well the guy charged with arson over that was Lex Woodlock. Mick can recall the trial quite vividly because he had a friend who had a business in the mall. According to Mick, at the time of the fire, Lex Woodlock was in debt. He owned the mall. He wanted to sell it, but he couldn't find a buyer. It was destroyed by fire. Everyone who knew about the fire, believed he lit it to get the insurance pay-out, so he could pay off his debts. A charge of arson was brought against him, but he got off. Some of the store owners lost their livelihood.

'Mick says Lex Woodlock is one of those shifty people who has his finger in a lot of pies.'

'That's interesting,' Kate remarked. 'But I still feel sorry for him if he has to spend eighteen years in gaol for a murder he didn't commit.'

'Oh well,' Magda said. 'Think of it as eighteen years for arson! That seems fair.

'Right now, I'm thinking about Auntie May: five years in the loony bin with probably another five to go. One time after I'd visited her, I decided I would go to Tijuana and get myself some Nembutal. I made some enquiries, only to learn it has a limited shelf life – about two years – and because I didn't intend to go loopy over the next two years, there was no point in purchasing any.'

'Where did you enquire?' Kate asked her.

'Smooth Egress. I'm on their mailing list.'

'How do you get on the mailing list?'

'They've got a post-office box in Adelaide. I'll give it to you if you're interested. As you can imagine, it's hard for the organisation to publicise itself. I'm a die-hard supporter of euthanasia, and I specifically don't say "voluntary euthanasia": poor Auntie May couldn't volunteer for anything!' Magda wrote the address on a piece of paper, which she gave to Kate.

'What else do you know about Nembutal?' Helen quizzed.

'Only that it's very effective,' Magda replied. 'I believe that Smooth Egress has couriers who go to Tijuana and bring it back to Australia and that if you know someone who knows someone, you can get hold of some.'

Magda didn't stay long. She'd really come to see Anne. As soon as she had gone, Helen charged to the magazine rack to look for Wednesday's edition of *The Canberra Envoy*, and there, on page 7, she found a tiny article reporting that Lex Woodlock's appeal had been rejected. 'No wonder we didn't see it!' she said.

She and Kate were now silent. The four women had been following the trial. They couldn't believe it when Lex Woodlock was found guilty. All the evidence seemed to be circumstantial and her body hadn't been found. After the guilty verdict, they then assumed he'd appeal and be acquitted.

'There's nothing we can do, Kate,' Helen said. 'You heard what Magda said about the fire: in a way, he *is* a criminal. Don't be upset because of it. You know first-hand how criminals can get off scot-free. Maybe some of the store owners who lost their business are rejoicing. Think of what people said to you, and apply it to Woodlock: "Lex, God will not give you a burden you cannot bear."; "Lex, God has forgiven the person who killed Colleen, so you must do the same."; "Maybe God wants you in gaol, perhaps he has a job for you to do in there."'

Despite what she'd said to Kate, Helen was feeling terrible about the fact that Lex Woodlock had been found guilty and sent to prison.

'Perhaps we could send the police a photo of Colleen holding a copy of today's *Envoy*,' Kate suggested.

'That's a thought. But that would give the cops a lead. We'd have to make sure our fingerprints weren't on any part of *The Envoy* we send. We'd have to buy paper to wrap it in, again making sure no fingerprints, and post it. It's too risky. I'll discuss it with Anne when she comes home.'

On her way home, Kate pondered what Magda had said about Nembutal. *Maybe Brett's a courier,* she said to herself. Also, she thought it ironic that Magda had given her Smooth Egress's postal address. *Why didn't I ask Brett for it?*

Anne arrived home not long after Kate had left. Helen told her all about Magda's visit, what Magda had said about Lex Woodlock and showed her the piece in *The Envoy* reporting that Lex Woodlock had no grounds for appeal.

Within a week of Anne's telling the prisoners they had to write their stories, they'd finished them. 'Goodness!' she exclaimed. 'I didn't expect you to finish them so soon! Some prisoners spend weeks writing, rewriting and fine-tuning theirs! I suggest you do the same. The organisation's very busy at present, so nothing'll happen before Christmas.'

'Christmas is two months away!' Colleen pointed out.

'That's right! So if Cinderella starts singing "You'll Be Home for Christmas", don't you believe her.'

Alison's number-one way of taunting Colleen was to sing hymns and songs to her. Her favourite hymn was 'What a Friend We Have in Jesus' and her favourite song was 'Everything's Alright' from the musical *Jesus Christ Superstar.*

The Second Christmas:
Christmas 1990

Kate's plan was to go to her brother's house and spend Christmas and New Year with him and his family. She'd wanted to leave Queanbeyan on the Saturday morning, but a friend of hers, Julie Mason, had invited her to a barbecue on the Sunday evening, so Kate had amended her departure time to be Monday morning instead. However, on Saturday morning, her phone rang, and the caller was Julie.

'Kate, I'm very sorry, but I'll have to cancel the barbecue. Kylie was hanging some balloons and fell off the ladder and hurt her wrist. We took her to the doctor, and he told us he was certain it was broken and that we should take her to the hospital. There's no way I could have the barbecue tomorrow now.'

Kate told Julie she was sorry to hear about Kylie's accident and said they'd catch up when she returned. She was all packed, so she decided to take off for her brother's place then and there. She phoned him to tell him she was leaving that day. She then threw her last few belongings in the car, locked the house and drove off towards Cowra. On the second of January, she was going to drive to Albury, where she was to meet two friends. The three friends had planned to take a two-week vacation in Tasmania. She was to be back in Queanbeyan on the eighteenth of January.

Helen's plan was to drive to Melbourne to have Christmas and New Year with her parents and her brother and his family. She then intended to catch up with some friends in Orbost and spend a week with them there. She was to be back in Canberra on the twelfth of January, and she and Kate were to restock Socamora on the nineteenth, by which date almost four weeks would have elapsed between supply deliveries.

Alison was going to spend Christmas in Nowra with her mother, sister and her sister's family. Her father had died in June, and as it was to be her mother's first Christmas without him, all the family had agreed to meet up in Nowra. Alison would be driving down there on Christmas Eve, staying in Nowra until the sixth of January, and then be off to Sydney to meet Daphne. She'd worked with Daphne in Perth, and the two of them had kept in contact over all the preceding years, despite the big physical distance between them. Alison and Daphne were to go to Chile, Bolivia and Peru on a twenty-one-day package tour.

Anne was to fly to New York and stay with a friend for a week. After her week there, she and her friend were to go skiing in Canada for three weeks.

Normally, the only one of the four women who took an extended holiday in January was Kate, but this year, all four were taking one. The only time that Alison's friend Daphne could get three weeks' leave was during the Christmas break. Anne's friend had finished his contract in New York. It was now Anne's last chance to visit him in New York, and because both of them were to be in the northern hemisphere, they agreed it'd be great to have a skiing holiday in Canada.

Christmas was on Tuesday, and the Saturday before, Anne and Helen were to replenish the supplies at Socamora. They were to leave extra food and water and to tell the prisoners to go easy on the water because they'd have to wait almost four weeks for the next visit to come around. After they'd ensured that the prisoners had everything they needed for a four-week period, Helen was to drop Anne off at the airport and then drive to Melbourne.

Anne and Helen ended up bringing the supplies to Socamora an hour later than planned. On the way there, they saw familiar flashing red and blue lights and couldn't believe their eyes. There'd been a car accident, and the two women then had to wait until all the debris had been cleared from the road. Just as they were carrying the last bag of supplies into the cabin and Anne was about to close the door, she saw a man approaching. He was about seventy metres away and was waving at her. 'Oh no!' Anne said nervously. 'Quick, put all the stuff in the cupboard: there's a man coming towards us. He's on our property!'

Helen immediately obeyed. She'd barely locked the cupboard when he was at the door.

'Hi,' he said. 'I'm Fred. I've bought the property next door. I saw your car, so I thought I'd come and say hello to my neighbours.'

Anne and Helen were startled. The cabin was almost half a kilometre from the boundary, and the stands of trees were thick. How had he seen the car? Was he really a new neighbour?

'That's nice,' Anne replied. 'I'm Anne, and this is Helen.'

'Hi! This is an interesting little place you have here,' Fred remarked.

'I'm not sure about "interesting",' Anne said. 'It's very basic. Did you climb over our fence to get here?'

'Yes, I hope you don't mind.'

'Well, it's not good for the fence,' Anne said in response.

'Is this your weekend retreat?' Fred quizzed.

'No, sometimes in summer we come here during the week after work,' Helen replied.

Fred was one of those people who just love to talk, and Anne and Helen couldn't get rid of him. They explained that Anne had a plane to catch, but he just kept on talking. Finally, Anne had to say, quite firmly, 'We *have* to go: I have a plane to catch.'

'Did you leave your ticket out here?' Fred asked suspiciously.

Anne and Helen were taken aback on hearing the question; they didn't know what to make of it. 'No,' Anne answered. 'We're just checking everything's in order before we go.'

'How long will you be away?'

This guy's unreal! Who is *he?* Helen said to herself. She wanted to tell him to stop being nosy and go home but decided to answer politely: 'Just for the Christmas break.'

'Would you like me to keep an eye on the property while you're away?'

'No,' Anne replied firmly. 'That won't be necessary: it's better you don't come on our property while we're away because you might be mistaken for a trespasser.'

'I don't think anyone would think your new neighbour's a trespasser!' he persisted. 'They'd probably realise I was keeping an eye on the place.'

'No one's kept an eye on it since we bought it, and we haven't had any trouble. Fred, we *must* go!' Helen said impatiently.

'Well,' he said, 'nice meeting you. Happy Christmas.'

'Happy Christmas to you, too,' Anne replied. 'Now, don't put too much strain on the fence when you hop over it or under it – whichever way you go.'

'I'll try not to. I get the distinct impression you don't like people climbing over your fences.'

Anne gritted her teeth. 'As I've already said, it's no good for the fence, stretching the wire and putting stress on the corner posts. If you pay a fortune to have a fence erected, the last thing you want is to see people standing on it. Now, we must fly. Goodbye, Fred.'

'Goodbye,' Fred said and headed towards the fence.

'Crikey, Anne. Look at the time! Let's go, or you'll miss your flight.'

Anne locked the cabin doors, and the two women sped in the car towards the airport, discussing Fred and what they'd do about the prisoners' supplies.

'Kate's not going to Cowra till Monday,' Helen said. 'I'll go via Queanbeyan. If she's not home, I'll leave a note at the front door. She always goes in the front door.'

'For extra peace of mind, after I check in, I'll ring her. If she's not home, I'll leave a cryptic message on the answering machine. Maybe I should ring Alison too.'

'There's no point ringing Alison. She was going to Linda's to help her get ready for a dinner party tonight, and she doesn't have an answering machine. Don't worry: I'll leave the note where Kate can't miss it, and I know she always checks her phone messages. I'm not concerned about Fred. Even if he goes snooping around, he won't find anything.'

'What I said about putting stress on the fence is probably a load of rubbish,' Anne admitted, 'but I wanted to give him a clear message he's not welcome to hop over the fence and visit us when he feels like it.'

'I hope he got the message,' Helen said and then bid Anne goodbye and drove on to Queanbeyan. When she arrived at Kate's place, she knocked on the door, but Kate didn't answer. Helen had some spare Christmas cards in the car, so after a moment's thought, she wrote on a card:

Dear Kate,
Happy Christmas!
Love, Helen

PS I have a horrible feeling I left some food in the cupboard at Socamora. Last time I was there, I saw a mouse. I don't want to encourage any more mice by leaving food about. Can you and Alison go and check for me? Sorry for the inconvenience.
H.

She put the card in its envelope, addressed the envelope to Kate, and then secured it behind the screen door.

Kate returned from her holiday. She opened the screen door and saw the envelope. *It's obviously a Christmas card,* she thought. She picked up the envelope and recognised Helen's handwriting. She was surprised because Helen had already given her a present with a card attached. She unlocked the front door and went inside. She saw that the light on the answering machine was flashing. Someone had left a message. *I really should've turned it off!* she mused. She pressed the button and listened to the message: 'Hi, Kate. It's Anne. Helen and I had to leave Socamora in a hurry, otherwise I'd have missed my flight. Can you and Alison go and check inside the cupboard? I think I left some milk in there. It'll be putrid by the time I get back.'

Kate was worried. What had happened? Why had Anne *really* wanted Alison and her to look inside the cupboard at Socamora? It had nothing to do with milk going putrid: they only ever took long-life milk. *No doubt the answer's in the cupboard,* she deduced. She then opened Helen's card and read the message in it, and after she'd read it, she started feeling very nervous. She figured that the matter must've been important if both Anne and Helen had had to leave her a message.

She rang Helen, but Helen didn't answer. Kate knew there was nothing she could do, though, because she had to obey the cardinal rule: 'Never go to Socamora on your own.'

She rang Helen again at six o'clock, and that time, Helen answered. Kate decided to disguise her voice, say she had the wrong number and hang up. She didn't want to discuss anything over the phone. Helen was now home. Kate jumped in her car and drove over to Helen's house.

She rang the doorbell, and Helen opened the door. 'Kate, how great to see you! Come in. How was your holiday? Kate, is something wrong?'

'I think so. Why did you and Anne want Alison and me to go and check the cupboard at Socamora?'

'Didn't you *go?*' Helen asked in a horrified voice.

'No. The barbecue was cancelled, and I left Queanbeyan on the Saturday. I didn't get the phone message and the card till I got home today. What's this all about?'

Helen was silent.

'Helen, what is it?' Kate asked frantically.

Again, Helen didn't reply.

'Helen, what *is* it? What's happened? Tell me!' By now, she was almost hysterical.

Helen finally spoke: 'The day Anne and I were going to Socamora to drop off the supplies, we were held up due to a car accident. We arrived much later than planned. Anne was about to close the cabin door when she saw a man approaching. He waved. He knew she'd seen him, so she could hardly close the door in his face. He told us he'd bought the property next to ours. Anne and I were surprised because we hadn't known it was for sale. You know how real-estate agents always put up a "For Sale" sign on country properties. Anyway, he started talking and talking, and we couldn't get rid of him. In the end, we said we had to go because Anne had a plane to catch. So we left without leaving the prisoners their supplies.

'While we were driving to the airport, we discussed what we should do. We knew you and Alison weren't leaving till the Monday. I said I'd call in on my way through Queanbeyan, and Anne agreed to ring you from the airport, as a double-check. We knew Alison was going out, and she doesn't have an answering machine, so there was no point phoning her. We never doubted for one minute you wouldn't find my note or get the phone message.'

Kate was now distraught. 'Helen, that means they haven't had their food and water topped up for five weeks! And you know what else it means – unless they managed to survive on dirt! Helen, I'm *so* sorry!'

'What for?' Helen asked. 'Don't have any guilt feelings – they didn't. Did Wayne Keys ever show any remorse? Did Lyn Cullen see anything wrong in releasing a rapist into the community? Despite Alison's long talks with Colleen, did she change her views about abortion? No, she continued to think it's acceptable to ruin women's lives by forcing them to be surrogates; that it's okay to let old people linger on for years, like vegetables. Remember what Magda said about her Auntie May? Don't give those three scumbags another thought!' Helen was very shaken, but she was trying to put on a brave face.

'Easier said than done ... I feel a bit sick,' Kate muttered.

Helen continued, 'What we'll do is this: we'll go to Socamora now; make sure everything's intact outside and inside the cabin; check for strange odours, but we won't go into the gaol. We'll wait for Anne and Alison to return. Then the four of us will go together.'

Kate and Helen hopped in Kate's car and headed for Socamora. They had a good look around the property and thought that everything looked intact.

Helen unlocked the cupboard. 'We'd better take the perishables home and throw them in the garbage; the rest of the food can stay here. Look, Kate, we made them Christmas hampers – plum pudding, wine, nuts, fruit-mince pies and fruitcake; this year, we even included a bon-bon each. The gun's in the far corner of the cupboard; we didn't know where to leave it. We could hardly leave it in your letterbox. I was nearly going to mention that the iron was in the corner, but Anne and I were sure you and Alison would find it. It's yours, you take it.'

She asked Kate whether she wanted to go to the Grongo pub for a drink, but Kate said she wasn't in the mood, so they drove back to Helen's home.

'Come inside and have a drink.'

Kate could stand it no longer. She had to say it: 'Helen, you know what this makes us?'

'No,' Helen replied. 'What does it make us?'

'Murderers. We've committed murder!' Kate cried.

'Not murder,' Helen stated matter-of-factly. 'Manslaughter – quite different. We didn't intend to kill them; it wasn't premeditated; it was an accident. We are four decent people who've rid the world of three pieces of scum. Think about it, Kate; think about what Alex McAlpine said. You once told me he was your hero: "If the legal system fails you, do it yourself."'

'That's not quite how he expressed it!' Kate remarked.

'Near enough. Think about what you went through; think about how Wayne Keys robbed you of your life. What *is* he? What's Lyn Cullen? Think about Alison, how she's suffered; how her life was ruined. The only unfortunate thing about this is we didn't throw Cullen in with Keys and then shoot his genitalia to pieces. You've told me more than once how you wanted to torture Keys and Cullen and then kill them. Well, you've tortured and killed them now. Good, an eye for an eye! I really believe that! Revenge is *good*! You believe it is too! We all saw a change in you once Keys was in the dungeon and you were getting your revenge; we all saw a change in Alison when Colleen had Gertrude taken away from her.'

Kate thought about what Helen had said. 'You're right, Helen, but I feel a bit nervous.'

'Kate, if they – whoever "they" are – haven't found the dungeon by now, they'll never find it. Think about it in a positive way: we don't have to take food to Socamora anymore, and we don't have to do their washing. I always thought if we slipped up on anything, it'd be their washing. How could we explain all that extra washing we were doing? Have another wine; let's get some pizzas delivered. Do you want to stay the night? I can lend you a nightie, and we always have a few spare toothbrushes.'

'Yes, I'd like that.'

Helen phoned for the pizzas.

'Now, let's not talk anymore about those maggots. Did you have a happy Christmas? How was your holiday? Let's talk about something important.'

Kate began telling Helen all about her Christmas and holiday, but she was having trouble concentrating on what she was saying. Her thoughts kept drifting back to the dead prisoners. As she was talking, she heard the doorbell ring.

'That'll be the pizzas, my shout,' Helen said.

I hope it's the pizzas and not the police! Kate said to herself.

While Helen was collecting the pizzas and paying the delivery boy, Kate thought about Anne and Helen: *They're so confident. I don't believe they've ever thought the police might find the dungeon, whereas Alison and I – especially Alison – aren't so confident!*

Kate and Helen ate the pizzas and drank some more wine. Helen could see that Kate was nervous about the prisoners' deaths, so she continued to put on a brave face in order to reassure her that everything would be fine. 'Kate, ages ago, I recorded *All About Eve*, but I haven't watched it. Shall we watch it now?'

'Good idea,' Kate replied.

Helen recharged the wine glasses, set the VCR rolling and sat down with Kate to watch the old movie. They both consumed quite a few drinks during it, and by the time it had finished, they were almost asleep, so they went off to bed.

Helen was already up when Kate awoke and asked her, 'Why don't we go to Julia's Eats for brekkie? The pantry's depleted; I have to go shopping.'

'Good idea,' Kate agreed. 'I'm going to have the big breakfast with the lot. I just love it.'

'Me too, and a large long black.'

It was a nice day, so they decided to walk to Julia's Eats. Once there, they placed their orders and sat down at a table to wait for the food to arrive.

'Re the little incident at Socamora,' Helen said, 'you can tell Alison, and I'll tell Anne when she returns. Here comes our food.'

'Yummy, the big breakfast: you can't beat it!'

They ate their breakfasts and ordered coffees, and when they'd finished them, they walked back to Helen's house.

'I'll go home now so you can do your chores and shopping.'

'Okay, Kate. But don't get yourself stressed over what's happened. The situation won't change because of stress.'

'I'll try not to,' Kate replied.

After Kate left, Helen felt ill. The enormity of what had happened hit her. She was experiencing delayed shock.

Anne returned home from her holiday on Monday and decided to give Helen a quick call at her workplace to let her know she was home. 'How is everything?' she asked her.

'Fine,' Helen answered. 'How are you? Did you have a good holiday?'

'Yes, I'll bring you up to date when you get home. I'll cook tonight – that's if I can remember how to. Boy, did I have a great holiday! Anyway, I won't keep you, bye.'

When Helen arrived home, she found Anne busy cutting up vegetables. 'Tell me all about your holiday,' Anne said. 'Then I'll tell you about mine.'

'Before I start, I have to tell you that Colleen, Lyn and Keys are dead.'

Anne could feel her legs starting to go weak and she stopped cutting up the vegetables. 'What happened?'

Helen proceeded to tell her about the mix-up with the food delivery. 'Kate and I have been to Socamora. Everything's fine outside and inside the cabin, but we didn't go into the gaol.'

'If you didn't go into the gaol, how do you know they're dead?' Anne enquired.

'Kate and I made the assumption.'

'If they *are* dead, I can't say I'm overcome with grief, but how can you and Kate be sure you made the right assumption? I read of a hunger striker who lasted fifty days.'

'Yes, but they take water,' Helen pointed out.

'They could've rationed their water.'

'Their water wasn't topped up: they can't possibly be alive,' Helen asserted.

'Some people go to incredible lengths to survive, like drinking their urine,' Anne reminded her.

'Kate and I thought we'd wait for you and Alison to return, and then all four of us can go to Socamora together.'

'When does Alison get back?' Anne asked.

'Not until the twenty-seventh, next Sunday.'

'She won't want to go to Socamora the day she gets back. How many days is it since the last delivery?'

'I need a calendar,' Helen stated, and located one. 'Thirty-six, thirty-six days since Kate and I made the last visit to Socamora. They can't possibly be alive.' She was adamant.

'But you know that the shelves are always stacked with baked beans, sardines, sweet corn, crisp bread, cheddar cheese, you name it. There's no saying how long they could've rationed the food. And don't forget, there's always heaps of tinned fruit and vegetables; they'd supply a lot of liquid. Are you sure you couldn't smell anything through the air vents?'

'Positive,' Helen replied emphatically.

Anne was glad Helen suggested waiting for Alison because she wasn't convinced that the prisoners were dead. The women had known for two months that the prisoners would have to go four weeks without deliveries over Christmas. During the two months, the women had been delivering extra food each time. They also knew that the prisoners were hiding food and water under their beds. Anne didn't want to go to Socamora and find the three prisoners on their last legs. She was frightened at the thought; she felt she could cope better with the sight of a corpse than of a human being at death's door. 'Well, there's nothing we can do now,' she concluded.

'Do you still feel like cooking?' Helen asked her.

'Yes, I'm starving. Let's be realistic, Helen. You and I know we could never have let them out; Alison and Kate must also know it. It was as if we were pretending the problem didn't exist; I guess that's why we never talked about it. Don't talk about it, and it'll go away. Maybe it *has* gone away.'

The two talked about their holidays while eating their dinner. There was no more discussion about the prisoners' deaths.

Alison's plane was due in at 9.05 am, and Kate drove to the airport to meet her. She was shocked when she saw Alison. She knew her friend had been up all night on a long flight, but she thought Alison looked truly sick. They drove to Alison's townhouse, talking about their holidays. Kate carried Alison's suitcase inside, and Alison remarked what a relief it was to come home and find everything just as she'd left it.

Alison had to be told about the prisoners' deaths, so Kate could see no point in delaying it. 'I won't stay long, Alison. I'm sure you want to unpack and have a rest. However, there's something I have to tell you: the prisoners are dead.'

Alison was about to say something, but before she could get a word in, Kate told her about the mix-up in taking the food to Socamora. 'Helen and I've been to Socamora. We checked outside and inside the cabin. Everything looks okay. We didn't go into the dungeon; we were waiting for you to return and then have the four of us go together.'

Alison was silent for a moment and said, 'I hope they've gone to hell! I hope the devil explained to them the reason they've been thrown into the fiery furnace!'

Kate was surprised at Alison's reaction; she'd been expecting her to be worried.

Alison started to cry. 'There's not a day in my life I don't think of little Megan. I can still remember the first time I saw her; she was lying in her little bassinet. The social worker didn't want me to see her again. She was worried I was going to keep her, and then that'd be one less baby for a loving family. It's beyond my comprehension how anyone can condone what I went through. If Megan had been born six months earlier, I wouldn't have even *seen* her. The "strongly adhered to" practice back then was that it was best if the relinquishing mothers – yes, that's what we were called – didn't see their babies. I wonder whether that letter Colleen wrote is intact. If it is, I'm going to post it to her family.'

Kate tried to console her, but knowing what it was to be inconsolable, she let Alison cry.

Suddenly, Alison said she needed to go to the bathroom. 'I think I've picked up something on the trip.'

When she returned, Kate asked her, 'Did it spoil your holiday?'

'No, it's only been the past three days I've felt sick. I'm not going back to work till Wednesday, but if I feel like this tomorrow, I'll make an appointment to see a doctor.'

'Are you sure I can't do anything for you?'

'Positive, Kate.'

'Ring me if you change your mind.'

'Thanks. I'm going to have a rest and then unpack.'

Kate could see that Alison was tired, so she said goodbye and went to Anne and Helen's house, where she found Helen the only one home. 'I've told Alison about the prisoners' dying,' she said to Helen. 'She almost seemed glad.'

'That's a relief,' Helen remarked. 'I thought she'd have a cardiac arrest. What's she up to?'

'She was going to have a rest and then unpack. She looks sick – very sick,' Kate said worriedly.

'I'm going to see her tonight, so I guess she'll bring me up to date.'

The next day, Alison was feeling worse, so she made an appointment to see her doctor. The doctor thought she'd probably picked up some bug in South America, so she prescribed Alison a course of antibiotics and gave her the rest of the week off work.

Kate and Helen saw Alison the following weekend. They thought she looked sicker than she had on the day she arrived home.

'Are you still taking the antibiotics?' Helen asked her.

'Yes, but they're not doing any good. The doctor said if there's no improvement after a week on the antibiotics, it's probably a virus, and I'll just have to let it run its course. But I can assure you, I don't feel too good. I don't feel like eating, and I feel quite nauseous.'

'I don't want to be rude,' Kate said, 'but you look a bit yellow. Could it be jaundice?'

'I've no idea,' Alison replied. 'I'll have to make another appointment to see Dr Trotter.'

Kate rang Alison on Sunday night and asked her, 'Are you feeling any better?'

'No, I'm ringing Dr Trotter tomorrow as soon as the surgery opens to see if she can fit me in.'

'I guess you'll let me know how you get on then. In the meantime, is there anything I can do for you?'

'No thanks, Kate. I'll ring you tomorrow night.'

Alison rang Kate the next night as promised.

'What did the doctor say?' Kate asked her nervously.

'She wants me to have some blood tests and an ultrasound, and she's given me another week off work. I'm going tomorrow at nine o'clock for the blood tests and one thirty for the ultrasound.'

'I'll visit you after work to see how you get on.'

'Thanks, Kate.'

The following day, Kate had trouble concentrating on her work; she kept thinking about Alison. As soon as she heard the bell ring, she packed up and drove to Alison's townhouse. She rang the doorbell and heard footsteps. *Good,* she said to herself: *Alison's home.* She'd thought Alison looked so sick the doctor might send her straight to hospital.

Alison greeted her. 'Come in.'

Kate became upset, seeing that Alison was clearly not well. 'Have you had the blood tests and ultrasound?'

'Yes,' Alison replied. 'I'm seeing Dr Trotter on Saturday; she should have the results by then.'

Helen drove Alison to Dr Trotter's surgery on Saturday. 'I'll wait in the waiting room,' she said. 'Hopefully there are some magazines I can read.'

Alison knew that Dr Trotter was always late. About thirty-five minutes after her appointment time, she heard Dr Trotter call her name out. She entered the surgery.

Helen was reading a magazine when she heard the surgery door being reopened. She looked up, expecting to see Alison emerge, but instead saw Dr Trotter, who looked straight at her.

'Helen Davis?' the doctor asked.

'Yes,' Helen replied nervously.

'Could you come with me?'

Helen felt her legs almost give way: the doctor's tone hadn't sounded good. She followed the doctor into the surgery, where she found Alison crying. A hundred thoughts flashed through Helen's head in half a second: *She can't be pregnant! It's still possible! Anyway, things've changed: she can get rid of it! AIDS, she can't have AIDS! She wouldn't be so stupid as to have unprotected sex on a holiday – would she? How else do you get AIDS? Syphilis? Do people still get syphilis? Why was she thinking sexual diseases? Alison wasn't like that! Poison fish? Poison arrow? That was it: slow-release poison arrow – unlikely! ... What is it?*

Dr Trotter looked at Helen. 'Your friend has advanced cancer of the pancreas.'

Helen almost burst into tears on hearing the diagnosis but managed to control herself, feeling she had to be supportive. 'What can be done?' she asked the doctor.

'Nothing, I'm afraid,' came the stern reply. 'To give Ms Roberts false hope would only be cruel. Pancreatic cancer is a very nasty type of cancer: by the time the symptoms are visible, it's too late to do anything. I've told Ms Roberts all the facts.'

'So what do we do now? Is there any chance the diagnosis is wrong?' Helen asked.

'None whatsoever,' Dr Trotter assured her. 'The ultrasound is quite clear. Pancreatic cancer is very aggressive. Ms Roberts has, *at the most*, five months to live. In six weeks' time, she'll probably not be able to care for herself. If she has no family members or friends who are willing to care for her, I can arrange for a bed in Bydees Hospice.'

Helen was appalled by Dr Trotter's bedside manner – or more correctly, by the absence of a bedside manner; the doctor seemed so cold and insensitive. Helen was confused about what she had to do next. Did she have to make another appointment? Was there a prescription to be filled? Alison was sobbing, and Helen didn't think it'd be very nice for her to have to walk past all the patients in the waiting room, so she asked Dr Trotter whether the surgery had a back entrance.

'No,' Dr Trotter replied, in an unsympathetic voice.

Helen took Alison to the car and then went back to the surgery to pay the bill. She collected the receipt and headed towards the car, not sure what she'd say to Alison. What do you say to a friend who has, *at the most*, five months to live? She opened the door and sat down. 'What do you want to do, darling?' she asked Alison, never having used that term of endearment with Alison before, but after the coldness of Dr Trotter, she felt that a bit of warmth was needed.

Alison merely said, 'I don't know.'

'Well, let's go to our place.'

They drove in silence. By the time they arrived, Alison was feeling dehydrated and went to sit on the couch.

Helen brought her a large glass of water, sat beside her, put her arm around her and said, 'We'll look after you.'

'Thanks, Helen. One good thing about my life is my friends: I have beautiful friends. I feel tired. Do you mind if I lie down?'

'Of course not,' Helen replied. 'The bed in the spare room's always made up. From now on, it can be yours. ... When you tell your mother, do you want to be alone, or do you want someone with you?'

'I haven't thought that far ahead. I'll tell Kerrie when I'm ready, and she can tell Mum.'

When Alison's friends heard the news, they were devastated, and none more so than Kate. Many of them offered for Alison to stay with them so they could look after her.

The news of Alison's cancer had delayed any plans about what to do with the dead prisoners. It was now the Saturday after Alison had had the cancer confirmed. She was staying with Anne and Helen, and Kate was also at the house. The four were psyching themselves up to go to Socamora. They didn't want Alison to go with them, but she was insisting.

Anne opened the forum: 'Does anyone know anything about a corpse, such as how long does it take one to decompose? What about the smell? I guess I'm trying to prepare ourselves for what we'll find, but I haven't a clue – *not a clue*! And this isn't the type of information that's readily available. In a way, their deaths are a load off our minds. It's now nine weeks since our last visit. Does anyone think there's the remotest possibility any of them could be alive?'

'No,' came the unanimous reply.

Anne continued speaking. 'I suggest, in the next few months, we demolish the gaol; make it look like a junk heap. We pull up the carpet tiles and the floating floor, concrete over the trapdoor, and lay ceramic tiles on the cabin floor.'

'Once that's done, we'll have no more anxiety over this dungeon,' Helen said confidently.

The other three women agreed whole-heartedly.

'Keys and Cullen dead,' Kate said. 'I always hoped their demise would be long, slow and painful. I hope it was. Thirty-one years ago, I had a goal. I can't believe I've achieved it. You three helped me achieve it.'

Alison, who hadn't spoken a word since Kate's arrival at Anne and Helen's house, other than to say hello, surprised them all when she said, 'I think it's a shame to waste the hole: we should throw a few more low-life forms down there.'

Helen was adamant: 'No, Alison. We can't keep this up, or we'll get caught; we've pushed our luck to the max.'

Anne and Kate agreed.

Alison continued though: 'I want to throw Gary Munkton, that hypocritical, bigoted Minister for Education, and Dawn Flaherty, the current national president of the Right to Esse, down there. And I'd like them to be joined by that horrible archbishop who gave money to Munkton's campaign and instructed his flock to vote for him.'

Anne and Helen spoke almost simultaneously: 'We can't push our luck any further.'

Alison was insistent, however: 'It's *not* luck; it's brilliant skill and careful planning that've led to these acts of justice we've performed.'

There was silence.

Eventually, Anne spoke: 'If we're going to Socamora, we should go now.'

Helen gave the first response: 'I don't think we need to go: Kate and I've checked it out. Everything's fine.'

Alison wasn't looking well, and she asked Kate whether she could take her home because she wanted to collect a few things before she went back to Anne and Helen's.

After Kate and Alison left, Anne said, 'Let's crack a bottle of bubbly to celebrate the burden that has been lifted from us.'

Alison

Kate helped Alison inside.

Alison sat down and asked her, 'Kate, will you do something for me?'

'If it's something I can do, of course, I will,' Kate replied.

'Will you meet me for a drink at the Prime Hotel, eight o'clock Wednesday night?'

'Sure. Whereabouts?'

'In the Partisan Bar.'

'Yes. I'll be there, eight o'clock, Wednesday night at the Partisan Bar,' Kate assured her.

'Isn't it ironic how we created the story *you* had cancer and now it's happened to me? Do you think I'm being punished for what I did?'

'Hell no, Alison! You mustn't think like that! No one really knows what caused your cancer. Why would you be the only one singled out for punishment? Why didn't *I* get cancer or Helen or Anne?'

'Maybe they didn't feel the stress as much as I felt it.'

'Well, I certainly did!' Kate said forcefully. 'And something Anne said to me while you were on holidays implied she's shat a few bricks.'

'A few! It's strange: now my life's ending, I don't want it to!'

'I wish I could change places with you,' Kate said. 'Now I've achieved my goal, I couldn't care less if my life ended tomorrow. What have *I* got to look forward to: old age on my own? I once saw an Olympic athlete interviewed about drugs in sport. She said the desire to win a gold medal at the Olympic Games was so great for some contestants, they'd take anything to win it, even if they knew they'd drop dead the next day. I know what she was talking about. When you have a goal, an obsession, and you've achieved it, nothing else matters.'

'Maybe I don't want my life to end because I haven't achieved my goal,' Alison sobbed.

'I thought you had,' Kate said, surprised.

'No,' Alison affirmed. 'Remember back in '88, when we told each other what our goals were? Yours was to throw Wayne Keys and Lyn Cullen in a dungeon, mine was to throw Colleen O'Day and Gary Munkton in a dungeon. I *have* to get Munkton in the dungeon.

'*Every time* I think of those people who think it's okay to take a woman's baby from her, I want to kill them! We condemn customs in other countries – cutting off thieves' hands, stoning adulterers, selling babies, paying for voluntary surrogacy – but for some reason, not paying for forced surrogacy is accepted in Australia. – By the way, who has the gun?'

Kate thought it strange that Alison should suddenly change her tune and want to know who had the gun. 'I do; I have it in my handbag. I brought it with me, just in case ... just in case they were still alive.'

'What were you going to do: euthanase them?' Alison asked.

'No ... Maybe ... I don't know. We read about incredible survival stories; I just thought they might be alive and as fit as Mallee bulls. Anyway, we never go to Socamora without the gun. Are you hungry? It's almost lunchtime. Do you want some lunch?'

'Yes,' Alison answered. 'How about you make us a sandwich?'

Kate and Alison had lunch together. Kate stayed on after lunch. It was almost three thirty when she decided she should go home.

'I must go home now. I'm going to Pam's for dinner tonight, and I said I'd bring a dessert, so I'd better go home and make it. Is there anything I can do for you before I take you back to Anne and Helen's?'

'I think I want to be on my own. I'll ring them and tell them.'

Kate was astonished. 'You can't stay on your own!'

'Kate, it's what I want,' Alison said emphatically.

Kate decided not to push the issue any further, not feeling she was in a position to determine what a woman in Alison's situation wanted.

'Are you going straight home?' Alison asked.

'No. I'm stopping off at the supermarket to get a few things.'

'In that case, you'd better leave the gun here,' Alison advised her. 'You know the rule about leaving the gun in a parked car: just because the scumbags are dead doesn't mean we can relax the rules.'

'That's for sure,' Kate agreed. She gave Alison the gun and said to her, 'Remember another gun rule: never leave the gun where it can be seen; hide it immediately. I'll see you Wednesday night. Give me a ring if you want anything.'

'I will,' Alison said, softly. She saw Kate to the door and waved goodbye.

As Kate was driving home, she had a strange feeling about Alison: what was she up to? She'd seemed different. *Maybe when you only have five months to live, you change,* she said to herself.

As soon as she arrived home, she rang Anne and Helen's number, and Helen answered. She and Kate agreed that if Alison wanted to be on her own, there was nothing they could do about it. However, Helen expressed her dismay that Alison hadn't told Kerrie or her mother about the diagnosis.

Kate arrived at the Partisan Bar promptly on Wednesday night and found Alison already there, talking to a woman Kate didn't recognise.

Alison introduced Kate to Marlene, whom she said she'd started talking to while waiting for Kate. Marlene was about to attend the Foreign Film Festival, and she told Kate and Alison about the film. 'It's based on a true story. It's about a priest who refuses to break the seal of confession. In the town where the priest lives is a serial killer. His target is old women. Each time an old lady is killed, the murderer confesses to the priest. The townsfolk are frantically trying to catch the murderer before he kills another old lady, but the priest won't tell them who it is. *He knows who the killer is, but he won't reveal it!* Eventually, the local policeman thinks he's found the culprit. The killer's tried, found guilty and sentenced to life in prison, but it turns out he's not the killer. Again, the priest remains silent. The wrongly convicted man spends nearly seven years in prison before it's discovered he's not the killer. I'm not sure about the rest of the story, but I do know that the wrongly convicted man returns to the town and confronts the priest ... Well, I must go. Bye, nice speaking to you!'

After Marlene had left, a man of about forty asked whether he could sit on the chair she'd vacated. As the bar was packed and there weren't many spare seats, both said he could. Alison started talking with him. 'The woman who's just left that seat was going to the Foreign Film Festival. She told us about the film. It's a true story. It's about a serial murderer who confesses to the local priest each time he commits a murder, but the priest doesn't report him to the police because confessions are confidential. Even when the wrong man is sentenced to life in prison, the priest says nothing. I wonder whether that'd happen today.'

The man laughed. 'Why don't you try it? By the way, my name's Ken.'

'Hi, I'm Kate.'

'Hi, Ken, I'm Alison. What do you mean?'

'Why not go to confession – don't ask me how you do that, though – and tell the priest you bumped off your husband and you want to be forgiven?'

Alison laughed. 'You'd want to be confident the priest wouldn't spill the beans if you confessed to a real murder!'

'You sure would,' Ken replied. 'You'd have to try him out first. Did your friend say how the film ended?'

Alison gave the response: 'She said the wrongly accused man returns to the town and confronts the priest, but that was all she knew about it.'

'If it was me,' Ken said, 'I'd insist the priest be sent to prison, and if he wasn't, I'd drive him to Lightning Ridge and throw him down an old mine shaft. I believe that if the judiciary doesn't hand out justice, you've got to dish it out yourself.'

'That's interesting,' Kate remarked, deciding she liked Ken. 'Have you ever dished out your own justice?'

'No. Fortunately, I've never been the victim of a crime, but I can assure you that if anyone hurt one of my daughters and was let off by some of those pricks of judges, I'd come after him with no end of vengeance, even if it meant I had to go to gaol. If people do the wrong thing, they should be punished. Do you come here often?'

'No, what about you?'

'Yes,' he replied. 'I often come here for a drink, but I've never seen it this crowded. It must be because of the film festival.'

'There's Senator Harwood. I wonder if he's going to the Foreign Film Festival,' Kate remarked.

'He stays here during the week. Lots of the politicians stay at the Prime during the week.'

'I didn't know that,' Alison commented.

Kate was surprised at Alison's comment because the fact that many of the politicians stayed at the Prime during the week was common knowledge among old Canberra residents.

Kate and Alison finished their drinks, and Alison announced that they had to leave. Kate walked with her to her car. As Alison was unlocking the door, she asked Kate to meet her at seven thirty the following Tuesday, again in the Partisan Bar.

'I will,' Kate agreed, 'but I'll see you before then.' She went home in good spirits, thinking, *Marlene's an interesting woman and Ken's 'a bit of all right'.*

Kate again met Alison in the Partisan Bar at seven thirty the following Tuesday. She didn't enjoy the evening nearly as much as she'd enjoyed last week's. Tonight, the bar was almost empty. She was hoping she might see Ken. She and Alison had a couple of drinks and made small talk. Kate couldn't get over how quickly Alison's health was deteriorating. She still hadn't told her mother or sister about the pancreatic cancer. The two women agreed to meet same time, same place next week.

It was much the same the following Tuesday: they had two drinks and left the bar.

'I'll go out the back door,' Alison said. 'I parked in the other car park.'

'Why?' Kate quizzed.

'I took a wrong turn, and rather than go around the block, I parked there.'

'It's very dark in that car park,' Kate reminded her. 'Let me drive you there.'

'No, thanks, Kate. I'll be fine.'

Kate reiterated the logic behind her suggestion: 'I don't like the idea of letting you walk down that dark alley on your own. Let me drive you there!'

Alison, however, was adamant: 'No, Kate, I'll be fine.'

'Okay, Alison,' Kate said. 'Bye.'

'Bye, Kate. Thanks for coming.' She made no mention of meeting the following week, so Kate assumed they wouldn't.

On Wednesday, Kate felt her legs go to jelly as she listened to the evening news and heard that Minister for Education, Gary Munkton, was missing. The ABC had received an anonymous phone call, and the caller had said, 'Munkton had had an unusual spasm at his mistress's unit and was still recovering from it.' He'd last been seen by the receptionist at the Prime Hotel the previous night, at approximately seven thirty. The police were investigating and were asking anyone who had any information to come forward.

Despite feeling concerned, Kate had a little chuckle about the 'anonymous phone call'. She didn't know whether or not Gary Munkton had a mistress, but she worked out that that part of the story had been an extra barb that Alison had obviously thought worth adding. She then found herself wondering whether Anne had made the anonymous call. Various thoughts came into her head: Was Anne in on the act? Did Helen know anything about it?

Her thoughts were interrupted when she heard the phone ring. It was Anne, and as soon as Kate heard her voice, she knew why she was ringing. Kate asked her, 'Are you in on it?'

'Hell no, Kate!' came the answer. 'Helen and I nearly *shat* ourselves!'

'Can I come over now?' Kate asked her.

'Of course,' Anne said. 'See you soon.'

Kate arrived at Anne and Helen's, and as soon as she was in the door, Anne asked her, 'Do you think it's Alison?'

'I do. He was last seen at the Prime Hotel. For the past three weeks, Alison's asked me to have a drink with her there. What do you think we should do?'

Helen gave the answer: 'I suggest none of us mentions anything about it to Alison. You know the old rule: ask no questions, get no answers. Although I must confess, I'd love to know how she did it! Don't worry, Kate. I'm sure Alison left no trails. After all, she's been in this business for nearly three years now, she's pretty cluey. All this aside, how are you?'

'I think I'm still in shock. I'm assuming Alison took him to Socamora. I'd like to know how she felt when she saw the bodies.'

'We've been thinking about that too,' Helen said. 'There's still the possibility it *wasn't* Alison, but I think the less said about the matter, the better.'

'I agree,' Kate said.

'Would you like to stay for dinner?' Helen asked her.

'That'd be lovely.'

No matter how hard the three women tried not to talk about Gary Munkton's disappearance, they always seemed to return to the topic during the dinner conversation. 'What cell's he in?'; 'Does the gaol stink?'; 'Is Alison going to feed him?'

Anne suggested they go to Socamora the following night and then to the Grongo pub for dinner. 'I want to check Alison hasn't left any doors or gates unlocked. Also, it's a while since we've been there. Daylight saving, we can fit in a game of badminton before dinner, but we're not going into the dungeon.'

Kate thanked Anne and Helen for their hospitality and went home.

Gary Munkton's disappearance was now headline news, and all the staff members at Kate's school were talking about it.

Helen said that everyone in her office was also talking about it. 'One woman said, "Oh, I do hope they find him: he's such a *nice* man!" I had to stop myself from saying, "Good riddance!"'

Anne said it was the talk of her office, although no one was especially upset. All her colleagues had a good laugh about the 'unusual spasm' and what might have caused it.

After Gary Munkton's disappearance, Kate stopped off at the local newsagent each day on her way to work to buy *The Canberra Envoy*, wanting to keep herself up to date about any developments. Three days after the disappearance, she opened the paper to see a letter written by Colleen O'Day, who'd disappeared in August 1989. It was a photocopy of the letter Colleen had written for Alison. Kate wondered what else Alison was going to do. However, she was no longer concerned because she'd devised her own escape plan.

She watched the news on TV that night and learnt that the police had called in a handwriting expert, who was certain the handwriting was Colleen's. Her husband and children were agreeing it looked like her writing, although they were remaining adamant, she'd never have written that type of letter. The letter had been posted at the Central Post Office, and according to the results of more tests, it hadn't been written recently.

After the 'letter incident', Kate, Anne and Helen wondered what Alison would do next. 'I half expect to open *The Canberra Envoy* and read that Archbishop Tool and Dawn Flaherty have disappeared,' Helen said.

'I feel uneasy about Alison,' Anne declared. 'It's a dreadful thing to say, but it'll almost be a relief when she goes to the hospice. Does she still have the gun?'

'Yes,' Kate answered.

'We'll have to get it,' Anne stated. 'Once she goes into the hospice, that's it. Imagine what'll happen if someone finds the gun. Do you know where she keeps it?'

'I'm going to see her tomorrow, after I finish work,' Kate replied. 'I'll make sure I get it. She's so sick and she's in a lot of pain, she'll *have* to go to the hospice soon. At least if she's in the hospice, she won't be able to commit any more crimes.'

As planned, Kate visited Alison after work, and she could barely keep herself from crying, seeing Alison looking so ill.

After the initial greetings, Alison spoke first: 'I've told Kerrie. She's coming to Canberra tomorrow. This could be our last conversation in private. Is there anything more you want to tell me?'

'I can't think of anything, Alison, but I must get the gun.'

'Yes, it's in the bottom of the soiled-linen basket, in a calico bag. Get it now. I know it's against the rules, but you'd better put it in your car because I'm expecting Judy; she's going to stay the night.'

'I intended to get the gun, so I brought my big handbag.'

As she was putting the gun in her handbag, Alison asked her, 'Will you make a promise to a dying woman?'

'If it's something I can do, I'll do it,' Kate assured her.

'Promise?'

'I promise.'

'You can do it,' Alison said. 'Please put Dawn Flaherty in our gaol.'

Kate hadn't been expecting to hear *that* request. She thought for a moment and decided it would be best to let Alison believe that Dawn Flaherty would end up in the gaol. 'I will,' she said.

'You said you've got nothing you want to tell me; is there anything you want me to tell you?'

'I don't think so,' Kate answered.

'Don't you want to know how I took Munkton?'

'No, I don't. You know our rule: ask no questions, get no answers! No answers mean you can't reveal anything.'

'It was so simple getting him,' Alison persisted. 'I won't be around much longer, so I might as well tell you. First of all, I committed the cardinal sin: I went to Socamora on my own. Using a rope, I managed to lift the trapdoor. I removed all the chains from Cell 1 and left the gate open. Naturally, I locked all the doors and screwed the cupboard in place before I left.'

Kate now felt angry with her, knowing that the rule was that no one goes to Socamora on her own.

Alison continued relating what she'd done: 'Before I went to the Partisan Bar, I rang the Prime Hotel, said I was Joan Fry, Minister Munkton's secretary. I said, "We're finalising a document that urgently needs his signature; can you give me his direct extension, so I can phone him as soon as it's ready?" The receptionist was very obliging and gave me the number. I thanked her and hung up. I dialled the number and he answered. I spun exactly the same line as we'd spun Colleen O'Day about the illegal abortion clinic. I told him where I would park and what sort of car I had, and he agreed to meet me there at eight thirty. He found me and hopped in the car, and I drove us to Socamora.

'On the way, I explained that the clinic was in a basement. When we got there, he willingly helped me remove the cupboard and lift up the trapdoor. I warned him that the clinic stank, and I gave him a lab mask to put on.'

'What's a lab mask?' Kate enquired.

'If we're doing experiments in the lab and we know they'll give off irritating fumes, we can wear a mask that fits over the nose and mouth. It has a little filter, and the mask itself has a pleasant smell. I always keep a few at home. I imagined that the dungeon would be pretty rancid, so I gave Munkton one and wore one myself.

'I went downstairs and unlocked the doors. I told him to come down and go through the first gate. As soon as he was in Cell 1, I closed the gate. You wouldn't believe it could be so easy! Then he saw Colleen's and Lyn's bodies. I told him they'd died because of botched abortions and that if they'd been able to have them in a sterile environment, undertaken by a qualified doctor, they'd still be alive.

'He started to say something, but I pointed the gun at him and told him to keep quiet and move to the back of the cell. I put three of the chains around the gate. I reckoned three would be enough. Then I left.'

'What was the state of the dungeon? What about the bodies?' Kate asked.

'When I went to Socamora to unlock everything, it was daytime, so the dungeon was pitch-black. I wore one of those torches you strap to your head, as well as the lab mask. I only stayed in the dungeon long enough to move the shelves away and open the cell gate; I couldn't bring myself to look for the bodies. When I went with Munkton, I saw the back of Cullen and O'Day's heads. That was all I saw.'

'Did the dungeon stink?' Kate quizzed.

'I can't say for sure. If it did, the mask was very effective. I guess I might as well finish the story. The day after Munkton disappeared, one of my work colleagues came to visit me. We were making small talk, and she mentioned Munkton's disappearance. She said she'd been at university the same time he'd been there. She'd lived in the same residential college that Munkton's girlfriend had lived in, and she said he used to sneak in and spend the night with her. She even told me her name: Deborah Eavers.

'Next day, I went back and said to him, "You'll stay in this dungeon till you believe that to make a woman go through an unwanted pregnancy and take the baby away from her, so she never hears another word about the baby is *inhumane*. You have a nine-year-old daughter. How would *you* feel if someone came and took *her* away, telling you she knew people who'd give the child a better life and that you mustn't be selfish; you must think of the child? It makes no difference if the child's nine years old or three days old!"

'But like stupid Colleen, he couldn't see the point I was trying to make. So I then got really angry and shouted, "You're going to hell because you're the father of an abortion!" He just stared at me. I said to him, "Deborah Eavers had an abortion, but she wasn't going to tell you because she knew you were such a bigot, you'd probably go to the police!"'

'Is that true?' Kate asked her in a startled voice. 'Did your colleague tell you that?'

'No, but I thought it was a good joke! You should've seen the look on his face when I mentioned Deborah Eavers! I described every detail of my suffering to him. I told him that because of the stress of worrying every day of my life whether my daughter was happy, I'd gotten cancer.

'He said, "That's not how you get cancer, and it isn't true about Deborah." I said it *was* true and told him that lots of the girls at Oakley College knew. He didn't know what to think!

'I was wondering what they'd used for contraception. I didn't imagine he'd use a frog, so I took a punt and said, "Maybe one night you forgot to 'get off at Redfern' or you panicked and thought God might kill you, just like he killed Onan, if you did." Well, he nearly freaked out! Then I recited some verses from Ecclesiastes. A girl at Karmoor was always saying them. I have never forgotten them: "I envy those who are dead and gone: they are better off than those who are still alive. But better off than either are those who have never been born, who have never seen the injustice that goes on in this world."

'I told him not to worry about his aborted child and turned to go. He asked me when I was going to let him out. I suggested he ask his god to let him out within the next hour and said, "If you're still here in one hour, you have to deduce that your god doesn't exist or else, like me, your god thinks you belong in this dungeon!"

'He started pleading with me to let him out; said he could see the point I was trying to make. I told him that was a lie. Then he mentioned his wife and daughter, and that finished me off: I looked him straight in the eye and said, "The best thing you can do is forget you ever had that daughter!"'

'What'd he say?' Kate asked.

'Nothing. Circumstances have caused me to change, Kate. As you know, I was once a kind, compassionate, extremely happy person. Now, I'm quite horrible: I enjoyed seeing the look of fear in Munkton's eyes. I told him I could hardly recognise him as the same spiteful, supercilious shit who used parliamentary privilege to insult and mock anyone who didn't believe what he believed.

'I must stop now. Use the same story about an illegal abortion clinic to get Dawn Flaherty, and once she's in the gaol, make sure you give her one hell of a lecture!'

'Yes, I will,' Kate assured her. 'And I know what you're talking about when you say you enjoyed seeing the fear in Munkton's eyes. Seeing someone you loathe, someone who's ruined your life, at your mercy, must be the greatest feeling anyone can have.'

'I agree,' Alison said. 'I can't think of anything else I want to tell you.'

'Good. I'll wait till Judy arrives.' Kate was relieved, not wanting to hear any more about Gary Munkton.

'You don't have to. Judy has a key.'

'No,' Kate insisted. 'I'm not leaving you alone.'

By the time Judy arrived, Alison had fallen asleep.

'I'll go now,' Kate said to Judy in a hushed voice. 'I didn't want to leave her on her own.'

'Thanks for waiting until I got here. Kerrie's arriving tomorrow.'

'I know. Helen's meeting her at the airport.'

After Kate had left Alison's house, she went to Anne and Helen's and told them what Alison had told her.

'So,' Helen declared, 'we can no longer pretend we don't know it's Alison who kidnapped Munkton. The past five days have been ridiculous: Alison didn't say anything, and we acted as if we didn't think it was her!'

'I don't want to have anything to do with Gary Munkton,' Anne said. 'Alison acted alone; he's *her* prisoner.'

'Does she intend to feed him?' Helen asked Kate.

'I didn't ask. I don't know what she intends to do with him.'

'Let's stop pretending!' Anne said in a distraught voice. 'Alison's in no fit state to do anything! And soon she'll go to the hospice. Munkton will die, and Alison's responsible for his death!'

Anne, Helen and Kate were now extremely distressed, and Anne was annoyed with Alison, having learnt she'd broken one of their rules: 'no one must do anything without consulting the other three.'

Helen met Kerrie at the airport, and Kerrie told her she was shattered, not only because of Alison's cancer, but because Alison had known about it for almost four weeks before she told her.

'I guess you also know that Alison hasn't told your mother,' Helen added.

'Yes, she wants *me* to tell her.'

'Kerrie,' Helen said, 'I don't want you to think we're heartless: all Alison's friends said she could stay with them, but she wanted to be on her own.'

'Yes, she told me that when I asked her who was helping her.'

When they arrived at Alison's townhouse, Helen told Kerrie she wouldn't go in with her. 'This is something between sisters. If you want me to go to Nowra to bring your mother to Canberra, let me know.'

'Thanks, Helen,' Kerrie said in response. 'And thanks for meeting me.'

That night, Kerrie rang Helen to say she was going to Nowra the next day to collect her mother.

Kerrie wanted Alison to stay with her on the Gold Coast, but Alison didn't want to. She knew no one on the Gold Coast, and she also knew her sister wouldn't be able to look after her in the final stage of her life. All her friends were in Canberra. She knew she'd always have at least one friend by her side.

Two weeks after Kerrie's arrival in Canberra, Alison went into the hospice. The doctor said she'd never seen such an aggressive case of pancreatic cancer in all her thirty-two years of practice.

The day after Alison's admission to the hospice, Kate visited her there, where she found her with no visitors. 'I told Mum and Kerrie you were coming to see me,' Alison said, 'so they've gone back to my place for a break; they've been here since nine o'clock this morning.'

Kate was surprised to see a Bible on Alison's bedside cabinet, and enquired, 'Whose is that?'

'A minister was visiting the woman in the bed next to mine. He smiled at me and asked me whether he could do anything for me. I said I couldn't think of anything. Then he asked me if I'd like a Bible. I wanted to read some more of Ecclesiastes, so I accepted it.'

Kate held Alison's hand, and they made small talk. There was another woman in the room, so the conversation was limited.

'Kate,' Alison said sadly, 'I always hoped I'd find my daughter. I think that's why I don't want to die. Maybe that was my goal. Maybe that was what I wanted to achieve. You achieved your goal.'

'Yes,' Kate agreed. 'I did. But didn't circumstances dictate unusual goals to us? I wonder what mine would've been if I hadn't been raped.'

'Is it really true you wouldn't care if you dropped dead tomorrow?' Alison asked her.

'As true as I sit here. I wish I could change places with you. I'm jealous of you.'

'You say that,' Alison said, 'but you can't be sure.'

'That's true,' Kate agreed, 'but I don't see any great future for me.'

'Set yourself another goal then: get Dawn Flaherty.'

'Can I make someone else's goal mine?'

'Yes, you can,' Alison assured her.

'I think you're right. What time is your mother and Kerrie coming to see you?'

'Mum's not coming back tonight; Kerrie's coming at six thirty. Dinner's brought around about six, so she'll come after that.'

'I'll stay with you till your dinner arrives. It shouldn't be long. It's almost six now.'

Alison's dinner arrived, so Kate kissed her and left. It was now ten past six, and Kate wanted to see Kerrie, who'd be arriving at six thirty. She knew that Kerrie wouldn't be late, so she decided to wait for her in the waiting room. When Kerrie arrived, Kate said to her, 'Hi, Kerrie. I just wanted to check if there's anything I can do for you.'

'Thank you, Kate,' Kerrie replied. 'I'll let you know. My younger daughter, Natasha, is coming tomorrow. She's staying for a week, and then my other daughter, Leah, is coming; she is staying for ten days. My husband, Jack, is coming after Leah goes back. Mum and I are staying ... Mum and I are staying to the ...' She started to cry, and when able to continue, said, 'I spoke to the specialist today. He said Alison has six weeks "at the most", to use his words. I'd love to meet you for lunch or afternoon tea. Apart from Helen, I feel I know so little about Alison's friends and her life in Canberra. Growing up, she was such fun. Then ... then ...'

'We've had some fun times together,' Kate remarked.

'I'm glad to hear it. So what about lunch or afternoon tea?'

'I'd prefer afternoon tea. Do you want to come to my place? It'd mean you have to drive to Queanbeyan, but I'm rather emotional, and I don't want to start crying in a restaurant or café.'

'I know what you mean. I'm happy to drive to Queanbeyan. What about the day after tomorrow? Natasha can stay with Alison while we have some time together. Mum's been very good, but she needs some time out.'

'Fine,' Kate said. 'What's say four o'clock at my place?'

'Thanks, Kate, I'll see you four o'clock Tuesday.'

Kerrie arrived at Kate's house for afternoon tea on Tuesday at four o'clock.

Kate ushered her into the lounge room, saying, 'Take a seat. I'll make us a coffee. How do you like it?'

'Black, no sugar.'

'The same as Alison,' Kate remarked.

'Yes, we have a lot in common.'

Kate made the coffee and placed Kerrie's cup on the same table she'd placed Alison's more than three years earlier.

'How long have you known Alison?' Kerrie asked her.

'Alison and I met on our first day at university,' Kate replied.

Kerrie looked surprised. 'You've known Alison since *uni*?'

'That's when we first met. We were the best of friends, but somehow, when we left uni, we lost contact. About three years ago, Alison spotted me in a crowd, and the next day, she rang me. I'd been living in Queanbeyan for almost twenty-seven years, and she'd been in Canberra for twenty, and neither of us knew. We started seeing each other, and after a month, it was like old times.'

'When I first met you, I thought I'd seen you before. Now, I recognise you from photos from Alison's uni days. You were in nearly all of them. That was so long ago. Poor Alison, she's had such an awful life. She deserved better. She ...'

'Kerrie,' Kate said, 'I know about Alison's baby.'

Kerrie started to cry uncontrollably. 'She nearly died having that baby. The young doctor was trying to avoid a caesarean. She was in labour for twenty hours. She had a reaction to the anaesthetic. She never fully recovered from the trauma. It left her bitter. What a wasted life! Kate, do you believe in life after death?'

'No, not one iota,' Kate asserted. 'Once you're dead, that's it, *finito*. It'd be nice to think there's something, though, because we'd have an explanation for "the meaning of life".'

'If Alison had been able to terminate that pregnancy, her life would've been completely different. The power the Right to Esse has is sickening! Speaking of the Right to Esse, remember that president who disappeared about eighteen months ago? What was her name, Clare O'Day?'

'I think her first name was Colleen,' Kate replied.

'I hope she's dead. I hope she had a painful death! Oh, Kate, what's the matter with me! Why am I saying such awful things!'

'Because you're overcome with grief and filled with hatred towards Gorgons like Colleen O'Day, who head up organisations that lobby governments to bend to their demands.'

'Well,' Kerrie said, 'while I'm saying evil things. If I ever find the people who took Alison's daughter, I'll tell them they ruined my sister's life! Last time I visited Alison, she told me she'd like me to put them in a dungeon. Do you know where I can find a dungeon?'

Kate didn't know what to think. Had Alison told Kerrie anything? She knew she had to change the topic of conversation. 'I'm afraid not! What about relatives? I know your father's dead, but what about aunts, uncles or cousins? Do you think Alison would want to see them?'

'All the relatives know about Alison's cancer; it'll be up to them to decide.'

Kate went to the hospice again on Saturday afternoon. The receptionist informed her that Alison had been moved to a single room and told Kate where it was. When Kate entered the room, she saw Alison's mother and Kerrie there. Alison seemed to be dying before Kate's eyes. Kerrie and her mother decided they'd go and have a cup of tea, to give Kate and Alison some time together.

Kate didn't know what to say. She couldn't ask the standard question: 'How are you?'

Alison was heavily sedated, and after the initial greetings, Kate almost vomited when Alison said to her, 'Kate, should I confess about Keys, Colleen, Lyr. and Munkton, and ask for forgiveness?'

'*What are you talking about?* What's confessing got to do with anything? You're not thinking there's an afterlife, are you?' Kate asked in a nervous and angry but hushed voice. 'You confess about the dungeon and we're all gone! I don't care about myself, but I care about Anne and Helen! *How could you betray your friends?*'

'I wouldn't reveal anything about the dungeon. I didn't mention the dungeon. You assumed my confession included exposing the dungeon.'

'Yes, I did.'

'Remember Marlene? The woman we met at the Partisan Bar? She told us about the film she was going to see – the one in which the man confessed to the murders, but the priest wouldn't say anything. The priest forgave him.'

'Have you lost your marbles?' Kate hissed, as quietly as she could manage. 'What's gotten into you? You know there's no afterlife, no God. If there is, where was *he* when you had to give up your Honours year? Where was *he* when you screamed for twenty hours in labour? Where was *he* when you had your baby taken from you? Where is he *now*? Don't get any ideas about confessing to the man who gave you the Bible. He's not a Catholic priest; he's a Protestant minister, and he doesn't have the seal of confession.'

'I *know* that, Kate!' Alison replied, almost annoyed at Kate's instructions.

'Well, who were you thinking of confessing to? Answer me!'

'I don't know. Maybe a priest could come here.'

Kate was furious with Alison. She couldn't believe Alison could be thinking like this. Alison always thought so logically. She must know any confession could spell trouble for her friends. It was most unlike Alison. Kate thought it might be the medication.

'If you want to take out some insurance for the next life – "the next life", what a laugh! – ask *God* to forgive you; in fact, I think forgiveness by God is automatic. Remember when I told you about that stupid minister who told me God had forgiven the men who raped me, so I must forgive them? I bet Wayne Keys and the other two didn't ask God for forgiveness, so you should be one hundred per cent confident you're forgiven, but if you've got any doubts, say, "Please, God, forgive me." That's all you have to say, and you're forgiven. Say it this minute, and don't give it another thought! But I still don't know why you're asking for forgiveness!

'I've never understood how God can forgive a person for hurting another person. I can't forgive you for something you've done to someone else. If I smash your head in, it's up to you to forgive me – and *only* you. Helen can't forgive me for something I've done to you.

'When I was five years old, a boy who was going to the same Sunday school as I was, had a tractor accident on his grandfather's farm. His left arm was severed just below the elbow. By the time he arrived at the hospital, he'd lost a lot of blood, and he was in a pretty bad shape. The accident happened on a Saturday. On Sunday, the head Sunday school teacher announced that Johnny Sykes had had an accident and was very ill. We were all to pray for Johnny's recovery. We were to pray for him *every night*. The following Sunday, the head Sunday school teacher was overjoyed to tell us God had answered our prayers and Johnny was no longer in a serious condition and would recover. Then one of the older boys stood up and said we should ask every church in Australia to devote ten minutes of the following Sunday's service to praying that Johnny's arm would grow back. Well, the head Sunday school teacher went off on this great spiel about how God had plans for Johnny and what a stronger person he'd be, and it was fortunate it was his *left* arm because Johnny's right-handed!' Blah! Blah! Rave on! But you and I know why she didn't want anyone praying for Johnny's arm to grow back because she knew it wouldn't, and why wouldn't it? Because there ain't no God! Sorry about the double negative – there *is* no God!' Kate hardly drew breath.

'Kate, have you lost *your* marbles?' Alison asked her with as much energy as she could muster. 'How could you possibly think I'd say anything to implicate you, Anne or Helen? I can't believe you'd think I'd do such a thing! You've really offended me!'

'I'm sorry, Alison, really sorry. It's just that if you were to say anything – I mean *anything* – to *anyone*, eventually the trail would lead to Anne, Helen and me.'

'Not necessarily, Kate. I'd make out I acted alone.'

'And where are the bodies? Your confession could still cause trouble.'

'You're right, Kate,' Alison admitted. 'I don't know what made me have that lapse. I need some more morphine. I can control my morphine now; the nurse set it up just after lunch.'

Alison's mother and Kerrie returned to the ward at five o'clock, and as soon as they were there, Kate left. She was now feeling quite nervous, so she decided to go to Anne and Helen's before returning to Queanbeyan. She was hoping someone would be home, and luckily when she arrived, Helen opened the door.

Helen could see that Kate was agitated and asked, 'What's up?'

'I'm worried about Alison!' Kate blurted out. 'I've just visited her. She was talking about confessing and asking for forgiveness. I had a stern talk with her, and I really think she's come to her senses and she'll do no such thing. Nevertheless, I'm worried she might start raving, under the influence of too much morphine. I don't care about myself, but there's no reason for you or Anne to be involved. She knows there's nothing after this life, yet for some reason, she wants to have two bob each way. She also said she's feeling guilty about Lex Woodlock.'

Anne, who'd overheard the conversation, entered the room.

'Hi, Anne. Do you know anything about the effects of morphine? Is it like alcohol? You know what I mean, *in vino veritas*?' Kate asked her.

'I don't know,' Anne said in a voice that indicated she was worried.

'I'm visiting her tomorrow night; I'll sound her out,' Helen said, also sounding worried. 'I'm concerned she is so heavily drugged, she's not thinking clearly.'

'She assured me she wouldn't mention the dungeon in her confession, but I think as a precaution we should demolish it ASAP and close up the trapdoor.'

'Confession or no confession, the demolition of the gaol is something that has to be done. Do you have any commitments next weekend?' Anne asked Kate.

'No,' she answered.

'Good, we'll go out next weekend. I'll buy two top-of-the-range spanners for us to use to dismantle the front of the cells. The most time-consuming part of the demolition will be smashing the brick wall between the cells. It'll also be dangerous; we'll have to be ultra-careful it doesn't fall on anyone.'

'Do you have any ideas how we'll do it?' Kate asked her.

'The mortar's reasonably soft,' Anne replied. 'I'll buy a masonry hand-saw. We'll divide the wall into large sections and saw through the mortar, and then push that part of the wall out. It won't take nearly as long to dismantle the gaol as it did to build it; in fact, if we work all day on both days, we can probably do it.'

'I think you're being a bit ambitious,' Helen remarked. 'It's also going to take a long time to smash up the concrete the bars are set in. How do you intend to do that?'

'With a wood splitter. You're right, Helen: I'm probably being too ambitious.'

'Also,' Kate said, 'Alison might think it's strange that not one of us visits her over the weekend.'

'What say you and I visit her Saturday night?' Helen suggested. 'That'll be enough. If you want to, Kate, you can stay overnight at our place Friday and Saturday night.'

'Thanks, Helen, I'll take you up on the offer, but remember: don't let it slip to Alison what we're doing. And I guess I don't have to remind you to buy some extra rubber gloves. I'm also concerned about stench. I'm not sure I told you, but Alison said she wore a mask over her nose and mouth when she went into the dungeon with Munkton; she'd gotten the masks from work.'

'Perhaps we could burn some incense,' Helen suggested.

'I'll make three surgical masks. They're quite simple: a rectangular piece of cloth with two bits of elastic at the back. And I'll buy some eucalyptus oil: we can put some oil on the masks.'

'Thanks, Kate,' Helen said. 'I'll bring a can of air freshener. You never know: it might help.'

'I wonder what state the bodies are in,' Kate said. 'As I've told you, Alison said all she saw was the back of Lyn's and Colleen's heads. I didn't want to press her for more information; I thought it'd be very insensitive of me to ask her about dead bodies when she's so close to death herself. I think it'll take us a few hours to dig the holes to bury them.'

'Yes,' Anne said, 'that won't be easy. We'll start digging near the toilet holes and showers. Hopefully it'll be a bit softer there. One last thought: is there any possibility Munkton's still alive?'

'No,' Helen and Kate both replied.

Having visited Alison at various times during the week, all three women were relieved she hadn't mentioned anything more about confessing or asking for forgiveness. However, they still didn't know how people who were heavily dosed up with morphine behaved or whether Alison would say anything 'right at the end'. They knew they had to be prepared in case she did.

Kate slept at Anne and Helen's house on Friday night. They rose early on the Saturday, had breakfast, packed some lunch and drove to Socamora. They arrived there just after eight o'clock. Helen climbed up on the roof and covered the solar panels with rugs so the solar lights would light up.

'I hope that Fred guy doesn't come snooping around,' Kate said.

'So do I. All we can do is keep the cabin locked,' Anne said as she unlocked the cabin doors.

Helen and Kate unscrewed and rolled away the cupboard and lifted up the trapdoor. They dabbed some eucalyptus oil on their surgical masks and then put them on.

Anne was first to descend the stairs, and Helen and Kate followed. Anne unlocked the doors and went into the corridor. They found that the smell wasn't nearly as bad as they'd been expecting. Anne walked slowly, and the other two women were soon standing beside her. All three felt nauseous when they saw the bodies. Wayne Keys was on his bed, his sheet pulled up to his neck so only his head was visible. Colleen was also in bed, her sheet up to her neck. Lyn Cullen and Gary Munkton were on the floor of Cell 1. Lyn was lying on the mattress from the top bunk, and Munkton was wrapped in a blanket. In short, all that was visible was four heads.

'The sooner we get these bodies buried, the better,' Helen choked.

'I agree,' Anne said. 'In the meantime, let's cover their heads.'

They moved the shelves away from the cell gates and unlocked the gates. Helen couldn't cover the exposed heads quickly enough. She entered Cell 1 and made sure no part of Colleen O'Day, Lyn Cullen or Gary Munkton was visible. Then she went to Cell 2 but found that Kate had already put a towel over Keys's head.

The three women were now standing in the corridor, all in a mild state of shock. All four prisoners' heads were indeed hideous.

'Well,' Helen said, 'I guess we should start the digging. Who's first?'

'Keys,' Anne responded.

They went into Cell 2 and ripped up the carpet near the shower; then they commenced the digging. They took turns using the tools, two each using a mattock and the other shovelling the soil away. The ground was hard, and they realised there was no way they'd be able to dig four holes deep enough to bury the four bodies in.

'Let's face it! At this rate, we'll still be digging come Christmas. I think we've removed enough dirt to cover Keys's body,' Helen said.

Kate and Anne agreed they had. However, the worst part lay in front of them: they had to drag Keys to his grave. They put on their rubber gloves and slid the mattress off the bed. They then dragged the mattress to the edge of the pit and tilted it until Wayne Gary Keys's body rolled off the mattress and into the pit. No one said a word.

Anne could hardly believe what she was doing and thought the other two must be feeling the same way.

They turned the mattress over, put it back on the bed and covered Keys's body with soil. The body was completely hidden, but it wouldn't be rocket science for someone to work out what probably lay beneath the mound of soil.

They then moved into Cell 1 and commenced digging there. When they thought they'd removed enough soil to cover three bodies, they stopped.

'Who goes first?' Kate asked.

'Munkton, he's closest to the hole. He's on a blanket. We'll drag the blanket to the pit,' Anne replied.

Colleen and Lyn were on a mattress. As the women had done with Keys, they dragged the mattresses to the edge of the pit and tilted them until the bodies rolled into it. Helen took the shovel, Kate the spade and Anne the rake, and they proceeded to cover the bodies.

After a while, Helen needed a break, and said, 'Let's get some fresh air.' Without waiting for an answer, she went up the stairs, and the others followed. They headed for the water tank and scrubbed their hands. In spite of what they'd just done, they hadn't lost their appetite, so they decided to sit on the grass and have lunch.

When they'd finished eating, Anne said, 'The worst part's done. Let's start dismantling the gaol. The first thing we should do is demolish the wall between the cells. We'll put a lot of the bricks on top of the bodies.'

After they'd flattened the wall, they decided they'd had enough and that they'd go home. 'We should be able to finish demolishing it tomorrow,' Anne said.

They went home feeling physically and mentally exhausted – and dirty. Anne's house had two showers. Helen and Kate showered first, and then went to visit Alison.

When they returned, Anne ordered Chinese food to be delivered for the three of them. They watched a movie on TV and went to bed.

The Sunday morning was the same as the Saturday morning: they rose early, ate breakfast, packed some lunch and drove to Socamora.

Once there, Kate and Helen got busy with spanners, unbolting the joins that were holding the front of the cells together. They were surprised at how quickly they were able to dismantle the grid. At the same time, Anne unscrewed the gates and doors and ripped up the carpet. Despite the good progress, though, it became obvious that Anne had been too ambitious: they wouldn't finish dismantling the gaol that day.

'We're not going to finish it today,' Anne announced. 'Can you two come next Saturday?'

'Yes,' Kate and Helen answered together.

They returned to Socamora to finish the demolition the following Saturday. Anne continued to give directions: 'Wreck everything; smash the shelves; dismantle the beds; take the water tanks off their stands and put an axe through them; empty the garbage bins; get the masks and anything else that's in the cupboard and drop them here. Make the dungeon look like a dump'

At 4.17 pm, Anne declared, 'I think we've finished.'

Kate ascended the ladder, and then Helen, and then Anne. The three of them pulled up the ladder. 'What we have to do now,' Anne said, 'is pull up these carpet tiles and boards, concrete over the hole and lay ceramic tiles on the floor. We'll take a break next weekend and do it the following week.'

They closed the trapdoor, wheeled the cupboard over it and screwed the cupboard to the wall. What each one was thinking the other two didn't know, but the limited conversation in the car on the way home was an indication of *something*: sadness, relief, guilt – who knew?

Three days after the demolition of the gaol was complete, Kate visited Alison, who again talked about asking for forgiveness.

Kate was livid. 'We've been through this, Alison! Stop talking like this or I'll put a pillow over your head and suffocate you! I'll say it was mercy killing! I don't care what happens to me, but I sure care about Anne and Helen, and so should you! I'll do anything to protect them! I still can't believe you can even think this way!'

'I'm sorry, Kate. I won't mention it again.'

'Not to anyone!' Kate demanded. 'Understand?'

'Yes, Kate.' Alison started to cry.

So did Kate.

'When I saw you angry, I got quite a scare,' Alison said. 'Would you really kill me?'

'Yes,' Kate replied. 'I always think Anne and Helen took a huge risk to help us. The thought that they might be punished under the law because you wanted to ask for forgiveness doesn't bear thinking about.'

'You're right, Kate. I won't mention it again.'

'Good! You and I have the proof there's no God! How can you be thinking like this?'

'I don't know, Kate. I only know I feel frightened, and I also feel guilty.'

Kate visited Alison regularly at the hospice and knew that one day soon she'd be losing her best friend. Finally, that horrible day came. It was a Tuesday, the twenty-third of April 1991. She arrived at the hospice, and as she started to go to Alison's room, she saw the look on the receptionist's face. 'Miss Scott …' the receptionist said.

'Oh no!' Kate blubbered, and she sat down and wept.

'About an hour ago,' the receptionist told her. 'Her mother and sister were with her. You've just missed them. They said they'd let you know. Obviously, you'd already left. I'm sorry to have to tell you this sad news.'

'Someone had to tell me. Goodbye, Mrs Gregory.'

'Goodbye, Miss Scott.'

Kate went to her car and started crying again. When she thought she could see through the tears, she drove to Anne and Helen's house, and Helen opened the door to her. As soon as Helen saw Kate, she knew Alison had died. She ushered Kate to a chair, and she too began to cry. Anne then entered the room. She was sad but didn't cry. She tried to console the other two. Not having any success, she decided it'd be best to let them cry, and she began to wonder whether the human body had a finite supply of tears or whether it kept making them forever.

Finally, when Kate and Helen stopped crying and were just sobbing, and Anne thought she could be heard above the sobs, she spoke to Kate. 'I think you shouldn't be on your own tonight: please spend the night here.'

'Thank you, Anne, I will. I'm not going to work tomorrow. Now I'd like to phone Kerrie.'

'Sure,' Anne said, 'go right ahead.'

Kate dialled Alison's number, and Kerrie answered, saying, 'Oh, Kate, I was just trying to get myself composed enough to ring you and Helen.'

'Thanks, Kerrie. You wouldn't have gotten on to me: I'm at Anne and Helen's. I went to the hospice. I already know. Is there anything we can do for you or your mother?'

'Not tonight, thanks, Kate,' Kerrie replied, 'but tomorrow we'd probably like a bit of support organising the funeral. My husband and daughters are arriving the following day.'

'What say Helen and I come over at ten o'clock?' Kate asked her. 'Is that too early?'

'No, that's fine.'

'Good, then we'll see you tomorrow at ten. Goodbye, Kerrie.'

'Goodbye, Kate.'

Kate put the receiver down.

'Do they want us to do anything?' Helen asked her.

'Not tonight. You and I'll go and see Kerrie at ten o'clock tomorrow.'

Anne made them a pot of tea. After they'd drunk their tea, they chatted for an hour, showered and went to bed.

Although Anne was saddened by Alison's death, she was also relieved: Alison hadn't been 'with it' in the end, and Anne had been worried she'd blurt out something about Socamora. Maybe she had.

All three women rose at about the same time and then had breakfast together.

Helen asked Anne, 'Are you going to work?'

'Yes. But if I can be of any assistance, just phone me. Now I must go. Bye, Kate. Bye, Helen.'

'Bye, Anne,' Kate and Helen said in unison as Anne was closing the door.

'Sometimes I can't work Anne out,' Helen declared. 'I know she's upset about Alison's death, but she doesn't show it. She's often accused of being heartless. It's quite unfair. Look how she felt for you, the injustice you suffered; she couldn't do enough to help you get your revenge.'

'I know,' Kate said. 'I think about it every day.'

'Kate, I know it sounds corny, but I can't put it any other way: Alison's suffering has ended, no more sadness for her. It's all over.'

'Well, *I* certainly think it's all over; I know a lot of people don't. They believe in life after death. It's hard to comprehend how intelligent people can believe such nonsense.'

'Not really,' Helen said. 'I think it's the intelligent people trying to find the meaning of life; the retards probably don't think twice about the meaning of life.'

'There isn't one.'

'I agree.'

Kate and Helen made small talk. At nine thirty, the phone rang and Helen answered it. 'That was Anne, calling to see how we are. That's what I mean when I say Anne's hard to work out: she goes out the door as if she has a heart of stone, yet she's probably been thinking about us since she left, and she phones to see how we are. She's a strange mixture.'

'I like the mix,' Kate said. 'I guess it's time for us go to Alison's house and see what we can do for Kerrie and her mother.'

Kate and Helen drove to Alison's house, and Kerrie opened the door to them. 'Come in, Kate, Helen. We've just finished wording the death notice. Mum and I are having a bit of a disagreement over the funeral: she thinks Alison showed some faith towards the end, but I told her it wasn't faith, it was fear. Fear indoctrinated into her by our stupid grandmother. Mum still thinks we should have a prayer or a hymn. I told her to respect Alison's beliefs – or lack of beliefs, whichever way you look at it. I've also reminded her that if there *is* a loving, all-powerful god, why did he ruin Alison's life? I think she's finally come around. Stupid Gran: the things she believed.'

'Some people who have a vivid imagination believe that when you die, something which can't be seen leaves the body, zooms skywards, and lives forever!' Kate said.

'It's called the soul,' Kerrie informed her. 'Gran reckons that when Pa died, she heard his soul leave his body.'

'It was probably a fart!' Kate remarked.

'Well, if it was, she wouldn't've heard it: couldn't even hear her own! She'd often humiliate us by letting one rip full-throttle in a crowded shopping mall – completely oblivious, silly old bag!

'During the holidays, I'd go and help her with the washing. I used to feel almost ill, hanging out size 18 bloomers that had skid marks ingrained in them. One Christmas, Alison was there, and she had a go at me for not telling Gran her undies should be sprayed with pre-wash, said she was going to subtly suggest it to her. I told her to unsubtly suggest paint stripper instead! Poor Alison was always trying to do the right thing by Gran. One of the first things she said to me when she found out she was pregnant was "What'll Gran say?" Here's Alison in this horrendous situation, and she's worried about Gran. I'm glad Gran's not here: she was one of those people who thought you confessed everything on your deathbed, to shorten your stay in purgatory. She must've brainwashed Alison, because she talked about confessing her sins. She started raving. She was going on about things she'd done, but it sounded more like things she'd *like* to have done. It was probably the painkillers talking.'

Crikey! Kate thought. *I wonder what it was!*

Oh, shit! Helen thought, and said, 'If it sounded way out, it probably was the drugs. So, what do you intend for the funeral?' She wanted to steer the conversation away from what Alison might have said to Kerrie on her deathbed.

'The funeral director's coming here at two o'clock. We'll finalise it then; still, I haven't a clue what we'll do. How long does a funeral last: an hour? half an hour? How can we spin it out to half an hour if there are no hymns, no prayers, no Bible readings? And I can't stand those funerals where everyone gets up and says what a great person the deceased was – as if anyone's going to get up at your funeral and say what a whopping lump of excreta you were and that many of us are glad you're dead. Although I did feel like saying something like that at Gran's funeral!

'She always had the TV blaring. She'd ask me to come and visit her, and when I arrived, she wouldn't turn the telly off. It was always the same: "Gran, turn off the TV!" "I just want to see the end of this program."

As soon as it ended, I'd say we could turn off the telly, and she'd say she just wanted to see the beginning of the next program. Then she'd go to sleep and start snoring and dribbling – a horrible sight. On her chin, she had about eight long, black, curly whiskers she wouldn't pluck. Even Mum told her she should remove them. Her response was "They're not offending the Lord." Have you ever heard such drivel?

'One night, I'd had it. I went to visit her, at her request, and she went to sleep. There she is, sitting in her chair, snoring, dribbling and farting, so I got some tweezers and yanked one of the whiskers out. She let out a blood-curdling cry. I said, "Pull out the other seven!" and went home.'

'That was very brave of you,' Helen commented.

'Yes, it was. You know, Gran really put unnecessary fear into Alison's life – always going on about "the good Lord" and "the treasures in heaven". Alison could never completely release the nonsensical idea that Gran might be right: that there might be a life after this one. I think that deep down, Alison hoped there was because her life on earth was such a waste. I also think she thought that maybe one day she'd find her daughter in heaven. She used to go to a wonderful support group, NoFourthR. Maybe you've heard of it.'

'We have,' Kate replied. 'Alison introduced me to it. I've attended many of their meetings in Canberra. They're a great group of people. They put out a monthly newsletter. I deliver some in Queanbeyan. You should read some of the stories – the *dreadful* things some children have been told – and as for the quotes from the Bible, I'm sure a lot of people are unaware of some of the atrocities God has committed.'

'Poor Alison, horrible Gran,' Kerrie said. 'I threatened to choke her once. I was still at school when Alison became pregnant. I was visiting Gran, and she talked about the good Lord working in mysterious ways and that I was to think about the joy the baby would bring to a lovely, childless couple, and she implied Alison was being punished for being naughty. Well, I went ballistic, and Gran actually became frightened!'

Kerrie burst into tears, and her mother heard the crying. She came into the room and tried to console her daughter but found the effort futile. She herself started to cry. The sight of the two grieving women didn't reduce Kate to tears. Secretly, she was jealous of Alison because Alison now had what Kate had wanted for more than thirty years. Kerrie and her mother eventually stopped crying.

'We still haven't worked out what we'll do about the funeral,' Helen said.

Alison's mother answered: 'The last funeral I went to, the minister emphasised the celebration of Betsy's life; I guess we'll have to do the same for Alison.'

Kerrie became angry. 'And what, pray tell, is there to celebrate about Alison's life? The first twenty good years can't compensate for the last thirty-two rotten ones! And Mum, Kate and Helen know about the baby: Alison told them – *your* granddaughter. Somewhere, you have a thirty-year-old granddaughter who should be at her mother's funeral. Why didn't you and Dad do more to help Alison have an abortion? Dad must've had contacts. Instead, you sent her to that effing hatchery in Sydney! "Celebration of a life"? What a joke! Do you celebrate someone's *existence*? "A life" and "an existence" are two completely different things!'

On hearing Kerrie's outburst, her mother started crying again. 'Kerrie, how can you say that? Your father and I gave Alison all the support we could. I don't want to talk about it anymore.'

'That's your way of dealing with every difficult thing!' Kerrie shouted at her. 'Don't talk about it! Throw it in the too-hard basket and hope it goes away! Why didn't *you* keep the baby?'

'Kerrie, do we have to go through this again?' her mother begged her. 'Particularly in front of Kate and Helen? Adoption seemed the best thing at the time!'

'The best thing for *you* and *Dad*!' Kerrie shot back. 'It wasn't as if you were on a walking frame! You were young and fit enough to bring her up! You're heartless, Mum! Think back to when Alison was born. How would you've felt if Alison had been whisked away from you as soon as she was born, with a curt "The best thing you can do now is forget you ever had this baby."? And your stupid mother supported the Right to Esse! I'd like to blow the whole effing lot of them to smithereens. You sent Alison and me to that bloody Sunday school because you didn't have the guts to tell your mother to get stuffed.'

Turning to Kate and Helen, Kerrie continued, 'One of my favourite ways of getting back at Gran was to find confronting verses in the Bible and ask her to explain. One, which I still remember and is very relevant right now, is from Ecclesiastes. The writer says straight out: "There is no way for us to know what will happen after we die."'

'I know you used to do that Kerrie and I thought it very naughty of you,' her mother said despairingly. 'My mother gained great comfort from her faith. She said that faith offered one hope.'

'Hope?' Kerrie echoed. 'What a futile way to live! Suffering the first half of the concert, *hoping* the second half'll be better; spewing on your entrée, *hoping* the main course'll be more palatable; walking down the street, *hoping* your head doesn't fall off! That's what religion's all about: eking out a life, *hoping, just hoping – no guarantee –* the next life'll be better! What rubbish! I'm sorry, Kate, Helen, but this is such an emotional issue for me!'

'You don't have to apologise,' Helen said sympathetically.

'Do you recognise Kate, Mum?' Kerrie asked her. 'Does her face look familiar? She was in all Alison's uni photos – the photos she burnt when her life ended.'

'Kerrie, you seem to think it's *my* fault Alison became pregnant.'

'Well, maybe it is! Maybe if you'd given us some sex education, it mightn't've happened, or you'd told Alison the dangers of playing Vatican Roulette. But I don't suppose you received much from your mother, did you? She'd've choked on the very word "sex"! Sanctimonious old prude! I used to think you and Uncle Dave must have been immaculate conceptions.'

'I sometimes think Alison coped with the pregnancy better than you did, Kerrie.'

'How can you say that?' Kerrie yelled. 'You show how little you know about your daughter! Alison survived by blocking it out. Maybe you think she coped because she never talked about it. That was because she *couldn't* talk about it; it was too traumatic. Talking about it almost made her suicidal. Sorry, Mum, but you know how I feel; I won't say any more.'

'Thank you, Kerrie,' her mother replied.

'We still haven't worked out what we're going to do at the funeral,' Kerrie said. 'I guess when the funeral director comes, he'll give us a few guidelines. I'm sure he's dealt with plenty of atheist funerals.'

'I feel I haven't been much help to you, Kerrie,' Kate said to her.

'You have, Kate,' she assured her. 'It's almost lunch time. Do you two want to have lunch with us?'

'Yes, that would be very nice,' Helen and Kate answered.

'Are you okay, Mum?' Kerrie asked her mother.

'As well as can be expected of a mother who's just lost her daughter.'

Kate and Helen saw the rage enter Kerrie's eyes. She glared at her mother and said to her, 'So, now you know what it's like to lose a daughter!'

Helen and Kate braced themselves for another tirade from Kerrie, but instead, she turned away from her mother and said in a whisper to them, 'I'll control myself.'

Kate and Helen had lunch with them, and then returned to Anne and Helen's house. Anne arrived home at three o'clock, saying, 'I couldn't concentrate, so I thought I should go home. How are Kerrie and her mother? I suppose that's a stupid question.'

'Kerrie gave her mother a real tongue-lashing,' Helen replied.

'What about?' Anne asked.

'Alison's baby. She told us, when she was walking with us to the car, that she's never forgiven her parents for not keeping the baby.'

'Did you work out the funeral details?' Anne queried.

'No,' Kate answered. 'We left before the funeral director arrived; I think Kerrie was going to leave it up to him. I've no idea how they'll make the service last ten minutes, let alone half an hour. Kerrie doesn't want people getting up and saying what a lovely person Alison was. I felt I was as much use as a one-legged woman at an arse-kicking party.'

'I'm sure they were glad of your presence, Kate,' Anne assured her.

'I'm not sure Mum was. Kerrie really dished out a tirade!'

'Maybe she was,' Anne commented. 'It might've been worse if you hadn't been there.'

'I've known Alison for twenty years. I met her on my third day in Canberra. The IT company I was working for was installing new software for Cural. I asked her where there was a good place for lunch. She said, "Follow me." We had lunch together and clicked from day one. She was one of my closest friends. I can't understand why she didn't tell me about the baby!' Helen said tearfully.

'She couldn't talk about it,' Kate said. 'The whole thing was just too traumatic! Poor darling. She also had a botched caesarean. That's why she never went out with guys, said she didn't know how she'd explain the great scar on her bloated stomach.'

Helen spoke softly, 'That was something I never understood because lots of guys wanted to take her out. Anne, remember Larry? He just about creamed his jeans every time he saw her, but he couldn't persuade her to go out with him. Other things are falling into place now. Communal change rooms, she always avoided them, and she didn't want to go to the public baths in Japan. The time she went to China, she insisted on paying the single supplement. Oh, the poor dear, living a huge part of your life as one big lie – how horrible.'

'It *is*,' Kate agreed.

Helen's grief then turned to anger, and her anger turned to rage. 'What was done to those women is unforgivable. The way they were sent away in disgrace to breed for other people! There's not a word in the English dictionary to describe the cruelty – you'd have to invent a new one! How about "nappicide": "the de-humanising of women". Is that a good definition? And the people who took their babies should be put in the stocks till they understand the atrocities they've committed. Someone should apologise to these women – not that it'd do much good. The Prime Minister should hold a National Day of Shame! Every Australian should acknowledge this shameful part of our history!'

'Maybe I should go and shoot Dawn Flaherty. Maybe I should knock on her door and, when she opens it, blast her head off. How many bullets do we have left? It must be ninety-three. I could kill ninety-two

Right to Esse scum and then shoot myself! What would it matter? Your life eventually ends; it doesn't matter if you end it sooner. Like people who leave a football match early: they know, or they don't care, what the score is. They want to leave early to avoid the traffic.'

'Where are you going to find ninety-two Right to Esse people?' Anne asked her.

'I'll go door knocking. I'll say I'm conducting a survey and ask the question outright: "Do you believe in abortion on demand?" And if they say, "No", I shoot 'em!'

'I'm feeling guilty I promised Alison I'd put Dawn Flaherty in the gaol,' Kate admitted. 'Maybe she was right: it is a shame to waste the hole. We should've thrown some more low-life forms in it! I should be the one to shoot Flaherty. I've nothing to live for. Fuck the world!'

Anne had never heard Kate swear let alone use the f-word. She didn't know what to make of the conversation they were having. These things were being said in a fit of rage, weren't they? She thought back to the first day all four women had gone to Socamora and thought how what they'd said in a fit of rage had come true. She sat beside Helen and put her arm around her. Helen and Kate, much to her relief, recovered from their outbursts of anger.

'Poor Alison!' Helen sobbed. 'All those years carrying that awful burden! Always creating some reason why she wouldn't go out with some guy: Frank had halitosis; Ray slurped his tea; James had no manners; Steve talked too loud in public; Tom had a comb-over; Terry danced with three legs. What a wasted life! What a fucking wasted life! Sorry about the language, Anne!'

'That's okay. Why don't the three of us go for a walk? The fresh air will do us good.'

The walk did prove to be therapeutic. When they returned home, they ordered some pizzas to be delivered.

Later in the night, Kerrie phoned to tell Helen and Kate that she and her mother were seeing a funeral celebrant at ten o'clock the next day and asked them to come.

When they arrived at the celebrant's office, Kerrie told them she was waiting for Margot, one of Alison's work colleagues. 'I have to face it: somebody – or somebodies – will have to say a few things about Alison. Maybe I should talk about her compassion for girls who were sent off to stud farms to breed for lovely, caring, barren shits. Maybe I should say, "In lieu of flowers, please make donations to Rebus." And "If there's anyone here who's a member of or supports the Right to Esse, you're not welcome at this funeral! Get! Piss off – now!"'

'Kerrie, be reasonable!' her mother said. 'You *know* you can't say things like that!'

'Don't underestimate me, Mum! Loathing can cause people to lose their reason!'

Just as Helen was about to ask Kerrie what Rebus was, Margot arrived. Kate, Helen and Margot agreed to write something about Alison and have the celebrant read it out; all agreed they'd break down if they had to read it. The celebrant suggested they sing two of Alison's favourite songs and that after the service, they have morning tea on the lawn adjacent to the funeral parlour.

After Kate, Helen and Margot left, Kerrie and her mother felt they'd put together an acceptable funeral for Alison, and Kerrie had agreed not to tell the Right to Esse to piss off. However, Helen was adamant she was going to write about Alison's compassion for women who'd had their studies or careers – and in many cases their life – ruined by having been forced to be surrogates.

Alison's funeral was held on Friday, and Anne estimated there were about 130 people there. She found herself wondering how many mourners would be at her own funeral. *The number of people at your funeral's hardly anything to worry about!* she told herself.

The Monday after the funeral, Anne left work early. She wanted to be home before Helen because Helen wasn't coping with Alison's death, and Anne felt that the less time Helen was on her own the better. She was therefore surprised to find Helen at home when she got there. 'How long have you been home?' she asked her.

'About an hour,' Helen answered. 'I had a run-in with Shelley, so I came home.'

'What happened?'

'Shelley came into my office and told me how sorry she was to hear Alison had passed away – "passed away", to use her expression. People seem to think it's less painful to say someone's "passed away" than to say someone's "died". I didn't want to talk to her, so I just said I was very upset, and I was glad Kate was coming to see me tonight. I'd once told her how I'd met Kate through Alison. Then she said that God had sent Kate because he knew he had to take Alison: "When God closes a door, he opens a window." So I asked her why he closed the friggin' door in the first place, and she said that one day I'd find the reason – everything happens for a reason. I was pretty angry by that stage, and I said, "What if your daughter – correction: the woman that some poor single girl was forced to give up – was raped? What would be the reason for that?" She said that Tammy wouldn't expose herself to that type of danger and most girls who get raped expose themselves to the risk. Well, you can imagine what that did to me! I had to control myself from picking up my in-tray and smashing it over her head!

'I said, "Most girls? What about the nice girls who don't expose themselves to the danger? What's the reason they're raped? So they'll get pregnant and give the likes of you a daughter, you self-righteous supporter of the Right to Esse!" Her face dropped a few centimetres. I knew she'd go running to Maree and get Maree to tell Roger that Helen had said horrible things to her, so I thought I'd get in first. Shelley's a real brown-nose, so I said, "You've upset me, Shelley: Allhue's policy on politics and religion is that they aren't to be brought into the office. I'm thinking of lodging a formal complaint." Now, can you believe this? Shelley started bawling and pleading and saying she didn't mean to upset me, so I told her I wouldn't say anything, and I packed up and came home. Why is it, Anne, that Christians like Shelley are always trying to find reasons for the tragedies that happen in a person's life?'

'I don't know, Helen. It's not Shelley's fault. From other things you've said about her, it's obvious she was brainwashed as a child and she can't distinguish her fear from her faith.'

'But now she's an adult, can't she work things out for herself? Can't she see religion's one giant, adult fairy story and give it the flick?'

'It's not that simple for people who've been brainwashed as children,' Anne pointed out. 'Look at Don; look at the people in Carol's support group at NoFourthR.'

'I guess you're right.'

'What time's Kate coming?' Anne asked.

'Six o'clock, but now I don't feel like cooking.'

'Don't worry,' Anne assured her. 'I'm happy to cook.'

'Thanks, Anne.'

For three weeks after Gary Munkton's disappearance, updates about it had been on the news and in the papers daily. However, as Anne had once told Colleen, people become bored with the same news and want to hear new stories. Two weeks after Alison's funeral, though, another small article about Munkton's vanishing appeared in *The Canberra Envoy*. Anne saw the headline. She read the article and was relieved to learn that the police had had to admit they had no leads in relation to the Honourable Mr Munkton's disappearance. She told Helen, and Helen started to cry as she let herself think about Alison's kidnapping of Munkton. 'All the time, she'd have been saying to herself, "Leave no trails!"'

Anne comforted her and told her it was good news for them and that they should be pleased to read it.

Helen agreed, but she still couldn't think of Alison's kidnapping effort without crying.

Kate

It was now four weeks since Alison's death, but Kate was still grieving and was constantly depressed. One night when Helen was visiting her, she said, 'I'm not sad Alison's dead; I'm sad she didn't die thirty years ago. If Alison and I had died when we were twenty-one, we wouldn't have endured all these years of misery; we would've died after having a short, happy life.

'When Rider Haggard's ten-year-old son died, Thomas Hardy wrote him a letter in which he said, "To be candid, I think the death of a child is never to be really regretted, when one reflects on what he has escaped." When I was at uni, there was a girl a year ahead of me who was killed in a freak boating accident. At the time, everybody said what a tragedy it was, and I agreed. Now, I don't think that way. If I'd been killed in a freak boating accident, everybody would've said the same thing, but if anyone had known the suffering I would've escaped, they'd have said how lucky I'd been.'

She then proceeded to tell Helen she didn't want to go on living. 'Alison's life was so unjust, and so is mine. Two lots of injustice are more than I can take. I get frightened when I think of going through old age on my own; I feel so lonely and sad.'

Although Helen was upset, she tried to console Kate, but Kate was inconsolable.

'I once heard an activist for voluntary euthanasia say, "Life's a party – but if you're not enjoying the party and you know it won't get any better, leave it." I agree with her,' Kate said.

'Kate, please don't say that!' Helen implored her.

'It's true, Helen. Sophocles said, "Death is not the worst thing; rather, it's when one who craves death cannot attain even that wish." I'm not scared of dying. There's nothing after this; there's no God. When I was young and went to Sunday school, I had a Sunday school teacher who talked about this "God of love" who was all-powerful. Well, he can't be both! Not a day in my life goes by that I don't think back to that terrifying night at the quarry and ask God where he was on that night. I prayed to him that night, begged him to save me, but he refused to help me. My life's been a crock of shit. I didn't deserve such a raw deal, and I do want to end it – leave the rotten party.'

'Kate, you don't mean it! You must come home with me: you can't stay on your own.'

'Thank you, Helen. You're one of the kindest people anyone could hope to meet; but going to your place is a temporary fix: tomorrow night I'll be on my own, and I'll be overcome with the same fear and sadness.'

Helen, now in tears and unable to bear seeing Kate that way, said, 'You can stay with Anne and me for a while.'

'Thank you, Helen, but eventually that would end too, and I'd have to return to this house and be lonely, sad and frightened.'

'Temporary fix or not, please come to our place tonight.'

'I'll be okay,' Kate assured her. 'I won't do anything untoward tonight. I promise.'

'Call me tomorrow morning before eight o'clock,' Helen instructed her. 'Make sure you do, otherwise I'll call you at a minute past.'

'I know you will.'

'One more go: are you sure you won't come to our place and stay the night?'

'I'm sure.'

Helen went to her car and drove home, sobbing all the way.

Anne was home and asked her, 'What's up?'

'It's Kate: she's so sad; she talked of suicide.'

'Oh no! Do you think she's serious?' Anne asked in a voice, that revealed she was very worried.

'I don't know.'

'Maybe you shouldn't've left her on her own.'

'She wouldn't come with me,' Helen explained. 'I did everything I could to persuade her to come to our place, but she wouldn't come. She assured me she wouldn't do "anything untoward tonight", to use her words. She said she'd ring me before eight tomorrow morning. If she hasn't rung by one minute past, I'll call her.'

Seeing Kate so sad and hearing her describe her life as a crock of shit had caused Helen to be very upset, and she now had to go to bed feeling extremely depressed. She tossed and turned all night, and although she kept telling herself that Kate would bounce back, she wasn't so sure.

The next morning, Helen woke feeling very groggy. She got up and went about her usual morning procedures, keeping one eye on the clock. When she saw it displaying 8.02 am, she dialled Kate's number and found it engaged. 'Anne!' she yelled. 'Kate's taken the phone off the hook! I'm going to her place!'

'Hang on!' Anne responded. 'Maybe she's genuinely talking to someone!'

'No, I have to go!' Helen insisted. 'That day I drove to Socamora with Keys in the car, I thought, if my heart beats any faster, it'll blow up! But that was nothing compared to how it's beating now!' She raced out the door.

When Kate's house came into view, Helen saw Kate in the front yard waving frantically to her. As soon as the car had stopped, Kate ran up to the car, most apologetic. 'Just as I was about to phone you, my phone rang. I thought it'd be you, so I answered it, but it was Yvonne, one of the kindergarten teachers. She wanted to tell me she wouldn't be in because her son was sick, and she was giving me instructions about what she wanted me to do for the relief teacher, going on about where she'd left the stencil; how many copies she wanted; where the coloured pencils were. I couldn't get rid of her.

'As soon as she hung up, I rang your number. Anne answered and told me you were on your way to Queanbeyan. I felt terrible. I thought of driving to Canberra, hoping I might see you and flag you down. But I thought we might miss each other, which was more than likely, given the divided sections, so I decided the best thing I could do was stay here. I'm so sorry you've come all this way for nothing. I feel really awful.'

'Don't feel bad about it,' Helen said. 'It hasn't been for nothing: you can tell me first-hand how you are.'

'Your arrival's done wonders for me: I realise how much you care. Now, I'd better say goodbye or you'll be late for work.'

One day, Kate announced she was going to apply for a teaching position at Queangolo High School. She'd seen the vacancy advertised in the *Gazette*. The position would be for only twelve months, while one of the teachers was on maternity leave. Kate would have to resign from her current job, but she didn't care, thinking, *Who knows what can happen in twelve months?* She obtained the position and went on to enjoy the teaching; she even talked about selling her house and buying a new, modern townhouse.

In June 1991, before attending a Lawfail meeting, Anne, Helen, Kate and Brett were having dinner with Jim Clunes and some other members of the organisation. When Jim had finished eating, he said, 'I know nothing about the new case. Angus Steele was going to drop off a copy at my house on the weekend, but he phoned to say he hadn't finished preparing it. Well, I'd better go to the function room and ensure all's ready. Helen, could I ask you to take the minutes? Moya Townsend's away.'

'Sure Jim, no problem,' Helen replied.

When Jim entered the function room, he found some other committee members there, but no sign of Angus, who was supposed to bring Mick along, so Mick could present a new case. It was now eight o'clock, so Jim opened the meeting and announced it'd be a short one because the committee had only one update to present, and Mick, who had a new case to present, hadn't shown up.

When Jim had dealt with the standard meeting procedures, he asked Jane Colton to give an update on the Deeta Gerber case. Jane was an active member of Lawfail and a very outspoken supporter of voluntary euthanasia. Deeta had been charged with murder, having removed the feeding tube from her son's stomach. Her son had been completely paralysed and constantly depressed and had wanted his life to end. Partway through the update, Jane informed the audience: 'We're getting tremendous support for this case from Smooth Egress—'

'Excuse me, would you mind if I interrupted?' Olga Mikhailovich called out.

'You already have, Olga,' Jane said in response. 'What do you want to say?'

'Why is this organisation having anything to do with Smooth Egress? As of this minute, I'm no longer a member of Lawfail. I'm leaving immediately, and I predict there'll be a few more who'll follow me.' She picked up her bag and left the room, but despite her prediction, no one else from the Religious Wrong followed suit.

Jane decided to continue: 'As I was saying, we're getting tremendous support for this case from Smooth Egress. Still, our biggest concern is that Justice Michael Kennedy's been appointed to the case. Justice Kennedy is of the same ilk as Olga, who's just stormed out. If ever there was a case for allowing the accused to choose the judge, this is it!

'About two and a half years ago, a man called Keith Davies presented a case at a Lawfail meeting I was attending. He spoke about the need for separation between the church and the law. It's clear what a joke our justice system is if the outcome of a case depends on what the judge's religion is!'

Jim thanked Jane and was about to declare the meeting closed when he saw Angus and Mick rushing through the door. 'Sorry we're late!' Angus said. 'There was a bingle on Farben Drive, and we were held up.'

'As soon as you get your breath, Angus, you can present the new case,' Jim said.

'Thanks, Jim,' Angus replied. 'I haven't had access to a photocopier, so I can't give everyone a copy tonight. I want to introduce Mick Woodlock. His brother Lex was sentenced to eighteen years' gaol for the murder of Colleen O'Day.'

Helen hoped no one detected the slight change in her body temperature and was careful not to make eye contact with Anne or Kate.

'Her body was never found,' Angus stated. 'All the evidence against Lex was circumstantial. The trial was a farce. Mick says his brother mightn't be an angel, but he's not a murderer. Many members of the legal profession aren't happy with the way the trial was conducted. Recently, there was an article about the case in *The Canberra Envoy*. Along with the article was a photo of Mrs O'Day. Now a woman's come forward and said she remembers seeing a woman who looked like Mrs O'Day hopping into the back seat of a car at the car park outside the Cactus Bar. It was a medium, white-coloured car. There was a woman outside the car and a woman in the driver's seat. This woman has a vague picture of the woman who was in the driver's seat, but not of the other woman. Mick, along with lots of other people, knows his brother's not guilty of this murder, and he's asking Lawfail to do all we can to help him prove he's innocent. That's about all I can say.'

A discussion followed, and Brett offered to coordinate the case, which henceforth was to be known as the Lex Woodlock case. Jim then declared the meeting closed.

As Kate and Brett were driving home, they discussed the new case. 'Kate,' Brett said, 'I know Lex Woodlock's not responsible for Colleen O'Day's disappearance.'

'How can you be so sure?' Kate asked him.

'The whole case against him was a joke!'

'That might be so,' Kate conceded, 'but how come you're so sure he had nothing to do with it? Perhaps you know who does have something to do with it. You once said, "I'd like to kill her and make sure no one finds the body."'

'You're not going to hold that against me, are you?' he asked. 'I know I was stupid to say it, but we agreed I wasn't serious at the time. Lex Woodlock's in gaol for a crime he didn't commit. Somewhere out there are two women who know what happened. I'm going to find them. What sort of a people *are* they? How can they live with themselves knowing someone's in gaol for a crime they committed? I tell you again, Kate, I'm going to find those women! Mick said that the police are putting together an identikit of the woman who was driving the car.'

'What if the identikit resembles several women?' Kate queried. 'How can you be so sure you've got the guilty one? Due to circumstantial evidence, you might get the wrong woman. An identikit's not much to go on.'

'It's a start,' Brett declared, however. 'I'll find them. You know how passionate Penny Jacobs is about the Dr Bloomer case?'

'Yes.'

'I'm the same about Lex Woodlock. I've read all the court reports, and I really believe he's innocent!'

'That's good, Brett. However, if I think you get the wrong woman, can I tell the cops what you said to me when we first talked about Colleen or the fact that Toni Crawford was mugged on the weekend you visited Tom in Wagga?'

'What! Pardon?'

'The weekend you went to Wagga to visit Tom, Toni Crawford was mugged.'

'I know. How do *you* know?' Brett asked.

'Alison saw it in *The Canberra Envoy*. How do *you* know?'

'Tom told me. It was in the *Wagga Wragg*. Kate, do you really think I'd do something like that?'

'I don't know, Brett,' Kate replied cautiously.

'I can't believe you could think I'd mug anyone!'

Kate laughed. 'You mean it wasn't you and Tom, and all this time I've been thinking what great blokes you were to rough up that despicable so-and-so? Now you've gone down in my estimation!'

Brett also had a laugh and said, 'I must tell Tom!'

They both then had a good chuckle. Nevertheless, Kate maintained a niggling feeling it was Brett and Tom who'd mugged Toni Crawford. They both loathed anyone who was associated with the Right to Esse and Kate had first-hand knowledge of what loathing could drive a person to do. She looked over at Brett. He was driving so she could see only his profile, yet she thought the look on his face was the same look she'd seen when he was telling her he hadn't gone to Tijuana. *Brett's a lovely man,* she said to herself. *Telling an outright lie would be difficult for him.*

When Kate arrived home, she rang Anne and Helen.

Helen answered, saying, 'I'm glad you rang because I was going to ring you. How do you feel about the fact that Brett's taking the case on?'

'Can I come over tomorrow night to talk about it?' Kate replied.

'Of course.'

Kate went to Anne and Helen's house the following night. Helen opened the door; Anne wasn't home. 'Come on in, Kate,' she said. 'So, do you think we should be worried about the Lex Woodlock case?'

'Brett says he's going to "find those two women". He also said the police are putting together an identikit of the woman who was driving the car. I hope we don't open the paper tomorrow and see an identikit of Alison.'

'Kate, don't say that! It's too horrible to think of!'

'Sorry! I wonder how the woman could've seen Colleen at the Cactus car park.'

'Did you have the courtesy light on?' Helen asked Kate.

'Yes, we did. We discussed the idea, but we thought it might look a bit suspicious if we asked Colleen to get into a dark car.'

'I agree.'

'I saw Colleen's courtesy light go on when she opened the door,' Kate continued, 'and she seemed to take ages to close the door.'

'Can you remember seeing anyone walking in the car park, or a car arriving or leaving? Its headlights might've shone on Colleen's face.'

'No,' Kate replied. 'The car park was as quiet as a mouse. Well, we thought it was; maybe we were wrong.'

'Well, there's nothing we can do about it,' Helen decided.

'What does Anne think?' Kate asked her.

'She's not concerned. She's more concerned about Colleen's kids. Anne sometimes takes herself on a little guilt trip about the fact that Colleen's kids lost their mother. I told her they were better off having no mother than a mother who fills their heads with nonsense.'

'Brett can work on the Lex Woodlock case,' Kate said. 'I'm going to concentrate on the Brian Cooper case.'

'I'm sorry I won't be able to come to the protest; I'm attending an off-site forum for two days. I don't think Anne can go either. She mumbled something about a prior commitment.'

'That's okay, Helen. I'll go home now. I didn't want to discuss anything about Lex Woodlock over the phone.'

'Fair enough. I'll see you out.'

Lawfail was now following the Brian Cooper case very carefully. Cooper and his girlfriend had purchased a new townhouse in Queanbeyan, and on the night of the purchase, they'd gone to their local pub to celebrate. The girlfriend had gone home just before eleven o'clock, but Brian had gone on to a mate's place and continued to party. He'd been very intoxicated when he left, at about two o'clock the next morning, and had gone home to the wrong townhouse. Having found the door unlocked, he'd entered, gone upstairs and raped the woman who was asleep in the bedroom. He'd been found guilty but given a suspended sentence. The judge, Justice Botham, had said the offence was Cooper's first; it hadn't been premeditated; Cooper had been under the influence of alcohol at the time; he'd shown remorse for the act; and his employer had said he was a hard-working, honest, reliable employee.

Kate couldn't believe the judge's summation.

A psychiatrist had said the victim was so traumatised she was having trouble making rational decisions and that her boss was considering she was no longer in a fit state to sit on the company's board. The woman had said she believed that her career was over.

Lawfail had organised for a protest to take place outside the courthouse and had set the time for it to commence at 12.45 pm so that people could attend it during their lunch hour.

Kate wanted Justice Botham to experience fear and didn't tell anyone what she intended to do. She planned to mount a protest outside his house one night. She thought he'd be terrified at having a mob outside his house in the early hours of the morning.

The first thing she had to do was publicise the protest. She thought about this for a long time, then an idea came to her. Four months earlier, she'd purchased a self-inking stamp whereby you could make your own stamp. She'd made a stamp bearing her name, address and phone number, but she'd never used it because she thought it looked untidy. She made the following stamp:

Show anger at Botham
Be outside his house
1.30 am, Wed 7th Aug
12 Jutta St. Queanbeyan
(memorise, destroy paper)

She then stamped it on two hundred pieces of paper, each piece measuring 6 by 3.5 centimetres.

Now she had to dispose of the stamp and decided that the safest method was to throw it in the river. At dusk, she drove to a secluded spot and threw the stamp in the Queanbeyan River.

She took the pile of leaflets to Lawfail's protest meeting, split the pile in two and subtly handed half to the woman next to her, saying, 'Take one and pass them on.' She then moved quickly to the back of the crowd and did the same there. She then left the protest, not knowing whether anyone would say anything about the notice on her little leaflets.

She watched the news that night and read the paper the next day. The protest had made headlines, but there was no mention of the fact that any notices had been distributed.

At 1.00 am on Wednesday, Kate decided to drive to Justice Botham's house to see whether anyone had turned up to the protest. She drove past the house at 1.25 am and was surprised to see five people standing on the footpath outside it. She drove down a nearby side street, parked her car and walked to the house. As she was arriving, she found that two men in balaclavas were leaving. One of them said, 'We've cut the telephone wire and turned off the electricity – that's our contribution.'

Within ten minutes, twenty or so people were outside the judge's house, and someone suggested, 'Let's scare the living daylights out of him!'

'Good idea!' came the universal reply.

One of the men went to a window – most probably the window of the main bedroom – and proceeded to tap on it, calling out, 'Wake up, Gerry! This is our first offence! We're a group of hard-working, honest, reliable people, but we're *not* intoxicated!'

Kate saw that someone had broken the lock on the back door and that people were now inside the house. She went in also. She and one of the other women had a torch. Ten people were now crammed into Justice Botham's bedroom.

The judge and his wife were clearly petrified.

One woman yelled, 'How does it feel to find intruders in your bedroom?'

Another shouted, 'How would you like a broom handle rammed up your arse?'

'Forget the broom!' another woman yelled. 'How about a shovel?'

Kate then saw that the woman, who was standing next to her, was holding a shovel.

Justice Botham was now pleading.

Kate yelled at him, 'You little creep! Not so brave now, are we? How does it feel to be on the receiving end?'

'How does the "end" feel "receiving it"? Come on, guys. Turn him over!' the woman holding the shovel shouted.

Everyone roared laughing.

'No!' the justice screamed.

'Don't bother then, guys,' the woman said. 'It seems he doesn't like that sort of thing! You're just lucky I'm a nice person, judge! You remember to tell all your judge friends I'm a nice person, hard-working and reliable! This is my *first* offence – although I'd call it a civic duty, not an offence. But I have to be honest: I'm *not* remorseful. I think I'll get a psychiatrist to say you're so traumatised by this incident you're having trouble making rational decisions and you're not in a fit state to sit on the bench!'

'You won't be in a fit state to sit on any bench if I get hold of that shovel!' one of the men yelled at the judge.

Again, everyone roared laughing.

'That'll be the end of your career!' the man added.

'And your rear!' another man put in.

The group was now hysterical, and Kate was on cloud nine.

Someone saw that the next-door neighbour's lights were on and said, 'Let's go: the cops'll be here soon.'

Kate was the last one out of the house, and two police officers arrived just as she and two other women were running towards the gate. One of the police officers was just about to grab one of the women. Kate picked up a chair and hurled it at him, knocking him over. The woman escaped. The woman who'd been carrying the shovel now dropped it, and Kate picked it up. 'Run! Run!' she yelled to the woman. The police officer was about to catch the woman, but Kate tripped him with the shovel. He got to his feet and grabbed Kate. Kate saw that everyone except her had escaped.

The police officers drove Kate to the local police station and charged her with breaking and entering, assaulting a police officer and hindering arrest. She spent the night in the lockup.

The next morning, the officer on duty gave her something to eat and allowed her to make two phone calls. 'I suggest you make one to a solicitor,' he added.

'I only want to make one call,' Kate declared and phoned work to tell her colleagues she wouldn't be in.

'When did the solicitor say he'd be here?' the police officer asked her.

'I didn't phone a solicitor. I don't know any solicitors.'

'We can provide you with some names,' the officer suggested.

'I don't want to phone a solicitor!' Kate responded.

'Then you're a very foolish woman!' the officer said.

'That's your opinion!' Kate shot back.

At ten o'clock, the senior sergeant arrived and began the interrogation. He also advised Kate to get legal advice, and once again she refused.

'What are the names of the other people who were with you when you broke into Justice Botham's house?' the sergeant asked her.

'I don't know.'

'What do you mean you don't know?'

'Exactly that. I went on my own. I didn't tell anybody I was going.'

'How come all those other people were there?'

'Ask them!'

'How come you all showed up at Justice Botham's house at one thirty in the morning?'

'I went to the protest meeting outside the courthouse the other day. I was standing there when I felt a nudge from behind me. A man put what felt like a small notepad in my hand and said, "Take one of these notices and pass the rest on." So I took one and passed the rest to the woman beside me and told her to do the same. I put the little bit of paper in my pocket. I didn't read it till I got home from work that afternoon. It was a notice about a protest at Judge Botham's house at one thirty in the morning on Wednesday. I wanted to show what I thought of Botham, so I turned up outside his house at one thirty.'

'And you mean to tell me you didn't see the person who gave you the piece of paper?'

'Yes,' Kate answered. 'He was behind me. It all happened so quickly.'

About mid-afternoon, the police allowed Kate to go home. She took a taxi to where she'd parked her car the previous night and was pleased to see it was still there. She hopped in and headed for home; she made a detour to the corner shop to purchase a newspaper.

When she arrived home, she took the mail from the letterbox, unlocked the front door and went inside. She couldn't identify how she was feeling, but she did know she was hungry and in need of a shower.

She opened the paper but found nothing in it about the break-in, so she realised that the paper had already been printed by the time the press heard about the incident. She decided to eat lunch, have a shower and sit down in her lounge room to contemplate her future. She knew she wouldn't get away with this one; it was very serious. She'd probably be tried by a jury; the judge would instruct the jurors to find her guilty and she'd be sent to gaol.

It was almost five o'clock now. She turned on the television to watch the five o'clock news. The invasion of Justice Botham's home was the headline story, and she was named. She waited for the phone to ring, wondering who the first caller would be. She knew that most of her friends watched the six-thirty or seven o'clock news, so she was surprised when a knock came on the door at five thirty.

It was Mr Basset, the school principal, and he said, 'Kate, I've just come to see whether you're all right. I was concerned you might be ill, and you live alone, so I thought I'd check to see whether you needed anything.'

'Really?' Kate replied. 'Ms Callaghan lives alone. Did you visit her last time she called in sick?'

'Er, no ... I thought you ... I suppose it's because you're a relatively new staff member ...'

Liar! Kate thought to herself. 'No,' she said. 'I'm fine; I don't need anything.' She didn't know whether to invite him in. She didn't want to but felt rude talking to him at the front door. She thought he wouldn't come into the house anyway: he was a very conservative man and wouldn't want anyone to think he'd been alone with Ms Scott. 'Do you want to come in?'

He hesitated and replied, 'Perhaps I should: there's something I want to ask you.'

'Well, come in then.' She directed him to the lounge room and said, 'Take a seat. Would you like a cup of tea or coffee?'

'No, thank you, Kate ... Kate, I heard on the five o'clock news that a Catherine Margaret Scott had been charged with breaking into Justice Botham's house.'

Kate knew that her school-teaching days were now over, so in response, she asked him, quite brusquely, 'Why didn't you say that's the reason you came here, making out you came to see whether I was okay when you probably couldn't care less if I was dead or alive?'

'That's not true, Kate. I *do* care about my staff.'

'Is that a fact?' she mocked.

'Yes.'

'You hid that fact well when Mr Johnson was battling with depression.'

'That was a very difficult situation for me,' he said in his defence.

'Well, my situation's not difficult: I'm innocent till proven guilty.'

'It's not that simple, Kate.'

'Why not?' she asked curtly. 'Just because I've been accused of a crime doesn't mean I'm guilty. I could accuse you of something, but that doesn't mean you're guilty.'

'What do you mean?'

'Exactly that! After all, we've been alone together in my house. I could go down to the cop shop and accuse you of assault, but that doesn't mean you're guilty!'

'But Kate, you've been charged.'

'I could put forward a good-enough case to have *you* charged.'

'Kate, what are you saying?'

'I think you heard!'

Mr Basset looked as if he was about to pass out. There was a painful silence.

I've said all I want to say, Kate said to herself.

Mr Basset broke the silence: 'Kate, it'd be best all round if you—'

He was interrupted by a knock on the door. Kate went to answer it and found Brett standing there.

Mr Basset nearly toppled off his chair when he saw that the visitor was Brett. Kate noticed Mr Basset's discomfort and assumed he had seen Brett on television. Three weeks earlier, as a publicity officer for Smooth Egress, Brett had been on television discussing a very controversial case involving the Robbins family.

Kate introduced the two men.

Mr Basset then rose to go, announcing, 'I'd better go home.'

'No,' Kate insisted. 'Don't go! We haven't resolved your problem!'

'I don't think it'd be appropriate to discuss it in front of your friend,' Mr Basset said.

'We can discuss it in front of Brett,' Kate replied. 'He's very understanding. Brett, just before you arrived, Mr Basset was saying how much easier it'd be for him if I resigned. Well, he didn't put it that way, but that's what he really meant. He was saying, "It'd be best all round." Don't you just love that expression? Whenever a person uses that expression, what he or she really means is: "It'd be best for me, but I don't give a rat's rectum about you!"'

'Kate,' Mr Basset said firmly, 'that's most unfair of you to say that.'

'Well, what *did* you mean? How can it be best for me if I resign? What do I live on?'

'I was going to suggest you take some leave.'

'What *sort* of leave? You know that teachers can only take rec leave in the school holidays, and I don't have any long-service leave. The only other type of leave is leave without pay, which means the question's still raised: what do I live on?'

'Kate, you know I'll have to contact the Department of Education about this matter.'

'No,' she replied, angrily, 'I *don't* know – I can't see why *you* can't resolve it!'

'What will the parents think?' he asked her. 'Try to see it from my side. Now I must go.'

Kate saw him out and closed the door.

'Pathetic old dork!' she said to Brett. 'He has no guts. Always worrying about "what the parents will say". Anyway, Brett, how are *you*?'

'My problems seem small compared with yours.'

'Oh, Brett, I'm not worried. The thrill of seeing Judge Botham nearly crap himself is beyond description. It'll keep me on a high for the rest of my life.'

'I can't see how you can get out of this,' Brett stated.

'You never know: I might get the jury's sympathy or get a suspended sentence – unexpected things can happen in a trial.'

Brett continued with his serious tone. 'It said on the news that you attacked a policeman with a shovel.'

'No, I didn't attack him. I used it to trip him.'

'Why?'

'Because he was about to catch the woman who'd been standing next to me in Botham's bedroom. I was like Horatius holding the bridge: I fought off the cops till everyone had escaped! Now, let's not talk about it. How are things with you? As I've said before, I think the way you presented the case for the Robbins family on telly was brilliant.'

'Going on TV and saying those things, I can hardly believe I did it,' Brett said. 'I feel as if I've come out of the closet.'

'Well done, Brett!'

Brett had been on a current affairs show to explain some of the Smooth Egress members' stance in relation to the Robbins family. Smooth Egress believes that anyone who is incurably ill should be able to end his or her life if he or she wished to. However, in relation to the Robbins family issue, the organisation was divided. The Robbins family, a couple and their twelve-year-old daughter, had been the victims of a home invasion that was too horrific to comprehend. The father had been on television and said that the family hadn't slept properly since the invasion. He said their daughter was so traumatised, she couldn't be left alone. All three family members were terrified and depressed all the time. He said they would never heal and begged Smooth Egress to send them some Nembutal. Brett had said that Smooth Egress wouldn't supply the family with the Nembutal, although many members, including himself, would like to help the Robbins family end their suffering. Someone had supplied the family with Nembutal, however, and Brett was now the prime suspect.

'I'm expecting it all to blow over soon,' he said. 'The cops have been hounding me for three weeks, but of course they can't pin anything on me. They won't be able to pin anything on anyone: whoever sent the Nembutal wouldn't've left any trails.

'I'm not as popular as I used to be. Some of the parents have complained to Ellen.' Ellen Kyte was the principal of Dolmar Primary School, where Brett worked. 'Some of them think I should be stood down until the police investigation's complete. "Stood down" – what they really mean is "dismissed", "sacked". As you know, Ellen's such a *strong* person. She sent a letter home to every parent, stating very firmly I hadn't been charged with, let alone found guilty of, any wrongdoing. She wrote in the letter that she'd heard defamatory statements from some parents about a staff member, and she reminded them of the seriousness about making that type of statement. I *love* Ellen: she's been *so* supportive.'

'It'd be different if Jack Basset was the principal,' Kate said. 'He'd be getting the parents on side, writing to all the politicians who are pro-life, and you'd be out the door. It's disgusting how a person's religious beliefs can dictate the path of another person's life.'

'That's true,' Brett agreed. 'One parent wrote to Ellen telling her, "The Lord decides when he takes us." She showed me the letter. Ellen said she felt like writing back and asking her whether the Lord also decides when a twelve-year-old girl will be gang-raped in her own home and her parents and pet dog tortured.'

'Changing the subject,' Kate said, 'how's the Lex Woodlock case going? I haven't seen the identikit of the woman in the paper.'

'No. I thought it would've appeared by now. Keep a lookout for it.'

'I certainly will,' Kate said, knowing full well why she would be keeping a lookout for it.

'Well, I'd better go home. Let me know if I can do anything for you.'

'Thanks, Brett.' She saw him out, said goodbye to him and wondered who, if anyone, would be the next caller.

That evening, many of Kate's friends came to visit her, and she received a phone call from Mr Basset, who instructed her not to go to work the following day. Kate knew it was now just a matter of time before she would be dismissed. Six days later, she received the official notification from the Department of Education. The 'guilty or innocent?' verdict was irrelevant; as far as the Department of Education was concerned, Kate had engaged in conduct inappropriate for a school teacher.

The next day, reporters and photographers from the *Queanbeyan Hermes* and *The Canberra Envoy* were outside Kate's house. She answered their questions, and they were gone within half an hour.

The following day, her photo was on the front page of both papers. From the photos, you could tell she was an extremely attractive woman and very photogenic. She looked gorgeous in both photos.

Anne thought the photos would be an aid to getting Kate some public sympathy, knowing that nobody likes an ugly woman. Anne looked at the photograph of Kate in *The Canberra Envoy* and found herself thinking that the woman in it looked hardly anything like the Kate whom Alison had introduced her to three years earlier. Now, Kate was almost glowing.

All Kate's friends were amazed at how calm she was about everything: losing her job, facing the impending trial and knowing she'd almost certainly be given a hefty gaol sentence.

After receiving her dismissal notice, the first thing Kate did was go to what was commonly known as the Dole House, and there she saw a lovely woman who told her that if she hadn't found employment within the next four weeks, she'd be entitled to unemployment benefits. She'd need to go in and fill out a form, and she'd receive a cheque in the mail within two weeks. She felt good when she heard that. She had no debts, so she knew she'd be able to survive by accepting the dole and drawing on her savings.

Her friends were very supportive, and they visited her regularly. During one of Helen's visits, Helen was surprised to see that Kate had a copy of *Mailex*, a magazine that was considered a bit sleazy. She couldn't resist asking Kate why she'd bought it.

'I buy it because it has a huge crossword puzzle in the back,' Kate explained. 'I love doing crosswords, and I sure have plenty of time to do them. I agree it's a bit of a low-grade magazine – all the things you can get through mail order. There's always a double page of war memorabilia. It's hard to imagine what sort of people buy some of the stuff. For example, would you believe you can get a replica of the phial Herman Goering had his cyanide capsule in? He's supposed to have hidden it in his rectum. Who'd want *that*? It even has the dimensions: twelve millimetres in diameter by forty-four millimetres in length. The mag costs $3.50, so I read some of the contents, to get my money's worth.'

Four days after the invasion of the judge's house, *The Canberra Envoy* and several of the smaller local papers featured an identikit picture of a woman who the police believed to be one of the people who'd abducted Colleen

O'Day. To the relief of Kate, Helen and Anne, at first glance, the face didn't look like Alison's. All three women studied the image carefully and agreed that if you knew Alison well, you'd be able to see a slight resemblance.

'We only see this resemblance because we know it *could* be Alison. I don't think anyone else who knew her would see any resemblance,' Anne stated.

'I agree. I don't think we should be worried about this, and if anyone *did* see a resemblance, I don't think they'd be game to say so,' Helen added.

Helen couldn't believe how long everything was taking for Kate's trial date to be set, although according to her legal friends in Lawfail, things were moving very quickly.

The night before the trial, Helen decided to visit Kate and found that Brett and another friend, Sonya, were there.

Helen was amazed at how calm Kate was. She knew that Kate would go to gaol, and when she thought of Kate being in gaol, she was reduced to tears. She used up all her tissues. Kate told her there was a box of tissues on her dressing table. When Helen went to the bedroom, she was shocked to see what she decided could only be a replica of the phial that Herman Goering had kept his cyanide in. She didn't know what to make of it. She wanted to open it to see what was inside it, but she was afraid to, thinking that if it had any powder in it, the powder would spill out, and Kate would know it'd been opened.

The thought then crossed Helen's mind that Kate might have 'tried it out', so she didn't want to touch it. Next, she thought about the phial's dimensions: were these types of phial 'one size fits all', could Kate use it if she wanted to? She couldn't ask Kate right then, because Brett and Sonya were there with her, so she decided to wait until they'd left.

However, Brett and Sonya were showing no signs of wanting to leave, and Helen was getting tired. She had an early start at work the next day and she had to give a presentation to some potential big clients. She'd gone to visit Kate to apologise for not being able to attend the first day of the trial. She said her goodbyes and hopped in her car. As she was driving home, all she could think about was the phial. The sight of it haunted her.

Kate had been charged with breaking and entering, attempted assault on Justice Botham, assaulting constables Duggan and Ryan, hindering an arrest – you name it – and she was to be tried by a jury. Malcolm had offered to defend her, but she'd refused. Everyone had been surprised at how fast the case was moving, and the reason it was moving quickly was that a judge had been attacked. The members of the legal fraternity had been furious, raving on about things such as 'people taking the law into their own hands'. They'd wanted to get Kate in gaol as soon as they could. The police had also been furious because they hadn't been able to catch any other people who'd taken part in the home invasion. They'd viewed, many times, the television footage of the protest that had taken place outside the courthouse and found that each participant they were able to identify had an alibi. The police had received two anonymous calls from women advising them that not everyone who'd taken part in the home invasion might've been at the protest outside the courthouse because some participants had received the notice in their letterbox. Kate deduced that the two women could only have been Anne and Helen.

The trial turned out to be almost a floorshow, and the trial judge, Justice Fox, was livid about that fact. He'd barely finished reading the charges when one of the jurors who'd already been sworn in stood up and spoke out of turn. He asked to be removed from the jury, saying he'd read all about the case in the *Queanbeyan Hermes,* and he now felt he couldn't give an impartial judgement because he thought Judge Botham 'had deserved what he got'. Another juror said she felt the same, whereupon several people in the public gallery gave a clap.

Justice Fox then dismissed the jury, the trial was aborted, and a new trial was to take place at a date yet to be set.

Helen wondered how long it would take to set the date.

Helen desperately wanted to know why Kate had bought the phial, but she didn't want to ask her over the phone. She decided she'd go to Queanbeyan, taking a chance Kate would be home, and ask her.

Kate seemed surprised to see her and said, 'Come in. I didn't expect you.'

Helen got straight to the point: 'Kate, there's something I want to know, and I hope you'll tell me. The night I went to get some tissues from your bedroom, I couldn't help noticing you had the Herman Goering replica phial on your dressing table.'

Kate laughed and replied, 'You came all the way to Queanbeyan to ask me that? I bought it as a symbol of *power* – not the megalomaniacal type of power Goering wanted – the power to control my own destiny. I won't give anyone the satisfaction or pleasure of deciding my fate!'

'What do you mean?' Helen asked her.

'Exactly that! It's symbolic, Helen: there's nothing *in* the phial. Look!' She opened the phial to show Helen it was empty.

'That's good,' Helen remarked and decided not to press her friend for any more information.

The new trial date was set – the sixteenth of October – and this time, the jury was sworn in without any problems. Kate saw she had many friends in the public gallery and smiled continually at them, much to the judge's annoyance.

The charges were read out to Kate, and she was asked how she pleaded. 'Not guilty,' she replied in relation to each one.

The judge then advised her to get legal representation and said he was willing to adjourn the proceedings to give her time to obtain a lawyer.

'If I'm guilty of a crime, I'm guilty,' she answered. 'When you tell me, I should have a solicitor to represent me, you spell out to me that something's inherently wrong with our legal system. Are you suggesting I might be "less guilty" if I have legal representation?'

It was clear that the judge didn't like Kate's stance one bit.

Every time the prosecutor spoke to Kate, Kate looked up at the ceiling. He was obviously finding her attitude very annoying and finally asked her, 'Is there any reason you can't look at me when I'm speaking to you, Miss Scott?'

'Yes, the spider veins in your nose make me feel ill.'

'The accused will refrain from such remarks!' Justice Fox said angrily.

'Just answering the question, Your Honour,' Kate responded. 'I'm telling the truth, the whole truth, and nothing but the truth.'

The prosecutor was obviously embarrassed, not to mention angry, and he shouted his next question at Kate.

She embarrassed him again by taking out a tissue and using it to wipe her arm and face, indicating he'd 'sprayed' her. Then she said, 'May I remind you I'm not hard of hearing? No. I *don't* know who turned off the electricity or cut the telephone wires.'

The prosecutor replied, 'May I remind you of the seriousness of perjury?'

'No. I'm aware of the seriousness of perjury.'

The prosecutor threw his papers down on his table and announced, 'No further questions, Your Honour.'

Justice Fox then addressed Kate and said, 'You may step down, Miss Scott. You are representing yourself, so are there any witnesses you wish to call?'

'Yes. I'd like to call Derek Botham.'

'You'll refer to the witness as Justice Botham,' the judge told her.

Justice Botham then took the stand, held the Bible and promised, 'The evidence I shall give will be the truth, the whole truth, and nothing but the truth. So help me God.'

Kate added, 'He wasn't much help on the seventh of August!'

On hearing the remark, Justice Fox gave Kate a stern rebuke, and the people in the public gallery tittered.

Kate addressed the witness and launched her questioning: 'I suggest to you, Justice Botham, that on the night of Tuesday the sixth of August 1991 or the morning of Wednesday the seventh of August 1991, you hired two men to cut your telephone wire and turn off your electricity.'

'That's ridiculous!' Justice Botham replied in a very loud voice.

Kate then made reference to the case that had prompted the attack, but the judge disallowed the reference. It now looked as if the trial would be over very quickly. Kate had been caught red-handed; she couldn't deny it. And she wasn't putting up much of a defence. It seemed every magistrate, judge and politician had spoken about the need for judges to make their judgments without fear of reprisals.

At three forty-five, the judge adjourned the case until nine thirty the following morning.

Kate's friends and supporters then gathered outside the courthouse, but Kate made it clear to all of them that she wanted to be on her own. The courthouse was within walking distance of her home, so she'd walked there, and although many people were now offering to drive her home, she said she wanted to walk. She said goodbye to everyone and walked away. When some of her friends saw her walking away on her own, they were reduced to tears.

That night, Helen rang Kate, but Kate didn't answer the phone.

Day two in court opened without any dramas, and by eleven fifty-two, it was all over. Everyone was expecting there to be a verdict by close of day.

The court was adjourned. Helen and Anne waited for Kate to join them. After fifteen minutes, however, it was obvious she wasn't coming. They went to a local café for lunch, although Helen felt so sick with worry for Kate, she didn't think she could eat.

While they were having lunch there, a woman of about Kate's age approached them and said, 'May I join you? I saw you talking to Kate outside the courthouse this morning. I assume you're close friends. I was at uni with Kate.'

'Please join us,' Helen responded. 'We've known Kate for about three and a half years. In that time, we've become very close.'

'My name's Fran Craig,' the woman said. 'As I've already told you, I was at uni with Kate. Like so many people you meet, I lost contact with her when we left uni. She obviously hasn't changed. She was always the life of the party, went in all the uni reviews and shows. She and Alison Roberts, what a pair! Did you ever meet her? No, I guess not.'

Helen wasn't in the mood to tell Fran that Alison had been one of her best friends and had died of cancer about six months beforehand, so she let the question pass and allowed Fran to continue reminiscing.

'Those two could turn any function into fun! I remember, one Saturday night, one of the girls organised a party at her parents' place. It looked like it was going to be a big flop. We were all standing around looking stupid and feeling painful, when Kate and Alison arrived. I don't know what it was about them – they had some sort of *magic*. Suddenly, we were all dancing and singing. Kate was – still is, I guess – a fantastic singer. She was pretty competent on the guitar too, a great folk singer. I loved to hear her sing … I wonder what time we should go back to the courthouse. The judge didn't give a time.'

Anne and Helen were surprised to hear that Kate was a good singer and guitarist, never having heard her sing or play; they wondered whether she even *had* a guitar. Helen felt only sadness and anger when she thought about what Fran had said. Poor Kate, her confidence for singing in public must've been destroyed due to the trauma; she'd been robbed of so much.

At one forty-five, the three women then made their way back to the courthouse, knowing that the jurors were expected to deliver their verdict sometime that afternoon. Helen was beside herself with anxiety.

What happened next was all a bit hazy. Kate wasn't under tight security because having honoured her bail conditions to the letter, she wasn't considered a flight risk. Most of the reporters and Kate's friends were milling around outside the courthouse. It was obvious that something was wrong inside, but no one knew what it was. Then came the sound of an ambulance siren, and soon the ambulance was in sight, siren blaring and lights flashing. It stopped outside the courthouse, and two ambulance officers raced inside.

'I hope it's Judge Fox!' Fran said to Helen. 'I hope the overweight old dork's had a heart attack!'

No one was allowed inside the courthouse. About five minutes later, the ambulance officers collected a stretcher from the van and went back inside the courthouse. By then, the police had arrived and had told everyone to move away.

One reporter called out, 'We're waiting for the verdict.'

Helen had a sickening feeling that something had happened to Kate. She recalled the conversation about the phial and could hear Kate saying, 'I won't give anyone the satisfaction or pleasure of deciding my fate.' She turned to Anne and said, 'I think it's Kate.' She couldn't bring herself to say the word 'suicide'.

One ambulance officer came out the door and headed for the van, and Helen rushed up to him and asked him whether it was Kate, but he ignored her; he hopped in the van and backed it as close to the back door of the courthouse as he could. Most of the crowd moved towards the back door.

Five minutes later, the officers emerged carrying the stretcher, which obviously had a body on it. The ambulance officers put the stretcher in the van and drove away – but there was no siren or flashing lights this time.

Helen kept trying to believe it hadn't been Kate on the stretcher.

Finally, a court official emerged and told everyone to leave. Helen approached him and asked for confirmation it'd been Kate who'd left in the ambulance.

However, all the official said was, 'I'm not at liberty to say anything.'

Helen persisted: 'If it *was* Kate, I need to know because I'm her next of kin.'

'Wait here, please,' the official instructed her and went back inside the courthouse.

What he'd said was all that Helen needed to hear. She started to weep uncontrollably. Anne tried to comfort her, and a policewoman then approached Helen and asked her whether she was Catherine Scott's next of kin.

Anne replied, 'We can supply you with that information: it's her brother, John Scott. He lives in Cowra.'

Anne and Helen then turned to go. Many of Kate's friends were still standing around, and Anne noticed Fran Graig. Fran looked at Anne, and Anne nodded. By that time, everyone knew that Kate was dead.

Helen and Anne left. Helen had a key to Kate's house and wanted to go there to see whether Kate had left a note. Anne convinced her it wasn't a good idea, so they went home instead. Once there, Anne contacted their mutual friends and told them that Kate had taken her own life.

The next day, the grim event was headlines in the local papers, and the blame game had started. According to the policewoman who'd been assigned to look after Kate, Kate had told her, just after the court had adjourned, that she wasn't feeling well, and she wanted to be on her own while she waited for the verdict. She'd asked if she could go the courthouse's sick bay, and requested she not be disturbed until the jury had reached a verdict. At one fifty-five, the constable had gone to check on her, and she'd found her, slumped in a chair, dead. There would now have to be an inquest into the death.

Helen couldn't go to work that day and asked Anne to stay home with her. Anne agreed, saying, 'I didn't intend to go to work today either.'

The two women were sitting in silence when they heard the doorbell ring. It was the postman, and he had two registered, A4-size envelopes. One was addressed to Helen, the other to Anne. Anne signed for both. She recognised the writing on the envelope as being Kate's. She handed Helen her envelope and opened her own. It contained a personal note, three copies of a letter and a copy of Kate's will.

'Listen to this,' she said, and she read out the note:

Dear Anne,

I cannot thank you enough for what you did for me.

I could not face the thought of gaol; I was not going to give Judge Fox the power to send me there.

I know there is no God; I have the proof because I asked him to save me that dreadful night at the quarry. Mrs Robbins said she also asked him to save them the night of the home invasion.

I achieved my goal. Seeing Judge Botham squirm that night was an unbelievable bonus. The look on his face was worth everything.

I would have liked to do something more dramatic, like Cleopatra did – perhaps put a king brown on my boob, but that was not possible. Remember the time we went to see the documentary on Peter Stiller?

His last words before he was hanged were 'Justice has been done. The feeling is euphoric. I have attained nirvana.' Believe me, Anne: it's true.

Enjoy the rest of your life. Don't cry for me, Queanbeyan! '… and the day you die is better than the day you are born.' – Ecclesiastes, chapter 7, verse 1.

Love,
Kate

PS I have written the same note to Helen. There was no point in trying to give them the personal touch because I wanted to say the same thing to both of you.

Helen started to cry, and Anne was close to tears.

'What else is in the envelope?' Helen asked her.

'Three copies of the same letter,' Anne replied, and she read out the letter:

12 Cummins Street
Queanbeyan NSW 2602
14/10/1991

Dear Anne,

NEVER EVER LOSE THIS LETTER. Put one copy in a bank vault and store the other two in different places. I know this means nothing to you now, but you might need it someday. If anything strange is ever discovered at Socamora, ALISON AND I DID IT. Thanks for agreeing to the trapdoor! We just didn't get around to storing any wine!
Love,
Kate
C. M. Scott

PS I have enclosed my driver's licence in Helen's envelope in case you ever have to verify the signature on this letter.

Anne put the papers on the coffee table, sat on the couch, put her head in her hands and wept. Helen had never seen her in such a state.

Helen's envelope contained the same papers – except the letters were addressed to her – and Kate's driver's licence. Through her tears, she read Kate's letters. By the time she'd finished, she was crying hysterically.

Anne was the first to stop crying. She regained her composure and told Helen she'd make some lunch.

By the time the lunch was ready, Helen had stopped crying and started to feel like eating. 'Do you think we should contact Kate's brother?' she asked Anne.

'No, Helen. We've never met him.'

'I wonder whether the funeral will be in Queanbeyan or Cowra,' Helen muttered. 'What if the brother wants to have the funeral in a church?'

'If he wants to have the funeral in a church, there's nothing we can do; we're just friends. He's the next of kin.'

'It doesn't seem all that long ago we went to *Alison*'s funeral,' Helen remarked.

Kate's brother John was feeling shattered, Kate having let him believe she was still teaching at Queangolo High School. She'd told him nothing about having broken into Justice Botham's house, or the trial, and because the events were considered to be local news, nothing had been published about them in the national news.

John and his wife, Barbara, drove to Queanbeyan to attend the inquest into Kate's death and to make arrangements for her funeral. John was well aware of Kate's stance in relation to matters of religion. He knew the horror she'd endured, and he himself often wondered why 'the good Lord' had permitted the terrible act that Kate had been subjected to. He made a decision to respect her atheism. Most of her friends lived in Queanbeyan, so he decided to have the funeral there.

Very little was made public about the cause of Kate's death. The coroner found that Catherine Margaret Scott had taken her own life by consuming a toxic substance.

Helen wondered whether John had been given any more information about the finding, but she didn't think it appropriate to ask him. She wondered about Kate's passport because Kate had had to surrender it to the police. Had the police given it to John? Had Kate made a trip to Tijuana? Helen conjured an image in which John and his family were going through Kate's belongings: the gun (did John know she had it?), the bullets, the Herman Goering phial. Then she told herself that Kate would 'leave no trails'.

It was standing room only at the funeral parlour, which was supposed to hold a hundred people, and during the service, a feeling of protest hung in the air. Most of the mourners were harbouring hostility because of the circumstances that had led to Kate's death.

Dear Mrs Kyte, the principal of Dolmar Primary School, where Kate had worked for years, attended, along with two Sixth Class students. They recited the sweetest poem, entitled 'The Flowers in Spring'. It contained nothing soppy about the fallacy that people are lovely once they're dead; it was simply a delightful poem about flowers. Although the two students had their parents' permission to attend the funeral, Mrs Kyte knew she was 'treading on thin ice' by taking them. She'd been prepared to make herself unpopular with most of the students' parents, who'd thought it entirely inappropriate for school children to attend the funeral of someone who'd committed a crime and taken her own life in order to avoid a gaol sentence.

Kate had often spoken about Mrs Kyte to Anne and Helen: 'Such a strong person; always willing to stand up for the underdog; always willing to take on the loudmouth clique in the P&C'.

There was no sign of Mr Basset at the funeral service.

One of Kate's friends, Greg, whom Anne and Helen hadn't met, sang 'The Wind beneath My Wings', which turned out to be a bit too emotional for some people present.

Several of Kate's other friends spoke about her, and Brett talked about the work she'd done with Lawfail and her passion for instituting a just legal system.

At the end of the service, the celebrant invited everyone to attend the burial at the cemetery. Most people did go, and it was an emotional scene at the graveside. The celebrant also mentioned that the mourners were welcome to go along to a function room in one of the local clubs, which Brett and some of Kate's other friends had hired, with John's endorsement, to celebrate Kate's life.

At the funeral service, Anne was standing near some teachers from Queangolo High School, and one of them told her that the teachers had better not go to the club because they were AWOL. Mr Basset had refused to give them leave to attend the funeral. 'That's the sort of hypocrite he is,' the teacher remarked to Anne.

When Anne and Helen went along to the club, Helen noticed that Fran Craig was there and sobbing. 'Oh, Helen,' Fran said, 'I can't believe this! Why would such a happy, contented person do this?'

Helen was in no mood to explain to her that Kate hadn't been a happy, contented person.

'Where's Kate's husband and children?' Fran asked her.

'She doesn't have a husband.'

'What happened to him?' Fran queried.

'She never married,' Helen answered.

'What?' Fran exclaimed. 'Never married? How come? It couldn't've been through lack of offers: she was so popular with the guys at uni! She was popular with *everyone*! She didn't have an enemy in the world! I'd just taken it for granted she had a family. Kate was a bit of a women's libber, so I'd assumed that was why she hadn't changed her surname.'

Helen was about to say, 'Alison Roberts never married, either,' but decided such a comment was irrelevant; instead, she said, 'You once asked me whether I knew Alison Roberts. She was one of my best friends. She died of cancer six months ago.'

'No!' Fran cried out and sat down and cried.

When Helen and Anne arrived home, Anne said she'd make a quick trip to the office because she'd gotten behind with a few things. Helen never ceased to be amazed by Anne. Helen knew how much Anne truly cared about people and she knew that Anne was devastated by Kate's death, but unless you knew Anne really well, you'd think she wasn't very upset at all.

All alone at home, Helen started thinking about Kate. Kate had wanted to end her life. She'd said she'd achieved her goal. In the end, Alison hadn't wanted to go, although she'd confided in Helen numerous times that she wished she'd 'just fall off the planet'. When Helen had asked her why, Alison never replied. Now Helen knew the reason: the thought of her daughter caused her depression every day of her life. What a way to have lived! Perhaps Alison was right: perhaps they should not have sealed off the gaol. Maybe they should've kept throwing scumbags in there.

Two days after the funeral, Kate's brother phoned Helen to confirm he was the executor of Kate's will and that she'd left her and Anne $10,000 each and Lawfail $5,000. He asked her whether he could come and visit her and Anne. He seemed keen to get the will sorted out as soon as possible. Helen didn't tell him that she and Anne already knew that Kate had left them the money; in fact, they were feeling a bit embarrassed about it. They thought that John and his family might be put out because Kate had made a bequest to two of her friends and to Lawfail, but it turned out they needn't have worried because John was perfectly happy about what his sister had done. Helen agreed to see him the next day at the house.

When John arrived, he was overcome with grief: 'Poor Kate. She ... she ...'

Helen had no idea what he was trying to say and found herself wondering whether she should tell him she knew about the fact that Kate had been gang-raped.

He then changed tack, however, and said, 'I'm glad Kate mentioned you and Anne in the will. After she met you two, she seemed to have a new lease on life; I don't know why, but she did. I'm also glad she left some money to Lawfail; it seems like a fantastic organisation. After I've seen the solicitor, I'm going to see Brett. I was so impressed with his speech – would you call it a speech? – at the funeral. I spoke to him at the club too. There should be a lot more Bretts in this world.'

There should be more Annes in this world too! Helen said to herself. *She was really the one who gave Kate the new lease on life – though to be fair to Brett, I bet he was the one who sent the Nembutal to the Robbins.*

John started to cry again, saying, 'Life's so *cruel* to some people. Poor Kate. She ... she ...'

Helen decided she'd tell him she knew about the sexual assault: 'John, I know that Kate was raped.'

'How come you know that?' he asked, shocked.

'She told me.'

'I can't believe it!' John said. 'She didn't want anyone to know – although many people did. It's hard to keep something like that a total secret. Do you know whether she told anyone else?'

'She told Anne and another friend, Alison Roberts, who died of cancer about six months ago.'

'Did she tell you anything about it?'

'Yes, she told us everything.'

'One of the rapists got off on a technicality,' John said bitterly. 'After the trial, there was a picture on the front page of the *Dubbo Messenger* of the solicitor who'd defended him: Lyn Cullen. I'll never forget that name. She was smiling from ear to ear. Dad and I wanted to kill her!'

'Why didn't you?' Helen asked softly.

'Pardon?'

Helen was immediately sorry she'd asked the question and said, 'Sorry, John.'

'Did Kate tell you that Wayne Keys, the one who was acquitted, and Lyn Cullen disappeared without a trace? Both of them came to Canberra and vanished. Keys disappeared in early '89, Cullen about nine months later. After Cullen disappeared, Kate was questioned by the police. The poor girl had to relive the whole nightmare!'

Helen was momentarily dazed because Kate had never mentioned she'd been questioned by the police after Lyn Cullen's disappearance. *Why didn't she tell us?* Helen asked herself. 'Er ... we ... we all knew about their disappearances; it was in the papers ... though Kate didn't tell us the police had questioned her. I guess she just didn't want to talk about it.'

'When I think of the people who ruined her life, I burn with anger!' John shouted. 'I hope they rot in hell!'

Helen barely heard his last sentence because she was obsessing about why Kate hadn't told her and Anne that the police had contacted her when Lyn Cullen had disappeared.

'I searched the house high and low, looking for a note,' John commented. 'I thought she might've left me a note. The only note she left was for a Sergeant Crowley.'

'Sergeant Crowley?' Helen asked, astonished. 'What did the note say?'

'I don't know.'

Helen had a feeling that John did know what was in the note, but that he didn't want to talk about it. Sergeant Crowley had been the officer in charge of the investigation into the Robbins's deaths. Helen was now having trouble concentrating: why would Kate have left a note for Sergeant Crowley?

John looked at his watch and announced, 'I have to get petrol, and I want to have a bite to eat before I see the solicitor, so I'd better go.'

Helen saw him out, and then sat down and thought about the note to Sergeant Crowley: *Maybe I was wrong to conclude that Brett had sent the Nembutal to the Robbins; it might've been Kate!*

When Anne arrived home, Helen told her that Kate had been interviewed by the police after Lyn Cullen disappeared and that she'd left a note for Sergeant Crowley.

Anne was also surprised that Kate hadn't told them that the police had contacted her and didn't know what to make of the note to the sergeant. 'Maybe it wasn't Brett or Kate who sent the Nembutal to the Robbins,' she said. 'Perhaps Kate was taking the rap for someone else. I wonder what else they found.'

Anne thought about Kate's brother, sister-in-law and nieces going through Kate's belongings, and she started wondering what she herself had around that she wouldn't like anyone to see after she died. Just thinking about someone going through her soiled linen basket repulsed her. Then she thought about the gun: where was it? Maybe John knew about it. She told herself to relax because Kate would have taken care of the incriminating item.

Helen knew she was too distressed to go to work the next day or the next, so she took a week off work. However, she was still very depressed when she returned.

Another Goal

When Helen came home from her first day back at work, she wanted to cook, even though Anne offered to. 'I need a distraction,' she explained. 'Do you want to make the coffee instead?'

Anne and Helen finished their dinner, Anne then poured the coffee, and they made small talk while drinking it. Helen then started to talk about Alison's and Kate's tragic lives.

Anne knew she had to be patient with her friend and told herself, *Let her run her course.*

'You know, Anne, I think Alison didn't want to die because she hadn't achieved her ultimate goal, which was to find her daughter.'

'I think you're right,' Anne responded.

'I'm going to make it my goal,' Helen declared. 'Somehow, I'm going to find her.'

Helen knew that Anne was unpredictable in that you could never be quite sure how she'd react. She thought Anne might tell her to forget about it and get on with her life.

To her delight, however, Anne agreed to the proposal, saying, 'That's a great idea, Helen! We'll make it *our* goal, something worthy to aim for. Remember Tony Dunn? "Don't let anything or anyone stand in the way of what you want in life. If you *truly* want something, you'll find the strength and the means to achieve it!" We'll start tonight. Where do we start?'

'We know she was born on the twenty-third of February 1961 to Alison May Roberts, at the Baldwin Street Women's Hospital in Sydney, and that seven days after the birth, she was given up for adoption. I loathe that expression: 'given up for adoption'. Seven days later, she was forcibly taken from her mother. I'll make some phone calls tomorrow.'

The following day, Helen contacted the Office of Births, Deaths and Marriages, but the woman there couldn't help her. Next, she contacted Baldwin Street Women's Hospital. The woman who answered the phone told Helen that the hospital wasn't at liberty to disclose any information, but then said, very softly, 'I'm not supposed to say this, but try Rebus. They're based in Sydney. Goodbye.'

Rebus ... Rebus, Helen pondered. *Where have I heard that name before?* She then remembered that Kerrie had mentioned it when they were arranging Alison's funeral. Helen had the Sydney telephone directory in her office, so she looked up the number in it. She found the number, although there was no indication of what Rebus was. She dialled the number and explained to Marion, the woman who answered, why she was calling. Rebus turned out to be an organisation of voluntary members who tried to help mothers find their baby and to help children find their mother. Marion was so nice. She took all the details Helen gave her and promised she'd get back to her.

Within half an hour, Marion phoned Helen to say she had some information for her.

Helen felt her heart rate double.

'We have a mother whose baby was born on that date wanting to find her child, but we don't have a child born on that date trying to find his or her mother. Consequently, I'm afraid I can't help you. I'm really sorry.'

'Can you give me the name of the mother?' Helen asked her.

'Once again, I apologise. I can't tell you her name. I hope you understand we have *very* tight privacy rules.'

'Yes, I *do* understand that. Could I push my limit and ask you whether the mother's looking for a son or a daughter?'

'A daughter,' came the reply.

'Thank you,' Helen said.

'I can assure you, Helen, that if Rebus receives any more information, someone'll contact you. I say this in all sincerity. We're committed to helping mothers find their children and vice versa. I hope that soon this inhumane practice of forcing women to be surrogates will be wiped out. It's more barbaric than plucking out the eyes of peeping Toms. I know what I'm talking about: thirty years on, and I still suffer from Post-traumatic Stress Disorder.'

'My friend was the same.'

'I hope that next time we talk I have some good news for you,' Marion said.

'Thank you, Marion,' Helen replied. 'Goodbye.'

'Goodbye, Helen.'

Helen decided to ring Anne to tell her she'd drawn three blanks.

'We'll have to use our own initiative,' Anne replied. 'Leave it with me.' Anne went on to enquire about placing an advertisement in the *Herald*. The size of the ad she wanted would cost $150. When she arrived home, she conveyed the information to Helen.

'If that's what it costs, that's what we have to pay,' Helen said. 'What sort of ad do you have in mind?'

'One similar to the ads solicitors put in the papers to ask a person to contact them. Something such as "Would anyone knowing the whereabouts of Megan Roberts [might no longer be known by that name] born Sydney, twenty-third of February 1961, ask her to contact Anne?" We're not giving up, Helen; we'll run that ad again and again. You and I aren't short of a dollar; we can afford it. We'll have to advertise in other papers besides the *Herald*. Do you think Kerrie would be able to give us any more info?'

'No, I'm sure she wouldn't. I think Kerrie was nearly as traumatised by the whole baby business as Alison was; she can't bear to think about it.'

'Fair enough,' Anne said.

They continued placing the notice in various papers, but no one ever responded to them. Helen became very despondent. 'Anne, in six days' time, it'll be the twenty-third of February. Does that date mean anything to you?'

Anne thought for a minute. 'No, it doesn't, though by the way you spoke, it should. What is it?'

'It's Alison's daughter's birthday.'

'Maybe we should place a birthday notice in the classifieds of some of the larger newspapers,' Anne suggested.

'That's a bit *off*, Anne!' Helen responded.

'No, I'm serious. I was thinking about putting something about my friend's beautiful baby who disappeared without a trace, was abducted or something to tell the reader the baby was adopted. You never know: someone might just see it and it'll click.'

'That's a brilliant idea! Sorry for saying your idea was off.'

'No offence,' Anne replied. 'Now, let's see whether we can come up with a suitable birthday notice.'

That task wasn't easy, however. They knew most newspaper editors were quite conservative about what they would allow in 'personal announcements'. Finally, Anne and Helen came up with a notice they thought would be acceptable and conveyed what they wanted to say:

HAPPY BIRTHDAY
To my friend's daughter
born 23/2/1961
at Baldwin Street Women's Hospital.
Taken 7 days later

Love
Helen

'The twenty-third is a Sunday,' Helen noted. 'We'll put it in the Saturday and Sunday issues. I'll put my work and home phone numbers at the bottom.'

When Helen rang the *Herald* to place the notice, the woman who answered the phone took the message without any questions. However, three hours later, Helen received a call from another woman who was questioning the notice. Helen explained that she belonged to a religion in which the practitioners believed that you didn't stop celebrating a person's birthday just because the person was no longer embodied and that it was customary to leave a phone number so mutual friends could contact each other and share in the celebration of Tammy's short life.

Two days after placing the 'Happy Birthday' notice in the *Herald*, Helen returned from lunch to find a note on her desk from Melanie to tell her that someone had phoned about a birthday notice. Helen suddenly felt numb. She raced to Melanie's desk to ask her about the call.

'It was a woman,' Melanie said. 'She asked to speak to Helen. I told her you were at lunch and asked her whether she wanted to leave a message. She said she was ringing about a birthday notice in the *Herald* and that she'd ring again.'

'Is that all she said? Did she leave a number?'

'No,' Melanie replied.

Helen couldn't concentrate on her work. She felt she'd hooked the big fish, only to lose it within a metre of the boat. She was also annoyed she hadn't put Anne's work number in the notice, reckoning that the woman might have rung Anne when she couldn't get Helen. Every time the phone rang, she felt her heart rate increase by thirty per cent. The time was now five thirty. She was still at work but hadn't received the phone call, so she thought she might as well go home.

As soon as she arrived home, she ran to the phone to see whether the answering machine had a message on it. There was none.

Anne arrived home, and Helen told her the news.

Anne responded with great enthusiasm, saying, 'That's *fantastic!*'

'Yes,' Helen said, 'but I thought I would've heard by now. What if the woman got cold feet? I'm also worried about something else: Rebus has a woman who's looking for a daughter born on the twenty-third of February 1961 at Baldwin Street Women's Hospital. Alison didn't tell us she was trying to find her daughter. What if it's not her? It's possible that two adopted babies were born on that day.'

'I suppose so,' Anne said. 'Alison didn't tell us *anything* about her daughter. We didn't even know she *had* a daughter till she said she wanted to take Gertrude home. Let's take one step at a time.'

Anne had hardly finished speaking when the phone rang. Helen raced to pick it up, reminding herself that Peter had said he'd ring on either Monday or Tuesday night to confirm arrangements for the coming weekend. When she heard the STD pips, she felt her legs turn to jelly, and when she heard an unfamiliar female voice ask, 'Is that Helen?' she had to sit down. 'Yes,' she replied.

'I'm ringing about a "Happy Birthday" notice that appeared in the *Herald* two days ago. You say the baby was taken seven days later. Do you mean that the baby died?'

'No,' Helen answered, 'I mean that the baby was adopted.'

'I had this sixth sense that's what was meant,' the woman said. 'I was born on the twenty-third of February 1961 at Baldwin Street Women's Hospital and was adopted when I was one week old.'

'My friend and I are searching for another friend's baby.'

'How come you're doing the searching?' the woman asked. 'Why isn't the mother searching?'

'I can't put it any other way, er ... er ...'

'Kirsty,' the woman said. 'My name's Kirsty.'

'Kirsty, our friend is dead.'

'Is she my mother?'

'Unless two babies were born on the twenty-third of February 1961 at Baldwin Street Women's Hospital and were adopted when they were one week old, our friend has to be your mother.'

There was silence, and Helen then heard crying.

'When did she die?' Kirsty asked.

'About ten months ago.'

'Did she ever talk about me?'

'She didn't talk about you,' Helen replied. 'She found talking about you too painful. But I can tell you there wasn't a day in Alison's life – her name was Alison – that she didn't *think* about you. She wanted so much to find you, but her life was cut short. My friend Anne and I decided we'd try to find you, to fulfil a sort of promise to your mother.'

She thought about the woman who was listed with Rebus and said, 'Kirsty, please let me say it's possible that two babies *were* born on the twenty-third of February 1961 at Baldwin Street Women's Hospital and were adopted: nearly all the unmarried mothers in New South Wales at that time had their baby at Baldwin Street Women's Hospital.'

'Oh, don't say that,' Kirsty blubbered.

'You're right. Forget I said that. Where do you live?'

'I live in Gosford. I'm a single parent. I have one daughter. She was unplanned, though I'd never tell her that. I often thought of my birth mother. I wanted to find her, but I didn't know where to start. After Gemma was born – my daughter's name's Gemma – and she was handed to me, I burst into tears. I thought of my birth mother; I thought of the poor woman. Fancy going through all that and have your child taken from you, so you never heard another word about her. There's so much I want to know.'

'It'd be best if we could meet,' Helen said. 'There are things that are better said face to face rather than over the phone.'

'I can't come soon enough,' Kirsty said.

They arranged to meet on the following weekend.

'Gemma's four, I'm not sure whether I should bring her. I can probably leave her with a friend.'

'It's fine with us if you bring her. We have plenty of spare beds. It's just that it might be easier for us to talk if she's not here. Gosh, that sounds awful, doesn't it? What I mean is: there are things you probably don't want her to hear till she's older.'

'I agree. I'll ring my friend Lana. Unless you hear from me again, I'll be knocking on your door about eight o'clock next Friday night.'

'Fantastic!' Helen said, and she hung up.

Kirsty left work early on Friday; she couldn't wait to meet Anne and Helen. She stopped only once, to have a cup of coffee and buy petrol.

At about seven thirty, Kirsty rang the doorbell and Helen opened the door. She looked at her and said, 'You *are* Alison's daughter!'

Kirsty burst into tears.

Helen and Anne showed her some photographs and told her all they knew about Alison. They gave her the addresses and phone numbers of Alison's mother and her sister, Kerrie. 'Now, Kirsty,' Anne said, 'tell us all about you.'

'I'm not sure at what age a child starts to remember,' Kirsty began, 'but my first memories are of a nice house and a doting mother and father. I grew up in Gilbarn. It has a population of about four thousand, so I guess you'd say I grew up in a small country town. My father was an accountant. My first memories are a bit hazy … but I'll never forget the day – it was a Saturday – that Mum and Dad told me I was adopted. They didn't use that word at first. I was ten days off my fifth birthday. My father worked on Saturday mornings, so Mum and I would wait till he came home, and we'd all have lunch together.

'After lunch, they usually took me to the park to play on the swings, and then we went on to visit my grandmother. This particular Saturday, I finished lunch, and Mum and Dad just sat there. The norm was for one of them to accompany me to the bathroom, supervise my teeth cleaning and then help me put on my sneakers. This day, Dad said, "Come into the lounge room, Kirsty: we want to tell you something." I was a bit scared: I thought Loanee must've died – for some reason, I called my grandmother Loanee.

'So, we all went into the lounge room, and I sat between Mum and Dad on the three-seater couch. Then Dad said, "Kirsty, there's something we must tell you." I was really quite scared by then. "Your mother and I aren't your real mother and father. Your mother wasn't able to have children."

'I didn't know what he was talking about. Then he and Mum went on with some great spiel about how the girl who'd had me knew she wouldn't be able to look after me, so she'd done what she knew was best for her baby and asked that her baby be given to a couple who couldn't have children but would love and care for her, and … that part's a bit blurry, sorry.

'I think I was in shock. Then they mentioned the word "adopted". I remember that because I asked them what it meant. I suppose they did their best to explain; nevertheless, I didn't quite understand. They told me that when I started school, some children might tell me I was adopted, so it was better they told me.

'Then Dad said, "That's enough for now. Let's get those teeth cleaned and shoes on and go to the park." So off we went to the park.

'There were always other children at the park, so I enjoyed going there. After my play in the park, we went to Loanee's. Loanee was Dad's mother. Looking back, I realise they must've told her they were going to "drop the bombshell", because when we arrived, Loanee had baked my favourite cake and we were going to stay for dinner.'

On hearing the story, Anne felt sad, visualising the confused little girl trying to work out the meaning of the word 'adopted'.

Helen was close to tears as she thought of how Alison had wondered whether her little daughter was happy.

'I was six before I understood exactly what "adopted" meant,' Kirsty said. 'And it was a good thing I was told I was adopted before I started school because everybody else seemed to know.

'When I was seven, my parents adopted a boy. At first, I was worried they wouldn't like me as much, and I didn't want "the baby brother", as he was referred to. But I realised that my fears were unfounded, and I used to push him in the stroller, and he was fun, till he went to school. He must've had rotten genes. I think he was in trouble the first day he went to school. He was a bully. He was always being sent to the principal's office. He swore at the teachers. He was expelled three times. He was uncontrollable at home. I was so embarrassed at school because of him. I was so unhappy having this revolting brother.

'As he got older, things got worse. He was violent. He was in trouble with the police. I was scared of him. When he started high school, he went from bad to rotten. Fortunately, I left home when he was ten; I went to Sydney to study Pharmacy.

'He caused my parents no end of trouble and, I might add, sadness. They held on to this ridiculous notion he'd stop his wicked ways and turn into the model son. They paid out that much money for legal expenses. He also caused me a lot of anxiety. I used to go to Sunday school, so I knew about God. There was a girl in my class who used to tell me that God punishes people who do bad things. I used to think my parents had done something wicked to have such a bad son. Now, I believe they have: taking newborn babies from their mother *is* a wicked thing. Yet at the time, I didn't realise it, so I guess I was pretty screwed up.

'After I started uni, I began to drift away from my parents. I didn't want to go home during the uni holidays. If someone invited me to their place, I accepted the offer. Graeme – that was the brother's name – was one of the reasons I didn't want to go home. After I graduated, I found work in Sydney. I worked in Sydney for two years and then moved to Gosford.

'I sometimes think of Mum and Dad. Graeme and I broke their hearts. They'd have been better off without us. A couple who can't have children should accept the fact and plan an interesting life without children. They shouldn't force some poor, unfortunate, single girl who has an accident to be a surrogate for them. How can anyone endorse such a sick, sadistic, uncivilised practice?'

'That's what your mother – your real mother – used to say,' Anne said. 'Do you have any contact with your adoptive parents?'

'Not much. Mum writes to me, and they phone me on my birthday. I still send them a card for their birthdays and gifts at Christmas time. But from what I know now, I don't think I'll be sending anything next Christmas. As for Graeme, I don't know where he is, and I don't *want* to know.'

'What do you mean when you say, "from what I know now"?' Helen asked her.

'You told me my real mother was listed with Rebus. I hadn't even *heard* of Rebus till about two years ago. Every time I raised the subject about finding my birth mother, Mum would start to cry. "*I'm* your mother!" she'd say. "Your father and I love you! We've done all we can to make you happy!" I mentioned it once to Aunty Ruth, thinking she might be less emotional about the whole thing, but she gave me a lecture, told me how ungrateful I was: "Look at all your mother's done for you! How *could* you hurt her like this?" I was better off not knowing. Dad and Loanee were the same. I was always taken on a big guilt trip; no one *ever* tried to see my side of the story.

'I told you that Mum and Dad phone me on my birthday. Two birthdays ago, when Mum phoned, I asked her whether she'd ever heard of Rebus. It was obvious she had because she couldn't answer yes or no. She started to get the vapours and reminded me, yet again, that she and Dad had done all they could to give me a happy life; said some things are better left alone. When she said that, I flipped out and told her it was a lie; told her she'd never had a baby of her own, so she didn't have a clue what it would've been like for the woman who'd given birth to me. If she was so concerned for my happiness, she would've helped me find my birth mother. I put the barb in by telling her it might've worked out if she had; we might be still good mates.

'I can't believe that my mother – my *real* mother – was looking for me all those years. And all those years, Mum – I don't know what else to call her – knew about Rebus and never told me. Right this minute, I hate her! I'll tell her someday that some things *aren't* better left alone! She was obsessed I'd find my real mother and ditch her! Well, I'm ditching her now! By the way, why doesn't Rebus advertise?'

'I asked the woman I spoke to the same question,' Helen replied. 'She said they sometimes do, but it's difficult for them. They operate on a shoestring budget, and a lot of people want to see them closed down.'

'I'm going to donate some money,' Kirsty said, 'especially for advertising.'

'It's not only the money side of it though. Most newspapers won't let them advertise; many people consider what Rebus does is illegal,' Helen told Kirsty.

Kirsty started to cry. 'Right now, I'm filled with hatred! What am I going to do?'

Helen comforted her while Anne spoke: 'Kirsty, I believe if someone's done the wrong thing by you, that person should be punished. What your adopted parents did to you and Alison *is* horrible. Alison never recovered from the trauma of having her baby taken from her. It's all very well for couples who adopt babies to try to justify what they've done, by saying abortion's illegal and these unmarried mothers put their baby up for adoption because they know he or she'll go to a good family – Blah! Blah! Rave on! But these couples *create* the demand. It's all about supply and demand. If there wasn't such a huge demand for these babies, maybe the abortion laws would be changed.'

'I don't think they would,' Helen commented.

'You're probably right,' Anne replied. 'Well, Kirsty, if you sever contact with your adoptive parents, don't feel guilty.'

'Anne!' Kirsty said. 'I can't believe you said that! Do you think you help yourself move forward if you pay back the people who've hurt you?'

'Yes, I do; I've seen it work. Payback, revenge, vengeance – call it what you like – are all euphemisms for justice, and everyone wants justice.'

'For the first time in my life, I feel I'm with people who think as I do. I was always told you have to forgive, but sometimes I couldn't see how forgiveness was possible. When I was in Third Class, a girl in Sixth Class had a serious accident on her bike: she went straight into the path of a car at an intersection. She spent a long time in hospital, and she was left with a permanent limp.

'After some investigation, the truth came out: two boys in the same class with her had tampered with the brakes on her bike. Nothing was going to happen to the boys because they were only ten. I'm not sure of the exact details, but the girl's father roughed up one of the boys when the boy was on his way home from the pool. I remember hearing Mum and Dad discussing what'd happened, and I made some comment about the fact I was glad about it because the boy had deserved what he'd had coming to him. Well, you should've heard the little moral lecture I received! The truth was: I *was* glad, really glad, but I couldn't tell anyone I was!'

'No one thinks that way in this house,' Anne assured her. 'We both believe that if someone does the wrong thing by you, that person should be punished.'

'Wow!' Kirsty exclaimed. 'It's so refreshing to hear someone say that! If I'd been able, I would've asked to be aborted rather than cause my mother so much sadness. Anyway, what's so fantastic about life? You only end up dying!'

'Exactly,' Anne said in response. 'A friend of mine and your mother's used to quote Sophocles: "To never have been born may be the greatest boon of all."'

'I totally agree,' Kirsty said.

Anne then made supper, and the three women continued talking.

Helen looked at her watch and saw that the time was almost eleven o'clock. 'Are you tired, Kirsty?' she asked her. 'Do you want to go to bed?'

'I'm feeling weary,' Kirsty admitted, 'though I'm sure I won't sleep – too much has happened tonight. I'm going to sleep with that photo of my *real* mother beside my bed. She has the most beautiful face. I just wish I could've met her.' She started to cry.

Helen put her arm around her and comforted her until she stopped crying. 'We'll put the photo on the bedside table.'

At eleven thirty, the women decided to call it a night and go to bed.

Anne was first to rise, followed by Helen and then Kirsty.

The women had breakfast together, and when they'd finished, Kirsty said, 'I guess it's time to contact my aunt. I'm so nervous. Do you have any idea how she'll react? Do you know her?'

'Yes,' Helen replied, 'we know her.'

'Do you think it'd be better if you rang her first?' Kirsty asked.

'If that's what you want, I'll ring her. But let's not delay: she might go out on Saturday mornings.' Helen rang Kerrie, and after explaining to her why she was ringing, she handed the receiver to Kirsty, saying, 'She can't wait to talk to you. We'll sit out in the garden and leave you to talk in private.'

Anne and Helen then picked up parts of the newspaper and went outside. They decided to sit near the barbecue, but neither of them could concentrate enough to read the papers. 'I hope it all goes okay,' Helen said. 'I know that Kerrie found it very painful to talk about.'

Ten minutes passed, but Helen and Anne saw no sign of Kirsty. Almost fifteen minutes had passed before they saw her emerge from the house in tears. 'I talked to her,' she said. 'She sounds lovely. I'm going to visit her – haven't set a date, but it's definitely going to happen. You forgot to tell me I have two cousins!'

'Yes, we did,' Anne said. 'I suppose we were so busy talking about other things.'

Kirsty flopped down into a chair. 'I called her Aunty Kerrie. I can tell she loves me. She's going to phone her mother and arrange for me and Gemma to visit her … I'm exhausted.'

'Just sit there and relax,' Helen said to her. 'I know one thing you have in common with your grandmother – your *real* grandmother.'

'What is it?' Kirsty asked.

'She was a pharmacist.'

'Really!' Kirsty exclaimed. 'Do you think those things are genetic?'

'Maybe. You have some beautiful genes in you, Kirsty.'

Kirsty started to cry and said, 'Talking about genes, do you know anything about my father?'

'No, Kirsty,' Helen replied. 'Nothing.'

They were silent for a minute, after which Helen asked Kirsty whether there was anything else she wanted to do.

'No,' she answered. 'I think I've done enough for one day. I'd love another cup of coffee, though, and then I'll head home. I can't believe this day's arrived!'

Anne agreed to make the coffee. Kirsty drank hers and then put her belongings in her car. There were teary goodbyes between Kirsty and Helen, and even Anne started to sob when Kirsty said, 'I can't thank you enough for what you've done. I'll see you again, won't I?'

'You sure will,' Anne replied. 'You and Gemma are welcome in this house anytime. I'd love to meet Alison's granddaughter.'

Kirsty hopped in the car and headed for Gosford, promising to keep regularly in contact: a promise she kept.

Back inside the house, Helen remarked, 'I feel a bit exhausted myself.'

'It's been a very emotional day,' Anne said. 'Why don't we go to the Grongo pub for lunch?'

'Good idea. We can stop by and say hello to Socamora.'

As Anne was driving them to Socamora, they discussed how horrible it must now be for Kirsty not to have a clue about her father.

In February 1992, Kirsty's visit turned out to be Anne and Helen's second piece of good news. The other happy event was that the letter that Colleen had sent her family had finally been considered new evidence in the Lex Woodlock case, and a judge had ordered a re-trial, during which Lex was found not guilty. Although Magda had told Anne and Helen about the fire that Lex was supposed to have started, and about the people who'd lost their businesses, Anne and Helen had continued to be very distraught that he was in gaol for having murdered Colleen.

Helen

Anne, her friends and Helen's friends agreed that Helen had changed after Kate's death. Helen had always been a great socialiser, but now, she was frequently declining invitations to dinners, the cinema, the theatre, picnics and other outings that in the past she'd have relished. She did continue attending meetings of NoFourthR and Lawfail, but her enthusiasm was clearly gone, and she often seemed depressed.

On the anniversary of Kate's death, Helen went to Queanbeyan to place a floral arrangement on her friend's grave, and on the anniversary of Alison's death, she visited the crematorium. She always returned home very depressed after the visits, and after one of them, she told Anne, 'I can't even pretend they're happy in la-la land.'

'Well,' Anne said in response, 'you can be happy their suffering's ended.'

Anne and Helen didn't talk much about their crimes. Friends were always hinting they should sell the block in the country. Helen suggested they build a tennis court on the block, so they could show some justification for keeping the property. However, building a tennis court was beyond their skills, and they didn't want to risk having construction workers on the block when the two women weren't there. They also thought about setting up a pitch and putt but decided they couldn't be bothered.

Once a year, the police in each state and territory held 'Missing Persons Week', and in the Australian Capital Territory, Gary Munkton was always top of the list. Anne and Helen usually felt a bit uneasy during that week, both of them having read that crimes had been solved twenty years after the person had committed them. The uneasy feeling didn't last long, though, because they remained confident that no one would find the dungeon and discover the bodies. And besides, they had the explanatory letter that Kate had written. Although neither of them thought it was all that convincing! Each year, the police could shed no more light on the disappearance of Wayne Keys, Colleen O'Day, Lyn Cullen and Gary Munkton.

It was an ordinary Sunday afternoon. Anne arrived home from a game of golf and saw a note on the table, from Helen: 'I've gone for a ride around the lake. Your washing finished, so I hung it out.' *Helen's so thoughtful,* she said to herself.

She changed out of her golf clothes, made herself a cup of coffee and sat down to finish reading the paper. It was then about four thirty. She wasn't sure what time Helen had left to go on the ride but felt she would've been back by four thirty. Then Anne thought Helen might have run into Rhonda or Jim because they often went for a ride on a Sunday afternoon. *Not to worry,* she thought to herself, *I'm enjoying reading the paper.*

As she was turning a page, she looked out the window, and that was when she saw it: a police car. It moved slowly past the house, did a U-turn and stopped right outside the gate. Two police officers stepped out – a man and a woman. She saw them open the front gate. She tried to think of some Q&As. She thought of Kate's letter, but before she could think any further, she heard a loud knock on the door. She could now do nothing but open it.

'Is this the residence of Helen Jane Davis?' the male police officer asked her.

'Yes,' she answered.

'I'm Senior Constable Michael Hawker and this is Constable Kaye Jones. Are you a relative?'

'No, I'm her flatmate, Anne Paterson.'

'May we come in, Ms Paterson?' Senior Constable Hawker asked her.

'Yes.' *Keep your cool!* she said to herself. *I know nothing!* 'What's happened?' she asked the constable.

'I'm afraid I have some bad news for you … Ms Davis is dead,' he replied.

'What?' Anne exclaimed.

'She was found about thirty metres from the bicycle path, half a kilometre north of the dam. It seems she had a heart attack and died instantly.'

'That can't be so! She was as fit as a Mallee bull! She didn't have anything wrong with her heart! She didn't have anything wrong with any part of her!'

'I can't comment on that, Ms Paterson. All I can say is, that's the initial finding. Of course, there'll have to be a coroner's inquest.'

'Why was she thirty metres from the bike path?' Anne asked him.

'We don't know.'

'Why would someone venture thirty metres off the bike path and then suddenly have a heart attack? Things aren't adding up.'

'I can't comment on that, Ms Paterson.'

'Maybe she felt pains in her chest and was looking for somewhere to lie down,' Constable Jones suggested.

'I'm sure everything will be revealed by the coroner,' the senior constable assured her. 'Would you have the contact details of her next of kin?'

'Yes. Her brother would be her next of kin; I have his address and phone number.' She walked over to the telex, wrote Colin's phone number and address on a piece of paper and handed the piece of paper to Constable Jones.

'The next of kin will have to officially identify the body,' Constable Jones said.

At that point, Anne came to realise that Helen was in fact dead. Her flatmate of thirty-five years was dead, so why wasn't she crying? What was *wrong* with her? *I'm in shock,* she told herself. 'I can't believe it,' she remarked. 'Where's Helen now?'

'In the morgue at Canberra Hospital,' Constable Jones replied.

'Oh no! Helen in the *morgue!*' She was now close to tears. 'Who found her?'

'A woman walking her dog. She said some birds flew over very low, and the dog chased them. She ran after the dog and saw your flatmate. It was a coincidence about the birds; she said she'd never have gone through the bush in that direction. Is there anything we can do for you? Would you like us to stay here till a friend comes over?'

'No, thank you, but I'd like to see where Helen was found.'

'That's not possible,' Constable Jones informed her. 'The area's been marked as a crime scene and cordoned off. We have Ms Davis's bike in our van. Can we leave it here?'

'Of course.'

As soon as Constable Jones wheeled the bike inside the gate, Anne noticed that the drink-bottle holder was empty. She thought that aspect very strange because Helen never went riding without taking water in the bottle. She was about to ask Constable Hawker whether they or any other police officers had taken it but decided not to.

'Well, Ms Paterson,' he said, 'if there's nothing else we can do for you, we'll leave.' The two police officers left.

Anne was now alone. She looked at the bike, decided to put it in the garage and went inside the house. Still, she hadn't cried. She wondered what the coroner's findings would be. She didn't believe that Helen had had a heart attack. She decided to ring Malcolm.

'I'll be straight over,' he said. 'See you in a few minutes.'

Within twenty minutes of putting the receiver down, she heard Malcolm's car pulling into the driveway. She thought about Malcolm and how he was such a dear friend: always reliable, nothing ever too much trouble. She opened the door before he had time to ring the bell.

He hugged her and gave her a kiss. 'I can't believe it!' he said. 'Helen was so healthy! Did she ever mention anything to you that she suspected heart problems?'

'Not a word,' Anne replied. 'She was a picture of health; she looked *years* younger than she was.'

'What did the police say?'

'Not very much at all. They told me Helen was found dead about thirty metres off the bike path, half a kilometre north of the dam. The cause of death was a heart attack, but the coroner has to be satisfied there are no suspicious circumstances. I gave the police Helen's brother's address and phone number. He's her closest relative. He can take it from there. I just hope he doesn't arrange some Christian funeral. I'm not sure whether he shares Helen's atheist views. I know there's a copy of her will in her filing cabinet, but I've no idea if she's left any instructions about arrangements for a funeral.'

Just then, she had a horrible thought: *What if Helen's family members contest the will in relation to Socamora? How can I be thinking these things? My friend and housemate of thirty-five years is dead, and I'm thinking about wills and funerals! I should be* weeping*!*

'Anne, what can I do for you?' Malcolm asked her.

'I want to see where Helen was found. The policeman said I couldn't go there because it's been marked as a crime scene and cordoned off, but I want to get as close a look as possible. Can you take me there?'

'Of course,' he answered. 'Who found Helen?'

'A woman walking her dog.'

As they neared the dam, they could see the police cars. They parked on the roadside and walked to the bicycle path. From the path, they could see the blue and white chequered tape.

'It doesn't make sense, Malcolm. Why would Helen scrub bash thirty metres through *that*? The policeman said it was a coincidence that the woman found Helen. Now I know what he means.'

Malcolm put his arm around her while she was looking at the place where her dear friend had died.

'Thanks, Malcolm, I suppose I can't achieve anything by staying here; we might as well go home. Can you make a few phone calls for me? Let Don and Carmel, John, Peter and Magda know. Tell them to let our mutual friends know. After that, there's probably not much more you can do.'

Malcolm made the phone calls, and both Anne and he knew they had to tell only a few friends and that within the hour, everyone would know.

That day, Anne received a steady stream of visitors and took numerous calls. At about seven o'clock, Malcolm suggested he'd collect some pizzas for the friends who were still there. Anne told him not to bother and that she'd make some toasted sandwiches instead; she had plenty of bread, ham, cheese, tomatoes and asparagus.

'Let me make them,' Magda offered.

Anne sometimes referred to Magda as her cultural companion. They'd known each other for more than twenty years. They often went to the art gallery, a movie or a concert together, but Magda wasn't interested in Lawfail or NoFourthR.

Anne agreed to the suggestion, saying, 'Okay. You know where everything is.'

Magda and Malcolm made the sandwiches, and when the visitors had finished eating, Magda packed the dishwasher and put everything back in its place. By now, the time was almost ten o'clock, and everyone except Magda had left.

'I'm dreading having to phone Kirsty tomorrow,' Anne said, 'but I know I have to do it. She adored Helen, and so did Gemma. Kirsty and Helen phoned each other at least once a week, and the three of them took holidays together sometimes.'

'Helen was a picture of health. I always thought she'd live to be a hundred,' Magda commented.

'So did I – well, at least ninety.'

'How old was she?'

'Sixty-one,' Anne replied.

'That beautiful skin!' Magda said. 'Not a wrinkle! She could've passed herself off for *fifty*-one. Would you like me to stay the night?'

'No, thanks, Magda. I'll be fine.'

'Well, would you like to come to dinner tomorrow night?'

'Thank you, Magda, I'd love to.'

'Any time after six,' Magda said. 'If there's nothing more I can do for you, then I'll take my leave, but ring me if you want anything.'

'Thanks, Magda. You're such a dear friend.'

'You have *many* dear friends.'

Magda then gave Anne a big hug and left. They'd all left now, and Anne was alone. She pondered the fact that she'd barely shed a tear over Helen's demise. She sat down on the couch to have a think. She found herself thinking about the past, something she seldom indulged in, believing that the past is the past – it's gone. She then thought about herself: why wasn't she crying? Throughout her life, she'd been told several times that she didn't have a heart. *Well,* she'd thought, *if I don't have a heart, it's not my fault: I was born without one!* She'd also been told she had no feelings. However, she knew she *did* in fact have a heart and she *did* in fact have feelings.

She recalled the day on which Kate had told her what they could do with the big hole on the Socamora property. Anne had been filled with rage and couldn't wait to throw those evil creatures in it. The first person to have told her she had no heart was Mrs James, her fifth-class teacher. She'd told her so because Anne had been the only girl in the class who hadn't cried when Mrs James had told the pupils that the principal's wife was seriously ill in the hospital. 'Holier than thou' Mrs James: off to church every Sunday; taking Scripture lessons when the ministers were absent; gushing over her pet pupils; ridiculing the poor kids who had difficulty with their spelling and arithmetic. Anne knew she had feelings: she'd often been so angry with Mrs James that she wanted to knock her lights out.

She then found herself remembering a leaflet that had been dropped in her letterbox. It would have been about fifteen years earlier, but it'd struck a nerve with her. It was an advertisement for a forum. Some guy was speaking on three topics. Anne had since forgotten the first and third topics but had never forgotten the second one: 'Are you incapable of loving?' She'd never forgotten it because she thought she was incapable of loving. *If I am incapable of loving, it's not my fault,* she'd told herself. *I was born that way, and I don't think I'll change if I listen to this guy!*

She thought back to her childhood and wondered how old a child is when she starts to remember things in her life: three? four? The first thing she could remember was playing in the backyard with her dog, a Labrador. She'd been happy then.

She thought about her mother. She'd liked her and admired her, but she didn't believe that she'd ever really loved her mother. She'd felt the same about her father. He'd been a really nice man, a good father and husband, and he'd taken care of his family, but she'd never felt she loved him. She thought about her brother and sister, and their spouses and children.

Raymond then came into to her mind. *Poor Raymond,* she thought to herself. *I broke his heart, but it wasn't my fault: I didn't love him.*

Her thoughts then turned to Kate and Alison, and she found herself boiling with rage. *Those beautiful girls! Their lives ruined!* She recalled the time that Alison had told her she'd seen a girl she thought might be her daughter. *The Right to Esse: that despicable organisation! If there's a hell, they'll all go there!* She thought about how Kate had suicided and how Helen had struggled with the meaning of life. Why couldn't Helen be like her and accept the fact that life *has* no meaning?

She started to cry and felt her eyes become red and swollen. She felt tired now. She looked at the clock and saw that the time was 11.04 pm. She decided to go to bed but found she couldn't sleep. She'd been in bed about twenty minutes when she heard the phone ring. She answered it, and the caller was Colin, Helen's brother. 'Anne, is that you?' he asked.

'Yes,' she replied.

'I'm sorry to ring you at this late hour, but I've just heard about Helen. I can't believe it. We went out for dinner and then to the pictures. When we arrived home, there was a message on the answering machine, from Constable Bloomfield at Lowther Police Station, and he asked me to contact him. My legs went weak. I thought Michael or Tanya must've had an accident. I rang the number, and he told me Helen had been found dead on a bike path in Canberra. I wondered whether you knew, but he told me you'd given him my contact details. Why didn't you phone us?'

'Police protocol, I'm not the next of kin.' Anne didn't know whether that was true, but she wasn't very close to Colin or his wife, Patty, and she hadn't wanted to be the one to tell them that Helen had died.

'Patty and I'll try to get a flight to Canberra tomorrow. If we can't, we'll drive up.'

'Let me know if you're flying,' Anne said. 'I'll meet you at the airport, and you can stay here. I suppose I'll go into work to tell them what's happened, so if you can't get me at home, try work.' She gave him her work number.

'Thanks, Anne. Well, there's nothing more Patty and I can do now. As soon as the booking office opens tomorrow, I'll phone ... By the way, Anne, how are *you*? You and Helen have been friends for a long time.'

'I'm very sad; however, I'm coping. My friends have been wonderful.'

'I'm pleased to hear that. Fly or drive, we'll see you tomorrow. Goodnight, Anne.'

'Goodnight, Colin.' She then went back to bed. Anne was one of those people who had no concept of insomnia, but tonight she discovered what it was.

She woke when the alarm went off at the usual time of six thirty but stayed in bed for a few minutes before getting up. She dressed, prepared a bowl of muesli and sat down to eat it. She pondered that normally by now, Helen would have appeared in the kitchen. When Helen took holidays, Anne didn't miss her; she'd enjoyed having the house to herself. This situation was different, though: Helen wasn't coming back, and Anne was feeling the loss.

She decided she'd go to work, tell the staff about Helen's death, see whether she had any urgent business to attend to, go home and wait for Colin to ring. She'd barely finished brushing her teeth when the phone rang, and Colin came on the line. He told her that he and Patty would be flying to Canberra that day and that the plane would be arriving at 10.35 am.

'That's fine,' Anne said. 'I'll be there to meet you.' She completed her ablutions and drove to work.

When she arrived, she found that Meg was the only person there. When she told Meg about Helen, Meg became visibly upset. 'Tell the others about Helen,' Anne instructed her, 'and if anything urgent crops up, I'll be at home, except between ten and eleven: I'm going to the airport to collect Helen's brother and sister-in-law.'

'Goodbye, Anne,' Meg said. 'And if you want anything, phone me.'

'Thanks, Meg.' She walked to the car and sat in it for three minutes before turning on the ignition. She found herself thinking again but remembered how dangerous it was to think because one became philosophical, and that wasn't her. However, she did think about what a kind and loyal employee Meg was. Had she ever told Meg? Yes, she had, she remembered – many times. Just like she'd told Paul and Richard and Rebecca and everyone else, when they'd earned the praise.

Anne was a good boss: she looked after her staff. Everyone liked her, except the whingers and the malingerers, but they never stayed long anyway. Anne had a subtle way of suggesting that those types of people were unsuited to the sort of work they were doing and that they'd be happier elsewhere. They always took her advice and left of their own accord.

She drove home and went inside the house. She hoped Colin would put a death notice in the paper because it was the easiest way to notify people who weren't in Anne and Helen's inner circle of friends. She knew she should inform the people at Helen's workplace, but she didn't feel up to making the call. She decided to read the paper until the time came for her to drive to the airport.

The plane arrived on time, and Anne recognised Colin and Patty as they were walking across the tarmac. They greeted her warmly and waited to collect their luggage from the carousel. Anne could tell they'd both been crying. It seemed to take forever for their suitcases to appear, but Colin finally spotted them. He grabbed them, and Anne directed him and Patty to the car. Colin put the cases in the boot, opened the back door for Patty and hopped in the front beside Anne.

'Did Constable Bloomfield give you any more details about Helen?' Anne asked him.

'He gave me a letter,' Colin answered. 'I'm to take it to the hospital as proof I'm the next of kin. Then I'll be asked to identify the body.' He was almost crying. 'I'm not looking forward to that part – oh, by the way, Michael and Robyn and Tanya are driving up when we know when the funeral will be. Robyn's mother will look after Sam and Doug.'

Michael and Tanya were Colin and Patty's children, and Robyn was Michael's wife. Tanya wasn't married; she'd been very close to Helen and shared Helen's belief that procreation wasn't a wonderful thing. Anne was pleased to hear that Michael and his wife were coming to their aunt's funeral. She'd been confident that Tanya would come but unsure that Michael would: birthdays and Christmas had been the only times Michael contacted Helen, and it'd always been Robyn who made the call or bought the present.

'Phone them and tell them they can stay at my house if they want to,' Anne said. 'It'll be a bit crowded, but we'll get by.' Normally, she'd have said 'our house' rather than 'my house', because although the house was in Anne's name, it was always 'Anne and Helen's house'. It seemed so strange for her to now be saying 'my house'.

'Thanks, Anne,' Colin said. 'It'll be good for us to be together.'

Anne continued, 'After you've formally identified Helen, you'll need to do a few practical things – put a death or funeral notice in the paper, find an undertaker and work out some sort of funeral. I suppose you know that Helen was an atheist –Atheist with a capital A.'

'Yes,' Patty replied. 'We know that, but ... but ...'

'We'll discuss it later,' Colin told her.

Anne knew that Patty was religious and that she'd want to have the funeral in a church. 'Here we are,' she said as they pulled into the driveway.

Colin carried the suitcases inside. Anne directed them to the spare room and asked them whether they'd like a drink. Both said they'd like a coffee, and Anne made them some.

When they returned to the kitchen, Anne poured the coffee for the three of them and started the conversation. 'I guess we have to discuss the practical things that have to be done. First of all, Colin, you have to identify Helen; I'll drive you to the hospital. Second, do you want to put a death and/or funeral notice in the paper?'

'Yes,' Colin and Patty replied in unison.

'When we come back from the hospital,' Anne said, 'you two can work out what to say, and I'll phone it through. I've checked it out. The cutoff for classifieds is six o'clock, so we have plenty of time. We also have to contact an undertaker and arrange the funeral. However, the big uncertainty in all this is the autopsy: the coroner has to determine the cause of death. I hate to say this, but before he releases the body, he has to be satisfied there was no foul play.'

'Did Helen ever mention heart problems to you?' Colin asked her.

'Never, Colin – *not once!* I find it very hard to believe that a person who's a picture of health can go for a bike ride; go thirty metres away from the path – for some unknown reason – and have a heart attack. Hopefully, all will be explained by the coroner. Perhaps we should go to the hospital now and get the really horrible part out of the way.'

'That's a good idea,' Patty said.

Anne drove them to the hospital, and once there, the three of them went into the waiting room, but only Colin went into the morgue. He completed the necessary paperwork there, and Anne drove them back to her house.

Colin and Patty sat at the dining table to write the death notice, Anne proofread it and phoned it through to the paper. She then got the Yellow Pages out, looked up an undertaker, and gave Colin the name and number she'd found so he could call him.

The undertaker came to see them that afternoon, but they couldn't set a date for the funeral until the coroner had released the body.

It was obvious that the emotional strain was taking its toll on all three, so Anne asked Patty and Colin whether they'd like to have a rest. They jumped at the suggestion.

'You two have a rest, and I'll go for a walk,' she said. She decided to take a long walk and returned home just after five o'clock to find Colin and Patty watching the news on TV.

The phone rang, and the caller wanted to speak to Colin. It was someone at the coroner's office to say that the body could now be released to the next of kin. All three were surprised to hear so. 'What did they say?' Patty asked Colin.

'Only that a doctor had examined the body and determined that the cause of death was a heart attack.'

Anne didn't know whether to feel relieved or not. She didn't believe Helen had had a heart attack.

The funeral would be on Wednesday. The time wasn't yet six o'clock, so Anne still had time to contact *The Canberra Envoy* for the funeral notice to appear in the next day's issue. There would be a service at the funeral parlour, similar to Alison's service. Patty wasn't happy about that aspect, but although Anne was adamant it was what Helen would have wanted, she was prepared to let Colin have the final say.

'I agree with Anne, Patty,' he said. 'Helen didn't believe in God, so it wouldn't be right that we had a religious funeral.'

'Couldn't we have at least *one* hymn or maybe a short Bible reading?' Patty queried.

Anne was starting to get annoyed with Patty. From things Helen had said about Patty, Anne knew Patty was one of those people who are used to getting her own way. *If she keeps this up, I'll have to say something*, she said to herself.

Colin gave the answer: 'No, Patty, we've decided to respect Helen's views on religion.'

Patty kept trying. 'There are some *lovely* hymns. To sing *one* hymn would be all right.'

Anne decided to take over. 'What hymn would you suggest then? A friend of mine was gang-raped. She never recovered from the trauma. She committed suicide. She used to say, "You can sing 'God Works in Mysterious Ways' at my funeral, or perhaps the one with those ridiculous lines 'Oh, what needless pain we bear, all because we do not carry everything to God in prayer.'" She said that while she was being raped, she prayed and prayed to God to save her, but for some unknown reason, he refused. Helen thought all religion's nonsense, and as for a Bible reading, forget it!'

As soon as she'd finished speaking, Anne regretted that she'd been so aggressive. However, Patty finally got the message, but she was not happy. She was almost sulking.

'Are you hungry?' Anne asked them. 'It's quite a while since you've eaten. Do you like Chinese food?'

'Yes, Anne, we do.'

'Good. I'll get some delivered for you. I won't join you though. I hope you don't think I'm rude, but before I knew you were coming, I accepted a dinner invitation from my good friend Magda.'

By the time the Chinese food arrived, Patty had recovered from her little sulk.

The next morning, the three had breakfast together, and Anne then asked, 'What do you two want to do today? Everything seems under control for tomorrow; there's nothing more to do. I was thinking of going into work; I think I'll be better at work than here at home.'

'You're probably right, Anne,' Colin agreed. 'Don't worry about Patty and me.'

'I'll give you Helen's keys. This one's for the front door, and of course, this one's for her car. Help yourself to the food.'

'Thank you, Anne,' Colin said, and Anne left for work.

She didn't have a very fruitful day in the office; nevertheless, she felt that the day passed quicker than it would've passed if she'd been trying to entertain Colin and Patty.

When she returned home, she found Colin and Patty watching the news. 'We always watch the news,' Patty said, as if apologising for having turned on the television.

Anne changed out of her work clothes and asked her guests whether quiche and salad would be okay for dinner. Both agreed it would, and Patty asked Anne whether she needed any help making the meal.

'No thanks, Patty. All I have to do is make a salad and heat up the quiche. My friends have been so kind. Carmel brought the quiche over.'

She prepared the meal, and when they sat down to eat, Patty took it upon herself to say grace. Anne saw the look of discomfort on Colin's face, but Patty went ahead and thanked 'the Lord' for the fresh, healthy food that would give them strength in this time of deep sorrow. Anne was always amused at the practice of giving thanks because one thanked the Lord for good things but didn't blame him for bad things – the bad things were your own fault. She felt like saying to Patty, 'You should be thanking *Carmel: she* made the quiche!' However, she had no intention of being antagonistic. She certainly didn't want Patty to get sulky again.

After the meal, Anne cleaned away the dishes and made a pot of tea. They'd just finished their second cup when they heard a knock on the door. Anne always felt irritated by people who knocked on the door when there was a doorbell.

'That must be Michael and crew,' Patty said. 'I'm so glad they've arrived safely.'

Anne went to the door. She herself was relieved to see the guests, remembering that the most recent knock on the door had been delivered by the police. She showed the family members to their rooms and made sure they had everything they needed. At nine o'clock, she said she'd leave the family to have time together and went off to her bedroom. It was too early to go to sleep, however, so she read.

They all woke about the same time, had breakfast together and then left for the funeral, which was to start at ten o'clock.

Everything went according to plan at the funeral service. All Helen's friends and work colleagues attended it. Tanya was the only family member who spoke. Colin had said he'd break down if he tried to speak about Helen in front of a crowd, especially when most of the people there were strangers. Kerrie had flown down from the Gold Coast and told Anne she could never thank her and Helen enough for having found Kirsty. Kirsty herself was devastated.

After the funeral service, most of the mourners went on to the Polly Hotel to have nibbles and drinks. When that part wound down, everyone left, one by one, and Colin, Patty and the other family members went back to Anne's house.

When they were sitting idly in the lounge room, Colin mentioned the will, saying, 'I know it sounds awful to be talking about the will, but it has to be sorted out.'

'Yes, it does, Colin,' Anne agreed. 'As far as I know, the original is with Bishop and Partners, and there's a copy in Helen's filing cabinet.'

'Maybe you should take a look, Colin,' Patty suggested.

'The only thing I know about the will is that Helen and I have a property near Grongo in joint names and that her half goes to me,' Anne commented.

'I didn't know about that!' Michael said in a surprised voice. 'Where's Grongo?'

'About a thirty-five-minute drive from here. I feel this is a family matter, so if you'll excuse me, I'll leave you to it. I'm going for a short walk; I'll be back in about forty minutes. See you then.'

Anne went to her room to change her shoes and get a jacket, and when there, she could hear some of the family members searching in Helen's room. The thought of them going through her friend's belongings upset her.

During her walk, she thought of Helen and Alison. *Poor Helen and Alison: they were always trying to work out the meaning of life!* She then thought of Kate, and for some odd reason, she found herself thinking how lucky the three friends had been to have passed away before becoming old. Next, she remembered what Magda had said about her Aunty May.

She pondered her future: would she have a stroke and end up a vegetable? would she get Alzheimer's? She didn't want to become an old lady. There were certain things about old ladies she didn't like. She recalled some of the things Kerrie had said about her grandmother and felt repulsed at the very thought she herself could end up that way. Where had Kate obtained the Nembutal? The coroner hadn't named the toxic substance that Kate had taken, but Anne assumed it'd been Nembutal. Would she herself have the courage to end it when she'd had enough? She'd never been sick in her life, and she didn't think old age would suit her. However, she decided there was no point thinking that way because no matter how unbearable life might become, it would end one day. She didn't want her life to become unbearable though; she wanted to quit while she was still on top. She thought about the Bible quote in Kate's letter: 'And the day you die is better than the day you are born.'

Patty wanted a Bible reading, she mused. *What a shame I didn't suggest that verse!*

She'd now been walking for twenty minutes and having told the guests she'd be gone for forty, she decided to do a U-turn and head for home.

When she arrived, she found all five guests sitting in the lounge room. Colin was the first to speak, asking her, 'How was your walk?'

'Good, thank you, Colin,' she replied. 'I felt I needed some fresh air.'

Patty was next: 'Did you know that Helen left you the house in Hughes?'

Anne was genuinely surprised to hear it, and answered, 'No!'

'You *must* have!' Patty insisted. 'She *must've* told you!'

'No, Patty, she didn't. The only thing we ever discussed about wills was Socamora: whoever went first would leave her half to the other one – and that's all I really care about.'

'I'd like to see Socamora,' Michael remarked.

'Okay,' Anne responded. 'We can go there. Let me know when you're ready.'

'I think we're ready now; let's make the most of the daylight.'

'Okay. Michael, you follow me,' Anne said.

Tanya suggested she go with Anne, and Anne was pleased at the idea. She liked Tanya and was looking forward to being able to talk to her in private.

During the drive to Socamora, Anne took care to ensure she didn't get out of Michael's sight. They came to the gate that bore the sign 'PRIVATE PROPERTY'. Anne hopped out of the car and unlocked the gate. She drove through and signalled for Michael to drive through. Then she relocked the gate and they drove on to the cabin.

Once there, Tanya commented, 'I wonder why Aunty Helen never told us about this! Did you know she owned a country property, Dad?'

'No,' Colin replied. 'To be precise, she owned *half* the property.'

Anne was now almost in tears, being at the place where she, Kate, Alison and Helen had undertaken their 'acts of justice'. Alison was gone, Kate was gone, and now Helen was gone. She unlocked the cabin door and said, 'Not much to see.'

'What did you and Aunty Helen do on the property?' Tanya asked her.

'Had fun with friends,' she replied. She didn't feel like talking and was relieved that Helen's family could see she didn't. She decided to sit on a chair outside the cabin and said, 'Feel free to go for a walk.'

'Where's the boundary?' Michael asked her.

'When you come to a fence, you're on the boundary,' she answered and watched as the five of them strode towards the fence. She noticed that Colin was apart from the others and surmised he wanted to be on his own, as he grieved for the loss of his only sibling. Anne then saw Patty turn around and head back to the cabin.

Once there, Patty sat beside Anne and started to cry. She stopped crying and started to talk about Helen. 'I didn't meet Helen till the night of our engagement party. She was working overseas, and she came home especially for the party. She was so sweet to everyone, and I could feel how happy she was for Colin. I thought how lucky I was to have such a beautiful sister-in-law. She had six months to go on her contract, and when it was finished, she was going to return to Australia. I thought she'd marry a really nice guy, we'd go out as a foursome, our children would play together, and we'd do all the other things extended families do. But that never happened.

'One Christmas, one of the aunts said she hoped Helen would soon find "Mr Right". Helen said, – I can still hear her – "I'm never getting married! Once a woman marries, she's expected to have children, and I'm not inflicting life on anyone!"'

'That must've been followed by a minute's silence,' Anne remarked.

'It was. Colin's mother tried to laugh it off as a joke, but it was obvious Helen meant it. I sometimes think, with much sadness, that Tanya agrees with Helen.'

I know she does! Anne said to herself.

Patty continued, 'After Colin's mother died, Helen, Colin and I were sorting out the cupboards. There were all these cups and ribbons Helen had won: Junior Athletics Champion, Senior Athletics Champion, Hockey Blue. There was a whole shelf of them, but Helen didn't want any of them. We still have them: Colin couldn't bring himself to throw them out. Jack and Freda were so proud of Helen. They had photos of her in the lounge room: Helen graduating with First Class Honours, Helen being presented with the H. G. Collis medal for outstanding achievement in system design. She had everything, Anne. She had more talent than any one person could ask for, though I could never really get close to her. Do you think she was happy?'

'I think so,' Anne replied, 'although she did allow herself to get depressed about things she had no control over. For example, if she read in the paper about a ten-year-old girl being sold off as a bride or young girls being forced into prostitution, she'd get upset – and I mean *really* upset. She was like someone suffering from depression. It never lasted long, but it was real.'

'How long would it last?' Patty enquired.

'Anything from fifteen minutes to an hour. She'd often ask, "Where was God when that was happening? Maybe the Archbishop of Canterbury or the Pope, knows." She—' Seeing that the others were now within hearing distance, Anne decided to stop talking.

By the time they'd returned to the cabin, the sky was almost dark, so they drove back to Anne's house. Anne heated up a lasagne that Malcolm had brought, and after they'd eaten it, Anne packed the dishwasher while the others watched TV.

At a civilised hour, she excused herself and went to her room. She didn't sleep well that night, and the reason was that despite the fact she had no heart, she was grieving.

She woke up early, and by the time the guests had entered the kitchen, she'd prepared everything in readiness for breakfast. After they'd eaten breakfast, Michael, Robyn and Tanya were leaving for Melbourne, and Colin and Patty were going to see the solicitor about Helen's will. They'd then be driving to Melbourne in Helen's car.

The will seemed quite straightforward: Anne was to receive the house in Hughes and, of course, Helen's half in Socamora. The rest was to go to Colin, Michael and Tanya.

'Before you all leave, I think there's something you should work out between yourselves. Helen sponsored two girls from overseas. Who's going to continue with the sponsoring?' Anne asked.

There was a moment of stony silence, after which Patty asked, 'How much is it?'

'Sixty dollars a month. It's through Child Watch.'

'I'm very wary about these organisations,' Patty griped. 'How can you be sure the money gets to the child?'

'Mum, it's with Child Watch. They're a reputable organisation,' Robyn said to Patty.

'I don't trust any of those organisations!' Patty snapped.

'Michael, maybe you and I could sponsor one of the children,' Robyn suggested.

Michael, however, said, 'I tend to agree with Mum, Robyn: I don't want to be sending off thirty dollars every month to buy whisky for some corrupt official!'

Patty then started up again, saying, 'Sometimes you have to be cruel to be kind. Those countries have got to do something about birth control! They can't continue to breed willy-nilly and then expect other countries to help them. Anyway, Helen should've mentioned it in her will; she should've set up a small trust fund.'

'I suppose she thought she could trust her family,' Anne said, using a tone of voice to show she wasn't hiding how disappointed she was with some of the family members present. 'Not to worry,' she said. 'I'll do it; I couldn't just *abandon* them – I'd be betraying Helen.'

'I agree, Anne,' Tanya said. 'How about you and I each sponsor a child?'

'That sounds like a good arrangement, Tanya,' Anne replied.

'Thank you, Anne,' Robyn said. 'And thank *you*, Tanya.'

Anne could see that Robyn wasn't happy with her husband's and mother-in-law's behaviour.

'Robyn,' Michael said, 'it'd be better to send thirty dollars' worth of condoms every month, wouldn't it?'

'How could you be sure they'd get to the people who needed them?' Anne asked him. 'They might be sent to a brothel for some corrupt official to use so he doesn't get AIDS.'

Colin was now anxious to close the subject and said, 'Thank you, Anne.'

The guests all said their goodbyes and left.

Finally having her house to herself, Anne heaved a sigh of relief and flopped into a lounge chair. However, she felt extremely sad. She didn't *want* the house to herself; she wanted her housemate back.

Anne

On the Saturday after Helen's funeral, Anne had a yearning to go to Socamora. She didn't know why, but she knew she wanted to go.

When she arrived at the locked gate, she was surprised and alarmed to see a car parked there. As she drove up to the cabin, she saw a man and two dogs outside it. The dogs were sniffing at the edge of the concrete slab, and the man was bending over, using his hand to scrape away the grass. She felt nervous. She couldn't see his face, but she knew she didn't like what she was seeing. She didn't know whether to turn around or keep going. She wished she had the gun with her. As she got closer, she knew she'd seen the man's face before but couldn't place it. Then it dawned on her: it was Don, the greenie. Now livid, she decided to park the car and approach him.

As she walked up to him, he said, 'Hi, Anne! How are you? I saw in the paper, that Helen died, and I thought you might be interested in selling.'

Anne made no effort to conceal her rage. 'Get off this property, you insensitive wretch! And if you ever set foot on this land again, I'll have you arrested for trespassing.'

'Oh boy! Sorry, Anne!' he responded and then added, 'By the way, what did Helen die of?'

'Just *get*!' Anne said in as loud a voice as she could muster.

When he'd gone, she decided she wouldn't go inside the cabin; rather, she'd sit outside it and admire the landscape.

She thought about the question Don had asked, which she hadn't answered. She just couldn't believe that Helen had died of a heart attack. She thought about how she'd heard of cases in which the doctor had incorrectly determined the cause of death, cases in which the body had been exhumed years later so the real cause of death could be determined. She also pondered how surprised she'd been that the coroner had released Helen's body so quickly. She thought about Socamora and what would happen to it when she died. She decided to leave the property to Alison's daughter.

Anne was now seventy-four. She was a fit and healthy woman for her age, and her mind was still as sharp as a tack. She was still playing golf, skiing, and going bushwalking and camping. She'd never suffered the 'senior moments' so many of her friends talked about: 'I've misplaced my keys!'; 'I can't remember whether I locked the door!'; 'I think I forgot to turn the iron off!'. She'd appointed a manager to run her business and she was now going to work only when she felt like doing so.

This day was one of the days on which she didn't feel like going in to work, preferring to go to the local shopping mall. While browsing in a bookshop there, she couldn't help noticing the number of autobiographies on the shelves and thought, *What an incredible ego these people must have, to think anyone wants to read about them!*

She read the blurb on the back cover of one of the autobiographies. *And why would you want to reveal such intimate details about your life?* she asked herself. *Who'd want to read about* my *life?*

She then thought back to a period in her life that she sometimes had trouble believing had really happened. She often found it difficult to come to terms with the fact she'd been part of those goings-on. Then she thought how they'd make a good crime story, and she suddenly found herself becoming very excited at the idea of writing a book about them. She now couldn't wait to start drafting the story, and she went home and commenced writing it.

While she was writing, she started thinking about how easy things had been back then and realised there was no way anyone could get away with such things today. In those days, when she'd helped commit the crimes, the number of the person calling wasn't displayed on your phone, Telecom – now Telstra – didn't itemise your calls on your phone account, and politicians weren't surrounded by security officers.

As always, Anne was pursuing many interests, and because completing the manuscript was a low-priority activity, she took about fifteen months to finish it. When she had, she thought to herself, *now all I have to do is think of a title.* It was then that something Alison had once said to her came into her mind. She vividly remembered the time that Alison was telling her and Helen about her baby Megan. Alison had said that to make a woman have a baby and take him or her away from the mother so she never hears another thing about him or her is sadistic. A title for Anne's book came to her: *The Right to Sadism*; but she thought that sounded 'off'. She did some more thinking and decided on *Justice Our Way.*

Postscript

I've told my story now. I've changed the names of some of the characters and either made up or changed the names of some of the places in order to hide the identity of the people I believe I don't need to identify. If I've betrayed anyone in writing this book, I'm sorry.

The reader might think that this writer is omniscient – and that was almost how things were in the days of the gaol at Socamora. Alison was the only one of the four women who kept her feelings to herself. One night when I was visiting her in the hospice, she shared all her doubts with me as well as her anxiety about the gaol.

The book cannot be published in my lifetime. I've purchased a new printer and a heat binder, and I intend to print and bind five copies and save two copies on CDs. I'll put the five printed copies and the two CDs in a safety-deposit box at the bank and append the details of the box to my will, which is kept at my solicitors'.

I'll bequeath the copyright of *Justice Our Way* to Lawfail so the members can perhaps publish it and make some money from it.

Maybe it's time this story was told. Maybe the victims' families have a right to know what happened to their loved ones. It could be told soon, because I've decided I don't want to be an old lady.

Anne Judith Paterson
January 2013